Intimate Strangers

Thelma Olshaker

THORNDIKE PRESS • THORNDIKE, MAINE

Library of Congress Cataloging in Publication Data:

Olshaker, Thelma.
  Intimate strangers.

  1. Large type books.   I. Title.
[PS3565.L8234I5   1984]   813'.54   84–2425
ISBN 0–89621–533–4 (lg. print)

Large Print edition available through arrangement with
Ballantine Books, A Division of Random House, Inc.

Cover design by Debbie Friedmann

INTIMATE STRANGERS

Chapter 1

Millicent Hart positioned the brown Mercedes into the only available parking space, turned off the ignition, and let her head droop against the steering wheel. Perspiration fell in droplets from her forehead onto her lap. The deft parking maneuver was accomplished, despite a racing heartbeat that drowned out all other sound on the swank, cobblestoned street of Georgetown.

The anxiety she had denied all morning became acute during the short ride to Dr. Bromley's office on N Street. Now it was drenching her carefully attired body in cold sweat. When the psychic tension subsided, total physical exhaustion took over.

I want to go home, she heard herself say out loud. *I'll soak in a long hot bath, and then Regina will bring me tea. I'll look out the window onto the beauty of Rock Creek Park and feel serene. I'll be whole again.*

How suddenly it had all changed, Millicent thought. This morning she had felt confident, almost optimistic about finally seeking help. But now, sitting in the car, oblivious to the fine autumn weather, Millicent again assumed the role of self-doubter. She could feel the nervous perspiration trickling down between her breasts. She silently asked herself why she had come and what could another doctor tell her that she didn't already know?

Why was Allyson determined to starve her young body to its bare bones?

Since Allyson's illness had been diagnosed, various theories were offered, and Millicent attempted to comprehend them all. She was told "Your daughter is suffering from a strange illness that we call anorexia nervosa. By not eating, she unconsciously achieves neurotic pleasure through working out her hostilities this way.

"Allyson in punishing her body to alleviate a sense of guilt.

"It would appear that your daughter has a pervasive fear of the responsibilities of adulthood and separation from the family. She clearly wants to remain in a dependent state and does this by starving herself and forcing you to give her your frantic attention.

"Often, anorexia stems from a subtle form of hostility between mother and daughter."

This was the kind of self-inquisition Millicent went through every time Allyson's condition worsened. It was not her idea to see a psychiatrist, but Dr. Graham, Allyson's current doctor, virtually insisted that Millicent get professional help to deal with Allyson's condition.

Millicent had always felt a bit smug about never needing to pour out her problems to strangers. She would listen uncomfortably as friends described their visits to the "shrink." She was incredulous that they would talk about their therapy as casually as though they were describing an afternoon at the hairdresser. She took a certain amount of pride, as her father did, in being able to handle any difficult situation herself.

"Let's keep it in the family," John J. Bolt would always say.

Ridiculous, daddy, isn't it? I'm fifty

years old and still scared about how you'll react when you find out that I turned to someone else for help. And you will find out. Even if I never tell you. But this time, my dear father, all your power and money can't set things right. I have to be the one to find a way of reaching my daughter in her own private hell.

The Federal-style townhouse was typical of the private residences of Georgetown. Millicent looked up at the quiet grandeur of the entrance. Slowly she got out of the car and climbed the stone steps, holding on to the iron railing as she cautiously made her way to the door.

For several moments she stood on the porch, reluctant to ring the bell. When she finally rang it, she was startled by a buzzing sound that indicated the door was open to her touch. Carefully she turned the knob and entered the hallway of the first floor. After closing the door, she turned and faced a carved winding staircase. At the top stood Dr. Frances Bromley, in the center of the landing.

"Come up, Mrs. Hart. I'm ready for you," called the psychiatrist cheerfully.

Millicent climbed the stairs, which

creaked with every step. She followed Dr. Bromley through a foyer that appeared to serve as a waiting room and entered a room to the right that looked more like a cluttered parlor than an office. Millicent stood motionless as her eyes took in the chintz flowered couch and the assortment of worn-out, overstuffed chairs strewn with needlepoint pillows. A large desk covered with papers and medical journals was in front of the bay window.

Dr. Bromley gave Millicent a pleasant smile and indicated a chair. Then she settled herself in a leather armchair a few feet away. Only a small table with an ashtray and a box of tissues was between them.

Millicent could hardly believe that this plump, grandmotherly woman was a renowned psychiatrist. Instinctively she looked to the wall, which was entirely covered with diplomas and awards. She squinted, trying to read the small print, more to reassure herself that Dr. Frances Bromley was indeed authentic than out of mere curiosity as to where the doctor had received her education and training.

When Millicent had spoken to her on the phone, she imagined a younger, more sophisticated woman, very unlike the person facing her, an elderly woman with gray hair pulled back in a neat bun.

"I have the feeling, Mrs. Hart, that you've been through a bad time before coming here." Dr. Bromley leaned forward, the expression on her face kind and full of compassion.

"How did you know?" asked Millicent with some dismay. "Am I that transparent?"

"Goodness no. It's just that your hairline is all wet and that lovely suede suit is spotted with perspiration. That tells me that you probably had quite an anxiety attack sometime between leaving home and arriving here."

Millicent shifted her position in the chair, suddenly relaxed and feeling more comfortable with the intuition and understanding of the psychiatrist.

"I don't know what hit me," she said easily, "but this awful wave of fear came over me while I was driving, and I felt as if my heart was going to jump out of my chest. For a few seconds, I couldn't breathe, then the water just poured out."

"Well, Mrs. Hart, as I understand it, after talking with Dr. Graham, you're here because your daughter is a very sick young lady. She's hospitalized at the moment with anorexia nervosa. Perhaps you're finding it terribly difficult to cope with the fact that she brought these awful circumstances upon herself?"

Millicent bit her lower lip, controlling her emotions. "Yes, I am having a terrible time, even after all these years . . . six, seven . . . in understanding why Allyson would continue to make herself, *will herself,* to be so sick. I'm sorry to say that I'm still dreadfully confused."

"Your distress and confusion are completely understandable. I can't imagine a mother feeling any other way."

Dr. Bromley's sympathetic words and tone melted the brave facade that Millicent had sustained for so long. A brief moment of tears quickly gave way to sobs of grief.

Dr. Bromley did not move, but behind the glasses, her clear blue eyes were filled with expression.

"Let it out, Mrs. Hart. Believe me, the old repeated maxim about having a good cry is no fable. It often works wonders."

"I feel so silly, so stupid for carrying on like this," said Millicent with embarrassment as she took a tissue from the box and tried to get control of herself.

"This is one place where you can act out whatever you feel and you won't be considered silly or stupid. My job is to help you to understand your feelings and come to terms with your distress, not to judge you. So I think we've made a good start, because already you're being honest with your emotions. Tell me about Allyson, Mrs. Hart. How old is she, and when did all this anorexia business start?"

"Allyson is twenty-three," Millicent began, then added, "but she looks a lot younger. More like fourteen or fifteen."

"That's rather late for the onset of the illness. Most girls are teenagers when it starts. So are you saying that it started a long time ago?"

"It probably started when she was seventeen, or maybe even earlier. It was in her first year of high school that we noticed she wasn't eating much and was beginning to lose weight. At dinner she would put enough food on her plate, but she'd just play around with it and make excuses for not eating. And she would talk about food and spend more time in the kitchen fixing odd concoctions, sometimes eating what she made and sometimes not. When she did eat, she would throw up. Her fascination with food, and at the same time her abhorrence of it, seemed strange, but we refused to recognize it as a psychological disorder."

Millicent took a deep breath and turned her head to the window. In her mind, she was trying to reconstruct a chronological order that would explain what had led to this strange illness. But her mind drifted into a fuzzy haze.

"Dr. Bromley, although this sickness has now been explained to me a dozen times and I've read all the literature about it, I'm still not sure that I understand what's going on. How can someone be obsessed with food and at the same time be repulsed by it?"

Millicent's voice became shrill and louder. "How can a perfectly wonderful, healthy child whose only problem in the world was being a little overweight go on a diet and end up as an emaciated skeleton who hates the world, and me, and her father and sister and brother, and most of all herself?"

Dr. Bromley's words were soft and slow: "Because, Mrs. Hart, being overweight obviously was not Allyson's only problem."

In her agitation, Millicent did not seem to hear this. "She weighs seventy pounds and says she wants to eat but just can't. What am I going to do?" She did not wait for an answer. "I can't let her die from starvation. And I certainly can't let her die from hate. Not my Allyson who had enough love for the whole world."

"I assume she's had psychotherapy?" Dr. Bromley asked.

Millicent exhaled audibly. "Yes. She's had individual and group therapy. She's had the best medical and psychiatric care, and at times she has improved. But for the past two years, she's been on a rigid ritual of controlled and methodical starvation. She's been in and out of the hospital and frankly, I don't know if she can take much more."

"And neither can you, is that right?" asked Dr. Bromley, trying not to sound critical.

"I don't think I have a choice," Millicent said. Her voice was so weary, it was almost pathetic.

"How has your husband reacted to Allyson's illness?" Dr. Bromley asked.

Millicent looked down and nervously started rubbing her fingernails with her thumb. With her head lowered, she answered: "My husband . . . my husband has thrown up his hands. I get the feeling he believes that by ignoring the sickness it will go away like a bad cold."

"What about the rest of the family? How are they reacting?"

Millicent lifted her hands to her chin. Despite her attempt not to sound accusatory, her tone nonetheless was bitter. "My mother is embarrassed by it all. Really embarrassed. In her milieu, it's not exactly country-club talk. My father tells Allyson 'to get hold of herself' as though it's as simple as that."

Millicent's eyes looked hurt and betrayed. "And Corinne and John, my other two children, have become openly resentful of all the time and attention that have been devoted to Allyson. And, of course, this has caused a great deal of dissension in the family."

"Are you telling me, Mrs. Hart, that you're feeling very alone and a little angry in carrying the burden of Allyson's illness without much support from your family?"

"I'm not sure," Millicent said quietly. Then her voice again took on an angry tone. "I honestly think, heaven forbid, that if

17

Allyson had some horrible disease like cancer, everyone could deal with it, strange as that may seem. They act as though there's some kind of stigma attached to this. My parents, everyone . . . they all say, 'Why doesn't she just eat something?' "

"My dear, this is a common feeling among families with an anorexic child. It's one of those taboo illnesses, like leprosy, that no one wants to talk about, and no family likes to admit having a child actually succumb to it. Sadly enough, the stigma that's been associated with anorexia has caused a great deal of misery to families like yours who can't possibly understand why some darling girl child of theirs would deliberately diet herself to death. And it does happen mainly to girls, young girls like your Allyson, who end up looking like they came out of a concentration camp. And it's a difficult process to reverse once it's gone on for so long."

"But, Dr. Bromley, Allyson was a bright, delightful child who never caused us any trouble and did extremely well in school. She was always such a good child, and she had everything."

"That's a common trait among anorexic

children, intellectually superior, excellent students. And it's also an illness primarily confined to adolescents of affluent families."

"Allyson was thoughtful and obedient in school and at home. She was so eager to please everyone." Millicent said this as though she were pleading for an accused defendant.

"A stubborn perfectionist, no doubt. But you see, Mrs. Hart, underneath, most of these young girls are overly sensitive, and they manifest compulsive and self-punitive behavior. In a word, they're self-destructive."

Millicent stared thoughtfully. Then she spoke with pain. "I never realized that until I went into her room one day and found her cutting up some skirts and blouses with such intensity that it looked like she was in a mad frenzy. She started yelling that she had to get rid of those clothes because they were for fat people. She would have destroyed her whole wardrobe if I hadn't stopped her. I had never seen her in such a hysterical state. That's the first time I realized fully that the diet she put herself on was turning into a serious sickness. God knows how long she had been feeling this way."

"This illness can lie dormant for a long time before the obsession with being thin comes into play. And that's usually in adolescence. It's as if, magically, if they had a perfect figure it would make them more acceptable people. But the diet that is innocently begun in adolescence soon takes an ominous turn."

"Allyson wasn't that heavy. Just a few pounds overweight. Why this compulsive drive for thinness?" Millicent asked as though Dr. Bromley had known Allyson when all this started.

"It's more of an antipathy to being fat. These children are mirror gazers. Truly. After a while, no matter how thin they get, to them, their bodies still have the image of fat bodies."

"Allyson would constantly look in the mirror and see a fat, ugly person no matter how much weight she'd lost. At first, we used to joke about it until it became apparent that she was using every kind of subterfuge to avoid eating. But paradoxically, Dr. Bromley, the intense preoccupation with food or cooking continued along with her bizarre eating habits when she did eat, which wasn't often."

Millicent's mind was full of random remembrances of Allyson's behavior, but she was unable to make any logical connection between the patterns and stages of her daughter's twisted development.

Dr. Bromley sensed this. "Do you have any idea how Allyson felt during this time, Mrs. Hart?"

Millicent struggled with the words. "It was . . . it was as if she was leading a secret life of guilt and fear . . . and desperation. I just knew she felt lonely and isolated from the world, and from us."

"Is that when you became so concerned?"

Millicent's voice was hopeless. "Concerned, but not enough. In spite of her disgust for food, Allyson was very active and seemed to have unlimited energy. That's why we didn't pay much attention to it in the beginning. Even the doctors misdiagnosed it. But then her hair started falling out and her skin became very dry. Eventually her periods stopped. She was always constipated and cold. When she was sixteen or seventeen, she didn't have an ounce of fat on her body.

"And then this restless activity began.

She was always starting something, getting excited about a new project, but never finishing anything; she lost interest very quickly."

Millicent paused, trying to remember the sequence of events. "She seemed happy about starting college. That was one of the good periods. She got into Wellesley, and we thought she was through with this dieting phase. She started eating more and making all sorts of plans for college. But the first time she went to college, she only lasted for six months. This was shocking, because we thought she was doing so well. She went back to school the following year for three months. I knew it wasn't working because she'd call home several times a week asking me to send her all kinds of exotic foods. I found out that she would gorge herself one minute and then make herself vomit after what she considered an eating binge.

"We then took her to Europe and later tried to get her to take courses at the local university. But mostly, she just stayed at home, in her own solitary confinement. She's been to many doctors and has actually gone through periods when for months everything pointed to complete recovery.

She's gained and lost weight and gained and lost so many times that I've lost track. But now she's back in the hospital and worse than ever. She looks like a skeleton."

Dr. Bromley attempted to sum up what Millicent had told her: "Allyson started dieting when she was about sixteen, but she did not become seriously ill until she went off to college. By then she was eighteen or nineteen, is that right?"

Millicent nodded.

"And from that time until now," continued Dr. Bromley, "she has been under the care of doctors and has been in and out of the hospital. But until this last serious episode, she had been doing better?"

Millicent nodded again but said nothing, as though she was too drained to explain further.

"Would you say, Mrs. Hart, that the times she was hospitalized were preceded by periods of depression? Did you or your family notice that Allyson acted more depressed or even showed exaggerated feelings of embarrassment about her condition just before these bad periods started?"

Millicent was slumped in her chair, her eyes vaguely staring into space. Her voice was controlled, almost tight. "Yes, I think she was depressed during these periods." She paused for a moment, as though she was hesitant about saying her next thought. "But my husband doesn't agree. Jeff thinks Allyson is getting a great deal of personal satisfaction from all our worry and attention. He believes Allyson is deliberately trying to pull the family apart, and the sympathy and concern he had have changed to anger and even indifference. Jeff says she's dangling us all at the end of a rope. And he can't deal with her hostility."

"Not many people can, Mrs. Hart. Especially when they don't understand where it's coming from. But there may be some truth in what your husband says. Anorexics can be very manipulative, and they have been known to cause family breakups. You see, their refusal to eat is seen by them as perhaps the only way they can exercise control and self-direction. This odd kind of control over their bodies gives them a sense of security. Their feelings of helplessness can turn into a form of power over everyone involved. But you must understand, my dear, that in their minds they are not deliberately killing themselves. It's not a conscious death wish."

As Dr. Bromley spoke, Millicent began to understand the awful truth of what the psychiatrist was saying. Again she remembered the conversations with other doctors. Her words came sadly from deep within. "Oh, I know. I've heard it all, all the theories, all the conscious and unconscious psychological roots. I can repeat them to you word for word. Even about Allyson's supposed regression to an infantile-maternal relationship. I . . ."

"Mrs. Hart," interrupted Dr. Bromley. "You probably know as much about anorexia nervosa as I do, but my knowledge is clinical while yours is personal. You've lived with it. If you've been through Allyson's problems with other doctors, why did you decide to come to me now?"

Millicent stared absently at the floor. When she looked up, her expression was pained, as though she had been wounded by the doctor's question. She shifted uneasily, not knowing how to answer. "I told you. Dr. Graham suggested that I see you. He was very definite about my part in supporting Allyson's therapy. He stressed that as a parent, it's important for me to be involved." She realized that she was running on in a nervous attempt to justify her presence in this office.

"Mrs. Hart. The doctor *didn't* make you come," said Dr. Bromley with firmness. "And the family therapy he referred to is very different from this."

"But he *did* recommend you when I talked to him."

"Is that the only reason you're here?"

Millicent's voice quivered. The fear of sudden inadequacy swept over her. "No. It's because I can't handle it anymore. I don't know how to explain what I feel but . . . I'm just afraid."

"You mean you can't handle the possibility that your daughter could die?" said Dr. Bromley with deliberate bluntness.

Millicent's eyes misted. "God forbid! I won't even allow myself to think about that possibility."

Dr. Bromley looked at her quietly for a moment. "Then what?"

Millicent groped for words. She didn't want to give the impression that she was asking for maudlin sympathy. She glanced at Dr. Bromley before she answered. Then she said honestly: "The depression. The confusion. The anxiety." She paused.

"Most of all . . . my guilt."

"Were you the one who first suggested that Allyson go on a diet?"

Millicent flushed. "Yes."

Dr. Bromley's eyes softened with sympathy. "Mrs. Hart, I don't think there's ever been an overweight youngster who hasn't been urged, nagged, by her mother to go on a diet. I know my own mother did. But the vast majority never become anorexic. I don't dispute your feelings of guilt. I only want you to know they are misplaced. Why are you punishing yourself for Allyson's condition? Why are you accepting all the blame?"

Millicent spoke slowly, with precision. "Because I have to accept the blame. The fault lies with me. I wanted Allyson so very much. She was the child of my dreams, the adored and welcomed baby who would hold my marriage . . . and my life . . . together. It was selfish, completely selfish. It never occurred to me that one day she would feel rejected and alien and isolated and somehow think herself unworthy of our love."

"I'm sorry, my dear, but I don't follow what you're saying. Why do you reproach yourself, after twenty-three years, for having this child?''

The words trembled on Millicent's lips. "Because I didn't *have* her. I adopted her. Then I *had* two natural children. I had no right to make her feel, as she puts it, like the 'unconnected one' — 'the blood stranger.' Allyson feels detached and forsaken by us because she's an adopted child. We've never rejected her, but she feels rejected."

Millicent paused for a moment. Her eyes clouded with a hazy sadness. "Do you know what she said to me yesterday?"

Dr. Bromley watched the tears stream down Millicent's pale cheeks. She could feel her pain. She waited, knowing she would hear a wistfully defeated voice.

"Allyson told me she's mourning her own death."

Chapter 2

It was peaceful in the Hart residence on Belmont Road. The stately house remained aloof to the anguish of its owner, very much as a religious temple is impervious to the troubled worshiper who receives comfort just from its inspiring presence. The frenzied pace of political Washington seemed far removed, yet the Capitol itself was only a ten-minute ride downtown. A few short blocks away was Massachusetts Avenue, the magnificent tree-lined boulevard of imposing embassies and old-world mansions. This was Embassy Row, where diplomats and politicians shaped international affairs over cocktails and sumptuous buffets.

Millicent lay on the brocaded lounge that was comfortably situated in front of the curved bay window in her splendid bedroom. The upholstery on the Louis XV chaise was slightly frayed, like most antiques of time-worn distinction. Everything around her spoke softly of wealth and class, from the elegant but understated furnishings to the expensive decorative accessories that never called attention to their costliness.

She often thought that this was the part of the day she liked best, the interval when she was not weighted by the pressures of conformity. The late afternoon was her time for reading and quiet thinking. The precious time to try to shut out the daily problems that had confronted her since Allyson's latest illness.

This was once her time for intimate talks with the children when they arrived from school, before the dinner hour, while the servants bustled downstairs with the evening preparations.

Her mind reached back to the time when the children were very young, just starting school. Allyson in first grade, Corinne in kindergarten, and Johnny in nursery school. They would rush upstairs, looking for Millicent, anxious to tell every new experience that had happened to them during the day. She remembered their laughter, their hurts too, but most of all their closeness.

When she dressed for social engagements, Allyson and Corinne would often watch, taking great delight in offering childish opinions on the proper selection of her clothes and jewelry. Even young John would dash in and out, boyishly mocking their feminine concern with fashion, yet not wanting to be left out of any family activity.

Her most contented times had been with the children. Now she wanted to remember. She had an overwhelming desire to recapture those good years and hold on to them, as though she had let some idyllic state slip by without savoring its sweetness.

Millicent looked the part of the pampered matron commonly displayed in society magazines depicting the lives of the world's fortunate few. She had been born with the proverbial silver spoon in her mouth, but her father's wealth had not brought her happiness. His money brought only material comforts and a husband who resented her for the very reason he had married her.

Soon it would be time to leave the

security of her familiar surroundings for the daily visit to the impersonal, aseptic environment of George Washington University Hospital. The doctor had restricted her visits to one hour in the early evening. But she would not think about that now, nor about her painful disclosures to Dr. Bromley.

She stared sightlessly out the window, seeing none of the beauty of the lustrous autumn leaves that had always endowed her with unexpected vitality. Instead she saw the young, vulnerable woman who had been herself twenty-seven years ago. A dreamy-eyed young woman, confident of the future, wrapped in the glowing ecstacy of marriage to the man of her romantic yearnings.

Unlike most girls of her day, Millicent had not married after college. At twenty-one, she graduated from Vassar with no marital prospects waiting. She worked in her father's business, in the accounting department, hoping that romance would come in an idealistic and mythical fashion.

She was not a pretty girl, and the corporal genes of her beautiful fair-haired mother were not passed on to her. Rather, they waited three years for her sister, Joan, who then quite naturally grew into a sought-after beauty. Instead, she inherited the olive skin and rugged features of her father. On John J. Bolt, the prominent nose and swarthy complexion were disarmingly handsome, adding to the sensual quality of his large, muscular body. On Millicent, the similar characteristics just didn't work in the same harmony. She lived out her entire childhood fully aware of her homeliness.

The expensive clothes, years of orthodontics, hairdressers, and ballet lessons did not enhance the looks of the shy young girl who knew she was constantly being compared with her glamorous and captivating sister.

Millicent was tall and thin, with gangling arms and legs that were great for tennis and swimming but a disaster on the dance floor. The debutante balls she obediently attended were the bane of her adolescent existence. Lacking sex appeal or even a girlish flair, the young men looked over the other girls but overlooked her. The embarrassment hurt, but it didn't shatter her. The experience was not inherently valueless. In fact, it added a delicate dimension of sensitivity to her character that offered another view of life.

But at this stage, it was hard to be philosophical about being a wallflower. The more her mother told her to stand up straight, the more she slumped, fancifully trying to reduce her awkward body to the acceptable standard of her peers. She desperately wanted the boys to lust after her as they did Joan and the other girls at school who had long blond hair, cheerleader bodies, and classic noses.

Millicent adored her dynamic and domineering father, despite the fact that he controlled his family with the same iron-fisted will he exerted over his corporate empire. What he owned he believed he possessed. But she took no great comfort in the fact that in his egocentric self-interest, John J. Bolt was proud that his older daughter resembled him physically.

She also inherited his intelligence. While he gained wealth and recognition by applying his keen mind to building his vast real estate and construction business, she gained his favor by excelling academically. Nevertheless, she would gladly have traded her high IQ for some of her sister's popularity. Millicent brought home the

A's, while Joan brought home the boys, an endless stream of adoring admirers who found her beautiful and exciting.

John J. Bolt would have preferred a son, as confirmation of his immortality and to carry on the business. But a daughter like Millicent was the next best thing to a son, so he treated her like one, up to a point. He discussed costs and construction plans and welcomed her presence at the office and at the conventions that bored his wife, Constance, but never did he consider her as his successor. John J. Bolt did not admire superwomen and barely acknowledged their existence with anything other than disdain. That would have diminished his image of the superman with the mystical, pure goddess at his side. This placed Millicent in the conflicting position of having her femininity questioned if she showed the aggressive and competitive traits that her father respected.

In her own peculiar way, Constance Bolt loved both of her daughters, but she found it difficult to relate to her introspective older child. It seemed that no matter how she tried to "fix her up" the uncomely, hard-featured young girl looked the same. They had no common interests, whereas

Constance and Joan saw eye to eye. They never tired of shopping and socializing together. They both possessed easy, outgoing personalities, and their money enabled them to fit gracefully into Washington society, which was a complicated mixture of powerful politicians and influential, established Washingtonians — the permanent families who were possessors of a proud and unique heritage and were fortunately unaffected by the "changing of the guard" on Capitol Hill.

Constance Bolt fancied herself social arbiter of these prestigious groups. She brought them together at her lavish parties, wined and dined them, then assumed the illusory position of being part of political history. It never occurred to her that senators and diplomats would go anywhere for free food and public exposure. Her most prized possession was her Chinese lacquered file box of monogrammed index cards detailing the fine particulars of the many exquisite dinners she had given throughout the years at her Tudor mansion in the Spring Valley section of Washington or at the elite Chevy Chase Country Club on Connecticut Avenue. She would proudly flick her cards and tell you exactly what the ambassador of Peru had consumed at her table five years ago. How many times had Millicent and Joan heard her say, "I would rather lose my diamond necklace than my files. Girls, always remember, in case of fire, grab The Box first."

The words of Dr. Bromley came back to Millicent as she mused on her past. In describing Allyson, the psychiatrist had spoken of "lonely children isolated from the world" and of "obedient girls eager to please and magically wishing to be accepted." Those words could just as easily have applied to herself. She hated remembering how she'd felt as a child.

Strange how time can reverse the order of things. The idea of herself as a shy wallflower made her smile. Millicent, in middle age, had acquired the confidence in her appearance that Joan had lost. The years had been good to her body. The graceless, unattractive young girl had matured into the stunning, willowy older woman. The swarthy complexion had not wrinkled with age. The sharp features had softened, changing her countenance to an alluring visage. The tall, flat body had become fully developed. Designer clothes and meticulous grooming complemented her majestic bearing. The irony of assuming the image of her mother's daughter did not escape Millicent.

Joan's pale beauty had been of temporary duration. The porcelain skin aged quickly from too much sun and alcohol. The once voluptuous young body now fought a constant battle with weight. The sparkling blue eyes had faded. The flaxen hair had grown coarse from bleach. Even extensive plastic surgery and heavy makeup could not undo the ravage of her dissipated life. Joan was about to be discarded by her fourth husband.

The ringing of the telephone interrupted Millicent's reverie. She hoped it wasn't her mother or father making their daily duty call to inquire about Allyson and offer more unsolicited advice and provincial analysis of the illness they would dearly love to ignore.

It was Dolly Henderson, announced the houseman, Homer. Millicent reluctantly picked up the phone, succumbing to the guilt of having refused her friend's frequent calls over the past weeks.

"Hi, Dolly. Good to hear from you," she said, trying to sound cheerful.

"Millicent, where have you been? I've been trying to get in touch with you for weeks. Lord honey, we all thought you had dropped off the face of the earth."

"I know, Dolly, but I've been busy going to the hospital and . . . frankly, I haven't been in the mood to talk." Depression crept into her voice. "There's nothing to talk about. Everything's the same."

"Too bad, love, and I don't mean to put you on the spot for not calling back. It's just that I've been worried about you and want to know if I can help. After all, problems are my specialty. God knows, I've had enough of my own."

"No, Dolly, but thanks. Thanks so much. I do appreciate your concern."

"I've got more than concern, Millicent. I've got big, broad shoulders to cry on, and you won't be the first to use them. What I want you to know is that I'm always available for pouring out your troubles. It does help, you know."

"You're sweet to offer, Dolly. But . . .

well, not now. I'm just not up to being with people."

"I'm not *just* people. I'm your friend," Dolly said, unable to conceal her hurt feelings. "I know sentimental confiding is not exactly your style, but don't knock a good heart to heart. Old Dolly has pulled many a friend out of the doldrums with an old-fashioned pep talk. Millicent, my dear, just don't forget that you *do* have friends, people who love you and want to help. And I have the utmost faith that this unpleasant little business with Allyson is going to straighten itself out. You'll see, she'll snap out of this sickness, just like that!"

What arrogance! Millicent felt the old irritation coming to the surface. So many others had made similar remarks. Why did people think that by glibly assuring you that your most serious problems would go away "just like that," you should take their word for it and feel relieved? They weren't doctors, and they certainly didn't understand the extent of Allyson's illness and the years of torment connected with it. What right did they have to profess faith in Allyson's recovery when hers was waning?

Millicent sounded cold and impatient. "I'm sure it will. And I do appreciate your caring. I really do. Look, Dolly, I hear Jeff coming in. I'll get back to you. Thanks again. 'Bye."

She regretted her feelings after she put down the phone. Was she overreacting to an innocent remark? Dolly had been a good friend, someone she could count on even though Dolly's frivolous personality sometimes made her appear callous and lacking depth. To Millicent she was neither, though at times, Dolly's affectations were hard to take. Their perspectives and life-styles were dissimilar, yet there existed a strong bond between them.

It had been established twenty years ago, when they met at one of Constance Bolt's political cocktail parties. Millicent still treasured Dolly's candid introduction: "I'm Dolly Henderson, and the only reason I was invited is because I'm the wife of the senator from New York. It appears that the two of us are the only ones here who are not running for office. Since we don't have to mingle, let's go find a quiet corner and talk. I have a feeling I'd love to be your friend."

Now Millicent realized she was keeping

Dolly at a distance. In truth, it had become more comfortable to withdraw into a desolate shell than to acknowledge her inner emptiness and reach out for emotional comfort.

She heard Jeff's footsteps on the stairs and wondered why he was home so early. She hoped it was his intention to go to the hospital with her.

Jeffrey Hart came into the bedroom, and they exchanged greetings and perfunctory kisses. Loosening his tie while in motion, he walked into his dressing room.

It had occurred to Millicent that it was an odd moment to feel passion. The sensuous part of her nature yearned for physical contact. Desire, as she used to know it, had somehow broken through the wall of depression. Millicent followed him and saw that he was removing his clothes, preparing to take a shower.

Jeff was tall, just over six feet, with broad shoulders. Though he was not heavy, he gave the impression of having enormous power in his body. His features were clear-cut with a chiseled quality that gave him the look of a mythical warrior. His light brown hair was graying at the temples. Of all his features, his eyes were the most distinguished. They were deep-set blue, observant and direct, and they acquired an audacious expression when he was very serious or angry.

Stripped down to his shorts, he walked into his adjoining bathroom. Millicent came from behind and encircled his still summer-bronzed muscular chest with her arms as she delicately kissed the back of his neck. He was still the best-looking man she had ever known, and it felt glorious to be close to him again. She waited for his response.

Jeff's body stiffened. "Not now, Mill. I'm in a rush."

Millicent ignored the slight. "Darling, I'm so glad you're home early. Will you come with me to the hospital? We can only stay there an hour anyway, and then we can go out to dinner or come home and have a quiet dinner here and spend the evening together."

He turned around. "I can't, Mill, not tonight. I have to dress and get back to the office. I have an appointment at six."

"You really can't, Jeff?" she asked, disheartened. Then she added brightly, "I tell you what, I'll go to the hospital and spend an hour with Allyson and then come to the office. By that time surely you'll be finished, and then we can go out to dinner."

"No, Millicent, we can't do that tonight, much as I'd like to. I have someone coming in with a land deal that I've been trying to wrap up for over a year, and we'll probably end up negotiating over dinner." He removed his shorts and headed for the marble shower stall.

Millicent took several steps backward. The disappointment showed on her face. "Can't someone else in the office fill in for you?"

Jeff stopped, his right hand gripping the shower door. His blue eyes were defiant. "Now you know that's ridiculous. Look, I've been trying to buy this land for two years. When it's almost in the bag, do you think that I'm going to hand it over to some hotshot junior executive to botch the whole deal? Why don't you tell that to your father and see how that great idea flies with him?" responded Jeffrey, aware of his sharp sarcasm.

Millicent was pacing in the bathroom, her hands behind her back. She answered penitently. "I'm sure father would also say

I'm being ridiculous. Of course you have to go." She paused and then said, "It's just that you haven't been to the hospital in over a week."

Jeff slammed the open shower door. He grabbed a towel and wrapped it around his lower body and walked a few steps toward Millicent.

"Would it make any difference, Mill?" he asked bitterly "Allyson wasn't exactly overjoyed the last time I went. Believe me, my presence won't change the situation. She's got good medical attention. She's in capable hands."

Millicent looked at him longingly and put her hand on his upper arm. "It's not just going to the hospital, Jeff. I wanted us to be together tonight. I've really missed you terribly these past few months."

Jeff moved away and faced the mirror, avoiding her gaze. "Millicent, I haven't gone any place." He said this with icy aloofness, indicating that she must be confusing the facts.

She moved beside him and touched his cheek, trying to get him to look at her. "Oh honey, we've both gone someplace else. We're living in the same house, but we might as well be miles apart. And that's just it, we are apart. I need you, Jeff, now more than ever. And I want you to need me. We have to face it together. The reality of the situation is that Allyson is very sick and we can't turn away from it. I'm not saying that we should stop living and just sit here and wring our hands and bemoan our fate. But you can't ignore it, either. And it can't be 'business as usual' all the time. It's a *real* crisis we're in."

He finally faced her, but with a mordant look. Caustically, he said, "Well then you'd better understand that I'm just one of those people who can't tolerate too much *reality*. We each create a world for ourselves in which it's bearable for us to live. I'm trying my damndest to keep that world going. So don't do me any favors by giving me your righteous lecture on how I should cope with life."

She put her hand out and ran her fingers over his hand, the one balanced on the sink. She said slowly, "But, Jeff, don't you realize that you're protecting yourself, like a child, from the fear of moral turmoil by not seeing things as they are?"

Jeff's stomach muscles tightened and he moved her hand.

46

Millicent stared at him, waiting for some sort of response.

Again he opened the shower door, but before he entered, he swerved around and returned her gaze. "Millicent," he said firmly and deliberately. "If you're strong enough to face life with 'things as they are,' then *good for you.* Be my guest and indulge yourself in all the pious reality you want. But don't tear down my defenses or my world." With an air of dismissal, he said, "And now I want to take a shower and get dressed and go back to 'business as usual,' because that's what I do best."

As Millicent was getting into her car, Homer hurriedly dashed out of the house to tell her that Corinne was on the phone. She rushed back in, glad not to have missed her younger daughter's long-distance call from Smith College in Northampton, Massachusetts. For the past two weeks, they had not been connecting, what with Millicent's erratic schedule and Corinne's frequent absences from the dorm whenever Millicent tried to reach her.

Millicent picked up the phone and said breathlessly, "Hello, darling, I'm so glad you caught me. I was just leaving for the hospital."

"Hi, mother, I've gotten your messages but whenever I called back you were always at the hospital or someplace." Corinne paused, letting the implication sink in. "Anyway, how are you?"

"Fine, dear."

"How are you, really?"

"Well, frankly, today . . . not so fine."

"Why, has anything changed?"

"Not really, and that's what bothers me. Allyson doesn't seem to be making any progress."

"All she has to do is *eat,* you know."

"Oh, Cory, not you too! It's not as simple as that. Don't you think she would if she could?"

"Mother, then you're saying that she doesn't know what she's doing. That she's crazy or something."

"Allyson is not crazy! She's just sick, psychologically and physically. You should understand that by now."

"Okay, mom, let's not get into a hassle about that again. What I wanted to tell you is that I'm not coming home next weekend as I had planned."

"Why not?"

"Because I've been invited to Harvard for a jazzy weekend by a super guy I met, and some of the girls from school are driving with me. And it'll be a good chance to see Johnny, too."

"I'm really disappointed. I was so looking forward to your coming in for a few days, and I'm sure your father was, too."

"How is dad? Is he home?"

"He's all right. No, he's not here. He had a business meeting tonight. He's been very busy lately. You're certain, then, that you can't come home? What about the following weekend?"

"You sound lonely, mother. Are you?"

"No, not really . . . well, maybe a little. It's just that I miss you and Johnny, and of course, Allyson. The house is very quiet these days. All the dinners and constant activity have suddenly stopped."

"Why don't you and dad entertain the way you used to? Why don't you have some friends in or go out more? Mother, you really should get out more. It'll do you good. You're letting your social life go to pot."

"Cory, how can I even think about entertaining at a time like this? I'm really not up to socializing."

"Well, mother, you can't stop living or give up your whole life just because Allyson has flipped out. You should be used to this by now."

Millicent could feel her back arch at this constant reminder of how she should live. *Cory, who could become so emotionally involved with strangers and far-out causes, did not seem to have any compassion for her sister.* Thinking this, Millicent was about to react angrily to Cory's flippancy but decided this was not the time for anger or a lecture.

"Sweetie," she said calmly, "this is not something you get used to. Am I supposed to stop being a mother just because things are rough?"

Cory was suddenly contrite. "I'm sorry, mom. I know you've taken the whole brunt of this mess. I guess your children just didn't inherit your understanding genes. And speaking of inherit, how're nana and grandad? I should call them, but I've been so busy. Nana sent me some perfume, and I never sent her a thank-you letter. She'll be sure to give me one of her famous lectures on manners if I don't. So do me a favor and tell her I got it and adore the *expensive fragrance,* and I'll douse my entire body with it at Harvard and smell like a true Smith girl. That should make her feel good."

Millicent was glad Cory couldn't see her look of disdain. "You always seem to know how to get around your grandmother. I'll give her the message. They're well. They'll be getting ready to go down to Palm Beach as soon as the weather turns cold. So you see, dear, everything does go on as usual. Europe in the spring and Florida in the winter, and everything else that's important in between."

"Do I detect a little bitterness? Where's all that compassion you're usually dishing out? After all, mother, they are old. And what could they do here anyway? I would think that you'd be glad to get them out of your hair for a few months."

Now it was her turn to be apologetic. "You're right, dear. I shouldn't expect everyone around me to feel as intensely as I do. But the truth of the matter is, I sometimes feel that I'm carrying this burden alone, although I know that's silly and not true. I realize it hasn't been easy on any of you, either. Oh Cory, I'm just getting caught up in self-pity, and I don't like myself for feeling that way. I guess your old mother is getting to be quite a drag."

"Never, mumsy. You just need something to pick you up, get that old spark back. You should take lessons from Aunt Joan. That lady sure knows how to live. You need a vacation from *that* hospital. How about a cruise, or a romp on the Riviera? You and dad ought to get away by yourselves, something romantic."

Millicent sighed, trying not to sound annoyed. "That would be lovely. Perhaps later in the year. But now isn't the time to run off."

"Mother. Got to go. Listen, as soon as I can, I'll run down for a weekend."

"By the way, Cory, you haven't even told me how you're doing in school this term. How is it going?"

"Tough. Very tough. I really need to hit the books this semester. That's another reason I won't be home so often. I've got a demon schedule this year. 'Bye, mom. I'll call you again, soon."

" 'Bye, Cory, and do drive carefully and give your brother a big kiss for me when you see him and tell him to call, too. Shall I . . . uh . . . tell Allyson anything? Any message?"

"Sure, sure. Tell her I asked after her. And I'll be down to see her sometime. Give dad and everybody my love. 'Bye, mother. Keep your lovely chin up."

"Good-bye, darling, wonderful to hear from you. Please call again. Keep trying, I'm really not out that much. Take care."

"You, too. I love you, mother."

"And I love you."

Chapter 3

The ride to the hospital was done in a mindless state. The walk through the long, winding corridors, the elevator ride to the fifth floor, were performed automatically with no awareness of place or destination. Millicent found herself approaching Allyson's room without any memory of how she'd gotten there.

Where had her mind been? With Jeff, of course, in a familiar fantasy: He was holding her hand and they were standing close together beside the children's beds, all three lined up in one room. Steam from a vaporizer filled the air. The children were young and sick with colds, but now they were sleeping peacefully as Jeffrey and Millicent smiled down on them. Still holding her hand, he would lead her to another room where they would talk for hours before falling asleep in each other's arms. But this room would be in another house, another place, where there were no children. It was a romantic mirage of tropical flowers and moonlight, separated from the real world.

Without too much introspection, Millicent realized the implications of her fantasy. *I accused Jeff of not being able to accept reality,* she said to herself, *of not facing up to life and here I am, doing just that. Trying in my mind to rekindle the ardent pitch of love and desire that was so long ago. An uncomplicated existence without responsibility and heartache. Or was I fooling myself even then about Jeff's love for me? Was the sexual attractiveness he professed enhanced by what I represented? Would he have married me if I had been only a secretary or an accountant in the office and not John J. Bolt's eligible daughter? Is this what made me look like a princess?*

When such thoughts came to Millicent, she felt an emptiness inside and forced herself back to something near normalcy and reason. She knew Jeff admired and respected her. He once told her that if anything ever happened to her he would never marry again, because no other woman could compare or take her place. She had been the most wonderful wife and mother anyone could ask for. He could discuss any business problem and she would immediately grasp it. She did believe there had once been real love between them. And that was why she could not accept the slow but steady disintegration of their relationship.

We each cope in different ways, she thought. *He plunges into work and I retreat into my imagination. Am I asking too much of Jeff? Am I looking for sensitivity and empathy while at the same time asking him to be strong and protective? If only we could call a truce to whatever is going on between us and sit down and talk about it.*

So what, in particular, had brought on this lonesome mood that she now found herself in? Wondering this, Millicent knew almost immediately it was that moment, just an hour ago, when she had desperately needed Jeff to share the pang of Allyson's sickness and the joy of still being close, and he had moved away. Moved away from the pain within her and the need for love.

Will that moment enlarge, she wondered, *and become long, lonely days and nights of emptiness? Real loneliness is not living alone*, she told herself. *It's living with a husband who makes you feel alone by isolating you from his feelings. It's just sharing space.*

Damn it! She cursed him in her mind, which was clearer now and full of resentment. *Don't you realize how lonely I am? Why can't you hold and comfort me and be a partner in this struggle? I can't go it alone.* She spoke to him as though he were there listening. *Jeff, why are you punishing me with solitude?*

Her meditations were interrupted by Miss Waverly, Allyson's nurse. Millicent stood at the door of the hospital room. Miss Waverly dashed forward from the chair near Allyson's bed and greeted her effusively. "Mrs. Hart. We've been waiting for you. We have had a rather good day. We ate a little Jell-O and some broth, and I do believe we're feeling a little stronger today."

Millicent was always taken back by Miss Waverly's way of reporting on Allyson's progress. The nurse consistently included herself, as though her duty called for complete alliance of treatment and response. It was as if the Hippocratic oath demanded that she become an extension of her patient.

Millicent's face lit up. Funny how such an ordinary thing as eating a little food could assume such importance and give so much pleasure. She went into the room with a big smile. "I'm so glad to hear that, Miss Waverly."

"Yes indeedy," said the nurse, who was very pleased with herself. "We had half a dish of strawberry Jell-O at four-ten and we kept down almost a cup of beef broth at five twenty-five. And I might add, with a cracker. Also, Dr. Graham called and said he would be in early this evening since he wasn't able to come by this afternoon, and I must say, he was most satisfied with our report. Now that you're here, Mrs. Hart, I'll just step out for a bit and get our chart up to date before the doctor arrives, and you and Allyson can have a nice visit."

Miss Waverly gave both Millicent and Allyson a wave of her hand and went slinking out as though she were on some wonderful mission.

Millicent watched Miss Waverly go and

turned to Allyson, a little anxious about what the expression on Allyson's face would be after that descriptive report. She walked cautiously to the bedside and bent down and kissed Allyson's forehead.

Allyson lay there with a look of disgust, staring toward the ceiling.

"Hello, darling, I hear you're feeling better," Millicent said as she took hold of Allyson's hand and held it between hers.

Allyson turned her face toward Millicent and glared. "No, mother. *We* are not feeling better. *She* is feeling better. *We* are feeling the same." Allyson folded her arms across her chest. "That old biddy is driving me up the wall. I'd like to kick her ass in, but I don't have the energy."

"Oh, Allyson, don't talk that way. Miss Waverly means well. Don't mind her peculiarity. She's really a very good nurse. Anyway, you really do look better."

As soon as Millicent said these involuntary words, her heart sank. She had made the same sort of remark to Jeffrey several weeks ago, the last time they had been to the hospital together. He had come out visibly shaken by Allyson's appearance. Millicent needed to reassure him, and herself, that Allyson did look better, and she said as much. Jeff's stunned reaction now intruded her thoughts: *"Look better! Better than what? A grotesque concentration-camp victim before she breathes her last breath? A cadaver on a medical-school anatomy table waiting to be dissected? Are you out of your mind, Millicent? She's wasting away to nothing and you're telling me she looks better!"* Then he broke down. Even in front of his wife, he had been embarrassed about crying and exposing his feelings.

Anyone who had known Allyson in high school would never recognize her now. Her long, brown, wavy hair had disappeared with the flesh. Little clumps of dark wool barely covered her scalp. The large, deep-set eyes were now of exaggerated proportion because of her gaunt face. She resembled one of those surrealistic paintings of children now popular in modern art galleries — stick figures with oversized heads and round, sad, ogling eyes. Her bare-boned body was as thin as a wafer and bore not the slightest resemblance to the slightly chubby form she had once inhabited as a sweet and serious teenager. Spindling, rawboned arms and legs lay limply on a sheepskin that protected her skeletal appendages from the slightest friction of a hospital sheet. But the most alarming sight was the fine layer of black hair called lanugo that had grown on her arms and stomach. Dr. Graham had told Millicent that this hair was a result of the loss of subcutaneous fat and was not uncommon on malnourished people.

What irony. Millicent thought, *that Allyson, who only wanted to look like a delicate storybook princess, should now be harshly reminded of her loss of femininity by this growth of hair.*

Millicent looked at Allyson again, and allowed herself the rationalization that the absence of intravenous feeding tubes was an indication that Allyson must be better this week. It was a welcome sight and colored her perception of Allyson's actual appearance.

Millicent moved closer to the side of the bed and gently stroked her daughter's forehead as she softly repeated the litany of praise and solicitude that had become a ritual during these hospital visits. It was the voice of the mother soothing the frightened child, banishing the unknown, childish fears. Allyson seemed to need this extra assurance and attention even at a time when she was being surfeited with care.

"Darling, your color looks good today. And I'm so glad the tubes are out. That must mean you're starting to get better. If you keep this up and have a few more good days, I'm sure the doctor will let you come home, and then we'll just fatten you up ourselves."

"I don't want to get fattened up, mother," Allyson said weakly but with conviction. "That's why I'm here, remember?"

"Well, I don't mean that literally," said Millicent, almost apologetically. "What I mean is that we'll be able to care for you well enough so that you won't need hospitalization. You see, dear, if you're able to increase the amount of food little by little, then I'm certain Dr. Graham will agree to your coming home."

"But what about the therapy sessions? The psychologist has been coming in every day trying to shrink my head to the size of my body."

Millicent ignored Allyson's cynicism and hurriedly went on to answer her question. "I think we can work that out, the therapy, I mean. You can be an outpatient here at the hospital or you can go back to your own psychiatrist," she said. "Don't worry about that now. I'm just glad to see improvement, and you *are* improving, Allyson. This time, you're going to make it. I just know it."

"Well, I don't know it," Allyson responded sardonically. "And if I don't feel I'm going to make it, then it doesn't make any difference what you or the doctor or anyone else tells me. At least, that much I've learned from therapy. I alone am responsible for my feelings. And right now I feel, well . . . what's the use? I've been on this roller coaster for years, and I'm never going to get off."

Allyson's sullen mood disturbed Millicent, so she took a deep breath and quickly changed the subject. "Before I forget, Cory called just as I was leaving the house. She asked about you and sends her love and will be down as soon as she gets a free weekend. And I expect Johnny, too. She sounds anxious to see you."

She tried to act casual and believable, but Allyson detected a false note. "How nice," Allyson snickered. "We can have a family party right here in the hospital. You, Cory, Johnny . . . maybe you can even get *my father* to come. And Miss Waverly can serve Jell-O and a glucose solution." With that, she turned her head toward the wall.

A pained look came over Millicent's face but she said nothing. However, a thought passed through her mind that she knew she had to obliterate: *When is it going to be my turn to vent my anger? When will I be allowed to release my rage? And at whom? What would happen if I turned to the wall?*

With effort, she resumed her soothing, salutary phrases in spite of Allyson's sullen mood. "Honey, you've got to believe that you are going to get well. Yes, you've had lots of setbacks. I know that, but, well, this time I just feel you're going to make it."

Allyson did not revert to the cutting sarcasm that usually followed Millicent's optimistic predictions. Instead, in a split-second change of personality, she became the gentle, sweet, repentant child. She turned around. She looked up at Millicent with her big dark eyes that were out of all proportion to her face. The face was sad, but the anger was gone. In a voice that was almost a whisper, she said, "You always try to brighten me up. Why do you put up with me when I cause you so much trouble? Why don't you just let me slip away? Why do you still have so much faith in me?"

Overwhelming love for her child engulfed Millicent. She took Allyson's hand and held it against her cheek. "Because I'm your mother and I believe in you. And maybe I get a sense of satisfaction out of beginning where others end. Or maybe it's the time of the year, that begins with burnished leaves."

"Mrs. Hart, I think you're a poet."

Startled, Millicent turned around. In the doorway stood Dr. Roger Graham.

Chapter 4

They sat facing each other across the green formica table in the hospital cafeteria, where Dr. Graham had suggested going for coffee. The hallway outside Allyson's room had generally been their place for brief consultations about the condition of his anorexic patient.

Millicent sat silent as he discussed the medical problems that can result from this strange illness — slow metabolism, low blood pressure, imbalance of electrolytes such as potassium, heart damage, kidney damage, sterility. She had heard it all before, numerous times from half a dozen other prominent doctors, but she still listened. Dr. Roger Graham had been called in only a few weeks ago, highly recommended just as the others had been.

She listened intently, oblivious to the

case discussion of the neurological team seated next to them, oblivious to the page-boy beepers that continuously interrupted spontaneous medical conferences and unappetizing dinners at surrounding tables.

She was barely aware of the sudden departures of men and women in green scrub suits under long white lab coats who left uneaten food when the beepers sounded and summoned. She hardly heard the scraping of metal chairs as doctors and nurses with dangling stethoscopes slung from their necks hurried out, or noticed the quick replacements that joined the small specialized groups that made up the dining space reserved for hospital staff.

She listened carefully and hopefully because this time, the sounds she heard were different. The dispassionate clinical tones and jargon she had become accustomed to from the other internists had filled her with despair and repressed anger. She wanted to shout at the stoic array of medical men who calmly shared their technical diagnoses and treatments with her as though that were her only interest.

She wanted to shout, "You're confusing

me with one of your colleagues who's interested in your fancy treatments. I am not a doctor. I am a frightened woman and this is my child you're talking about, not a case history. Her body is slipping away into nothingness and you're not weeping with frustration and grief! Your medical knowledge and clinical concern are not enough. I don't want a reserved and cautious opinion. I want a total commitment, a promise that you'll make her well."

But, of course, she never shouted at them or allowed her anger to demand what she rationally knew they could not and would not give her. She only thanked them, over and over again, for their attempts and failures, and paid their bills. Her intimidation was practiced. She had been going through this for six years. Each time, her mind emptied of hopes as she watched her daughter inextricably sink down the black well until the new doctor came on board.

This time she heard another voice, unlike the others. The medical terms were the same but there was a distinctive element, an intonation of a mood that she had never perceived in the other doctors.

She felt an uneasy state of blended concern and sensed his uncertainty and apprehension. This was an emotional moment. His distress infused with hers. He spoke of Allyson as her child, not merely as his patient. And when he communicated his empathy, he very naturally grasped her hand in his. The reassurance of this gesture calmed her whole body.

As she walked away from the hospital, Millicent thought of Roger Graham. Automatically, she compared him with Jeff and realized there was no comparison. His face was strong rather than handsome. He was shorter, thinner, paler than Jeff. His features were sharper, too. Age? Undeterminable. Forty? Forty-five? In all, rather undistinguished, except for his voice. It was full and resonant with a quality that she could not describe even to herself. She searched for the right descriptive word for his voice, but all that came to mind was physical power, and she wondered about that. He had somehow caressed her with his sonorous tone.

She got into her car and was about to head for home but decided to drive to the Watergate, just a few minutes away from the hospital. John and Constance Bolt had lived there since the time they gave up the big house in Spring Valley, the very fashionable and then very restricted enclave in Northwest Washington.

Millicent had not seen them in almost two weeks, feigning excuses so that she would not have to face them in her depressed state. She was of the generation when children were conditioned to please their parents, not aggravate them. They had been taught to keep their private fears and heartaches to themselves and to bring only their success stories to their parents. She also became part of the generation where parents relentlessly tried to please their children.

It had become a complete turnabout. The revelation, which should have been obvious, only became startingly clear the last time she had visited her parents. She had found herself staring at the large family portrait in the living room, as if she were really seeing it for the first time. The huge painted rendition was of her mother sitting magnificently gowned in a red velvet chair with her father standing properly beside her. Millicent and Joan, perfectly groomed in organdy dresses and bows, and with mechanical smiles, sat stiffly on cushions at their parents' feet. That painting represented her childhood. A world where adults called the shots and the children jumped to attention because they knew their place. And that place did not come with the privilege of laying a guilt trip on dear old mom and dad. Heaven forbid! They would have sent you packing to boarding school, very far away. And no anorexia nervosa to make them look into themselves and ask what went wrong. The "starving children in Europe" cliché would have been thrown at you at the first uneaten morsel. *I sure as hell got caught in the middle,* Millicent had said to herself as she focused on those two obedient little girls in the picture. *Look what happened to you, little girl! You went from the adult-oriented world to the child-oriented world in one continuous motion and brought the guilt right along with you. You got dumped on from both ends.*

Allyson's physical condition could not be hidden, but Millicent's mental state was another matter. She was expected to assume a happy exterior even with the anguish she carried inside. Burdening her mother and father with personal problems was unthinkable. In keeping with her world of privileged status, she was supposed to keep a stiff upper lip and bear life's suffering without complaint. John and Constance Bolt had taught her the importance of noblesse oblige — high rank imposes obligations of honorable behavior. A proper public image demands a denial of emotional conflict.

Her parents still exercised control in many subtle ways, especially her father, and they were not about to clutter their well-ordered lives with uncomfortable thoughts. They were naturally concerned but not sensitive. Maintaining the good life consumed all their passion.

The Watergate, which became well known as a result of the Nixon political scandal, is an architectural landmark in Washington, as well as an exclusive status symbol for its prominent residents. With its galleries, boutiques, health spa, expensive restaurants and other high-priced amenities, it is a convenient fortress for its cosmopolitan clientele. International flair is a trademark of the decorating schemes of more than a few of the apartments. For many who reside there, the Watergate is merely a second or third lodging in a string of homes. Cabinet members, industrialists, wealthy foreigners and members of Congress use it as a pied-à-terre while doing business in the capital city. No one would have to leave the complex on Virginia Avenue to enjoy a rich social life.

As Millicent entered the spacious, sumptuously appointed Watergate West, she mused to herself about whether it was an apartment or a museum. The interior designer had created a background that enhanced an already distinguished collection of furniture and paintings by combining an unorthodox mixture of selective luxury with extreme eclecticism, not just to suggest luxury but to flaunt it. The distinct feeling was one of pretentiousness. The Bolts had obviously become interested in grandeur for its own sake. They were the privileged Americans who had survived wars and depressions with fortunes intact.

John J. Bolt had not been born of wealth, but he always knew he would acquire it. He set out to become rich, and circumstances and timing provided the opportunity. By the time he was thirty, there was no trace of his middle-class background. Constance came from a respectable southern family with more heritage than money. Together they gave the impression of having been spawned by generations of distinguished ancestors.

The maid greeted Millicent in the entrance hall, which heralded the theme of the Bolts' collections. The finest eighteenth-century Chinese and English decorative arts provided an exotic note. Chinese wallpaper of flowers and birds complemented the delicate porcelain pieces resting on an Irish hunt table.

The entrance-hall gallery was only the beginning. The living room was dominated by two great and rare objects: a Chinese ten-panel coromandel screen and an elaborately carved George II drop-front secretary. Both of these splendid acquisitions mingled perfectly with nineteenth-century blue and white porcelains that filled the room without smothering it. The bright lacquered walls of the living room formed a fine contrast to the dim glow of the expansive dining room across the hall, which provided the illusion that generous entertaining still took place. Dramatically sited on Rockcreek Parkway overlooking the Potomac River, the large angular balcony seemed to jut out over the water, giving the appearance of setting sail for some far horizon.

Constance Bolt presided over her elegantly decorated apartment as an actress presides over a stage.

It was almost 7:30, and the darkness was descending earlier each day. The autumn air was cold and damp, but it was uncomfortably warm inside the apartment. Millicent always took notice of how hot her parents kept the place and how seldom they opened the windows. Through these windows she could see the flickering lights of airplanes flying north above the river.

Constance and John Bolt were finishing dinner. They were seated at opposite ends of the long table. Millicent walked into the dining room and greeted each with a kiss and a smile. Her parents looked surprised by her visit and lost little time in telling her how neglectful she had been. Every visit seemed to begin on a note of nervous apprehension. This Tuesday evening was no different. Millicent braced herself.

"Well, hello there, *stranger*," said John

Bolt, in a flip, sarcastic way. "Thought you had taken a trip around the world without saying good-bye." This was an often used expression of his, and it never ceased to wound her. He embraced her lightly, unaware of her stiffening anger. Millicent sat down at the table, between them, and waited for the lecture she usually got from her mother after a long absence.

"Millicent, what a pleasant surprise, and a rare one these days," said Constance as she arched her eyebrows and looked hurt. "Your father and I were just remarking how little we've seen of you. It's probably been weeks. And you don't even call. If we didn't call you, we'd never hear from you. I don't know what keeps you so busy."

Millicent heaved a sigh. "Well, that's why I thought I'd drop by this evening. I just came from the hospital, and I realized that I hadn't seen you lately. So I thought it would be a good time for a visit. But it looks as if you're dressed to go out."

Constance looked splendidly put together, her blond hair neatly waved.

"In fact, we do have a little social engagement. Nothing special. Just another symphony reception at the Kennedy Center. They're getting rather dull. I'm really tired of these endless fund-raising parties, but I still feel it's my civic duty to support our city's cultural endeavors, and so I go. You know how desperate they are for money. How are you, dear? And how is Allyson?"

Without waiting for a reply, Constance turned to the mirror on the side wall, patted her stiff coiffure and remarked casually, "Millicent, you really ought to do something about your hair. It needs styling or something. You're letting yourself go, dear. I noticed that the last time I saw you weeks ago."

There it was again. The disparagement and insensitivity to my problems. Dammit! Millicent said silently as a prickling rage swept through her body. *Why can't my own mother give me just a little of the support she so generously lavishes on her "cultural endeavors"? She lives here like a hothouse flower, immune from contact with the real world. And then scolds me like a child for spoiling her environment with a less-than-perfect appearance.*

"Mother, I really haven't had the time or the inclination to worry about my hair,"

Millicent responded, trying not to sound annoyed. "No one notices my hair at the hospital."

John J. Bolt pushed away his coffee cup and said, "Oh, you were at the hospital? Yes, yes, of course. I hope Allyson is better. I think that new doctor will get to the heart of things. Had him call and give me a report, and he seems to know what he's doing. Checked him out, too. Good man, that Graham. Mark my words, he'll get her straightened out. I told him to spare no expense and to call in some good consultants. I even suggested the Mayo Clinic, but don't want to interfere."

Oh, I bet you checked him out, thought Millicent. *Just like you do everything else.*

Millicent felt the anger ebbing from his guilt-provoking greeting as she became more acutely aware of her father's constant need to maintain control over every situation. *He enjoys the role. Poor father,* she said to herself. *You need to have power over everything, as if to remind us of the man you once were.*

"Yes, father, Dr. Graham does seem to be very good. I think there's been some improvement since he's been taking care of Allyson." Millicent paused and cast her eyes downward. "I'm really sorry I haven't been in touch. I know I've neglected you both lately, but I've had so much on my mind."

"Well, we've had a lot on our minds, too." John J. Bolt's statement was made like a lecture. "Don't you think we're just as concerned? Of course, we are. But we still attend to the needs of our family. We don't for a minute let important things slide. You've got to keep a clear sense of perspective about these matters, my girl."

"I'm sorry, father. I do know how concerned you are."

I'm doing it again, Millicent realized. *I seem to spend half my life saying I'm sorry, apologizing for things that aren't my fault. Good God, how are they able to produce this unreasonable burden of guilt? Somehow they all manage to make me feel guilty. Mother, father, Jeff, the children, Joan. How have I failed them? What have I done that makes me feel so sorry?*

She became aware of Constance's reproachful voice. "You must understand, Millicent, that this whole ugly business with Allyson has put a terrible strain on us, too. Do you think it's easy for us to stand by and watch that child suffer? We worry ourselves to death. We do all we can. We would do *anything* to make her well. Believe me, I'm not even in the mood to go out tonight. But for the sake of everyone, I keep up appearances."

Millicent was more bewildered than hurt. How could they possibly ignore what she was going through and expect her to be sympathetic to their feelings. So many thoughts were taking shape at once: *I've lived so long with this ridiculous sense of obligation, and I'm sick of it. And why don't I ever say anything? What makes me cower like a bad little girl? I'm old enough to be a grandmother and I act like a child — dependent and weak, and still wanting them to bless me.*

But she kept silent and let her parents run on about how difficult it was for them to carry on when "one of their own" was in trouble. And then she changed the subject and offered her mother what she hoped would please her.

"Oh, mother, before I forget, Cory called from school and said to be sure to tell you how much she adores the perfume you sent her and to thank you for it."

"Well, I'm not looking for any thanks, but a brief note once in a while would at least assure me that she has the manners a well-brought-up girl should have. Maybe I'm old-fashioned but . . . anyway, I'm glad she likes it. Perhaps it will be an incentive for Corinne to discard those frightful jeans and put on a proper dress every so often. Millicent, do you realize that she goes out on dates with those dirty pants on? She told me so. Corinne is such a beautiful girl. I can't for the life of me understand why she tries to make herself look unattractive. You know what, I think I'm going to send some of that marvelous Patou perfume to Allyson in the hospital. Yes, that's exactly what I'll do. You'll see, it will cheer her up. A good scent always does wonders for me when I'm feeling down. Isn't that so, John?"

"That's so, Constance. And a nice piece of jewelry can really bring you up," answered her husband with a wry smile, remembering all the lovely baubles he had given her to compensate for his indiscretions.

Millicent arrived home drained from the visit with her parents. She had gone there as the dutiful daughter, determined to keep the peace and bring them a thread of good news about Allyson. But their lack of understanding and implicit demands of her reverential attention, even at a time like this, had only stirred up old wounds. She was annoyed at herself because she realized for the hundredth time that she was afraid of their disapproval.

What do they want from me? They give nothing of themselves and want everything. And it's always been that way.

They'd never shown any interest in what she felt ever. She was awkward amid the all-female atmosphere at the swanky private girls' schools they chose for her — from National Cathedral to Vassar. She had been smothered with the constant attention to ridiculous details: her hair, her clothes, her posture, her manners, her looks or the lack of them. Did they realize what it was like always being compared with her beautiful mother and ravishing sister? And then the expectations of a suitable marriage that would produce a certain life-style and proper children. Until she married Jeff, she had done everything they wanted with ingratiating regard for their wishes. She had lived up to their idea of a well-brought-up daughter. Jeffrey Hart, with his humble background, wasn't exactly what they had in mind as a suitable match, but they were smart enough to realize that the society boys weren't breaking down her door. And anyway, her father needed a hard-working, obsequious "son" to come into the business. He knew he could mold him to "their way." In fact, he rationalized, a poor boy would be grateful for the marvelous opportunity, and that kind of deferential relationship suited John J. Bolt just fine.

What do I want from them? Millicent asked herself. *Their love, their reassurance, their concern for my feelings, their approval. Always their approval.*

"Oh damn!" she cursed out loud. *I seem to want that from everybody, and when it isn't forthcoming I get so disappointed and upset. I've got to stop wishing they were what they are not and never will be. Is it so much easier to complain about mother and father than it is to become the person I want to be? I want to be independent, free from feeling injured by their petty criticisms. Instead, I suffer their disapproval and make a career out of complaining about them. And why do I need them in my corner at this stage of my life? What's the use of trying to make them*

understand? At their age, they're not going to change. The change has to come from me. The trouble is that I've never challenged their rules, and that's what's kept me absolutely paralyzed. I've got to stop living in the past. All it takes is courage and determination. But God knows, I haven't had much of that lately.

Millicent was determined not to sink into another morass of anxiety and self-pity. She decided to read the book on economics she had bought weeks ago and had put aside because her worried mind could not give the book the total concentration it merited. It was a subject that had always fascinated her, and she had been sorry that she hadn't studied more of it in college instead of the liberal arts frills she had been talked into. She would read in bed and wait for Jeff and persuade him to love her again.

But her impassioned yearning and desire to reassert her love for him were not to be fulfilled that night. Millicent waited, ready to offer herself fully and completely, but fell asleep long before Jeff returned from the all-consuming transactions of the evening.

Chapter 5

Millicent awoke with a start the next morning. The place beside her was empty. Jeff had quietly left the house without disturbing her. She had overslept and was disappointed that she had missed seeing him. Today, as she had last night, she wanted to reaffirm her devotion to him and magically make things right. Sitting on the edge of the bed, she was depressed by the thought that she had missed the opportunity. She had been anxious to share the good news about Allyson with Jeff, as though this little bit of improvement in their daughter would somehow strengthen their tenuous relationship. Now the anticipated joy in that moment had been missed.

As she showered and dressed, Millicent thought that for the first time in many months, she didn't want to spend the day by herself. She had given up her volunteer work since Allyson's latest hospitalization. Working with battered women and their underprivileged children provided an added satisfaction to her life. But she now found she was unable to handle other people's problems. So the days became empty.

Today she felt the need of a friend, female companionship, in whom she could freely confide or just spend a few hours of diversion. She needed to reestablish the comfortable relationship she had once had with Dolly Henderson. Not that she wanted to pour out the most intimate details of her troubled life. That was uncharacteristic of her. It was just that she wanted to be with someone who was sympathetic and easy to talk to. She even wanted some of Dolly's crazy chatter and that misplaced enthusiasm that usually proved contagious.

Dolly answered the phone with her grouchy morning voice. "Who is calling at this ungodly hour? Speak up and identify yourself."

"Dolly, it's me, Millicent."

"My dear, I don't hear from you in weeks and now you call and take me away from the only decent dream I've had in months."

"Dolly, I spoke to you yesterday."

"Yes, that's right. I remember — you turned down all my attempts at getting you out of that house and away from that hospital for even an afternoon of cheerful relief."

"And now I'm sorry I didn't take your offer. Give me another chance and have lunch with me today. You were right, I do need to get out."

"Well now, surprise of surprises, an apology and an invitation." Dolly was clearly beginning to wake up. "Mill, is there something special on your mind, something you want to talk about?"

"Not really, Dolly. I'm just feeling better, and I'm taking your advice about seeing old friends. Can you make it for lunch?"

"I'll have to switch a few appointments around, but sure, I'll make it. I'm thrilled you called, Mill. There is something special you want to talk about, isn't there?"

"As a matter of fact, there is. I need

your opinion and perhaps your help in sorting things out."

"I thought so," said Dolly in an all-knowing tone. "What exactly is on your mind?"

"We can discuss it later," said Millicent. "right now I'm just interested in seeing you. How about meeting me at the Jockey Club around twelve-thirty? I'll make a reservation."

Dolly arrived at the Jockey Club elegant, trim, and self-possessed but late as usual. She came sweeping through the posh French restaurant in the Ritz-Carlton Hotel like a dazzling model on a runway. Whatever the new look in fashion was, Dolly had it first. She wore a black-and-white houndstooth suit designed by Yves Saint Laurent that she claimed was "seriously structured," in keeping with the latest trend. Her white silk blouse was ornately ruffled at the throat and cuffs and gave the outfit a regal look. Gold chains dangled from her neck and wrist, and when she walked, they noisily called attention to her entrance. Louis, the gracious host, led her across the plank-pegged floors to the table where Millicent was waiting with a bloody mary.

They embraced warmly, and Millicent realized how good it was to see her old friend. Dolly, despite her faults, was part of her past and had remained a friend just because she had always been there.

Dolly Henderson was an arrogantly handsome woman of undisclosed age. She had a Latin look that disarmed people when she spoke. Her acquired top-drawer accent made her sound as though she were talking with marbles in her mouth and had spent her youth sailing around Newport with the Vanderbilts. It was rarely possible to detect that Dolly wasn't "to the manor born," or that she hadn't learned how to speak at Miss Porter's Finishing School as had her close circle of friends. Only when she was angry or nervous could she be caught off guard, and then a faint trace of the old Brooklyn accent came through.

"Darling, it's marvelous to see you again. At least I think I see you. My God, you still need a guide dog in here. One of these days I'm going to break my neck before lunch and sue the bloody establishment for impersonating an opium den." She paused and gave the room a sweeping glance. "Oh, but I do love this place. It's the ultimate in sophisticated dining, and that's so important, you know." This Dolly said between clenched teeth in a low, precise voice.

They drank cocktails and ordered lunch. Dolly talked non-stop from the paté maison with toasted Syrian bread through the salmon mousse covered with sauce verte and surrounded by artichoke hearts right down to the biscuit tortoni with nectarines.

Millicent eagerly listened to all the frivolous news and gossip that Dolly poured out. It was fun, for a change, to be with someone who didn't make her feel as if she had to account for her emotions.

"Tell me, Millicent, now that I've gotten all the 'important' news over with, what is it you have to tell me? I told you before that I'm the one to come to with your troubles. Deep down, although most people don't think so, I'm a good listener. I also know when to keep a confidence. Remember, I've been through this scene myself."

There was a peculiar nuance in Dolly's conversation, as though there was something on her mind that she was waiting for Millicent to disclose first. Millicent sensed this and wondered: *Is she referring to Allyson? Probably, what else is there? Except my relationship with mother and father, and that's old hat to her.*

"Well, Dolly, Allyson's illness has been the kind of trouble that I wouldn't wish on my worst enemy." Millicent found she could say this easily to Dolly.

"Mill, you don't have an enemy in this world, and you know it."

"I wouldn't be too sure of that. Lately, I've had the feeling that somebody up there doesn't like me." Millicent said this with a mirthless laugh. "But I think she is a little bit better. Only a little bit, mind you, but enough to make me feel hopeful."

"Oh, that's good to hear, sweetie. *Jeff* must be so relieved too," said Dolly with deliberate emphasis.

"I only wish he knew . . . we haven't been, well, what shall I say, communicating very well lately. I wanted to tell him last night or this morning, but I never saw him and . . ."

"You mean he never came home? You poor thing, to have *this* on top of all your other problems."

What does she mean by "this"? Millicent wondered. *Does she know something that I don't? Was she hinting at something that she couldn't bring herself to say outright? Maybe I'm just imagining some ominous inflection. After all, she's always been overly dramatic.*

"I mean, I didn't get to see him, and I guess that along with Allyson's illness . . . well, I seem to have a bad case of the empty-nest blues. Now that's something I used to read about and laugh about. Well, I'm not laughing now. It does hit you when all the kids leave and you're all alone, rattling around in a big, empty house."

Dolly was eagerly sympathetic. "Well, you shouldn't be alone, not now of all times. Men are all alike, Mill, even the best of them. When you need them the most, that's when they split for greener and younger pastures. It makes me sick to hear about this."

There was no mistaking Dolly's words now. The expression in her eyes said she was referring to Jeff.

Millicent leaned forward and swallowed hard. "Dolly, what *are* you saying? I have the strangest feeling you're trying to tell me something."

A quizzical expression came across Dolly's face, then her eyes widened in disbelief.

In contrast to her haughty composure when she entered the restaurant, Dolly was now overcome with confusion. She felt sick. She squirmed in her chair and opened her hands wide as though she were pleading her case. Her voice lost its lofty accent.

"Millicent, I thought you knew. I thought that was why you wanted to see me today. I just assumed you had to talk it over, and . . . when you suggested the Jockey Club, of all places, well I was sure you knew . . . . Oh my God . . . what have I done? You mean, you didn't know?"

With this unexpected innuendo, Millicent's stomach muscles tightened and her heart began to beat rapidly. For several tense moments, the two women looked at each other miserably.

With difficulty, and with a quivering voice, Millicent finally said, "No, Dolly, I didn't know, and I still don't know. What in heaven's name are you talking about, and does it have something to do with Jeff? It does have to do with Jeff, doesn't it?"

Dolly fumbled through her purse, her

hands unsteady, and came up with several twenty-dollar bills. She threw them on the table and motioned to Millicent to get up. "Oh Mill, let's get out of here. I'm a mess. I thought surely you knew. It never crossed my mind that after all this time, you didn't call me just because you had to unburden yourself and get some advice and tell me about last night and Jeff and . . ."

Half standing, half sitting, Millicent grabbed the arms of the chair and slid back into the seat. "Last night!" she said incredulously. "I was home alone most of the evening. I wasn't even with Jeff. I was waiting for him. He had a business appointment. He was with a client and . . . you mean he wasn't with a client?" Dolly's stricken face brought Millicent close to tears. "Dolly, what is this all about? Tell me!"

Chapter 6

Dolly told her.

They sat in the upstairs drawing room, both women visibly nervous. Dolly lived in Kalorama Square, that bastion of many-storied luxurious townhouses with a security system that had everything but a moat filled with snapping alligators to ward off inner-city residents who might be curious as to how rich people were different.

With more composure than she had had in the restaurant, Dolly was still pleading her case. "I simply cannot get it through my head that you didn't know. Millicent, believe me, I would never, never, have said a word if I hadn't been absolutely positive that that's what this luncheon date was all about."

Millicent was anything but composed. "No, it wasn't, Dolly. What made you think that's why I called? I don't know what I said or did to give you that impression."

"Oh, come on now, Mill! You call me for the first time in ages saying that you want to see me, the very next day after I called you practically begging to take you away from that house and the hospital, where you've isolated yourself for weeks. You refuse any company or friendship or help with your problems. And then, the very next day, you call and say you want to see me and act very mysterious as to what it's all about and then suggest meeting at the Jockey Club, of all places. So, of course, I assumed that you knew about Jeff being there the night before with a beautiful woman, having dinner with her, and then being seen going in the elevator together, obviously up to her room in the Ritz-Carlton, and that you found out and were mad as hell and wanted to go back there for some strange, ironic twist and talk about it with me." Dolly was breathless after this long explanation.

Millicent looked at her curiously. "How would I find out, and even if I did, why in the world would I suggest going to the Jockey Club if I knew Jeff had been there with someone else? That's just about the last place I would ever want to go. That would really be rubbing it in, especially since Jeff always thought it was too dark and secluded for a restaurant. What I'm saying is that he likes bright, bustling restaurants and . . . oh, Dolly, I'm not even making sense." More upset, Millicent shuddered and clasped her hands.

Dolly became more excited and defensive. "But that's exactly what went through my mind, the fact that *it is* dark and secluded and an unlikely place for him to be seen in, not one of your big downtown table-hopping scenes where he usually takes clients. Oh, Mill, I guess I just projected my own warped sense of revenge, thinking what I would do in a similar situation. In fact, what I did with my 'long lost husband' when he was screwing around with every Capitol Hill cutie in Washington was to follow his amorous trail through every restaurant, bar, and hotel in the city. I got some kind of secret, spiteful pleasure from being in on his romantic hiding places, hoping to catch him and at the same time afraid I would. But you're not me, and I should have known that your mind isn't filled with the same evil thoughts I'm consumed with."

"Well, they are now," admitted Millicent, with a lump in her throat. She stood up and nervously paced the room, hardly aware of the surroundings but conscious if her pounding heart.

Dolly regarded her compassionately, and when Millicent's face became even more troubled, she made another stab in her own defense.

"Look, Mill. This whole thing is a big, stupid mistake. I've got a big mouth and a suspicious heart. Perhaps I assumed too much and had no business being the harbinger of bad news. God knows, you've got enough problems to deal with. But I swear to you that I really did think you knew about Jeff and that you just needed that shoulder I offered you to lean on. Men are not exactly my favorite people these days, your husband included, if you don't mind my saying so. But you are my dearest friend and I value your friendship. I wouldn't deliberately hurt your this way for the world. You've got to believe me, Millicent."

Millicent sat down beside her. She took a few quick breaths in an effort to calm down. "I do believe you, Dolly. Now let's forget the whys and wherefores and get down to what this is all about. I still have only bits and pieces so tell me what you know straight out. And at this point, don't spare me. Not knowing everything is worse than knowing a little and imagining more. So begin at the beginning."

Dolly nodded and took a gulp of the scotch that was fortifying her. "Late last night I got a call from Cissy Benson . . ."

"The self-proclaimed watchtower of infidelity," interrupted Millicent in a voice that had a crusty edge.

"Well, Cissy does seem to have a knack for being in the right place when any hanky-panky is going on," said Dolly, stitting up straighter in her chair, her face becoming animated. "Anyway, Cissy called and told me that she had dinner at the Jockey Club last night with some out-of-town friends who happened to be staying at the Ritz-Carlton, and they unexpectedly decided to eat at the hotel. Of course, the food is first class and so are the prices, and the chef is touted as some culinary whiz with magic French hands who can turn pigs' feet into a culinary delicacy like . . ."

"Dolly," snapped Millicent, "forget the food and the chef. The Jockey Club doesn't need an endorsement, and I don't need any local color. Please get on with it."

"Well, Cissy had to go to the ladies' room. As she was groping her way through that unlit maze of tables and waiters, she tripped against one of the tables and knocked a woman's purse off. Rather startled, she glanced around and saw a gorgeous young woman staring right into her face. Then she saw the man who was with her. He was bending down to pick up the purse just as a waiter dashed over with one of those darling little candle holders that they use there instead of light bulbs. The light from the flame was right on the man's face, and the man was Jeff. Cissy claims he didn't see her, but she saw him perfectly and the woman, too. She made a beeline to the bathroom before he straightened up, and when she came back in, she avoided them. However, when she left the restaurant, she made it her business to go right past them. But they were so busy talking they didn't even notice her."

Dolly paused, wondering whether she

should repeat the part about Cissy seeing them go into the elevator together and how Jeff had his arm around the woman's shoulder and they were laughing and very much engrossed in each other. Cissy had been loitering in the lobby with her friends, saying their good-byes, and Jeff and his "friend" came out and sauntered past her. And as Cissy said, where else could they have been going in the elevator if not up to the woman's room. Perhaps the remark had made no impression, Dolly thought, and she decided not to mention it unless Millicent pressed her. No sense in adding salt to an already painful wound, Dolly surmised.

While Dolly talked, Millicent sat lost in thought. She could not remember when she had felt so low.

Dolly knew this and tried to make amends.

"You're right, Mill. She is the town gossip and obviously takes great delight in exposing the high and the mighty. So, of course, she couldn't wait to call me, and she probably knew somehow that I would eventually spill the beans to you. But, honestly, I wouldn't have if this odd chain of circumstances hadn't taken place. I

101

mean, if you hadn't called me the very next day, I wouldn't have said a word to you or anyone else. And now that you know, what are you going to do?"

Until now, Millicent was in a state of shock. The question brought her out of her reverie and made her angry. "Do? What do you expect me to do? You throw this at me out of the blue, as if you're telling some juicy gossip about a movie star or someone I never heard of, and then expect me to know . . . I don't know what!"

Millicent put her head down between her hands and sat silently. Dolly got up and went to her side. She put her arm around her friend and felt the depths of Millicent's misery. "Oh, Mill, I'm so sorry," she said.

Millicent looked up. Her anger subsided. "So am I," she said forlornly. "So am I." Then she asked quietly, "What can I do? What should I do?"

Dolly sighed and moved slowly toward the couch, slumping into it dejectedly, her feet curled under her. With a faraway look she said, "You're asking the wrong woman, love. My marriage broke up because I demanded answers, and all I accomplished was to send that husband of mine hopping into a younger bed."

Millicent looked at her in amazement. "You mean you should have just ignored it and let him have his fling?"

The expression on Dolly's face became bitter. "Well, it wasn't exactly a fling. It was more like an extended vacation of lustful self-indulgence. No, you can't ignore it. At least I couldn't. But I should have found a way to live with it, or ride it out as other politicians' wives do. Look, it comes with the territory when you marry important, successful men who are in the public eye. They're a pushover for every adoring female and consider every fatuous compliment as an invitation to show off their sexual prowess. All that power does silly things to men. So yes, I should have stuck it out somehow. But that's hindsight. At the time, I didn't have anything but outrage for the *famous Senator Henderson,* champion of the people, who was hustling more than votes from every pretty little hometown constituent who got a typing job in his office." Suddenly Dolly softened. "And fair is fair. I did the same thing to Lloyd's first wife. So what was I so sore about when he turned around and did me in just like he did to her? I got kicked in the behind the same as Mrs. Henderson number one, only this time it was my behind and it hurt like hell. When your pride is on the line, Mill, you do things you can become very sorry for later. Sure I had my pride, but pride isn't very good company when you're lonely. I found that out pretty fast after he took off."

Millicent considered what Dolly said. "Now that you've told me, you're saying to forget it?"

"I don't know what I'm saying, Millicent. This happened five years ago. I'm just telling you how I feel now, and if I had to do it all over again, although there's still a part of me that hates the bastard, I would probably wait it out until he got too old to get it up anymore. But frankly, at the time, I thought he was already too old. I didn't know that men go through a crazy phase of honestly believing they've grown a second penis to take the place of the one that's atrophied and about to fall off. Young, ambitious girls can make them believe they could hump a camel, because these men are consummate egotists and have to believe it. And God knows, once upon a time I was one of those political groupies myself. I would have told a ninety-year-old congressman that he had four balls if that would have gotten me a place on his bandwagon."

In spite of her absorption with her own immediate problem, Millicent reacted instantly to Dolly's self-deprecating remarks and came to her friend's defense. "Stop talking like that, Dolly. You're making yourself sound like a slut. You and Lloyd had a good marriage until he got carried away with his self-importance and power. And you didn't steal him from his first wife. He very willingly left her and ran after you. You're accepting too much blame. He was the cheater, not you."

"Look who's talking!" said Dolly with a side glance of scorn. "I can look at you right now and imagine what you're feeling. You're full of suppressed emotion, probably rage. But when I look into your eyes I see pain, not anger, Mill. You haven't said one nasty remark about Jeff. You haven't hurled one legitimate invective at his lecherous soul since I told you. I'll bet you a fifty-dollar lunch at the highly popular Jockey Club that right now, right this minute, you're wondering what you did wrong to throw him into the arms of that gorgeous *client*. Your well-organized and understanding mind, my dear Millicent, is saying: 'How did I shatter his fragile ego, or what qualities do I lack that would make him turn to someone else at a time like this?' Don't tell me you're not blaming yourself instead of sticking pins in his jockey shorts! I know you too well, Mill. You're big on tolerance but low on outrage. Your gut is overstuffed with guilt, but for you there's always room for one more bitter pill to swallow. So join the club, my friend, and become a quiet forgiving dumpee."

Millicent became thoughtful. No use denying what Dolly said, because it was all true. Instead of being angry at Jeff, she was feeling unexplainable guilt. "Did you forgive Lloyd?" she asked.

"Not really. But I did forget a lot of the bad times. And when the bruises healed and the wounds closed, all I clearly remembered were the good old days. And I sure as hell miss them."

"Then where do I go from here?" Millicent asked without recrimination.

"Home, sweetie."

"But, Dolly, the martyr role doesn't

suit me."

Dolly threw back her head and with a cynical smile said, "Sure it does. It suits us both or we would have given our wayward spouses what for a long time ago and taken a little roll in the hay ourselves.'

Millicent didn't respond. She stared at her friend with disbelief. Did Dolly know about Jeff's past, too? Was she referring to those unhappy years a long time ago? No. How could she? I didn't even know her then.

Her eyes filled with tears. "I really love him."

"I know you do, Mill. And strangely enough, I think I still have a lot of feeling for Lloyd. My hostility is mostly talk. I'd probably take him back in a minute if I had the chance. Face it, chum, we're just born-again victims."

The third Mrs. Henderson would have scoffed at that remark, but the first Mrs. Henderson would have agreed. It all depends on where your place in line is.

Dolly consoled herself with another drink and the thought that Millicent would have found out sooner or later. She sat for a long while in the drawing room that resembled an Irish garden in full bloom. Floral prints designed by Sybil Connolly covered the fabric walls. Primroses, violets, and poppies spread from floor to ceiling. Deep red roses and delicate pansy prints in yellow and lilac swept over the upholstered furniture without interruption. Baskets and pots of flowers filled all the rooms of the precisely decorated house. Dolly was a romantic and did her best to preserve the illusion of romanticism that had been the mainstay of her fantasies as a girl growing up in Brooklyn.

She had come to Washington in her twenties to escape the dreariness of being poor in New York, the worst possible place in the world to be without substantial funds, and to avoid the pressure of marriage to "one of her own kind." She was young and bright and pretty, with the vitality of her generation of Italians. But she felt suffocated by her strict religious background and by the unsophisticated Catholic boys she was allowed to date only after they had been carefully scrutinized by her old-fashioned parents.

She broke loose, much to their shame and dismay, by coming to Washington. She landed on Capitol Hill in the farthest corner of the secretarial pool. But when a lovely brunette with big dark eyes looked up with an adoring smile, it was not too surprising that the representative from New York noticed her and took her "under his wing." She worked her way up in Congressman Henderson's office rather quickly. He represented the "silk stocking" district and was already a forty-year-old political star. He was also married to a woman he had married before he became important.

Lloyd Henderson was desperately ambitious, but so was Delores Maria Angela Carusi. No sleazy motel rooms or late working nights on the office couch appealed to Dolly, as she was now called. And the old line about "my wife doesn't understand me" or "she hasn't grown with me" never penetrated her rigid sexual mores. Free sex, in Dolly's mind, was unethical. She believed in the strict work ethic — a good day's pay for a good day's work.

She doled out her sexuality in small doses, just enough to excite the soon-to-be-powerful senator from New York, but not enough to be taken for granted. She wasn't about to be kept dangling with deceptive promises or expensive little rewards. The only reward she wanted was his name. She knew her social status could only rise as Mrs. Lloyd Henderson, and early in the relationship, she decided to settle for nothing less. She wanted to serve tea to the senate wives as the hostess in her own house.

Lloyd Henderson thrived on excitement. So the aspiring socialite titillated the aspiring senator until he willingly capitulated and got his docile and unexciting wife to give him a divorce and take the kids back home. But only after he had won his senate seat.

Dolly got her house and all the glorious perks that go with political prominence. For sixteen years, they lived the agreeable life with distractions galore — an endless round of lunches, teas, and dinners with famous people, including those in residence at the White House. Being backup to her husband became her life's main occupation, and she found it enormously satisfying. No children were born of this marriage. The senator already had two whom he rarely saw. And Dolly's life was so full of outside interests that she never considered the need for the inner fulfillment that children bring. There was money too — from where, she never questioned. The senator had "good" connections, and lucrative business deals "just fell into his lap."

Dolly was not disappointed that some of the emotion disappeared in the course of the marriage. In fact, she regarded the passing of passion with relief. She had grown tired of acting as though she was on an amphetamine high every time the senator got sweaty palms and a rapid pulse. But not the senator. Lust was his ego reinforcement, and what he could no longer perform in the bed, he could imagine in his mind. So when a young divorcee with the same social aspirations that Dolly once had came along with bedroom tricks that made Lloyd Henderson feel like a hormone-drenched adolescent, their longstanding relationship ended with bitterness and a financial settlement.

Dolly raged and cried. She had spent most of her adult life worrying about her charm instead of developing a career, and now she was out of the only job she had prepared herself for. But the survivor in her eventually gained control, and she intelligently assessed her empty single existence in terms of other similarly situated women. Where would she go if she needed a job?

Turned out by their successful breadwinners, where do once secure middle-aged women go when their only career skills are the fine points of shopping and entertaining? What do they do with their class and pride? Dolly decided that a life devoted to being a superb hostess, an elegant dresser, a polished political partner, should count for something.

An employment agency for social has-beens was the answer. With her substantial settlement she started Elite, Inc. She hauled out her old aggressiveness and milked her contacts and got enough displaced women to pay her a fee to find them suitable employment. She found them positions as fashion consultants, interior decorators, travel specialists, shopping advisers, entertainment connoisseurs, and any other jobs that called upon their finely honed and tasteful skills learned in the world of the haut monde. In a few short years, her fancy employment agency became highly successful, and Dolly Henderson became a woman of independent means and status.

That was what Millicent had had on her mind when she called Dolly. Besides wanting the pleasure of her company, Millicent wanted Dolly's advice on possible employment for Allyson. If and when she recovered from this latest bout with anorexia, Allyson would need a job, something to keep her busy and make her feel useful, and a contrived position in the family business would never work.

But the unexpected revelation of Jeff's latest escapade had diverted her attention. The subject of employment for Allyson had never come up. Millicent's attempt to focus on the hard facts of her muddled existence now became further blurred. The humiliation of other people knowing about their private lives was almost harder to bear than his faithlessness. She could only guess at the truth, and she did not want to know for certain the extent of her husband's involvement with this woman because she was too numb to contemplate the future. In a way, her realism was slipping and she was conscious that she was hanging on to reasonableness by a slim thread. Another complication in her already entangled life suddenly loomed as staggering.

Millicent left Dolly's house dejected and wondering, as Dolly had predicted, where she had failed. There was a rush of remembrance, and the heaviness in her chest felt like a millstone. She realized that everything put together sooner or later falls apart. She had been through this before, in the early years of their marriage, and the hurt had been devastating. But she had dealt with it then and had thought Jeff's libertine days were long over. Now she was too drained to even figure out what to do.

She arrived home and was surprised to see Jeff's car in the driveway. *Is he dressing to go out again or did his conscience bring him home early?* she wondered. The thought of facing him now gripped her with anxiety. She knew she could not handle it. She turned the car around and headed for the hospital.

Miss Waverly met her in the hallway and gently stopped her from entering the room.

"Now don't get upset, Mrs. Hart, but we've had a bit of a setback. I tried to call you at home, but I couldn't get in touch with you."

Millicent pressed her hands to her face and gasped, "Oh my God, what's happened?"

"Nothing alarming. It's just that the patient has been in a depressed mood today and will not take any nourishment. Dr. Graham and the resident are with her now."

Millicent was aware of the change in Miss Waverly's words and tone. The nurse sounded detached when she referred to "the patient," as though she were already separating herself emotionally from the inevitable and dire consequences.

She rushed in and saw Dr. Graham and the resident physician hovering over Allyson, who was lying motionless. They were examining her and at the same time persistently coaxing her to respond to their presence.

Dr. Graham looked up imploringly, and Millicent hurried to the bed. She stroked the limp arms and patted the lifeless hands. "Allyson honey. What's the matter? You seemed so much better yesterday. Did anything happen? Tell me, sweetheart. Is there something you want?"

Allyson continued to stare at the ceiling as though she were in a catatonic state. But Millicent persisted. "Darling, listen to me. I know you can hear me. You've got to eat something. Just try. You need to regain your strength. We'll all help you. Just tell us what's bothering you today. And I have some great plans for you that I'm anxious to tell you about. I've been thinking about what you'll do when you get out of the hospital. We really need to talk about it. Allyson, baby, talk to me. Please talk to me."

Allyson did not move, but a single tear slid down her cheek.

Dr. Graham beckoned Millicent to come out in the hall. She followed him and leaned her back against the wall for support. She felt as if her whole body was out of control, as if sections of it were missing, torn away. In a fleeting second, as she stood with Roger Graham in the unusually still corridor, she had the sensation that her body was reacting to her mind. She had the momentary impulse to let go of everything. The instinctive discipline and patient endurance she had been clinging to so tightly were slipping away. Her whole life was out of control.

She became aware of Dr. Graham's soothing voice and strong arm around her shoulder, holding her up. With his arm firmly supporting her, Roger Graham slowly led her down the hall past the nursing station to a small waiting room that was fortunately empty of visitors. He guided her to a lounge chair and pulled one of the straight-back chairs close to hers. "Mrs. Hart, I really don't know what happened. It's as if she turned off her mind and body and put herself into a comalike state. But she's not in a coma and this could be a very temporary condition. However, she's turning inward, and we're going to have to put her back on intravenous feeding if she doesn't react soon. We have to ward off any irreversible kidney damage."

Millicent sat quietly for a long while, trying to grasp the meaning of all this. Finally, the disappointed words came: "I was so hopeful yesterday."

"So was I," said Dr. Graham sympathetically. "But we have to separate the hope from the reality. Something deep inside her is taking hold, and since we don't know what it is, we are just going to have to proceed with standard medical support and get her functioning again physically. I do have a few ideas, and I'll try them for whatever they're worth."

"What do you mean? A new treatment?" Millicent asked hopefully.

"No, there's no new treatment. We're just going to have to be a little unorthodox about getting her out of this trance she seems determined to be in. If I had to guess, I would say that this catatonic stupor that Allyson's regressed into could be a neurotic reaction to anxiety and depression. It's a form of selective inattention or denial whereby a person blocks out those environmental details that generate unpleasant feelings." Suddenly Dr. Graham looked embarrassed. "I am sounding like a psychiatrist, aren't I? Nevertheless, what's important now is to try to pull her out of it."

Millicent caught her breath and clutched her hands tightly. "You mean she may not come out of this state?"

Dr. Graham shook his head. His voice became reassuring. "No, no, Mrs. Hart. We'll get her out of it. The problem is to keep her out."

As Millicent entered the house,

exhausted and confused, she silently said, *Help me*. Her belief in God had been formed in direct opposition to her father's irreligious philosophy, which rejected sustenance and strength from any unworldly presence.

She started up the stairs just as Jeff opened the library door. "Millicent, where have you been? I've been waiting for you."

Without turning she answered coldly, "At the hospital."

Jeff followed her up to their bedroom suite. "Why didn't you come in the house before? Homer said you drove in the driveway and then turned around and left. I came home early to go to the hospital with you. Millicent, stop moving. Look at me. What's the matter? Is Allyson worse?"

She turned and faced him. She was deadly pale. "Yes, she's worse."

His voice was strained. "How much worse? What happened?"

Without apparent emotion, she answered: "I don't know what happened. She was better yesterday and today it's as if she's in a coma. She's not talking. She's not moving. She just stares. But the doctor said it's not a coma. What's the difference? She's out of touch with reality and seems to be sinking into oblivion."

"Should I go to the hospital?"

"No. There's nothing you can do. They told me to leave. They'll call us if there's any change." Millicent walked to the chaise and slumped down.

Jeffrey went to her and put his arms around her trembling body. "Don't worry, honey. She'll come out of this. She'll be all right. You're not alone, Mill. We'll see this thing through together."

Angrily she turned on him. "Then why do I feel so empty and alone?"

Taken by surprise, he glared at her. "Are you still mad because I didn't go to the hospital with you last night?"

"It's not where you *didn't go*, it's where you *did go*," she blurted out. She hadn't meant to say anything. It just came out, and she was sorry because she wasn't up to an ugly scene or excuses or even an explanation.

He jumped up from the chaise lounge. "For Christ's sake, what *are* you referring to?"

She dreaded what she had unwittingly started. She fell silent, but Jeff was not about to postpone this discussion.

His body became taut, and he stood

hovering over her, his hands boldly on his hips. His jaw was rigid as he waited for her to answer him.

She turned away and remained silent.

Carefully but firmly, he reached down and put his hand on her chin and forced her to look at him. "Millicent, let's have it. I know you're upset, very upset about Allyson, and I am too. But obviously there's something else that's bothering you. I'm sorry about last night. I wish we could have been together, but it couldn't be helped. So what is it?" His hand fell to his side.

She rose from the chaise, and his eyes followed her as she paced aimlessly throughout the bedroom. With a sudden stop, she stood riveted in place and faced him. She wanted her voice to be calm, composed, but when the words came out, they were filled with anger and sarcasm: "It's where you were last night and who you were with. I'm sure you thought you were being discreet, but you were not discreet enough, Jeff. You should have taken *her* to your office, or perhaps a cozy out-of-the-way hotel. You should know by now, Jeff, that Washington is really a very small town and everyone here knows everybody else's business."

With a thud, he slapped his fist into his other hand and rolled his head back. "Holy shit! So that's it. One of your goddamned nosy friends thought she was blowing the whistle. Which man-hating bitch was it who probably called you bright and early to report that I had dinner last night at the Jockey Club with some beautiful dame?"

For a long moment, Millicent remained frozen in position. She responded with what amounted to an uncomprehending stare.

Jeff approached her. His face was only inches from hers. His voice was demanding. "Okay, Millicent, out with it. Who told you about last night?"

Millicent stood in front of him, stunned. Their roles had reversed. Her tone was incredulous. "You admit it?"

He returned her stare. "Of course, I admit it. I was seen, wasn't I?" he answered sarcastically. "And she probably told you that I went up to her room, which I did, to conduct *business*."

She had expected remorse or an implausible explanation from Jeff, but certainly not anger. Why was he now turning it on her? Why wasn't he even the least bit defensive?

No sooner had she contemplated this than his whole mood changed. The strain left Jeff's face and he looked at her lovingly. Then he pulled her to him and cradled his head in her shoulder.

Millicent was bewildered. Conflicting thoughts were going through her head. Her eyes were a curious mixture of surprise and fear. "I have the feeling," she said contritely, "that I've been caught up in some twisted gossip that I had no business listening to. Jeff, am I imagining something stupid and idiotic?"

Still holding her, Jeff looked into her eyes. His voice was gentle. "I think so, hon. I was having dinner with a client, just as I told you."

She moved away from him and sat down on the edge of the bed. She gazed up at him. "She's a client?"

"Yes, she is," Jeff replied matter-of-factly. "She's Cynthia Ross, the widow of Al Ross."

"That young woman was married to Al Ross?"

Jeff nodded. "That's right. They were married only a short time before he died.

The whole estate is tied up in legal knots, with his former wife and children contesting the will. Cynthia's got control of all that land in Virginia that was almost signed, sealed, and delivered before Al died. At this point, I think I'm going to have to take the whole damn Ross family to a lot of dinners before I figure out who actually owns the land."

"But why did you go to the Jockey Club?"

"Because she was staying at the Ritz-Carlton and that's where she wanted to eat. I would have taken her to Paris for dinner if she would have signed on the dotted line."

"But does she have the right to sell it?"

"As it stands now, she does. That's what our lawyers tell us. Al Ross created a joint tenancy when he married her, and by the right of survivorship, she gets the property. And that's what the other heirs are fighting about. So until I hear differently, she gets to go to dinner whenever and wherever she wants."

"Oh Jeff, I'm sorry. I feel awful about this. Am I coming completely apart?"

He came and sat beside her, his legs spread, his head slightly bowed, his hands tightly clasped. "You can't, Mill. Not now. Allyson needs you."

"She needs you too. Jeff."

There were tears in the corners of his eyes. His voice was shaky. "I know, but I can't seem to help. It's a crazy situation that I just don't understand, and when I don't understand I feel helpless about what to do. It's as if this whole business with . . . her . . . is unreal, and I feel . . . well . . . removed. Sometimes I feel it was all a mistake. Maybe your father was right and we should never have adopted her."

Millicent's heart missed a beat. She sat up stiffly. "Don't say that, Jeff! Please don't ever say that again. He wasn't right! She's ours. She always has been and always will be, and if we even dare question it, then that will be a form of rejection, and that's what she's possibly feeling. Oh, Jeff, you would never say that about Cory or John, that we shouldn't have had them. So don't say that about Allyson. She's our child, the same as the others, and we must never let her feel otherwise."

Jeff stood up and paced around the room in a pensive mood, unobtrusively wiping the corner of his eye with the back of his hand. Then he went into his dressing room.

Millicent lay back on the bed and let her shoes drop to the floor. She felt melancholy and anxious. Waiting for the phone to ring, hoping it would not, deciding whether to call the hospital, thinking about Cynthia Ross and what a fool she had been. She realized how confused she felt, and to her amazement she realized how passionate she felt. This whole emotional episode had produced an excitement in her body that made her feel shameful. What was happening? Was she losing her mind to be filled with so much desire at a time like this?

Jeff came out of the dressing room in his robe. As if he read her mind, he turned off the lights and lay down beside her. It was going to happen in moments and she held her breath and trembled. He undressed her slowly, almost methodically, and as his fingers stroked every part of her taut body, the tension subsided and she responded with as deep a sensuality as she had ever known. She kissed his open, willing mouth and slid her head down to his thighs. Her hair fell loosely around his groin and she could feel the warmth of his erection on her cheek. She kissed his penis obsessively and gently put her lips around it. Then he held her in his arms and tenderly touched her swelling breasts and gradually moved his hands down to her clitoris. The rapturous sensations mounted within her, closing out the abnormal world, and she begged him to enter her. As he moved rhythmically to and fro, she moaned uncontrollably until her entire being quivered at the moment of orgasm. She clung to him as they relaxed almost breathlessly.

They had come together through her grief and his guilt. It was a day of sorrow and a night to remember.

Chapter 7

At half past eight the next morning, Millicent awoke with a start. For a split second, she did not know where she was or even the approximate time of day. Her thoughts were like gliding clouds, fading in and out of the heavens. For five minutes, she sat hunched on the edge of the king-sized bed, trying desperately to put her mind in order. She had never remembered feeling so disoriented.

Allyson lying in the hospital was her first concrete thought. She could not decide whether to call the hospital or just go there. They had not called her during the night, which could mean one of several things: Allyson was better; her condition was the same; she was worse and they did not want to tell her.

Should she dress first or call first?

Should she dress and go without calling? Should she wake Jeff and tell him to call? She realized he wasn't there. Her mind was in a fog, and a harrowing headache pounded her forehead so incessantly that she could barely find her way to the medicine cabinet and the aspirin.

She gulped down two tablets and splashed her face with cold water. She found herself staring in the bathroom mirror, and the memory of last night returned in a flash. Instantly, a creeping sensation of embarrassment and fear climbed from her legs to her arms until she was covered with gooseflesh.

Never had sex reached such heights of ecstasy and plunged her into such frightening depths. Unlike other times, the sex had not left her glowing and content. There had been something uncontrollable about it, as though a button had been pressed and her passion had been let loose, wild and shocking. She felt as if her senses had been manipulated and she had been artfully maneuvered into erotic play.

Millicent had never experienced this sensation, and she cringed at this moment of realization. Panic set in from her mental perplexity. She knew she had to do something, make a move, make a decision. But a clouding of conscious thought prevented her. She got to the hallway and called for Regina, the maid.

"Mrs. Hart, what are you doing running around in your nightgown?" Regina asked. "You don't look so good. Where do you think you're going like that?"

"I have to get to the hospital."

"Well, ma'am, they'll put you in a bed right fast if you go like that."

"Then I have to call and see how Allyson is."

"Mr. Hart already called. He told me to tell you nothing's changed much. He left a while back to go down there."

"I have to get dressed, Regina, but somehow I can't. I feel so mixed up."

"You look mixed up, and no wonder, with all that's goin' on. Come on back in your room and I'll help you."

Regina helped Millicent to dress and insisted she eat some breakfast. Homer told her that he was driving her to the hospital, as she was in no condition to drive herself. She nodded submissively. It was a relief to have someone tell her what to do.

Millicent arrived at Allyson's room and saw the day nurse, Miss Borkin, sitting by the bed watching her patient sleep. When she looked up and noticed Millicent, she put her fingers to her lips to request quiet and tiptoed to the door. They went into the hall.

"How is she, Miss Borkin? Has anything changed? I don't see the intravenous."

"They took it out early this morning. Dr. Graham was here and so was your husband. She had a rough night but she seems a little better, more alert and not in that stupor she was in yesterday."

"Has she eaten anything?" Millicent asked anxiously.

"Yes, she has. In fact, just before she fell asleep I fed her some soup, and she didn't try to refuse it."

"Thank goodness she ate something. Miss Borkin, she was so sick yesterday that I . . . well, I thought she might not make it."

"Yes, I know," said Miss Borkin sympathetically. "Yesterday was the worst. Dr. Graham was here a long time last night and so was the psychiatry resident. But today, there's definitely a slight improvement. I don't know what the doctor did, but whatever it is, today she's better. Forgive me, Mrs. Hart, but you look terrible. You're as white as a sheet. Come in and sit down. I don't think it will disturb Allyson."

Millicent allowed Miss Borkin to lead her into the room, to the chair that was farthest away from the bed. She looked at the nurse sheepishly and said, "As a matter of fact, I don't feel too well. But I'll be fine. I'm just a little disoriented."

"Well, these past few days have been very traumatic. It isn't any wonder you're not feeling well. Can I get you something?"

"No thank you. I'll just sit here a while. Perhaps Allyson will wake up. I'll wait."

"I'm going to the nurse's station and get you a cup of tea, Mrs. Hart. I think it will do you good. You just sit here and relax. I think Allyson is resting comfortably."

Millicent put her head back and thought about last night. She knew it had happened. Unlike any time she could remember, she knew she had completely lost her inhibitions in an unrestrained burst of emotion. She had the sensation that she had stepped out of herself and the lovemaking had happened to someone else.

The intimacy had never passed through her flesh.

She watched Allyson sleep, and her mind turned from the present to the past. She thought about the times she had watched her as a baby, in blissful sleep. Those were lovely times, and she tried to hold them in her mind. But disquieting half memories intruded. Those few years before Allyson came to them had been turbulent ones.

Millicent Bolt was capitavated by Jeffrey Hart the minute she laid eyes on him. No more than a month after he had been hired by Bolt Construction Company, Millicent saw him. Immediately, Jeffrey Hart stood out from the other new employees. His astonishing good looks were out of character in the stuffy office setting. His bulging muscles noticeably outlined the business suit he was unaccustomed to wearing. Millicent found herself staring at him, and when he looked up and flashed a perfect smile, her heart skipped a beat and she blushed self-consciously. His luxuriant head of sandy hair fell over his forehead in tiny wisps. He was about twenty-three, Millicent surmised, and surely the handsomest young man Bolt Construction had working for them. The thought crossed her mind that Miss Wilson of personnel must have hired him on looks alone.

Actually, Jeffrey Hart was hired on the recommendation of his college coach, who had known John J. Bolt when both men were students at Notre Dame. Jeff had been a high-school football star in Bethlehem, Pennsylvania. He went to Penn State on an athletic scholarship, confident that football was his passport to a world that was not constricted by steel mills and small-town provincialism. The prospect of spending the rest of his life as a steel worker like his father was depressing. He counted on his athletic ability to bring him the financial security he had never had and the recognition he thrived on. But his college football career, although promising, was not outstanding. After four years, he still needed a job. His coach steered him down to Washington, D.C., to his old college buddy, and Jeffrey Hart gave up his dream of a professional football career for a routine job in the building industry.

Jeff's pursuit of Millicent was the talk

of the office and half of Washington. The lowly employee, handsome and ambitious, pursuing the boss's daughter who was neither pretty nor pretentious, caused enough of a stir to make her father take notice and send her off to Europe for the "cure." But for the first time in her life, Millicent would not be dissuaded by her father's entreaties. She wanted Jeffrey Hart for life, and it didn't matter why he wanted her.

The starry-eyed adoration persisted, and her father reluctantly accepted the inevitable and made Jeff vice-president in charge of new construction, while her mother prepared an elaborate wedding that Millicent did not want. She wanted something small and intimate, not the gala society affair that had become an art form with Constance. But Constance could not be dissuaded either, so the wedding of the year was held at the Mayflower Hotel, with five hundred of the Bolts' "nearest and dearest" and a small contingent from Jeffrey's hometown in Pennsylvania.

They married and waited for children, as was the order of things then. But none came. Millicent had grown up insecure about her femininity, and Jeffrey had grown up insecure about his background and self-worth. When she didn't become pregnant as planned, and the pressure to have children permeated their existence, their relationship grew tense.

Jeffrey Hart was determined to show John Bolt that he was worthy of the great man's daughter, and Millicent was determined to prove to herself that her husband had not married her for all the wrong reasons.

As Jeff struggled at the top of the corporate ladder, Millicent valiantly wrestled with the role of housewife, a difficult role to make credible without housework or children. As Jeff became more adept at convincing himself that he was indeed worthy of his lofty position, Millicent became more unsure of herself and feared she might lose him.

Humble, young, diffident Jeffrey Hart quickly got the taste of money and power and liked it. With John J. Bolt as his role model, he gradually took on the stereotyped characteristics of the corporate executive — he gave orders and he took women. Both actions came easily as he gained confidence in his ability as the hotshot Washington real-estate developer and shed the advantaged but derisive title of son-in-law. He became very good at his job. John J. Bolt didn't believe in giving anybody a free ride, not even family. Sooner or later, he called in the chips and expected payback for his generosity. Jeff more than carried his weight as the business continued to prosper in the real-estate boom. As was customary, John J. Bolt got a good return on his investment. More than that, Jeff idolized him.

The womanizing was neither promiscuous nor public, nor was it meant as an insult to their marriage. To Jeff, it was more of a sophisticated affectation that developed by association with successful men who regarded infidelity as a traditional activity befitting gentlemen of their privileged class. Jeff also became a wine snob and an art collector with the same purpose.

The dalliances with attractive women also bolstered his inherently fragile ego, which often teetered precipitously from being suddenly thrust into a world of pressure and prestige unlike any he had ever known. In those early years, he did not recognize that he was trying to make a statement.

Millicent busied herself with fixing up their home, a luxurious wedding gift from her parents, and working part time in the company. Unlike Constance and Joan, she had always been keenly interested in the family business and had eagerly soaked up the knowledge of the economics of the Bolt enterprises that her father obsessively imparted to any intelligent and interested listener. No doubt she would have been a likely successor to John J. Bolt had she been a son instead of a daughter.

But with Jeffrey now a company executive, her presence there was threatening to him, and she bowed out gracefully at the advice of Martha Carrington, her father's indispensable secretary of twenty-five years.

Martha had been Millicent's friend and confidante for as long as she could remember. Even when Millicent was a child, she had been like a mother to her. Martha had also been John Bolt's mistress, a fact that Millicent did not register because she chose not to see this part of her father's life.

The sharp-tongued, highly efficient woman still retained vestiges of the beauty she once was. She presided over the offices of the Bolt Building on K Street as if the enormous profits accrued to her. For she was more than a secretary. Martha knew every facet of the real-estate business, and the other employees deferred to this acerbic woman who had a computer memory for land transactions as though she were an extension of the boss. She gave orders to everyone, and took them from no one.

Martha usually dressed in expensive basic black, with the adornment of good jewelry, courtesy of John J. Bolt. Her jewels were almost the equal of those of Constance Bolt. John had been generous to both his wife and his mistress. Since she was nineteen her world had been the Bolt Construction Company and her long, clandestine affair with its founder. Those were her two loves. And in the years that followed, when John's attentions waned because of age and family pressures, all that was left for Martha was her job and the charity work that she kept a secret.

Underneath Martha's caustic and hard exterior, however, was a heart of gold. Through the years, many employees had been the recipients of her generosity in time of need. She was perceptively mindful of those in trouble and gave willingly of her material and emotional resources. But she always did this privately. She preferred to retain her image as a tough woman.

She loved Millicent too, like the daughter she never had. Martha was always there for the shy young girl, giving the comfort and strength she had acquired from her own unfulfilling affair with John Bolt.

It was Martha who had suggested to Millicent that she should consider adopting a baby, after Millicent confided to her the fears she had about Jeff's wayward habits and his insatiable desire for top-drawer status. Millicent saw her husband fanatically assuming a role she had spent years trying to shed. It seemed that they were exploding toward opposite edges of the universe. In a long talk with Millicent, Martha pointed out that a child might reinstate their relationship and add another dimension to Jeff's life. Since Millicent wanted a baby more than anything else in the world besides Jeff's love, she embraced the suggestion with jubilation.

Jeff did not share Millicent's enthusiasm for the adoption. In his eyes, adoption was an affront to his manhood, despite the fact that the doctor had assured them both that they were physically capable of having children. It just hadn't happened. Jeff was also perfectly content with his new life-style and did not have the same burning need for parenthood. But since it meant so much to Millicent, he went along with her wishes and they applied to an adoption agency.

When John Bolt heard about this, he hit the roof. To him it was unthinkable that a child, parented by strangers, should become a part of his family. He gave them a long lecture on the importance of "blood line and heritage" and the grievous eventualities that might someday confront them. He almost convinced Jeff that it would be a drastic mistake. But Millicent was adamant. She desperately wanted a child and eventually persuaded her father to bestow his blessing when she uncharacteristically opened up to him and alluded to Jeff's philandering.

Rather than become upset as she had expected he would, her father laughed it off and assured his daughter that it meant nothing. In fact, he was surprised at her concern and thought she was overreacting to what he considered part and parcel of man's urbane image. He felt that philandering in no way diminished a husband's love for his wife. But he couldn't bear to see Millicent not have the one thing she wanted, so he reluctantly accepted her decision to adopt a baby.

Oddly enough, when Allyson came to them, John J. Bolt immediately fell madly in love with the adorable child, and his earlier qualms seemed to disappear as he assumed the role of proud grandfather. Even Constance, who also had reservations about the adoption, became the effusive and demonstrative grandmother, bragging to everyone about the baby's progress as if no other child possessed such capabilities. Constance bragged about everything she was involved in.

Allyson brought into their lives a sense of harmony and order that Millicent had only dared to fantasize about. As Martha had predicted, the baby added a new dimension to Jeff's life. He seemed to settle down and to be at peace with himself. Allyson was a tiny charmer and everyone adored her, especially Millicent, who found motherhood the most rewarding experience of her life.

When Allyson was eight months old, Millicent was totally surprised to discover she was pregnant. The doctor was not surprised. He told her that it often happened. Women who for years cannot conceive, adopt a child, then they become pregnant without even trying. Whether it happened because of the absence of pressure and anxiety or because of biological changes, he could not discern, but it happened four times. Corinne was born fifteen months after Allyson was adopted, and John Bolt Hart came along a year after Cory. Two more pregnancies terminated in miscarriages, and the irony of the situation escaped no one. Everyone knew how much Millicent had wanted a baby and how long she had tried to have one, but now it seemed as though she couldn't stop. Jeff had found a new contentment in their marriage and his lovemaking with Millicent was rekindled to the exquisite and uninhibited pleasure of their honeymoon.

Cory and John were welcomed with the same exultation as that which greeted Allyson. Though Millicent loved all three children dearly, there was a special place in her heart for Allyson, the child who had brought so much happiness and had pulled their lives together. She tried never to show favoritism, but it was there, nevertheless. What she did not realize, because she did it subconsciously, was that she often bent over backward to assure Allyson that she was no different from her sister and brother.

They moved into the bigger, sunny house on Belmont Road and Millicent was content with raising her family and doing the volunteer work that Martha Carrington persuaded her to become involved with. Martha's concern with the plight of battered women, long before it was exposed as a serious and despicable offense, was her secret charity. Martha diligently worked with the few women's groups then in existence. These groups were equally appalled by this neglected violation, because at the time it was considered neither a crime nor worthy of public outrage. Male abuse was regarded as a private family matter, a husband's or lover's God-given prerogative.

Millicent generously gave financial assistance to help Martha and a few other volunteer workers set up a shelter where battered women could seek refuge for themselves and their children when the abuse became intolerable. But Martha convinced Millicent that money was not enough. Personal involvement was needed. So Millicent spent two days a week at the House of Hope, tending to these mistreated and discarded souls, offering her help and support.

It was during this period of her life that Millicent came to understand that she was one of the lucky people of this world. She had taken for granted all the substances of life these miserable women never had — money, position, security, pride, dignity — the wherewithal to control your own destiny, all because of an accident of birth. Not that people of her class were without their own miseries, but it was not the same. It was different in that material resources can lessen the agony of misfortune. At least people of her means had enough glorious compensations in their lives to offset the suffering. These sad, troubled women had few choices and no such comparable satisfactions to relieve the wretchedness of their existence. As Martha would tell her, "All people have troubles, rich and poor, but the poor have so much more."

At the shelter, Millicent gained an awareness of how unfair destiny is, and she never again took for granted her good fortune. She was determined to pass on to her children the lesson she had learned during the years she worked at the House of Hope — that each one of us has a moral obligation to give back to the world something of value, something of ourselves. She sadly doubted whether she had adequately imparted this philosophy to her children. Only time would tell.

Millicent was brought out of her reverie by Miss Borkin's footsteps as the nurse came into the silent hospital room. As she heard Miss Borkin's voice, Millicent wondered how long she had been lost in solitary thought.

"Mrs. Hart, Mrs. Hart. Here's your tea. Drink it. You'll feel better. Oh, were you asleep? Did I disturb you?"

Millicent blinked and rubbed her eyes, trying to erase the images of her dreamy state.

"No, Miss Borkin, I wasn't asleep. I was just sitting here thinking. Thank you for the tea. Perhaps it will help. Does Allyson show any signs of getting up?"

A small voice came from across the room. "I am up, mother."

"Allyson! I didn't realize it."

"I know. I was watching you. You looked like you were far off in another world. What were you thinking about?"

"Nothing much. Just indulging myself with memories. How are you, honey?"

"I don't know," said Allyson weakly. "I'm here, so I suppose I'm OK."

Millicent got up from the chair and went to the bed. She stroked Allyson's forehead and held her hand. "You're better than OK. You're talking to me, and yesterday you weren't. Do you remember yesterday?"

Allyson shrugged her small shoulders. "I don't remember much of anything. I don't even know when yesterday was."

Millicent tried to contain the anxiety in her voice. "Well, yesterday wasn't a very good day for you, dear. We were all here but we couldn't reach you. And Daddy was here this morning and so was Dr. Graham. Do you remember that?"

Allyson squinted, and wrinkles appeared on her gaunt face. "Sort of. Yes, I saw Daddy. I'm glad he came, but he didn't look good. Neither do you. Mother, you

147

look so tired." Allyson's voice abruptly changed from mature to childlike. "Oh, Mommy, I'm causing all of you so much trouble. You must hate me. Everyone hates me. I wish I were dead."

Millicent's body became rigid, and a chill went through it. She was emotionally and physically drained. She wondered how much longer she could coddle and coax her daughter back to the world of the living. This young woman was forcing herself back into a child's body and then into nothingness, as though she were trying to reverse the order of life.

How much longer, Millicent asked herself, could she sustain false cheer and suppress anxiety and continue with the excessive solicitude that had become second nature? She was ashamed of her doubts. So, again, she used artful persuasion.

"Now you stop that, Allyson. I don't want to hear that kind of talk. Hate you? Who could ever hate you? We love you dearly. Life is precious, and your life is more precious to me than anything else in this world. You have no right to give it up."

"It's my life. I can do what I damn well

please with it," responded Allyson with a sudden burst of hostile energy.

Millicent had to hold herself in check to repress the instinct to shake Allyson. Her voice was louder than usual and it startled Allyson. "Of course it's your life, and I want you to live for yourself. But if you can't do that now, please live for me. That's all I'll ever ask of you, Allyson." Then it became hardly audible as she pleaded, "Just live for me."

Allyson covered her face with her hands and quietly whimpered like a homesick puppy while Millicent again reverted to soothing tones and words. Then quite suddenly Allyson cut it off and assumed an adult turn of mind, but one with belligerence.

"You sound like Dr. Lyons, mother. Have you been talking to him?"

Millicent was caught off guard. "Who is Dr. Lyons? No, I haven't spoken to him. I don't know who he is."

Miss Borkin interrupted. "Dr. Lyons is the psychiatry resident, Mrs. Hart. He was in last night and again this morning."

Millicent's eyes brightened. "Oh, I'm glad to hear that. He must have helped you, dear. I'd like to meet him."

"Don't bother," said Allyson, expressing disgust. "He didn't help me, and I told him not to come back. He's horrid. I don't want to see him again."

"Allyson, give him a chance. What can it hurt to talk with him?" The thought occurred to her that she had said those exact words a dozen times before.

Allyson looked at her grimly. "How would you like some smart-ass psychiatrist picking your brains apart all the time? I'm sick and tired of their psychiatric crap. I've seen so damn many shrinks I could open up my own clinic for the mentally deranged."

Cautiously, Millicent asked, "What did you tell him? You really didn't tell him not to see you again, did you?"

Allyson pulled herself up and glared at her mother. "Didn't you hear what I said? I told him to go back to the sixth floor with the other sickies and then go fuck himself!"

Millicent swallowed hard and turned to Miss Borkin in amazement. The nurse shrugged and looked equally embarrassed. She turned back to her defiant daughter. "Allyson! You didn't say that to the doctor! Why are you talking like this? I've never heard you use such language!"

Allyson ignored the reprimand and dismissed Millicent with her silence.

Unknown to them, Dr. Graham had been standing just outside the door listening. When he walked into the room, he had a smile on his customarily serious face.

"Well, I see the patient is in a bad mood today," he said sardonically. "At least that's better than no mood. What's got you so mad today, Allyson?"

Allyson looked at Dr. Graham in utter disgust. "You know damn well what it is. What did you think you were pulling on me by sending that fucked-up doctor in? Aren't you smart enough to treat me? Don't think I don't know what you're doing. I'm not a child."

Millicent froze in disbelief and shame, as though the words were coming out of her mouth instead of Allyson's.

Dr. Graham was neither offended nor sympathetic. "Then stop acting like a child and do what we think is best for you. Dr. Lyons said he was coming back, and I strongly advise you to see him. I consider him part of the treatment, and at this time, young lady, I'm in charge."

Millicent waited out in the hall while Dr. Graham examined Allyson and wrote his orders on the chart. "Dr. Graham, I'm so sorry. I don't know what got into her. Allyson has never been like that before, no matter how sick she was. Believe me, she's not herself. She's not like that at all. It must be a reaction from yesterday. She's always had the sweetest disposition in the world."

"I believe you, Mrs. Hart. And there's no need to apologize. Frankly, I'm encouraged by her behavior. At least she's showing some animation, and I much prefer that to how lifeless she was yesterday. Don't worry. She'll calm down." He scratched his head and looked puzzled. "Dr. Lyons must have really gotten to her."

"Who is this Dr. Lyons?" Millicent asked. "And what could he have done to make her act this way?"

"He's a psychiatric resident at the hospital. He's a young man who is, well . . . a little on the unorthodox side. He does rub some people the wrong way, and he is not for every patient. But he has already had very fine training, and I like him and think he's very effective in dealing with young patients. I don't know what he did or whether she'll even respond to him or talk to him again. At least he got her out of that stupor, and she did take some nourishment today. I'm grateful for that. What the long-range prognosis is, I still can't say. But right now, Mrs. Hart, I think you'd better start looking after yourself. Pardon my saying this, but you don't look very well."

For a second, Millicent was jarred by his unexpected reference to her appearance. Afraid that the unshed tears would fall, she laughed nervously. "Heavens, I must look like the wrath of God. Dr. Graham, you are about the fifth person who has said that to me this morning. I'd better get to a beauty parlor."

"No, I have a better idea, " said Dr. Graham as though on impulse. "Come have lunch with me. I have an hour before a staff meeting. We can go across the street."

Millicent hesitated awkwardly, trying to think of a way to say no — her instinctive reaction — to the surprising invitation. "I didn't know busy doctors took time out for lunch."

"I usually don't, but today I'd like to. It seems right. Will you join me?"

She asked herself what to say, now unsure of her immediate reluctance. The mixed emotions confused her. She did not know whether she should accept just to please Dr. Graham, to whom she felt a sense of indebtedness, or whether by going she would actually be pleasing herself. Millicent was aware of some kind of imperceptible intimacy that had been moving beneath the surface of their relationship, but she wasn't sure how to handle it outside the safe and invulnerable atmosphere of the hospital.

Then she remembered her appointment with Dr. Bromley. "I'd like to join you, Dr. Graham, but I just remembered that I have an appointment with Dr. Bromley that completely slipped my mind." She thanked him for referring her to Dr. Bromley. "Give me a rain check on that lunch, Dr. Graham. Will you?"

"Without a doubt, Mrs. Hart."

The dilemma had been resolved. But only for the moment.

Chapter 8

"So from what you've been telling me, Mrs. Hart, yesterday you thought Allyson was going to die and today you are more hopeful than ever. Despite her hostility, you seem to think there's a good chance she's going to make it."

"Yes, that's about it, Dr. Bromley."

"But you still seem so upset, my dear? Why is that?"

Millicent uncrossed her legs and unclasped her hands. She fell silent for a moment. Then with difficulty she said, "I don't know. I feel as if I'm going to jump out of my skin."

"And your conscience tells you that's wrong. That you should be jumping for joy."

"Yes. That's exactly what the still voice inside my head keeps telling me."

"But your mind is also clogged by guilt feelings that you can't express," prodded Dr. Bromley.

"I'm not sure what's going on today. I woke up feeling strange and disoriented." Millicent paused, struggling with her next thought. Automatically, her hands clutched her stomach. "Besides that, I have this awful, empty feeling in the pit of my stomach . . . like a barren spot . . . and I feel lonely, terribly alone."

Dr. Bromley raised her eyes. They had been focused on Millicent's hands. She asked, "Do you have any idea as to why you are feeling this way, so empty and alone?"

Millicent shook her head. "No, not exactly, I just feel that I'm coming . . . I think the expression is unglued. Yesterday I was certain that the world, my world, was coming to an end. It was awful, but it was certain. Now that some of the pressure has been lifted, I'm faltering. My strength, determination, or whatever you want to call it, is going."

Dr. Bromley leaned forward and asked softly, "Could what you're feeling be a reaction to the realization that Allyson is probably going to recover?"

Millicent looked perplexed. "No," she said simply. "I should be feeling just the opposite, happy and relieved."

Dr. Bromley stood up and put her hands to her mouth as though she were preparing for a speech. She walked back and forth, and Millicent watched her. The psychiatrist stopped abruptly.

"Does it occur to you, Mrs. Hart, that this is a turning point in Allyson's illness and that possibly, she is finally going to give up being a child and become the adult she actually is, that is, as far as age goes? After all, at twenty-three most girls are reasonably independent — married or working or both." Dr. Bromley turned to Millicent, watching for a response.

Millicent's stare was clouded. She felt very uneasy and squirmed in her chair. "I'm not sure I understand. What has that to do with Allyson? She's been ill for so many years. She can't be compared to other girls of her age." Without intending to, she said angrily, "She shouldn't be compared to other girls. Her situation is completely different."

Dr. Bromley went to her chair and moved it closer to Millicent. She sat down and gestured with her finger. "But that's just the point, Mrs. Hart. Whether she should or should not isn't the issue. Parents cater to the needs and demands of little children because it's expected of them and because it's right, it's necessary. But taking care of an adult, even your own child, is not the same. It's a burden that is too prolonged and interferes with your own life. It carries a great deal of resentment."

Millicent was irritated, but she said politely, "I don't feel that way at all, Dr. Bromley. I'll take care of her just as long as she needs me. It's more than a duty. It's what I want. You don't stop caring for a child just because she reaches a certain age. There's no cutoff point."

"Of course there's no cutoff point for caring," Dr. Bromley agreed, well aware of Millicent's irritation. "But there definitely is a cutoff point for physically having to attend to a grown child in the same way you did when she was a little girl. There comes a time when mothering is over and total responsibility for another adult is not only an imposition but is inappropriate."

Millicent refused to accept this. "But we're not talking about just another child.

Allyson is my daughter and she's very sick. So what difference does it make whether she's five or twenty-three?"

"It makes all the difference in the world, Mrs. Hart. It's out of keeping with this phase of your life. As long as you saw Allyson as a child, talking like a child, looking like a child, acting like a child, you could accept your responsibility without any qualms. Now, today, it's not so clear-cut. You saw a little improvement, and you saw her assert herself as an adult and rebel against your mothering. Some deep feelings apparently came close to the surface. And you're probably feeling pretty angry about devoting your entire life to a sick adult."

Millicent looked away from Dr. Bromley and held her hand to her forehead, her chin almost resting on her chest. She stayed silent for a long time, letting the psychiatrist's words sink in like the slow drip of water permeating a stiff sponge until it becomes saturated and soft.

"Then if I am angry, as you say, then I hate myself for feeling that way. That is a weakness that I just can't tolerate. I've been very fortunate all my life, Dr. Bromley, in never having had to worry about money or security. I have had worldly possessions that other people just dream of. And to feel anger just because everything isn't perfect, because everything isn't just the way I would want it to be . . . well, I consider that a terrible weakness in my character, a real failing.''

Dr. Bromley was acutely aware of how quickly Millicent's attitude turned from anger to depression. ''Then let me convince you that it's not a terrible weakness and you have not failed. We are all fallible human beings made up of every emotion imaginable — love, hate, anger, compassion. There's good in the worst of us and bad in the best of us, and who knows for sure, anyway, what is good or what is bad or what's a weakness or what's a strength.'' With a slight smile on her face, Dr. Bromley gestured with her finger and said, ''So allow me a little professional license and let me give you an order. Stop trying to change your feelings. It's very unproductive. There are many things we can change in this world, but feelings . . . well, that's not so easy. That comes about in a different way, very often from a change in relationships.''

Millicent looked pensive as she tried to

come to grips with what the psychiatrist had said.

In this reflective mood, she almost jumped out of her chair when, quite suddenly and without the least hesitation, Dr. Bromley asked, "How is your sex life?"

"What!"

"Forgive me for being so blunt, my dear, but sex is such an integral part of a person's feelings that it's important that we talk about your sexual relationships. And I think now is a good time."

Millicent was still taken aback. "What has that to do with Allyson?"

Dr. Bromley replied calmly, "I really don't know. Maybe nothing. But since you are very concerned about your feelings, it might be well to explore your feelings about sex. You're at a tough age. Do you and your husband have sex often?"

Millicent took a deep breath and forced herself to say what was on her mind: "Dr. Bromley, forgive me for being impertinent. But I find this terribly embarrassing, and, well . . . irrelevant. I didn't come here to talk about my sex life. I came here for help in coping with a sick child who has a strange illness, who is suffering, I'm

161

told, from some kind of identity crisis because she happens to be adopted. Somehow, I feel responsible for what has unexpectedly turned into a very sad situation, because I did the adopting, not she. I see no reason to discuss my sexual relations or feelings in that regard. I respect your expertise in this field, but frankly this is a bit much."

Millicent became cooly silent, and after a few moments of deliberation, she stood up and addressed Dr. Bromley. "So if you'll excuse me, I think I would prefer to end this session, and I'd like to cancel my other appointments."

"I'm sorry, Mrs. Hart. I did not intend to offend you. You're certainly free to go. I wish I could have been of more help to you."

Millicent avoided Dr. Bromley's gaze as she picked up her coat and purse and started for the door.

"Good-bye, Mrs. Hart. Try to remember, my dear, that being a victim is a hard habit to break."

Millicent turned around and stared at the psychiatrist. She paused for a moment, threw her coat and purse on the table, and returned to the worn leather chair.

For the rest of the hour she described every moment, every touch, every feeling of that delirious and extraordinarily uninhibited sexual encounter that she had experienced with Jeff last night. How a frenzied rapture had taken hold of her and would not let go until every part of her body was satisfied. How Jeff had stroked her into divine submission until, inextricably, she melted like ice. But the whole experience was as complex and full of contradictions as the act of sex itself had been. Instead of making her feel warm and loved, it made her feel strangely weird, and the feeling still persisted.

After pouring all this out to the doctor, Millicent had a wonderful sensation of freedom, as though she had been purged and forgiven. Dr. Bromley listened without comment until Millicent's last sentence: "Before last night, we had not had sexual relations for a long time, months and months."

"So you think last night came about because of your need for each other at a time of great crisis concerning your daughter?"

"It may have been just that, or it may have been a combination of that and my false suspicions about Jeff and another woman."

Millicent was astonishingly composed and candid. She related to Dr. Bromley what Dolly had told her about Jeff being seen with a client, Cynthia Ross, and about his past affairs with other women.

"And so you suspected that he was starting to run around again. How did that make you feel?"

Millicent thought hard and then answered in a straightforward manner: "Afraid and rejected, and very much alone."

"Just like Allyson feels, Mrs. Hart?" Dr. Bromley asked incisively.

Millicent was startled and bewildered. She looked at Dr. Bromley entreatingly, as though she were begging for an explanation.

"You see, my dear, we all experience the same emotions. Not at the same time and not necessarily from the same set of circumstances. We are all different, and yet, paradoxically, all the same. Young and old alike. Youth has no corner on the market of feelings."

Incredulous, Millicent asked: "Are you saying that, somehow, what I'm feeling, that what I've felt . . . I don't even know quite how to put it . . . this confusion and turmoil . . . that I am identifying with Allyson?"

"That's a possibility. Or perhaps, she's identifying with you. That's another possibility."

Millicent became annoyed at this imprecise and divergent answer. Her voice rose. "Well, what is it? What am I feeling? Tell me what I am!"

"I can't, Mrs. Hart. You will have to find that out for yourself. All I can do is help you along the way. We can talk more about this subject next time. Meanwhile, think about it. I would also like to hear about your other children. So next time, tell me about them. I like to know all about a family."

Chapter 9

Dolly Henderson was waiting in the library when Millicent arrived home. The glass of sherry provided by Regina did not make her any less impatient or fretful.

She sprang up the minute the door opened. Virtually no time was spent on small talk. When Millicent came into the library, Dolly immediately confronted her with apologies and self-remorse.

"I didn't sleep all night, Mill. I feel positively awful about this nasty little business with Jeff. I just kept wondering whether you were having a terrible fight."

"Dolly, there was nothing to forgive except my own stupidity for listening to idle gossip that was . . . well, is, groundless."

"You mean he really wasn't out with another woman? Cissy made the whole thing up? That son-of-a-bitch liar!"

"No, she saw him with a woman, a client. And I know who the woman is, and it was a perfectly innocent business dinner. The fact that the woman is young and pretty . . . well, you don't pick your clientele by age or looks. So don't worry. Jeff and I are fine. Really, Dolly, that's not number one on my list of worries. We've had a very bad time with Allyson since I saw you."

"Oh, Mill, I'm sorry," said Dolly, instantly compassionate. "What happened? She's worse, isn't she?"

"She was yesterday. I honestly thought we were going to lose her. But today she's somewhat improved. At least she's showing signs of life, mostly in the form of anger."

Although it was still early afternoon, Millicent was exhausted from the tension of the day. She put her head back against the library couch and closed her eyes while Dolly talked on.

"God, love, I don't know how you stand it. Every day another crisis. It's as if the girl is tantalizing you to death with her ups and downs. And to think that I caused you all that aggravation on top of what you already have. When I see that crack-brained Cissy I'm going to tell her once and for all what a horse's ass she is and tell her to take her next piece of juicy gossip and go stick it. Really, Mill, that woman is utterly impossible."

Millicent felt so weary. She pressed her lids together and responded in a half whisper. "Forget it, Dolly. It's over. She's probably a very unhappy person who relishes malicious gossip to make up for her own inadequacies. She must be very lonely. Frankly, I feel sorry for her, and so should you."

"God, Millicent, is there no limit to your understanding? I'd get nothing but pleasure from telling that vicious magpie to go to hell, and you feel sorry for her! But you're right. Forget Cissy. She's not worth talking about, and I'm certainly relieved to hear that nothing happened between you and Jeff. God knows, I would never want to be thought of as the instigator of someone's divorce."

Millicent opened her eyes abruptly and sat up. "Dolly, there isn't going to be any divorce! And I don't want to talk about it anymore."

"Of course not, dear," said Dolly,

watching the change of expression on Millicent's face. "Let's forget it, shall we?"

Strange, thought Millicent, *I just told Dr. Bromley how lonely I feel, and now I would give anything if Dolly would leave and I could be alone.*

But Dolly was not leaving. In fact, she settled into her armchair, tucked her feet up beneath her, and sipped her sherry.

Comfortable and inviting, the library abounded with mementos of the Harts' life and interests and contained contrasting pieces of furniture, giving the grand wood-paneled room an informal atmosphere. Bookcases covered one whole wall. An eighteenth-century English secretary stood in a corner. A Steinway piano, the top cluttered with family pictures, was to the left of the intricately carved fireplace. Propped against the back of an antique chair was a slightly dusty violin. A chess set was spread out on a cherrywood table. Covering the center of the floor was a Portuguese needlepoint rug, and oriental rugs were scattered about. The sofas and chairs were a mixture of warm leather and bright prints.

Dolly was now relaxed. "Did you just

come from the hospital, Millicent?"

"No, I was there this morning."

"Then where were you? I've been here almost an hour waiting, and . . . Jesus, don't answer that. What am I doing questioning you? I used to do that to Lloyd all the time. My psychiatrist tells me that I have this insatiable need to know every detail of people's lives. It's all mixed up with insecurity and my suspicious nature. But I'm overcoming it. I've finally stopped asking sales clerks what religion they are."

Try as she would, Millicent couldn't visualize Dolly honestly examining her psyche with a psychiatrist. Nor could she imagine a psychiatrist taking Dolly seriously. Yet she was curious to know what Dolly thought about treatment, as if she needed assurance that she was doing the right thing herself by seeing Dr. Bromley.

"Dolly, has it helped you to go to a psychiatrist?"

A look of satisfaction crossed Dolly's face, giving the impression that this was her favorite subject. "You bet it has!" She took a swallow of sherry before she said, "I don't think I could have gotten through that year after Lloyd left without him. A husband playing around is one thing. But actually leaving you for another woman . . . well, that's positively the worst kind of rejection. My ego hit an all-time low, but that wonderful man, my psychiatrist, absolutely saved me. Anyway, I'm just one of those people who will probably have to go to a shrink the rest of my life. Lord, Mill, I've associated with the lah-de-dah set for so long that I can't remember who I was, or understand who I am now. Honestly, life is nothing but a constant fight to endure, and if I didn't have someone professional to talk to, I would have been wacko long ago." Dolly's voice was choked with sincerity.

Millicent was surprised and touched by her friend's frankness and insight. This was a Dolly Henderson she seldom saw, serious and without affectation. She said kindly, "So it's really helped you to see someone."

Dolly was completely candid. "Oh yes, it's helped tremendously. I understand so much more about myself than I ever did, especially why I was so desperate to marry Lloyd and why I couldn't bear losing him. How my god-awful dreary and repressive background affected my need to become somebody important and even a little outlandish. Mainly, I've come to accept myself, weaknesses and all." She heaved a sigh and squared her shoulders. "But I still need constant reassurance. I'm not strong like you, Millicent. I'm hard, but I'm not strong."

Because she suddenly felt very protective of her, Millicent defended Dolly's own self-analysis. "Don't underestimate yourself, Dolly. You're as tough as they come. You came through a very bad time. You've kept your sense of humor, and that's more than I've done."

Dolly got up and came to sit beside Millicent on the sofa. When she spoke, her eyes flickered and she seemed to step out of character. Her voice was anxious and had lost its cultured inflection and lighthearted ring. "But you don't need crutches or constant support the way I do," she said. "You have inner strength that everyone knows about; everyone can feel it. You don't have to ask someone for the answers. You find out for yourself. You know who you are and you can always . . ." She stopped abruptly and put her hand to her mouth. "Mill, are you thinking about seeing a psychiatrist?"

Millicent looked away from Dolly's

stare. She felt a twinge of genuine discomfort and flushed. She hadn't anticipated the question and was reluctant to tell anyone she was seeing a psychiatrist. Although she had told Jeff, she hadn't even discussed with him the real reason she was going.

But Dolly was persistent. "Millicent, are you really thinking about seeing a psychiatrist?"

The room was very quiet. Outside, the autumn leaves were blowing against the windows. The gray October sky was getting darker. Millicent realized that her silence was answering the question.

"I already have," she finally admitted. "I'm not as strong as you think. I do need help."

The expression on Dolly's face was one of shock and satisfaction. "What do you talk about? Who are you seeing? Is he good?"

Millicent stood and walked over to the fireplace. Picking up a blue Chinese porcelain frog on the mantelpiece, she began turning it around in her hands as if it was a new acquisition to the room. In point of fact, it was one of a pair, a wedding gift from Martha Carrington, and both frogs had always been there. She put the object back in its place and turned around.

Even as she spoke, she realized she sounded guarded and defensive. "He's a she, Dolly. She's good. Dr. Graham recommended her. What do we talk about? We talk mostly about Allyson."

Millicent walked back to the sofa and sat down. She could see that Dolly was impatiently waiting for more of an explanation.

"What else is there on my mind these days but Allyson? But the doctor wants to know more. In fact, today she asked me about the other children, and do you know that I'm ashamed to admit that in the past few weeks I've hardly thought about them except when they call."

Dolly rearranged the heavy gold chain that had twisted around her neck. "Well, that's certainly understandable. One sick kid can absolutely take up all your time. Thank God I never had children. I just don't have the stomach for it. Only governesses should be mothers. I couldn't possibly put up with all you've had to go through. It's no wonder you need psychiatric help. Children can shorten your life faster than alcohol and drugs. But I'll tell you something, sweetie. If I ever did have a daughter, I'd want her to be just like your Cory. Now that's a girl after my own heart. Free and independent, with both feet on the ground. She's her own person."

"She's always been like that, unrestrained and unrestricted, as if she were exempt from any sort of control. Free and easy, I guess. Although, believe me, she wasn't easy to bring up. Not like Allyson or Johnny. She was always finding something to rebel against, and we usually gave in to her because she's so darn clever and could wrap us around her little finger with all that logical reasoning she would throw at us. She could even con my father, and you know that takes some doing. Remember that time she got father to buy her a car for her sixteenth birthday by convincing him that the school bus wasn't safe? And the time she almost got expelled from National Cathedral — I think she was only fourteen — with that speech she gave in the chapel on the sexual repressions forced on young girls by a private Episcopalian school. Heavens, she was a handful!"

Dolly shook her head wearily as she

reached over to the coffee table and poured herself another glass of sherry. "All children are, Mill. That's why British parents ship them off to school in the provinces as soon as they're toilet trained. And I'm firmly convinced that's why English women have such marvelous skin. No worry lines from the little darlings. They always manage to keep their children well hidden. You remember Lloyd's cousins Malcolm and Virginia Henderson from London. They swear they have five children, but no one's ever seen any of them. I just take their word for it that they're actually alive. But oh God, that Virginia has fabulous skin."

Millicent smiled. "Well, anyway, Cory's matured and she has turned out well. I'm thankful for that. You're so right, Dolly. Cory is a true free spirit."

Cory was not free today. Corinne Bolt Hart had been arrested for disturbing the peace. She had been dragged off to jail kicking and shouting invectives at the two policemen who were taking her into custody. When they asked for her name and address, she answered, "No comment."

Cory left the rarefied confines of Smith College in Northampton, Massachusetts, and drove to Boston for an abortion. There was a Pro-Life group demonstrating with banners and chants in front of the abortion clinic, trying to persuade the young girls who went in to turn back and give life to their unborn babies.

A somber, black-clad priest stopped Cory and told her that a disagreeable task is its own reward, to which Cory replied, "Up yours, Father."

When he placed his firm hand on her shoulder and told her in his sermonlike voice that she would "perish in hell" for eternity for the murder of her innocent fetus and that there was still time to repent for her sins, Cory swung around instinctively and knocked his hand from her body with a swift karate chop. The surprised priest lost his balance and fell face down into a pile of leaves and mud. Within thirty seconds, there was pandemonium. The Pro-Abortionists and the Pro-Lifers were embroiled in a small riot, and a crowd quickly gathered.

The curses and the blood flowed freely until the Boston police arrived and escorted the more obvious offenders into the paddy wagon. Cory, her nose bleeding profusely, was sitting on top of a devout two-hundred pound woman who had hit her in the face with her "Save the Babies" placard after Cory had made the obscene gesture of extending her middle finger up in the air just two inches from the woman's nose.

Cory stayed in the lockup all day because she would neither post bail nor give the police any information. She was furious at this restriction of her freedom. Her pregnancy was the succulent fruit of a victory celebration with a Yale football player after the Harvard-Yale game in early September. Cory saw no need to reveal her condition to the Yale gridiron star. She had not been prepared for the spontaneous and amorous encounter and blamed only herself for getting caught. Furthermore, she saw no need for his involvement or his patronizing advice, which to Cory epitomized male chauvinism in its most superior, degrading form.

She thought of herself as fiercely independent and in touch with the common people. As she later stated to the president of Smith College, becoming "unpregnant" was of no concern to anyone but herself, and a public-supported abortion was a critical liberty to be shared by all women.

Cory regarded capitalism as undemocratic but gave little thought to where her financial support came from. Her ideas of equality and justice were commendable in theory, and her altruistic causes, such as increased social welfare, gave substance to her life but were in reality inconsistent with her luxury-style world of unlimited resources and wealthy companions. In fact, lack of consistency was her dominant and most disarming characteristic and was regarded by some as her most charismatic quality.

Unquestionably, Cory was a leader, and the worst part of being in jail was the separation from her followers, friends who were constantly charmed by her nonconforming behavior. Cory generated awe. Bootsie Maguire of Locust Valley, New York, and Palm Springs, California — and Cory's most ardent admirer — had accompanied her to the abortion clinic but returned to Smith in a state of panic when Cory was arrested. Bootsie excitedly informed everyone on campus of the day's wild events, and within minutes, President Patricia Brewster was on the phone to Washington to apprise the incredulous Hart household of Cory's incarceration. President Brewster then dispatched the college's attorney to Boston to deal with the legalities of extricating Cory from the Boston jail and keep the shocking incident out of the newspapers. The lawyer obtained her release, but the information he was forced to reveal hit the evening papers. A picture of Corinne Hart, beautiful but tousled in torn jeans and very mad, appeared under the caption: "Society Girl Clobbers Pro-Lifer."

While Cory was brooding in jail her brother, John Bolt Hart, Harvard sophomore, was getting married. He and Sandy Witcowski were being united in matrimony by a Justice of the Peace in Cambridge, Massachusetts. The attendants at the modest ceremony were Justin Albritton III and Sandy's two children, Darlene, age seven, and Stanley, age five.

Sandy was beaming in her new blue suit, a startling contrast from the waitress uniform she wore on duty in McGinty's Bar and Grill. She looked older than twenty-seven, and the new bridegroom looked younger than twenty. They stood together, a striking exhibition of unlikeness. The antithesis of their backgrounds and life experiences was visible even to the Justice of the Peace as he wished them well and thanked Johnny for the generous wedding fee.

John Hart bore no resemblance to his father in looks or personality. He was tall and gangling, and when he was sixteen, he and Elliot Carver, who was very short and fat, were secretly thought the most unpromising athletes at St. Albans School for Boys, a Washington institution with a reputation for athletic accomplishments as well as academic excellence. Try as he would, Johnny never developed proficiency in sports. In spite of lessons and persistence, he still remained awkward on the playing fields, much to the consternation of his father and grandfather, who were always pushing him to try harder. Johnny had the touch of gentleness, a trait that did not endear him to the impressionable young girls of the sister school of National Cathedral nor to the rough and physical boys in his class. That he excelled in his studies made him popular only with the teachers.

So he remained an introspective loner, and his first year at Harvard was not significantly different from prep school until he met Sandy Witcowski. Johnny brought with him to college the same feelings of inadequacy and low self-esteem that he had had as an adolescent. Ironically, with all his worldly goods, opportunities and clever mind, he felt inept in relationships, especially with women.

His father was his idol and at the same time his enemy. Unintentionally, Jeff made him feel insignificant in accomplishment and unmanly by comparison. Johnny wanted to look like Jeff and to be like him, but because he was not, he retreated into an ethereal shell that was in complete opposition to all the paternal expectations that had been laid out to him since he was a small boy.

Sandy was only the second girl with whom he had had a sexual experience. The first was a virgin from Mt. Holyoke he met on a blind date arranged by his roommate, Justin. She was as shy and as inexperienced as he. They came together out of a mutual desperation to rid themselves of the stigma of their virginity, but the whole encounter was a bumbling disaster.

Johnny thought of himself as the most inadequate male in the whole college population of the Boston area, and his first sexual experience did nothing to erase that impression. Somehow, his feelings of sexual inadequacy became a confirmation of his inability to live up to his father's expectations as heir apparent to the Bolt-Hart enterprises.

Until he met Sandy toward the end of his freshman year, he felt queer and lost, and even more lonely when surrounded by the cream of college students.

Justin was neither handsome nor accomplished, but he had an ego as big as his father's pharmaceutical factory. He could not understand Johnny's desire or willingness to entangle his life with a waitress when all those lovely coeds were available. He tried to discourage his love-struck roommate, but Johnny viewed this incongruous relationship with a ready-made family as synonymous with maturity. Besides, Sandy wanted a husband, not a lover, and Johnny thought he was doing the right thing for her.

Johnny had been attracted to the flirtatious Sandy from the first day he and Justin had gone into McGinty's, the popular drinking place in Cambridge. Her looks were just ordinary, but her open and spirited personality captivated him from the first time she waited on him, and he kept going back. As he became more familiar with her, he realized that she possessed no more — and probably less — than average intelligence and that she was lacking in deep insight, good taste, and refinement. But she made him feel wonderful, sexy and manly. She was unlike any girl he had ever met, and her earthiness both embarrassed and excited him. Their lovemaking was the realization of all his adolescent sexual fantasies.

Sandy was somebody he didn't have to measure up to, someone who stroked his fragile ego and in no way forced him to compete for superiority. Johnny found himself drawn to her as to the forbidden playmate from the wrong side of the tracks, especially when he was moody or depressed about what was expected of him. Without realizing the implication, she was part of his strategy to be downwardly mobile. Johnny was uncomfortable with his heritage. Although he was interested in business and had the head for it, he was reluctant to step into Bolt Construction as a career. He felt the stirrings of ambition but kept them hidden. Without fully understanding, he felt that he should reject the values and occupations of his father and grandfather. So he shied away from business courses and chose liberal arts.

The fact that she was older than he, and divorced with two children, were the least of their differences. He knew nothing of her world, and she had only dreamed of his. Johnny had never reveled in the common upper-crust forms of rebellion such as flunking, cheating, boozing, or trashing expensive cars. But with this marriage, he had achieved the consummate rebellion. Sandy was the kind of girl Ivy League men slept with but never married.

Chapter 10

It was a terrible scene and Millicent was in despair. Cory sat curled up in a large, overstuffed chair in the library, sulking and avoiding the grim faces of her parents and grandparents.

John J. Bolt slammed the Boston paper down in a rage. "I don't believe it!" he shouted. "I simply do not believe it! Corinne, what in God's name possessed you to go to that abortion clinic and get involved in that brawl?" he asked.

Cory looked up in disgust. "For the obvious reason that anyone goes, to get an abortion. I didn't plan on having a fight," she answered sarcastically.

His white hair seemed to stand up in all directions, and his cheeks puffed in and out. "It's disgraceful enough that a young girl like you, a college girl, should, uh

. . . get into trouble . . . out of wedlock, but . . ."

Cory interrupted him. "The word is pregnant, grandfather."

John Bolt ignored the indirect derogatory intimation that was meant to emphasize his antiquated sense of morality. "But to go to a public place for an abortion! Well, if that's your idea of throwing dirt in our faces, you very well succeeded, young lady." His face became red and blotchy, and his thick gray eyebrows seemed to recede into his forehead. He turned in a huff and went to the bar to refill his whiskey glass, before proceeding with the interrogation.

"Your grandfather's right, Corinne," said Constance, on the verge of hysterics. "You've disgraced us all publicly and deliberately. How could you? I am certain that the boy, whoever he is, would have been willing to marry you. Or one of our doctors could have handled the matter privately. Something could have been arranged. But not this!" She dabbed her eyes with the lace handkerchief she had been twisting in her lap.

Cory bolted upright. "None of you have been listening to me. You don't seem to get it through your heads that I don't *need* you to *arrange* anything. I don't want to get *married*. I *don't need* to get married. I wouldn't marry that oversexed jock if he was the last man on earth. I don't even remember what he looks like."

"That's disgusting, girl!" roared John Bolt.

Jeff was seething. "Perhaps he even raped you, is that it?"

Cory glared at Jeff and said with contempt, "No, *father*, he didn't *rape* me. And have you heard that this is almost the end of the twentieth century? Sex is now permitted between consenting adults. And you seem to forget that I am an adult, over twenty-one, and I can do just what I please. And, furthermore, I don't have to sit here and listen to this crap about how I brought disgrace on the precious family name."

With that Cory got up and headed for the door. Jeff pushed her back in the chair, and she plopped onto the soft cushion with an unexpected and amazed expression.

Jeff stood over her and glared. "Oh, yes you do have to listen, because as long as you're a member of this family and you're enjoying all the sweet benefits that go with it, you *are* going to listen."

Cory opened her mouth to protest, but he cut her off.

"When you act irresponsibly you reflect on all of us, and don't you forget it."

Cory didn't react. She just stared.

Millicent was sitting in a corner looking helpless. She desperately wanted to say something compassionate and concilatory that would relieve the air of hostility that surrounded her younger daughter. She felt she should say something in her defense, put her arms around her, act as the buffer between Cory and the angry attacks that were only serving to confirm Cory's worst feelings about her family. She even hoped for an expression of contrition from Cory that might evoke a momentary softening of the dour faces of her mother and father, and Jeff. She struggled to offset the accusatory tone of the others, but all that came out was a cliché question that provoked Cory to turn on her.

"Cory honey, why didn't you come to me and talk this over? We used to be able to talk. I feel as if I don't know you."

"You don't!" Cory shouted. "Come to you? You haven't been around for a long time!"

Millicent looked at her in astonishment. "And just what does that mean?"

"You know exactly what it means! I don't have to spell it out. You've been so preoccupied with Allyson that you haven't had time for anyone else."

It was so unfair that Millicent couldn't answer. She started trembling. It hurt that her own daughter would make her feel guilty about taking care of her sister. But she realized it was probably true, at least in Cory's mind. She said nothing and turned away. It was useless to explain or defend what she had been through with Allyson for the past six years.

Jeff turned and pointed his finger at Cory. "Now you just wait a minute, young lady. Don't you dare turn all this around and start blaming your mother for your promiscuous behavior and stupidity. You're a big girl, and it's time you took a little responsibility for your own actions."

Cory was indignant. "You're so right, dad. I am a big girl, bigger than you think, and that's just what I intend to do, take full charge of my own affairs. But *you* just wait a minute. *You* brought me here to decide my fate. I didn't come home begging for your advice or protection, and frankly I don't want it. I am perfectly capable of handling this myself, and my biggest regret is that all of you found out and took it upon yourselves to meddle in my business."

Cory looked over toward Millicent and saw her forlorn face. Suddenly she was ashamed of how she had attacked her. She held up her hand in a conciliatory way.

"Look, everyone, I'm sorry for all this mess. Can you understand that I had no intention of broadcasting the fact that I was going to have an abortion? That woman attacked me, and I was only defending myself. Yes, I was stupid, in more ways than one. I should have walked away from the whole ridiculous scene. But it's done and I'm sorry, and if you'll leave me alone, I'll work it out."

"But, Corinne dear," said Constance, dripping with dignity, "we *are* your family and we feel that your burden is our burden. We want to stand by you in your time of trouble. It's just that it's so public, and when people start talking, you know how sordid this kind of thing gets."

Cory was losing patience. She wanted this whole episode to end. "Oh, nana, you sound like a nineteenth-century novel.

Who cares if anybody talks? What do you want to do, banish me to some hiding place to keep my condition a private family disgrace?"

"Well, I may be old-fashioned," said Constance with feigned defensiveness, "but virtue doesn't go out of style. The problem still exists and you do have your reputation to think about. Yes, my dear, reputation is still very important. Just what *are* you going to do?"

Cory let out a sigh and ran her hand through her hair. "I am going to take my *reputation* and go back to school and have the abortion, quietly I hope. And then play in the hockey finals. That's what I'm going to do. And they can print that in the papers, too, in headlines, if anyone's interested, which I seriously doubt."

"Oh you are, are you?" asked John Bolt haughtily. "And what makes you think that Smith would have you back after all this notoriety, and in your shameful condition? I wouldn't think they would look too favorably on an unwed mother as a student in their venerable institution. My guess, my girl, is that you will be asked to leave, with all haste."

Cory looked at her grandfather with an

incredulous expression. "You've got to be kidding, granddad! Ask *me* to leave? In that case, they'd have to get rid of half the student body at one time or another. Believe me, they don't give A's for virginity. In fact, I think the school should set up their own abortion facilities to take care of their *own* girls so we innocent little preppies don't have to go to the big bad city to get fixed."

John Bolt was aghast. He glared at her in shock before he spoke. "I don't like hearing those things coming from your mouth, Corinne. It's this permissive generation of yours that's undermining the sinews of our whole society. I'm surprised at you spouting that liberated garbage. I know you wouldn't be talking like this if those man-hating revolutionaries were not allowed to parade around campuses and prey on young girls. Don't think that I don't know how they brainwash you with this new-fangled independence and push it down your throat. They are Communists, and all this women's independence propaganda is nonsense. Why, they have no more respect for women than the man in the moon. Just want to drag this country down to their disgusting level. And you should be smart enough to realize what *they* are doing."

Cory had been listening to her grandfather with renewed impatience. She sat tapping her fingernails on the arms of the chair.

When he stopped talking she shouted in exasperation, "Jesus, you want me to take responsibility for my own behavior, but you can't stand my independence. Well, you *good people*, you can't have it both ways. Please do me a favor and let me take care of myself. I'll do just fine, and your pure, aristocratic hands won't have to be stained with my dishonorable deeds. And, grandfather, put your mind at rest. Smith will take me back with open arms. The faculty strongly believes that youth is fundamentally good, and besides, they need the tuition and are counting on you for a nice, fat endowment. Believe me, it isn't easy to get kicked out of school these days."

John J. Bolt peered over his glasses. "Don't you be flip with me, Corinne." He snapped his fingers. "I don't want to hear anymore."

Cory shrugged, folded her arms, and cast her eyes down.

Jeffrey was infuriated by her rational approach to contemporary life. He could not conceal his wrath for the daughter who had once been the apple of his eye, his spoiled darling who was now making a mockery of their serious concern.

"Haven't you one ounce of feeling for what this family has been put through during the past few years? For what your mother and I have had to put up with, the anguish even your grandparents have suffered? And now you dump this crisis in our laps, and despite your high and mighty independence, *we* have to deal with it."

Cory looked up with fury. A nerve had been touched.

"You just hold it right there, dad. *You* are not going to make *me* the scapegoat for this family. There sure as hell has been plenty going on, but I'm not about to be your whipping boy who's going to suffer the stress and strain so you all can present yourselves to society as one glorious American unit. You want to avoid your problems by making *me* a problem? No way! You already have your scapegoat. You've got another daughter to take the heat off, to divert all of you from the real problems and the underlying hostility that's been pulling you apart. You just keep her good and sick, and that will call a truce to all the private little wars I damned well know were going on before I was even born. Just let *her* suffer so the rest of you can maintain some kind of genteel family stability. *She's* your victim, not *me*. And she's welcome to it!''

Regina and Homer could not help hearing the loud, emotional harangue that was taking place in the library. Homer went about his work, maintaining the cool demeanor of the good servant he had been for eighteen years, without comment or expression to indicate that anything was wrong in the household.

Later, when the house was quiet, when John and Constance Bolt had left, when Jeff had gone to bed feeling sick from the confrontation with his daughter, Millicent crept softly downstairs because she suspected Cory was alone in the kitchen.
Ever since Cory was a child, the aftermath of a scolding was milk and cookies. Not many years ago after they'd had an argument, she told Millicent that she

considered it a child's compensation for being the underdog.

"Cory, I thought I'd find you here."

Cory did not react to her mother's presence. Only the crunching of cookies could be heard.

Millicent came into the kitchen, filled the tea kettle with water, and took a cup and saucer from the cabinet. She stood by the stove, waiting for the water to boil, and watching her daughter. Cory sat in oversized pajama tops, her blond hair piled loosely on top of her head, her face firmly set in deep thought.

Millicent poured herself a cup of tea and joined Cory at the kitchen table. "You want to talk about this evening, honey?" Millicent asked.

"Not really," said Cory stiffly. "What else is there to say? You all act like I committed a crime and should pay a penalty. I was careless and dumb, that's all."

"We were dumb, too, for the way we acted. And I guess I was the dumbest of all for letting them gang up on you. But it was that publicity that did it. And you must remember, Cory, that becoming pregnant when you're not married and getting an abortion may not seem like much to you, but to your grandparents, it's nothing less than a catastrophe. And I have to admit, I'm not used to the idea myself. It's really not something to take lightly."

Cory leaned back in her chair. Her mouth was set in an obstinate way. "Mother, don't think I'm taking this lightly. I'm not. I just don't see where it's anyone's business but my own. It's something I have to deal with in my own way and according to *my* conscience, nobody else's."

Millicent sighed but said nothing. How could she refute this? In fact, she envied Cory for standing up to Jeff and John Bolt, something she'd never had the courage to do. She sipped her tea, wondering what she could say to get closer to Cory.

Cory sensed this. The brief attitude of belligerence had left her, and she reached out and placed her hand over Millicent's.

"Mom, I'm sorry for the things I said, especially about not . . ."

Millicent finished it for her. "About my not being available? I didn't realize it, Cory, at least not to any great extent. I guess Allyson's illness has been hard on everyone."

"Well, it hasn't been easy for anybody, but the truth of the matter is that you've had the full brunt of it. All of us — dad, Johnny, grandad, nana, and me — well, we go about our business doing what we want. Our lives haven't changed that much. But yours has. You're the one who has been put through the ringer, and I suppose we haven't given you much help or sympathy."

"Honey, I don't want sympathy. Allyson is the one who needs it, from all of us." Hesitatingly, Millicent added, "I don't agree that she's been used as a scapegoat. If you and everyone would just realize that she's sick, really sick, and show her the same compassion that you would show to anyone who is suffering . . . well, that's all I want." She looked wistfully at her daughter. "You and Allyson used to be so close, Cory. What happened?"

Cory sat back and folded her arms. "She pulled away, mother, a long time ago. And maybe I did, too. You see, you can't go along wrapped up in other people's lives indefinitely, especially in their misery." Then she added bluntly, "The plain truth is, sick people can get very tiresome."

Millicent flinched but was not surprised by this statement. Cory usually said openly what other people repressed. They went to bed without ever discussing what had really been bothering Millicent: Why had Cory said that Allyson was being used as a scapegoat?

For days afterward as she thought about it, Millicent was bewildered and confused. The shock of Cory's words turned into anger. But when the anger ebbed, she could not dismiss the pathetic picture Cory had painted of them as a family. She relived the whole ugly scene, which culminated with Cory storming out of the room after her father and Jeff had continued with their tirade of recriminations and righteous indignation. It left all of them in an explosive and exhausted state.

She couldn't believe that what Cory said was true. Even in her worst moments of self-loathing for Allyson's illness, she knew she had been a good mother. Perhaps too good, according to John Bolt.

She remembered what her father said to her after Cory left the room: "Millicent, I warned you long ago that no good would come from your liberal ways of bringing up these children. Allowing them to do just as they please without a tight rein! So now you see how the chickens come home to roost, and you can well ask, 'What went wrong?' "

She was furious when he said that, but now she doubted her whole philosophy of child raising. *Was it wrong to allow your children to think for themselves? she asked herself. Permitting them to experience and experiment, was that giving them a false sense of freedom? Giving them luxuries and privileges without exacting repayment, was that corrosive to responsibility? What have I done to mess things up so badly? And why do I still take my cues from mother and father? Why was I a part of that dreadful scene? Why did I allow it? And what could possibly have made Cory say those awful things about Allyson being a scapegoat and our using her illness to take the pressure off our real problems? Could it possibly be true that Jeff and I never had to come to terms with our own conflicts as long as Allyson was sick? That it served to keep up the pretenses that whatever was wrong between us was a result of Allyson's sickness and not our* own problems? Do we really use our children to deflect us from thinking about ourselves? God knows, I've always done everything possible to avoid a battle with Jeff, and of course with father. Oh, how I've avoided ever making my father angry! And what if that had been me who came home from college pregnant? How would I have handled it? Certainly not like Cory, who ended up telling them all to mind their own damned business. I wouldn't have come home, except in a box, because I would have killed myself first. Absolutely and without a doubt, I would have taken poison rather than face father and tell him I was having a baby. Talk about shame! Who had babies in those days? Married women and bad girls — sluts, tramps, poor naïve girls who were sent away to homes for unwed mothers and were then branded for life with the scars of their disgrace.

Father would have shown no mercy. I would have killed myself, and Cory went back to play in the hockey finals! God, how the world's changed in only one generation.

Chapter 11

It was strange. Millicent felt awkward in Jeff's presence, both of them unable to tell each other what was on their minds. The silence between them loomed like a powerful wall. Each was frustrated, unable to understand the other, unable to discuss their daughter's actions without creating more dissension. His remoteness and work schedule increased after the incident with Cory. The tension built.

Cory had the abortion, played in the hockey finals, and went on with college life as though nothing of great importance had taken place. Cory had dropped a bomb and left them to pick up the pieces.

Several days later, Millicent sadly related the bitter scene to Dr. Bromley but deliberately left out the final denunciation her daughter had made. She could not bring herself to tell the psychiatrist how Cory had accused them of subconsciously perpetuating Allyson's anorexic condition. That was a shattering charge she could not deal with, at least not now.

But she did reproach herself by expressing the gnawing suspicion that somehow the pregnancy, the abortion, the terrible scene at home, would not have happened if she had been alert to the needs of her daughter.

"I can't help feeling," she said with remorse, "that if I had just been there for her, really available to her, this whole messy situation would never had happened."

Dr. Bromley said, "In these days, a twenty-one-year-old woman does not come to her mother for permission to have sex. As for birth control, I daresay that your daughter knows more about it than you do."

"Oh, I know that," said Millicent, biting on the nail of her thumb, "but at least she could have confided in me about her decision to have the abortion."

"What would you have done if she had, talked her out of it?"

"I don't know, perhaps."

"Then perhaps Cory didn't want to be talked out of it. Can you accept the fact that she is grown up and trying to be independent and this was, rightfully, her decision to make?"

Millicent was not convinced that she should not feel guilty. "But I still feel that somehow I failed her by . . . by not paying attention."

Dr. Bromley confronted her with this guilt. "By letting Allyson eat up all your maternal attention, is that it?"

Millicent sighed regretfully. "Cory said as much. That's what she accused me of. That's obviously where I failed."

"You talk as if you're dedicated to failure," Dr. Bromley observed. "You've got to stop taking the blame for your entire family. You are neither demon nor their savior. Remember, you are a product of your upbringing just as Cory is of hers. You became a mother with an established background and parents of your own, and above all, with memories. You are still thrown into terror when you have to deal with your parents." Dr. Bromley leaned forward, resting one elbow hard on the arm of the chair. She looked into Millicent's eyes questioningly.

"Millicent, tell me what is going through your mind."

Millicent denied her own thoughts. "Nothing much. I'm just thinking about Cory."

Dr. Bromley challenged her. "I doubt that. I think you are thinking of something else, and I also think you are very frightened."

A shiver went through Millicent, and she curled up in her chair as though she were withdrawing from the fear.

Dr. Bromley's voice was calm but persistent. "Tell me what is going through your mind, my dear."

Millicent stared straight ahead and answered flatly, "My father."

"What about your father?"

Suddenly the rage erupted. "Dammit! Why did I let him badger Cory with his righteous morality? And why did Jeff side with him? Why did I let my father take control of the situation when I'm her mother? I'm her mother! He had no right to take control!"

"Then why did you let him?" asked Dr. Bromley.

A helpless expression crossed Millicent's face. "Because . . . because I'm still overwhelmed by his power, his superior power."

Dr. Bromley bent her head questioningly to one side. "Did you feel, while you were sitting there watching this argument, that *you* were in Cory's place, that *you* were the one who was being threatened?"

Millicent's eyes grew wide with the startling revelation of the psychiatrist's knowing exactly how she felt. She tightened up, just feeling the sheer force of her father's dominance.

Dr. Bromley continued to prod her. "While you were watching this scene, this power stuggle between your father and Cory, and your husband, did you feel that *you* were the one who was being accused, attacked?"

Millicent felt as if her whole body was shriveling in the chair. When she spoke, her voice was barely audible. "Oh, yes. Don't you see, he still scares me to death. I can't fight him. He's too . . . too . . ."

Dr. Bromley finished it for her. "Your father is too strong for you. Is that it? And you expected Cory to crumble as you would have crumbled, and you were petrified and powerless to do anything?"

Millicent put both hands to her face and

nodded, again and again.

"Millicent, my dear, let go. Once and for all, separate from him. You will not deteriorate. He is not your authority anymore."

Millicent looked at the psychiatrist with uncertainty.

Dr. Bromley went on to explain: "You've been locked into what we call a dependent-hostile relationship with your father, and it's been very frightening for you to separate and become an independent person with an identity of your own. In a way, it's a safe place to be, but it never gives you the opportunity to grow."

Millicent sighed inwardly as she absorbed the implication of the doctor's statement. "It sounds like you're talking about Allyson."

Dr. Bromley did not respond. After a few moments of silence she asked, "And where does your mother fit in? Are you still so attached to her, too?"

Millicent shook her head. Her answer was decisive. "No, not my mother. I left her long ago."

Dr. Bromley looked directly into her eyes. "How?" she asked.

"By making the decision," Millicent

said slowly, "that I would never be like her. In fact, I made a conscious effort to be just the opposite of her in every way. I hope I've at least accomplished that."

In the weeks ahead, the sense of being somehow apart from others did not leave Millicent. The feeling of becoming "unglued" had taken on a dimension of isolation. She was not encouraged by Dr. Graham's optimistic prognosis of Allyson's progress. It was already November and she was still in the hospital.

Jeff grew more distant, but she told herself it was due to his increased responsibilities while her father was wintering in Palm Beach. Jeff was actually more of an extension of John Bolt than his own children were, and the two men had come to depend upon each other in an odd, inexplicable way.

Johnny seemed distant too, at least different, when she last spoke to him, but she could not clearly discern the change. She sensed an avoidance on his part to talk about anything personal. She begged him to take a weekend off and fly home, but he offered one excuse after another until her instincts told her that something had altered the course of his life. But after the painful confrontation with Cory, she was reluctant to press him for the answers that would ease her anxious doubts. If Millicent had any idea of the real state of Johnny's changed life, she would have been more than vaguely troubled.

She was overreacting, she told herself. Johnny was probably involved with a girl friend, and knowing his shyness, he would not want to discuss the relationship. Interfering had become tricky, and she proceeded with caution. So she did not push him. She realized that she was thinking of herself, too. If anything was wrong, she almost didn't want to know. Her composure was fast breaking, and she needed to protect herself.

But she also needed to talk to someone who had a warm link with her past. Despite her sense of inadequacy, Millicent wanted to be reassured that things were going to be right again, just as a child seeks comfort in the darkness. She needed not to feel so lonely.

They sat in the overly done French provincial living room off Martha Carrington's apartment, which looked more like the home of a rich widow than that of a spinster secretary. Antiques and treasured mementos filled the spacious rooms with the high ceilings. It had been a long time since John J. Bolt had been there for clandestine moments of pleasure. He always left an extravagant ornament until the apartment became a vestige of expensive memories.

The living room, where Martha and Millicent were having tea, was a cluttered room that gave the impression that the owner coud not bear to part with a single possession that kept the past alive. It was as if the objects were autobiographical: silver gilt rectangular boxes collected by Martha's mother along with indistinguished pieces of crystal; her father's collection of old clocks; unusual Chinese porcelain bowls from John Bolt; rare figures of painted birds, also from John Bolt; French upholstered furniture and fine antiques acquired on pleasure trips to Europe; and various gifts from appreciative clients.

Martha poured formally from the elaborate tea service, now rarely in use. "Millicent, it's been a long time between visits. I've thought about you and worried about you, and I've even been a little mad at you for neglecting me. But no matter, you're here now and I'm glad. I've missed you. How's Allyson, or shouldn't I ask? Jeff doesn't say much at the office, and your father has been passing it off as if she'd had nothing more than a bad case of chicken pox for six years. I'm not exactly anyone's confidante these days, so you tell me. After all, you . . . all of you, are the only family I have left, and I don't like to be kept out of things."

"Martha, what's there to tell? It's pretty much the same old story. Allyson is still in the hospital. I don't see what they're doing for her there that we can't do at home. Thank heavens she's not starving herself, but she's far from cured."

Millicent moved forward on the antique velvet settee and took several sips of tea. Martha sat facing her on the other side of the coffee table that held the tea service. Her eyes glazed with concentration as she waited for Millicent to continue.

"Allyson has made progress with the help of a psychiatrist whom I've never met because he doesn't want to see me yet and whom Allyson constantly tells me she hates. It doesn't make any sense, Martha.

212

I honestly don't know what's going on there, but Dr. Graham assures me that she's getting better and will be home soon. Soon, I've learned, is a word that can mean a week or six months or a year. Frankly, I'm not optimistic about her progress because I've been through these so-called good periods so many times before. And when she does come home, who knows when the whole business will start up again? I'm afraid to get caught up in their enthusiasm. I've been disappointed too often."

Martha peered over the rim of her tea cup. "So you make your daily visit and another year will go by and all of a sudden you'll realize that your whole day revolves around getting ready to go to the hospital." Martha put her cup down and glanced uneasily at Millicent. "But that's not all that's on your mind, is it? What else is worrying you? Is it Jeff?"

Millicent focused her eyes in the tea cup. Aimlessly, she stirred the tea as she answered. "Yes and no. It would be rather nice to spend our twilight years together. He seems to be working harder than ever."

"Well, I can vouch for that," said Martha as she took a cigarette from the coffee table and inserted it into an ornate silver holder. "Your husband has been determined to outdo your father, and he has certainly succeeded. The company is more prosperous than ever. They are definitely cut from the same cloth. You know, Jeff's even getting to look like J.J. He's stubborn like him, too. But that's not your immediate problem. I can tell. Which other kid, Johnny or Cory, is driving you up the wall?"

Millicent stood up and walked restlessly around the room.

Martha took a long drag on her cigarette and waited for Millicent to answer. When she didn't, Martha asked again, "Is it Cory?"

Millicent clenched her teeth. Then she said, "Yes, it's Cory."

"Oh Lord, is she pregnant or some stupid thing like that?" asked Martha cynically as she waved her cigarette in the air.

Even with her back turned, Millicent flushed with embarrassment. "She was," she finally responded. Millicent turned around and sat down again. "She had an abortion." She winced when she said it.

"Don't look so grim. From what I hear,

it's not exactly the worst thing in the world these days, and it's certainly not unusual. Believe me, Millicent, it won't ruin her life. It's not like it used to be."

Millicent shifted uneasily on the edge of the settee. "I know that, although I have to admit that it still shakes me up. Martha, I just haven't bridged that generation gap, and I rather guess my own feelings about premarital sex and abortions made me less than sympathetic. You won't believe what an awful mess it all turned out to be."

Martha sat back. "Tell me," she said with a gentleness in her voice.

Millicent told Martha the details of Cory's homecoming in a detached, factual manner. But when she got to the part where Cory accused them of using Allyson as a scapegoat in order to deal with their own troubles, she broke down.

Martha came and sat by her and put her arms around her as she had so often done when Millicent was a frightened, unhappy child.

"You know, Millicent, many years ago I put you on the road to motherhood and you always told me that it was the greatest thing that ever happened to you."

"It was, Martha," said Millicent as she

wiped away the tears. "It gave me a purpose in life beyond anything I had ever had. For once, I felt important and needed. It felt so good to be giving. Lives depended on me. But something got twisted along the way. It seems that all of a sudden, even though it wasn't sudden at all, one by one . . . my family . . . my life . . . came apart. Allyson got sick, now this with Cory, and I suspect that not all is right with Johnny."

"What's wrong with *that* kid?" asked Martha with surprise. "I always thought he was the quiet one who never gave you any trouble. Why are you worried about him?"

"I don't know. I just sense something is bothering him, and not knowing what it is bothers me."

"Then why don't you ask him?"

"Because I can't ask anymore. They're grown up. I've got to get uninvolved from them."

Martha slapped her hand on the table. "Well, that's about the first sensible thing you've said. When are you going to get back to your own life?"

"But, Martha, that's what's driving me crazy," said Millicent miserably. "Is Cory right? Do I use my children in a way that keeps me from getting back to my life because there's really nothing to get back to? Without their problems, does my reason for living stop?"

Martha sat up with a start and pointed a finger at Millicent. "Millicent Bolt Hart! You're talking like a fool and, furthermore, you're indulging in disgusting self-pity. Don't you dare reach middle age exhausted in mind and body! You've got a marvelous-looking, virile, successful husband, who despite the fact that he and I could not be in the same room for ten minutes without having an argument, is probably one of the most desirable men in Washington. You've got money, position, friends, health, brains . . ."

Millicent interrupted. "And three immature adult children . . . well at least two, who are so screwed up that I don't know what's going to become of them."

Martha peered at Millicent and spoke sharply. "Now you just hold it there! Where the hell is it written that everything should turn out rosy? Why should your children be any different from other kids, and when did you take out a patent on perfect children? OK, so it's been hard

217

and they've given you a rough time and Allyson *is* temporarily screwed up with this absurd sickness. But, my God Millicent, you're not the only mother who has suffered! And you're also not the only parent who has poured her guts out and gotten kicked in the teeth. Life isn't easy, my girl, and I don't think God ever intended it to be."

Millicent lowered her head in embarrassment as Martha reminded her about all the positive things in her life and about the other parents who had suffered. For a long while she was quiet.

Then she looked up into Martha's face. "You make me feel ashamed, Martha. I guess what it comes down to is that I'm as selfish as the people I criticize for wanting it all. The money isn't enough, all the material things aren't enough, a husband isn't enough. I want faultless, super children who won't give me any heartache and who will make me proud."

Martha's face became soft and the frown of disapproval disappeared. She patted Millicent's folded hands. "Oh, Millicent dear, we all want it all. Who doesn't? Don't be ashamed of that. Just face the fact that it's not going to turn out that way. We all come to realize that what we have is not what we hoped for but *that* we *can* still make the best out of a second-best situation. Success is never absolute and neither is failure. And this business with Cory . . . well, there may be some truth in what she said. But I don't think Allyson is volunteering herself as a sacrificial offering. It's not a conscious decision on her part, nor on yours. Sometimes things just happen. And sometimes the strongest link assumes the weakest role."

"What do you mean?" asked Millicent, genuinely puzzled by Martha's statement.

Martha answered, sounding uncertain. "Oh, I don't know exactly what I mean except that I have the feeling that Allyson isn't as weak and dependent as you think. There's something deep down inside of her that will emerge one day if she can ever get over this state she's in. All that good mothering you gave her for so many years has got to count for something. You'll see, it hasn't been wasted."

Millicent smiled, and squeezed Martha's hand. "You're very dear to say that. Thank you."

Martha shrugged and took another cigarette from the silver box on the table.

Millicent finally relaxed and thought back. "Isn't it ironic, Martha, that I wanted to become pregnant more than anything else in the world. That I believed my life and my relationship with Jeff were fading because I couldn't have a child. I felt totally inadequate as a woman. And now my daughter becomes pregnant by someone she doesn't want a relationship with, someone she barely remembers and certainly doesn't care about, and passes it off as an inconvenience. Abortion wasn't in my vocabulary. I barely knew anything about it. I had never even heard about anyone having one except in those trashy magazines that were passed around in school. That was a seedy side of life that was completely foreign to me. It was illegal, like stealing. People who did it were criminals, and I never questioned the morality or justice of it. And somehow my mind still thinks of it as dirty. I have this outdated value system, and I know I'm wrong."

"Well, you're right about its being dirty. It was dirty then, but only because women were made to feel dirty and had to sneak around in filthy back alley places to have it done. But the consequences of not having an abortion were even worse. Single women couldn't have babies, and they didn't need a law to forbid it." A shadow of gloom came over her. "Society punished you in its own ways."

Martha got up and walked to the window. She stared earnestly at a fluffy cloud formation, and then the furrows in her brow squeezed together as though an old wound had opened up and she was suddenly in pain. She turned so Millicent would not see, but Millicent had seen the anguish of grief that came upon the face of her old friend. As if her mind had flowed with Martha's, she said, "Martha, I've said something to make you miserable. What is it? What's wrong?"

She could have replied, *You think you're the only one who knows about suffering. Just consider yourself and your daughter lucky that times are different. You've got choices. What did I have?* But instead, she merely stiffened in an effort to regain self-possession and said, "Nothing's wrong, you silly girl. All this heavy talk gives me a headache. I'm not getting any younger you know, almost into senility if you listen to the people at the office."

"No, Martha. You're not going to put

me off. I've spent my life coming to you for help without ever giving you the opportunity to open up to me. Well, I'm not a child anymore, far from it, and it's about time I paid you back in kind, even just a little. So tell me. What's the matter? I may not be able to help much because I'm in such a sorry state myself, but I can at least listen. Please, Martha, you've listened to me for so long. Let me listen to you."

Martha turned on her heels and reacted with mock resentment. "Millicent, what in heaven's name has gotten into you? What makes you think people can reverse roles and that turnabout is fair play? I don't like spilling my insides to anyone, even you. That's not my style. I am a voyeur by nature, a prying observer, and I intend to remain that way. Let's get back to your problems. That suits me better."

But Millicent persisted. She loved Martha and wanted just once to share her feelings. "Martha, you've been like a mother to me. I've told you all the things I could never tell my own mother. I've burdened you enough. Think of me as your daughter and let *me* comfort you."

Martha's proud bearing, always impenetrable, faltered slightly. A vulnerable expression crossed her face. "You were like my daughter, weren't you?" As she said this, her eyes became glazed as though memories had been stirred. She returned to the chair across from Millicent and sat down stiffly, her body erect, both feet flat together on the floor, her hands folded in her lap like a prim little girl.

An unnatural smile settled on her lips. "You know, Millicent, I used to pretend you *were* my daughter. I really did."

Suddenly Martha became animated. "Do you remember the times I took you to the theater and to concerts? God, I used to enjoy that. You were such a bright child, you understood everything. Didn't we have fun?" Her laugh was tense.

Millicent shifted uncomfortably in her seat. Something was peculiar, she mused, but she couldn't focus on what it was. She could, in that moment, see that Martha's personality had changed and she regretted begging her to unburden herself.

Martha leaned forward, an unaccustomed broad smile on her face. "Do you still have that fan I bought you after we went to see *Madame Butterfly?* You just had to have a Japanese fan, and I took you to the museum shop. Do you remember, Millicent? It was a gorgeous thing, silk with flowers and birds?"

It was so unlike Martha to indulge in maudlin nostalgia that Millicent could barely respond. "No, Martha, I don't have it. It was lost, misplaced, long ago."

"What a pity," said Martha wistfully. "It was so lovely." Martha looked longingly toward the window, staring but not quite seeing. "We *were* just like mother and daughter, weren't we?" she said in a distant voice.

This was a woman Millicent had never seen. The haughty, arrogant terror of the Bolt corporation looked suddenly frail and pitiful as she dug back into the past. There was an oppressive quiet. Millicent sat agonizing and groping for words that would relieve the tension that was building up.

Quite suddenly, Martha jumped up and dashed to the desk on the other side of the room. Frantically, she searched the contents of the drawers. It was apparent to Millicent that she was looking for some special article that had been placed inside and long forgotten but was now of paramount importance.

With a look of delight, Martha found what she wanted. It was a picture, and for a brief moment she hugged it to her breast. Then, quickly, she brought it to Millicent and thrust it into her hands.

"See," she said. "I knew I had it. You remember when we took it, don't you? Isn't it marvelous?"

Millicent's eyes narrowed as she studied the picture. It was a photograph of Martha and John J. Bolt with Millicent between them, all standing in front of the new Bolt Building on the day of its dedication. Millicent was about twelve years old then. Martha looked young and radiantly beautiful, and John J. Bolt stood proud and handsome. Millicent searched her mind but could not remember the day the picture was taken.

Martha leaned over as Millicent stared at the picture. "Wasn't that the most exciting day, Millicent? Remember the party and the photographers. At the time, it was considered the most modern building in Washington. We planned it so carefully, every piece of brick and glass."

Millicent now remembered the opening of her father's building on K Street, and the lavish party, but she could not remember posing for the picture. The little girl in the photograph hardly looked familiar to her. Millicent looked up dubiously and handed back the picture.

Martha's face was fixed in a taut smile. Coyly, she bent her head to one side and laughed lightly. "No matter who I showed this picture to," she said as she blushed, "everyone thought you looked like me."

Martha went to the desk, carefully wrapped the photograph back in its old tissue paper and put it in the drawer. The color had drained from her face and the smile was gone. An expression of deep sadness had taken its place. Then she walked to the window and fixed her eyes on the billowing clouds gliding through the gray sky.

Oh, my God! said Millicent to herself. What is going on with her? What did I set in motion that's causing her to act so strange? She seems to have regressed into a world of unrequited dreams. Funny, she really and truly has always thought of me as her daughter. I guess I sensed it but never really understood the extent of her longing until now. She looks so desolate. I've got to help her.

Millicent went to the window and stood by Martha. "Martha dear, I've upset you. Do you want to talk about it? What did I open up?"

She responded sadly, "A lifetime of regrets."

"That you never married and had children?" Millicent gently asked, realizing that she had never asked that question before.

"That I never could," said Martha plaintively. She began to pace up and down nervously. Suddenly she stopped and faced Millicent. "Don't you see," Martha said with an air of helplessness. "Cory had a choice. I never did. What choice did I have in those days?" she added guiltily.

Millicent put her fingers to her mouth in surprise. "Oh, Martha, now I understand. You had an abortion yourself, a long time ago, didn't you?"

Martha hesitated. "Yes, a long time ago." Her voice was a half whisper and filled with melancholy.

"And you had put it away and now I made you relive the whole painful experience again with all this talk about Cory. Oh, Martha, I had no idea. I never intended this. How could I know?"

Martha showed no reaction. She began to pace again, rubbing her palms together. She looked as if there was so much that had to be explained. Suddenly Martha began to talk, and her memories came out in bits and pieces, disjointed, out of sequence, formless miseries of the past.

"You see, I wanted the baby. I really wanted her but he said it was impossible, unthinkable. That I would not only destroy my life but his as well, and his family's, too. I knew the shame that would come from having her and I was even willing to go away, far away, but he was adamant. Oh, he was unrelenting. I finally gave in. I had to. Don't you see, I had to. What choice did I have? None, absolutely none. He sent me to that miserable place in Baltimore. It was so degrading, so everlastingly humiliating, even though they were paid plenty for taking her from me. He saw to that. He made all the arrangements but never showed his face. I went alone and came back alone. He told me it was our 'silent secret' and that I had proven my love for him. I did love him so. You see that, don't you? He wouldn't even talk about it. 'Bury it, Martha, bury it deep,' he said. And I did. I let them take her."

As though she had come to the end of a prepared explanation, Martha stopped and stood silent and motionless in the middle of the room. Eventually, she walked stiffly to a lounge chair and plumped down wearily. Perspiration dripped from her forehead. Her eyes had a glassy cast. Martha sat gazing into space.

Millicent, overwhelmed by the realization that Martha was coming apart emotionally, stood speechless for what seemed an eternity. Finally and impulsively, she asked aloud what had been in her mind as Martha talked. "You had an abortion, Martha. Why do you call it 'her'?"

Martha looked up and gave Millicent an inscrutable look. The agony in her voice was chilling. "Because I miss *her*. I'll miss her every day of my life." And quite suddenly she burst into tears and her chest heaved with uncontrollable sobs.

Millicent put her hands to her mouth to muffle a gasp. She rushed over and knelt beside Martha, gathering the pathetic figure around the waist, offering words of consolation in hushed tones.

As the anguish of grief subsided, Martha stopped crying. She clasped her hands and looked anxiously at Millicent as though there was more to explain.

Millicent returned a look of profound sympathy that urged her to go on, having no idea of the connection between Martha's secret guilt and herself.

"And you realize, of course, that I had no choice, no choice at all," Martha brooded again. "Cory could have had the baby and brought her up and loved her. But I couldn't. And how could I leave him? He needed me. And how could I ruin your life?"

Millicent looked at her incredulously. "My life! My life?"

"Certainly. All your lives. You and Joan and Constance, the company. Oh, yes, the company. He said it would destroy . . ."

Millicent jumped up, her face contorted. "Oh, my God! Oh, my God! You mean it was *my father* who . . ."

With that Martha seemed to come back from the dead as though her faculties were instantaneously restored. "Lord in heaven! What have I said? What have I done? Oh my dearest, as God is my witness, I never meant for you to know. Never! Never! Never!" She ran from the room screaming the words.

Chapter 12

It would never again be the same between Millicent and Martha. As often happens with good friends, great secrets divulged in emotional dark moments become awkward barriers in the light of day when life once more resumes its normal but repressive pattern. To inadvertently reveal something private during horrendous melodrama is to foreclose the bonds of intimacy to the point of estrangement.

In the weeks that followed, Millicent came to accept the startling revelation without piercing shock. She tried to reestablish her relationship with Martha. She called her and went by the office, attempting to console Martha with understanding and without recrimination. Ultimately, she even tried to act as though nothing had been said. But it was to no avail. Secrets once told cannot be untold. Their meetings became a painful ceremony. Martha had bared her troubled soul. Her protective armor had been penetrated. She resorted to even more irreverent wit as an avoidance of familiarity, and her coworkers got the brunt of an acrimony that masked a deeper sense of loss.

In the middle of November, Millicent found herself more alone and isolated. The raw winter weather was approaching, and it affected her mood. It went from a gradual sense of acceptance of her problems to high irritability. She was impatient to get her life together, as though it were hanging in limbo without any course to follow.

It was during this time that Millicent received a frantic overseas call from her sister that left her in a quandary and added to her depressive state. The call came from an exclusive spa in the south of France, and it took Millicent ten minutes of repeated questioning to get Joan, who sounded drunk, to stop babbling incoherently and tell her where she was.

"Millicent, why are you asking me so

many questions?" Joan squealed over the phone. "I told you, I'm in some sort of spa in France, someplace down south. I can't think of the name right now. Oh, what the bloody difference does it make? I need ten thousand dollars right away."

"Why are you there, Joan, and where's your husband, uh . . ." Millicent groped for the name of Joan's fourth husband, the painter.

"Jean Claude," Joan offered with bitterness. "God knows where that rat is. He took off with everything and left me high and dry." She started giggling. "But not so dry."

"Why are you there, at this spa? Joan, can you hear me?"

"Of course, I can hear you. I'm not deaf," she said with agitation. "I'm here because my friends said I needed rest and relaxation. They brought me. I've got so many dear friends." Her voice trailed off. "You just don't know how tired I am. Millicent, you won't believe what a frightful year I've had. I lost all my luggage in Paris, and Fifi died."

Millicent was reluctant to ask, but she did. "Who's Fifi?"

"My darling poodle," Joan said with a

whimper. "You know, the one Simone gave me. The poor thing died of fright, and it was all that bastard Jean Claude's fault. He dropped paint on her and then that thief . . ."

"Joan, why do you need so much money now?"

"To pay the spa. What do you think? They're getting positively pissy about being paid. And I need to stay until I get my strength back. You will send it right away, won't you, Millicent? The doctor is simply wonderful but terribly impatient."

"Joan dear, why don't you come home? We'll take care of you. I'll send a ticket and arrange for someone to get you on a plane."

"No, you don't understand!" Joan yelled. "I can't come home! It's not my home! My nerves are shot. I need to rest." Her voice became calmer and childish. "I like it here. I'm having marvelous massages. Please, Millicent, please send me the money. You will, won't you, right away?"

Millicent sighed helplessly as she gave in. She got through to the doctor in charge, learned scarcely more from him about Joan's condition except that she was drunker than usual, and promised to send the money and inform the trustees of her sister's whereabouts.

She considered calling her mother and father but she could not bear to remind them of this daughter whose outlandish behavior was the scourge of the Bolt family. Her mother's reaction would most probably be, "what in the world is that child up to this time, and what did you say her husband's name is?" Her father's reaction would be to stiffen up, turn somber, and with resignation tell her, "Call my lawyers and send the money."

So with a heart filled with sorrow she made the arrangements to send the money, promising herself that she would go there within the next few weeks if Allyson continued to improve.

She had not seen Joan in almost two years. It had been one of her whirlwind visits to the States that left Millicent and the Bolts exhausted and not too unhappy upon her departure. Joan had a knack for stirring things up, and her detailed narratives of foreign escapades were outlandishly alien to their ordered lives. She would arrive in Washington exuberant and happy to see everyone and then depart hastily and unexpectedly, thinking she could leave behind her bad feelings about herself.

It was difficult for Millicent to think of Joan with compassion because the past interfered with the present. The pathetic creature her sister had become was a paradox of their youth. There had been no apparent rivalry, just one-sided envy. Joan was beautiful and sought after. Millicent was not.

Joan could have married anyone and she did. Carter Smith was high society, and this first marriage merged wealth and position with more wealth and position and was blessed by both families. That it ended in divorce three years later came as a surprise to the society watchers and the respective families. It seemed such a perfect match. But Joan grew tired of the blond young boys who hung around, and when she arrived home unexpectedly from Jamaica and caught Carter in the shower with an especially young one, she took off for Europe. Joan's second marriage to a titled Englishman, long on nobility but short of funds and twice her age, was considered the passing fancy of the whimsical rich. Oddly enough, the union lasted nine years, but only because the once impecunious lord was unaffected by his young wife's antics now that he was totally and laboriously immersed in the all-consuming task of documenting his family's patrician lineage. The majestic chronicle was his life's passion, and he felt fortunate to be able to work on his archives since the distasteful pressures of unemployment had been lifted with the marriage, which could go on forever as far as he was concerned. But Joan met a handsome Italian actor of dubious talent who persuaded her to transfer her assets to him. This third marriage ended when he reached a modicum of success in second-rate films. He discarded her on the Italian Riviera, a stone's throw from the French Riviera, where she took to alcohol and young lovers with a vengeance. The French artist came on the scene when she needed a conspicuous admirer and consort and he needed a patron. Joan had put distance between herself and the family like an adolescent trying to achieve independence. But she lacked the confidence to survive on her own resources and sought husbands to care for her.

She had never had children and never

wanted any. Millicent wondered what Joan ever really wanted out of life, but the merry-go-round, jet-set world she went in and out of offered no clues. So the family dealt with her on a crisis-to-crisis basis.

Millicent went to the Bolt Building just before 5:00 P.M. to make the financial arrangements and have the money dispatched to France. She hoped to see Jeff before he left for his business trip to New York. During the week she had seen so little of him. His standoffishness bothered her terribly, and she wanted to clear the air or at least restore some warmth between them. She thought it would be nice to take him to the airport before making her evening visit to the hospital, although she suspected the company limousine would already be there waiting.

When she approached Jeffrey's office, she heard loud, angry voices and burning words and knew instantly that Martha and Jeff were at it again, disagreeing on what was probably an innocuous company policy. Millicent turned and started to move out of range until the argument was over, but Martha came out of the office fuming and muttering under her breath and strode right past her without a glance.

Millicent entered as Jeff was breaking a pencil in half.

"Did you hear that? That woman is going to drive me crazy! I'm working on million-dollar deals and she comes to me with idiotic requests about personnel. I swear, I'd gladly give her anything if only she would retire."

"Oh Jeff, you know she'll never do that. This is her life. It's all she has. Try to be more understanding with Martha. Underneath she's a good woman."

He moved closer to her and took her gently by the shoulders. "Millicent my love, she's a witch! But I'll try to be understanding and kind to her because you want me to be and J. J. wants me to be and because I have no choice. She'd probably put a curse on me." He kissed her lightly on the forehead.

Millicent flinched for a second, surprised by this gesture of warmth. Her bruised pride had been soothed and she realized how little it took to lift her ego. *I always come around to him,* she said to herself as she looked into his face and smiled.

"What brings you down, honey?" said Jeff as he returned to his desk and began gathering papers. "I'm sorry but I've got to leave in a few minutes to catch a plane to New York."

"I know, but I had to get a check sent off to France."

A smirk came across Jeff's face. "I bet it's a big one and I bet I know who it's for. What's her problem this time?"

Millicent held up her hand to ward off any further comment. "Jeff, I don't care to discuss it. I just wanted to do it and not think about it because I can't cope with one more dilemma. I'm taking the easy way out."

Jeff was more than sympathetic. "You should, honey. I agree. We've got enough. Your sister's a hard nut to crack. Did you tell J. J.?"

"To change the subject, Jeff, would you like me to take you to the airport?"

His voice was full of disappointment. "I'd love it, but the car's waiting downstairs and my bag and briefcase are already in it. Anyway, Harry McIntyre's coming along. But I'll call you tonight and again tomorrow, and if things go well I'll come back a day early and not go into the office. In fact, I'll make a date with you, Mrs. Hart. We'll spend the whole day together, doing whatever you want. I promise. Honestly hon, I know it's been hard on you but we've never been busier, and with J. J. away, I just can't seem to get out from under. But I miss just being with you, and if you'll put up with me a little longer, I'll take you away to an exotic place for some old-fashioned romance and show you how much I love you."

"When have I heard that before?" asked Millicent with a trace of sarcasm.

"No, sweetie, this time I mean it. We will get away. Just the two of us. Besides, I need a rest. This pace is killing. I can hardly wait until Johnny comes into the business and relieves his old man of some of the pressures. You can't trust a business like this to strangers, no matter how competent they are. You need family at the helm. So will you save up some loving and keep it warm until I get back?"

He kissed her affectionately and held her in his arms as if he couldn't bear to be separated for even a few days. It was tender and lingering and she wished she could hold on to this moment forever. Before he went out he threw her a kiss and said, "Give this to Allyson, from me." With one gesture, he touched her heart.

After he left, she sat in his large executive chair feeling her mood of despondency begin to melt away. *I'm so easy to please,* she thought. *Is that good or just plain stupid? A warm touch, a loving kiss and a hug, some caring words and I'm mad for him again. The unexpected always happens just when I've adjusted to the reality of the situation. Why am I so happily surprised by Jeff's loving moods? Because for a long time they've been so rare, or have I been as unavailable as he's been? Oh, what's the use of trying to figure it out. I like it because I feel as though my life is coming together again. I love it, and the spark is still there and we've got to start enjoying each other.*

She sat there dreamy minded, playing with the ornately carved letter opener on Jeff's massive desk and remembering the lovely feeling of his embrace. Pink telephone message slips were scattered on the desk, and she absentmindedly glanced at them without giving the typical abbreviated, indistinct notes much thought until she saw the word "flowers" on one of them. The message was written by Jeff's private secretary: "Mr. H. Flowers to C. R. tak c/o. Deliv to Mayfair Reg at 8. Din

Res at 9 Le Cirq."

Without any sense of recognition, she pushed the slip into the pile of other pink slips and got up with a sigh because her reverie of detachment had been interrupted. It was time to go to the hospital.

Millicent was greeted by the effusive Miss Waverly, who was overflowing with good news: "Mrs. Hart, happy the sun shines on us today. We were able to eat meat, real meat, and we enjoyed it, I'm sure. Lamb chop and half a baked potato with a pat of butter and a spoonful of fresh garden peas and a cup of delicious custard. Would you believe? Oh, we are progressing so well, and tomorrow we shall have chicken croquettes with lyonnaise potatoes and yellow squash."

"How nice, Miss Waverly, how very nice." Millicent never knew how to respond to the nurse's opening progress reports. She actually spoke the way a menu was written.

Allyson was sitting up in bed silently mimicking Miss Waverly's prissy face. It was the first sign of her sense of humor Millicent had seen in years.

Miss Waverly looked from one to the

other with a sly grin. "Now I know we have a lot to tell you, so I'll just slip out for a short break and a wee sojourn to the little girls' room. We won't be long."

Allyson looked as if she was about to vomit.

"Allyson, don't say it," Millicent cautioned her with a smile.

Allyson raised her eyebrows as if she didn't know what Millicent was talking about. "Say what, mother?"

"That you can't stand her," said Millicent. "You're right. She's very odd. But put up with her. It won't be much longer."

"Oh, I don't mind her. She's very funny, really. And I'm getting terribly involved in her life story. Each day is another ridiculous chapter. Do you know that her father was a Baptist minister in Georgia and sold peach tonic to his congregation? And he made it himself and it was called Father Polk's."

"No, I didn't know that," said Millicent, a little taken aback by Allyson's change of attitude toward Miss Waverly. "Well, I'm pleasantly surprised that you've accepted her. She's not a bad sort. And what's with all this food she's getting into you?"

Allyson shrugged. "No big deal. I'm getting better so I'm eating. Isn't that what I'm here for?"

"Of course, sweetheart, and I'm very pleased. Has Dr. Graham said when you can go home?" Millicent asked carefully.

"Yep. He says any time I'm ready."

"Great! When should we plan it? Tomorrow? Day after?"

"Nope," Allyson responded decisively. "Not yet. Michael says I'm not ready."

Millicent could not contain her indignation. "And who is Michael and why aren't you ready?"

"I mean Dr. Lyons, my psychiatrist. He says I'm not ready to take the big plunge."

"Allyson, what is this all about? And I thought you hated him, this Dr. Lyons."

"I did," said Allyson curtly. "That was last week. This week I hate him less."

"And why haven't I met him? Why won't he see me?" asked Millicent with a hurt tone.

"Don't take it personally, mother. Michael says it's psychiatrically detrimental to our relationship. He wants to deal with my problems alone and not be influenced by parental concern."

"You sound as if you're reading from a textbook."

"I am. He gives me lots to read and then we spend a lot of time arguing about it. He wants to free me of my repressions so I can establish my identity. He's very argumentative, you know, and extremely hostile."

Millicent stared at her, astonished. "The psychiatrist is hostile! That's the limit. How can he possibly treat you?"

"With hostility," said Allyson, matter-of-factly. "He's very unorthodox and not at all Freudian like my last one."

"Oh, Allyson, I really don't think this is in your best interest. He sounds peculiar."

Allyson was annoyed. She straightened up in bed and folded her arms across her chest. "He's not peculiar, mother. He's just different. And I am getting better. Didn't Little Miss Pitty Pat Waverly give you a glowing report?"

Millicent moved close to the bed and gently touched Allyson's cheek. She looked down at her lovingly. "Tell me, Allyson, is the reason you don't want to come home because you feel safe here?"

Allyson looked up and gave her mother

a puzzled look. "Safe?"

"Yes, safe and protected."

Allyson turned and stared straight ahead. She hesitated before replying. "I don't know. Maybe."

"What are you afraid of?"

Allyson looked pensive and deliberated before answering. "Michael says of losing my childhood."

"You lost that a long time ago," Millicent remarked thoughtfully.

"Not according to him or the books I've been reading. Apparently I'm still hanging on to it," Allyson said as she sighed. "Just like Aunt Joan, wouldn't you say?" She cocked her head up as she looked for a reaction.

Millicent seemed visibly disturbed. "No, not at all like Aunt Joan. You've just had a hard time growing up, that's all. But you'll get there. You do feel better, don't you?"

"Who knows?" There was uncertainty in her voice. "Sometimes I do and sometimes I don't. But I must be, because I get hungry now and I feel more alive and Michael says just to 'go with it.' So I am."

"Well then, why can't you come home and see him at his office?"

"He doesn't have a regular office. He's full-time at the hospital. He sees people here. He's a resident."

Millicent continued to question her, not realizing that Allyson was clenching her teeth. "Then why can't you come here, to the hospital, for your appointments?"

Plainly irritated now, Allyson said, "Why do you ask so many questions?"

At once, Millicent became contrite. "Because I feel I should. I'm sorry."

"That's one of your problems, mother," remarked Allyson with a patronizing air. "You always have to find logical answers for everything. You should go more with your feelings. Not everything has an answer. You're stuck in a certain emotional and psychological pattern."

"Oh, really now!" responded Millicent with piercing irony. "And are you *stuck?*"

"Of course." Allyson paused and took a deep breath. "That's been my trouble. I've been stuck in denying my potential for growth. Staying stuck brings rewards and emotional payoffs like avoidance of responsibility and failure. Choosing self-abnegation protects a person like myself from fear and anxiety."

"I'm impressed," said Millicent with

sarcasm. "You certainly have become proficient in analyzing yourself."

"I've had a lot of practice, mother. After all, who's gone to psychiatrists as long as I have?" Allyson asked, not expecting an answer but with a twist of her voice that dug right into Millicent's gut.

"And what does your Michael say about getting 'unstuck'?" asked Millicent, coming back at Allyson as if they were debating the issue.

"Courage and determination," she answered emphatically. "Michael says you can choose to get unstuck by putting your past behind you. Deal with the present. All it takes is courage and determination, that is, after you begin to understand yourself."

"Well then, now that you both have that figured out, what keeps you from coming home?"

Allyson suddenly lost her vigor and maturity and became subdued. She smoothed her gown over her knees. Her voice was shaky. "Because I don't have the courage and determination yet. I'm still stuck. I don't want to fall apart, not again. But I just may. You see, I'm an emotional mess."

Millicent was heartbroken by this plaintive self-reproach. She cradled Allyson in her arms as a brace of strength, not as a gesture of comfort. "No, my angel, you're not going to fall apart. I won't let you. You're getting some insight into your problems and that's the first step. You're different this time, darling. You really are. And Dr. Lyons must be helping you or you wouldn't want to remain under his care. No, Allyson, you're not an emotional mess at all. You just suffer more than others."

Allyson looked up with teary eyes. "Mother, your optimism is unreal. But it's what keeps me going. That and Michael's ridiculous half-baked theories."

Millicent smiled down at her. "You do like him, don't you?"

Allyson acted as if she were shocked. "God no! I can't stand him. He's gross, with all that psychological bullshit. But he keeps me from getting bored. And he's really smart. Smart but nutty. I don't know how he ever became a psychiatrist," said Allyson, blushing like a teenager.

Millicent tried not to smile. "That settles that, then. I'll stop asking you when you're coming home," she said, knowing when to back off. "I'm certain you'll be ready soon and you'll know when you are, you and Dr. Lyons."

With a sudden shift, Allyson asked, "Mother, how's Cory?"

The question took Millicent by surprise. "Fine, I guess. Why do you ask?"

"Because of the abortion."

"How did you know?"

"I just know."

"Who told you, Allyson?"

"She called me."

Millicent paused before asking, "Did she say anything else, about it I mean?"

Before Allyson could reply, Miss Waverly came slithering into the room with a silly grin on her face and a change of freshly starched uniform on her angular body. A bright print handkerchief, pleated, was attached to her pocket with a large safety pin. "We've had a nice visit, haven't we? I can tell. Mrs. Hart, I love your outfit. You do have the most beautiful clothes and the figure for them, too. I rather have a flair for fashion myself. Isn't our little girl just moving right along? Dr. Graham writes such nice little notes on our chart."

Miss Waverly was making Millicent

uncomfortable and Allyson found it amusing. Giggling, she pulled the sheet over her mouth.

"By the way," Millicent asked the nurse, "has Dr. Graham been in today?"

"No. He called and said he'd be in this evening." A frown came to Miss Waverly's face. "That poor man doesn't get a minute's rest. Has to make most of his rounds in the evenings because he's so busy in his office during the day. I honestly worry about him. Will you wait to see him, Mrs. Hart? He should be here in about an hour or so."

Millicent hesitated. "No, I think not. I'll stay a few more minutes and then go home. I'm rather tired myself."

Miss Waverly clasped her palms together as though she were praying. "If that's the case, then we'll just walk down to Ross Hall. There's a lovely lecture and film on hypnotism, and Allyson said she wanted to see it. It's good for us to move about."

"You two go right ahead," said Millicent as she picked up her coat and purse. "I'll be going. Good night, dear. I'll see you tomorrow. Oh, I forgot something." Millicent bent down and kissed Allyson on the cheek. "Daddy said to give this to you."

Allyson's face lit up.

Millicent walked through the lobby of the hospital, which was crowded with evening visitors. She headed for the revolving doors, watching them whirl around, depositing a visitor with every quarter turn and waiting for an empty space to exit. Random thoughts were going around in her head as though in synchronization with the circling door.

And then there came a moment of intense awareness, a chain reaction of associations put in motion by one isolated word that suddenly came into her mind — *Ross*. Backing away from the revolving doors, she turned toward the waiting room on the right, bumping into the people behind her. She found an empty chair in a line of chairs in the waiting room and sat down absentmindedly, connections whirling around in her head.

She heard herself speaking: *Ross Hall. Miss Waverly said that's where the film and lecture is. Flowers for C. R., the note on Jeff's desk said. C. R. is Cynthia Ross, and the Mayfair Regent is that posh hotel in New York that Dolly always talks about, where Le Cirque Restaurant is. The company has a suite at the St. Regis, so why the Mayfair? Because he's going to meet her there and the flowers will be delivered at eight o'clock and they'll have dinner at Le Cirque at nine and he won't call because they'll be together tonight. And he's not coming back a day early because he'll tell me the meetings didn't go as well as he had expected. Damn him! What am I going to do?*

Suddenly Millicent was aware of the woman in the next chair, staring at her. Flustered, she got up and walked toward the elevator. Without knowing why, she went back to Allyson's empty room and sank into the plastic lounge chair, exhausted with a drowsy numbness.

She took a deep breath. The humiliation was as shattering as if the liaison had been publicly announced. *Why would he deceive me that way?* The questions were pounding her head. *What could possibly make him act as if going away from me for a few days was an unbearable separation when all the time he was thinking of being with someone else? There was affection gleaming in his eyes, all right, but all the while he was calculating in his mind. No, Millicent, there's nothing between us. She's just a client. A pretty young widow, but just a client. Damn it! He hasn't changed. He's just become slyer. Where the devil does he get off with that rot about spending a day together, just the two of us, and I've missed you so much and I want to put romance back into our lives? How would you feel if I was with another man? Would it matter? Why do you need her? Why don't you need me?*

She sat there pulling him apart in her mind, the anger exploding inside. She was hardly aware of the passing of time until she heard footsteps approaching the room and then saw the weary face of Dr. Graham peering around the door, looking for Allyson. He seemed surprised to see her.

"Mrs. Hart. Didn't think I'd find you here. Where's my skinny patient?" Immediately he was embarrassed by his choice of words.

"Gone with Miss Waverly to a lecture. They'll be back soon."

Dr. Graham walked over to Allyson's bed and sat down wearily on the edge, facing Millicent. "I haven't seen you for a while, and I apologize for not being in touch with you. I've been getting by later and later each day. I really intended to call you this week. I'm truly sorry. I've just been so busy. I guess it's the time of the year for everybody to get sick at once. Anyway, it's good to see you, and I do want to fill you in on Allyson's progress. First off, what's your impression of how she's doing?"

Millicent was completely composed. Upon seeing Dr. Graham, her irate indignation had been properly sublimated. "I think she's better. She's certainly livelier and more talkative, and she *is* eating. So I think it looks promising this time." She looked up at him for confirmation.

He tried to sound reassuring. "I think so too, although with her history, I'm almost afraid to tell you that. I know how many times in the past you've been told she's better only to have another, more serious setback. I don't want to get your hopes too high, but I've been conferring with Dr. Lyons and he really feels she's moving in the right direction even though she's got a long way to go."

"Where do we go from here, Dr. Graham?"

Roger Graham put his hand to his chin and rubbed it back and forth. After a few moments of thought he said, "I'm not sure, Mrs. Hart. We take it one day at a time. I intend to keep her here at least another week and gradually increase the amount of food intake and see how she responds to a normal diet. I've got to be sure that all her vital organs are functioning normally again, or at least near normal, because another episode like this could be, well . . . we won't even talk about that. I'll also want some more tests to determine just what damage has been done. And if Allyson agrees, I want her to continue seeing Dr. Lyons as an outpatient, or we can talk about another therapist."

Millicent shook her head. "No, Dr. Graham. For now I think another therapist is out of the question. Allyson has seen her share of them and they've all been good, but my instincts tell me she should stick with Dr. Lyons for now. Although, heaven knows, it's hard to see how he's accomplishing anything with the surly attitude she has toward him. She's never had this kind of relationship with a doctor before. It's so . . ."

"Familiar but irreverent?" Dr. Graham filled in with a smile.

"Yes, very familiar and very hostile. She calls him by his first name, as if they were classmates and then talks about him with complete disrespect. It sounds as if all they do is fight."

Roger Graham laughed. "They probably do. Dr. Lyons is a battler, and he's not your run-of-the-mill psychiatrist. I told you before, he's very unconventional, but that might be why he's been successful in treating her. And I think she respects him a lot more than she'll let on. He's really a brilliant young man."

Millicent looked uncertain. "What disturbs me, Dr. Graham, is that he's made no attempt to talk to me or my husband, and Allyson says he doesn't want to see me. In fact, I called him and he never returned the call. All of the other psychiatrists got us very much involved in her treatment."

Dr. Graham shrugged and gave her a puzzled look. "Well, I don't know what to say about that, Mrs. Hart, except that after talking with Dr. Lyons, he seems to be pretty much concerned with Allyson's dependency on you and it appears that he wants her to establish an identity of her own."

Millicent stood up and stretched her arms down at her side. When she spoke again, it was in a tone of resignation. "She said the same thing to me. Look, what's important to me in the last analysis is what he can do for her. I'm perfectly willing to go along with any treatment, no matter how unorthodox, just so I know it's helping her and, of course, that the doctor is competent."

Dr. Graham was quick to come to Dr. Lyons' defense. "Oh, he's competent all right. He wouldn't be here if he weren't."

Millicent nodded and smiled. "Then that's good enough for me." She buttoned her coat and picked up her purse from the chair. She put on her gloves as she spoke. "Dr. Graham, I've been here a long time. I think I'll just get out before they come back, which should be momentarily. Why don't you give me a call at the end of the week and let me know what the tests show and when you think she'll be able to come home." She held out her hand to say good-bye.

He took her hand in his but found himself saying entreatingly, "Don't go.

Why don't you wait for me, then we can talk some more, after I've seen Allyson."

Millicent didn't know what to say. She looked down and smoothed her gloves but didn't answer.

"Are you expected at home, Mrs. Hart?" he asked and then wished he hadn't.

Millicent looked momentarily downcast. "No, I'm not. I'll wait downstairs in the lobby."

He came down about a half hour later, his smile was a flash of surprise and pleasure, as though he had seriously doubted she would be there.

"Allyson was good tonight, really good," he said, genuinely pleased. "Her improvement seems to be in proportion to how nasty she gets. But she's gained five pounds this week, so I can put up with her disposition."

"Oh, Dr. Graham, what's happening to her personality?" Millicent's expression showed concern. "She's so, as you say, nasty, and aggressive."

He steered her over to a chair in the lobby as he tried to explain. "She's more like a defiant child throwing around her newfound independence, Mrs. Hart."

They both sat down, and Millicent unbuttoned her coat and let it drop off her shoulders. He stared at her for a minute and then continued: "She's going through a crash time frame all in one fell swoop . . . of childhood, adolescence and adulthood . . . and she doesn't know where she is yet because she's been in another world for so many years."

Millicent leaned toward Dr. Graham and asked earnestly, "How will it affect her, psychologically I mean?"

He opened his hands in a doubtful gesture. "I don't know. Let's leave that to Dr. Lyons."

"I'd really like to talk to him, Dr. Graham. I wish he'd see me."

"He will, when he's ready." Dr. Graham paused and then asked quickly. "By the way, are you hungry?"

Millicent looked surprised at the question and wondered if he thought she looked sick. "No, not really," she replied.

"Did you have dinner?"

"No, but then I don't remember having lunch, either." She put her hands to her face. "Do I look awful again?"

He laughed. "No, of course not. I just

think we should definitely do something about that, I mean about your not eating. We don't want another anorexic on our hands," he said jokingly.

Millicent sighed coyly. "No fear. I'm a gorger. I eat in spurts but not when I'm upset. Then I lose my appetite."

His voice became infused with enthusiasm. "I haven't eaten all day either but I'm starved, so I'm calling in that rain check you promised. Have dinner with me."

Millicent's instinct was to say no again and offer an excuse, but Jeff came into her mind and she knew there was nothing to go home for.

"Thank you, I'd like to. Where shall we go?"

Roger Graham seemed to heave a sigh of relief. "Let's see. What do you feel like?"

"I don't really know since I'm not hungry. Nothing fancy."

"How about walking over to a little French place on Pennsylvania Avenue that's noisy and crowded but has atmosphere?"

Millicent gathered her coat and laughed. "That's just what I need now, atmosphere. Let's go."

Chapter 13

"For someone who wasn't hungry, I did very well by the bouillabaisse. I'm ashamed to admit it, but I think I also ate all the bread." Millicent looked shame-faced as she held up the empty bread basket.

"No, I had one piece. But who's counting? You see, you really did need some food and I . . . needed your company. I don't like eating alone, and I can't remember when I've enjoyed a dinner more."

It had been a very relaxing dinner, despite the noisy, chaotic atmosphere of the small restaurant. The eclectic French ambience gave it a cheery feeling. No mention of Allyson or personal matters was exchanged between them. It was casual and comfortable, with lots of conversation and laughter about nothing in particular. Ordinary subjects without significant meaning took on an unexpected pleasure. For both of them it was an escape of mellow sweetness.

For Millicent, it was a respite from unhappiness and anger. The awful emptiness that had engulfed her at the realization of Jeff's betrayal was gone. She felt lighthearted and giddy, like a girl on her first big date. A startling thought crossed her mind: *I haven't had dinner alone with a man other than Jeff or my father in twenty-seven years.* And then her heart began to flutter with excitement as she looked across the table at Roger Graham, who was asking her if she would like more wine.

She was surprised at how positively she responded. "Oh yes, by all means. It's wonderful. I haven't had this much to drink in . . . I can't remember when." *With the slightest encouragement, I could float right into your arms,* she thought, as she held up her glass.

Millicent was aware that Roger Graham was looking at her with more than a faint glimmer of interest. As she picked up the vibrations, she was shaken by her own involuntary reaction — a tingling sensation that went up her legs, so strong that she squeezed her thighs together to repress the sensuous urge.

She envied women who could be casual and mature with men other than their husbands. At this moment, she felt about as unsophisticated as she remembered herself at one of the many debutante balls she was forced to attend.

Roger Graham spoke her name only after the second bottle of wine had been consumed and Millicent had properly noted the lateness of the time. "Millicent, I don't want this evening to end. Come back to my apartment with me for just a little while."

Millicent reddened and fidgeted with her napkin. "Why Dr. Graham, I couldn't possibly do that. We really hardly know each other. What would people think, and what would be the point of it? And aren't you married? And, of course, I am and . . . I'd love to."

The unexpected and surprising departure and arrival of pleasure caught him off guard, and he laughed out loud.

"Great! But will you do me a favor?"

"Ah, here it comes," said Millicent,

with a coy turn of her head. "Strings attached, huh? Okay, since you've given me this lovely dinner and plied me with God knows how much wine, how can I possibly refuse? What can I do for you, doctor?"

"Please call me Roger, because with the way I feel right now, it would be highly unprofessional for us not to be on a first-name basis. Are you ready, Millicent? Shall we go?"

"I'm ready, *Roger.*" She felt bashful saying it.

They arrived at his building, the Columbia Plaza, a modern high rise of concrete and glass near the Kennedy Center. Hardly a word was said between them as they parked in the underground garage and took the elevator to his pleasant but sparsely furnished apartment. The easy, agreeable mood that had accompanied their dinner was absent during the near-silent ride to his apartment, as though a good idea had lost its flavor on second thought.

It was an awkward few minutes of polite hospitality on his part: "Let me take your coat; excuse the mess, I wasn't expecting company; won't you sit down; can I fix you a drink?"

On her part it was "Thank you; oh, don't bother to straighten, it looks fine; thank you, but I can only stay a little while; no thank you, I think I've had too much to drink already."

Then clumsy silence again, not easily dealt with.

Millicent walked nervously around the living room, commenting on the few pieces of primitive art.

Roger made small talk about never getting around to buying more furniture.

She gravitated toward the window and complimented the view. He agreed that it was the best part of the apartment.

The conversation was getting increasingly stilted, and Millicent felt foolish standing there. She wanted to leave but did not know how to do it graciously. Idly, she wandered around the room for a few minutes, then sat down on the modern leather sofa.

He looked at her anxiously and then followed her to the sofa, seating himself a few feet away from her. They were a picture of self-consciousness, like two high-school kids on a blind date.

With an irresistible compulsion, Roger moved closer and kissed her lightly on the lips.

Her face registered astonishment.

"That was to break the ice," Roger said almost apologetically. "I figured that if I didn't say or do something soon, you'd walk out. And I really didn't know what to say. I'm sorry. Do you want to slap my face?"

After a long moment Millicent smiled, and the stiffness disappeared. "No, I don't want to slap your face. I'm probably a lot older than you but I'm not from the Victorian age when that was what a woman was supposed to do when a man took such liberties. In fact, it was rather sweet and you're right, it did break the ice. I was getting very uncomfortable about being here."

"And now?" he asked.

"I don't know how to answer that. I feel I should go, but I guess I really don't want to." She hesitated. "I must admit that I was feeling a little . . . well, lonely at the hospital. And it's been such a pleasant evening and I found you so easy to talk to that . . . I guess I didn't want the evening to end, either."

"I'm glad," he said, "and I like your being here."

"Frankly, I've never been to a man's apartment," Millicent confessed, wondering why she felt the need to say that.

"Frankly, I've never had another woman here. You're the first."

Roger leaned back against the sofa and spread his arms around the frame and said with a touch of melancholy. "You know, lonely people don't have to stay lonely. Have you ever given any thought to that?"

Millicent's impulse was to ask what he meant by that. Instead, she lowered her eyes and said, "By the way, there's a question I should ask that will probably put me right back in that Victorian era I said I wasn't in."

"Go ahead and ask. I won't pass judgment."

Millicent weighed her words carefully. "Does a wife come with this apartment and if so, is she likely to walk in?"

Roger sighed and a shadow of unhappiness crossed his face before he answered. "Yes and no. I am married, but my wife is presently in Boston at a meeting and won't be back for several days."

As though reality suddenly set in, Millicent told herself that she definitely must leave. *Being here is ridiculous,* she said silently. *Furthermore, it's unreal. What in the world am I doing with Allyson's doctor, in his apartment, at night? We look like two pathetic souls sitting here trying to establish some sort of relationship that should never be anything but professional. I feel like a character in a play about two lonely people looking for a brief encounter.*

Millicent straightened up, trying to regain the dignity she thought she had lost. "Roger, I really must go. It's getting late. I'm sure you have to get up early tomorrow."

He gave her a pleading look. "Please don't, not just yet."

"Really now, where is this all leading to? I must . . ."

He took her hand and said quickly, "I hope, Millicent, into my arms, because that's where I've wanted you to be practically from the first time I met you."

Her eyes grew wide and her mouth fell open. She could barely respond, but she knew she must. "Roger, if I tell you that that shocks me beyond anything I can imagine, would you believe me?"

He lowered his face with embarrassment. He could feel the heat climbing up his neck. "Yes, because it shocks me to hear myself saying it." He looked up at her. "Millicent, I'm a reserved forty-two-year-old doctor, sort of on the shy side, married twelve years and have never played around, never."

At first she was awed by his ingenuousness, then she remembered Jeff's placating words of only a few hours ago and she felt like a fool, ready to be taken in again.

Because she was doubtful and flustered, her voice took on a tone of sarcasm and she asked him derisively, "Then can I presume correctly that your sudden surge of amour is due to the frequently quoted male excuse that your wife *doesn't understand* you, and I came along when you desperately needed a little understanding?"

"Oh no, quite the contrary," he said with sincerity. "She understands me perfectly. The problem is, I don't understand her."

Despite her misgivings, Millicent did not leave. Roger Graham told her about himself and about his wife, Janet. Millicent found it easy to empathize with him. She didn't understand this woman at all, because their worlds were totally alien.

They had met when both were residents at Massachusetts General in Boston. As dedicated young doctors with similar upper-middle class New England backgrounds, including fathers who were doctors, they simply gravitated toward each other. Neither had had much experience with romantic relationships, though they sensed they were compatible through their daily contact. Their careers were the most important things in their lives, and they shared identical goals and beliefs. They were both unobtrusive in social relationships, modest and retiring in dealing with people other than patients. They got along beautifully, seemingly an ideal match. Neither of them wanted children or craved great wealth, and they felt no professional competition between them. They came to Washington when Roger got a fellowship in medicine at the Georgetown Medical Center and Janet got a research grant at the National Institutes of Health. They lived in a small apartment in the Maryland suburbs near N.I.H. and then moved to downtown Washington when Roger opened his office. It made no difference to Janet where she lived, just as long as it was close to an airport. Her consummate and brilliant devotion to genetic research had elevated her to a position of authority, and she spent half her life writing papers and flying all over the country presenting them to eminent medical groups.

When she was home and not at work she was pleasant, loving, perfectly content and made no demands on her husband. Whatever he wanted was fine with her as long as she could pursue her research exhaustively.

Millicent sat on the couch, her legs curled up under her, and listened to Roger pour out what had been securely bottled up in him for years. Roger sat with his legs stretched out in front of him, his arms folded across his chest, and found himself talking to her as he would to a close and dear friend.

"What I don't understand about Janet is that she's never changed." He looked at Millicent as though he expected a reaction, then he went on, his voice sounding more burdened. "She has no desire for material possessions or diversions. She doesn't want a home. One apartment is as good as the next. She doesn't want clothes or *things* or people. And I do. As I get older, I find I do want more things and I need contact with people. People outside of the office and the hospital. We both make enough money to buy a nice house and entertain and take vacations and do some exciting things with our lives that we never did before. But she doesn't feel that way." Roger stopped for a minute and lifted his hand in a gesture of acknowledgment. "Yet she never puts me down for what I want. In fact, she encourages me to buy or go where I want and do what I want, and she's genuinely pleased if I go to the theater or take a few days off and fly down to Bermuda for some diving. I'd even like to have a boat and a house on the water. I think I would really enjoy sailing. Something about it has always intrigued me. When I tell her, she says fine, as long as she can work while I sail. That's all she ever asks of me, to let her work and go flying around giving her scholarly papers." He paused and shook his head. "I don't understand Janet anymore. Is that all she wants out of life? Yet she seems to understand me and even sympathizes when I tell her I want more out of life than to just see sick people every day. She's the most contented person I've ever known and oddly enough, the most caring." He stopped and ran his fingers through his hair, and when he continued, there was an edge of desperation in his voice. "But little by little, I'm going bananas."

"She also sounds like the most liberated woman I've ever heard of," said Millicent, after listening for a long time without comment.

Roger shook his head. "I don't think that even occurs to Janet. This is the way it's been her whole life. Her parents let her do whatever she wanted because all she wanted to do was study and become a doctor. And I have to admit, that was one of the most appealing things about her when we met. The fact that we could both pursue our careers without encumbrances or fanatic driving ambition for lots of worldly goodies. It was a marriage of true minds, and for her, nothing has changed. For me, it has, Millicent, I find I get very lonely, and it's not just because Janet is off to God-knows-where every other week." His voice slowed down to a dismal pace. "I'm lonely when she's here, too. Something's missing."

Contemplating her own marriage, Millicent felt a momentary sense of empathy with Roger. But she was not ready to share it.

"Roger, I'm not the one to supply what's missing in your life. God knows, I can barely hold my own life together. There's very little left in me to give to someone else, to another man."

"You don't realize how much you do have, Millicent."

She gave him a puzzled glance. "Why are you even attracted to me? That's not exactly what I mean," she corrected herself. "Why, seeing me just in the hospital, under the most peculiar conditions, would it even occur to you that something could happen between us?"

He took her hand and with his brought it up to the side of his cheek, and she felt the roughness as he tenderly moved her fingers to his mouth. After a few moments, he looked at her lovingly and said, "Because I'm a dreamer. And I've been dreaming how wonderful it would be to have someone like you care about me . . ."

"Like I care about Allyson?" She finished what she believed was his thought. "Allyson is my child. That's a different kind of caring. You can't give that kind of love to anyone but your children."

Roger shook his head in protest. "I don't want that kind of love, Millicent. I'm not looking for mothering. I guess I'm looking for someone to share loneliness." He hesitated for a moment. "And I don't think you'd be here tonight if you didn't want that, too."

Millicent pulled her hand away from his and turned her head, avoiding his eyes.

Roger waited for her to speak and when she did not, he asked, "Isn't there something missing in your life, too?"

She faced him squarely, but her answer was vague: "Roger, there's probably something missing in everyone's life. Life rarely turns out the way you expect it to."

Her mind, meanwhile, was throbbing with other thoughts: *Oh, yes, Roger, there is something missing in my life. Like your wife, my husband is totally involved in his work. But unlike your Janet, my husband is rejecting me for another woman. He doesn't see in me what you*

278

do. And the fact that you do, that you feel this need and think that I could fulfill it, is very flattering, coming at a time like this. In fact, the thought rather excites me, because I'm feeling very lonesome and shut out.

She heard Roger's plaintive voice and it brought her out of her thoughts. "Millicent, if two people have a void in their lives, is it so wrong for them to reach out to each other for something . . . even for an intimate moment?"

Looking at him with futility, she said softly, "But don't you see, Roger, that's all it could be, a brief interval of intimacy between strangers who are lonely. Nothing more."

"Isn't that enough, for now?"

"Perhaps it would be under different circumstances. But I have to rely on you for taking care of my daughter. We have to see each other in an entirely different situation. I don't think I could handle that."

"You're much too logical, Millicent. Why think about that now?" His question came out more like a statement.

Roger got up and took off his jacket and loosened his tie. His shirt separated and the sight of his muscled chest, his flesh and tufted hair, gave her a momentary tingle that rippled through her entire body and almost dislodged all the reservations that were spinning around in her confused mind.

Even though she suddenly felt drawn to him, an inner restraint kept her from succumbing to his need. She realized she was not ready for him as he was for her. She stood up quickly and straightened her skirt. "Roger, I must go now. Will you take me to my car?"

Millicent was barely awake when the telephone rang. Seconds later, the buzzer on the phone sounded for her. She cleared her throat and blinked her eyes, trying to remove the remnants of sleep before answering.

"Hello."

"Millicent, how are you on this wonderful morning?"

"Sleepy. Who is this?"

"How soon they forget," Roger answered with mock disappointment. "I rather thought I had made some kind of impression last night."

"Doctor . . . Roger, is that you?"

"Yes, Millicent. Will you accept my apology for last night?"

"For what?"

"For being an insensitive clod and coming on too strong."

"No apology necessary. Forget it, Roger."

"I don't want to, really. It give me an excuse for asking you to have dinner with me so I can say I'm sorry in person. Will you? Will you have dinner with me tonight?"

"Roger, I couldn't possibly do that."

"Why not?"

"Because there's no point in pursuing this. And you don't have to be sorry about last night. Despite . . . despite everything, I enjoyed being with you. Let's leave it at that."

"Please, Millicent, just have dinner with me. I promise we'll talk about nothing more personal than Allyson's weight chart. In fact, it will be a professional consultation between doctor and patient's family. Will you come, for the sake of your child?"

She gave an ironic laugh. "You're very persuasive, Dr. Graham. All right, we'll meet for a 'professional' dinner."

This was a stunning moment in Millicent's life. She knew in her heart that seeing Roger outside of the hospital could never again be just professional. He was already part of her dream. She had to concentrate on the conflict that was pulling equally.

I want a respite from family responsibility. I want to escape from the eventlessness of my days — the hospital, the meaningless chores, the waiting, the emptiness. Allyson's looking for her identity? Well, I'm looking for mine, too. Did I lose it in a blink of time or slowly, over many years? It's either been buried or denied, but I want it back. I want an identity separate from the children and Jeff. I want to try having experiences without involvement, to grow, to change, to expend energy on myself — to acknowledge my desires. I've suddenly discovered that the rules have changed and you don't have to be dependent on a husband and family to realize fulfillment. There's a whole new world out there saying you don't have to devote your life to impossible situations. Fantasies can come true. Break with the past and find yourself!

But how? How do you chuck fifty years

of programming? How do you live with the remorse of deceit? And how do you live with the passion of old age? Where do you get the courage to embrace independence when you've made a special bond of dependence, first with your father and then with your husband? Who will take care of me if I let this man love me?

She forced herself to confront her feelings.

Chapter 14

Jeff did call. Complications had come up. The meetings would continue for at least another day, possibly longer. He was sorry he couldn't return as planned, but business is business. He missed her. He would make it up to her. As soon as he got this deal squared away, he would take time off. No, he was not enjoying himself. Just meetings all day and night. He would call tomorrow.

She listened with a feigned sympathetic ear, and he seemed relieved by her understanding tone. Her decision had been made easier. Seeing Roger again had stronger justification.

Dolly called, too. "Millicent, you've got to help me out tonight."

"What's wrong, Dolly?"

"Everything. I'm in the most frightful

predicament. I'm having a dinner party tonight, all politicos, just to keep my hands in their grubby little pockets. The amorous congressman from Indiana is coming, sans wife, whom of course I had invited but was told she was indisposed or off for the cure or some such thing, and so I didn't count on her coming. Just expected *the Honorable* Carl Hagan alone. And now he calls and asks if he can bring his divine lady friend. Imagine that? Just bold as brass he asks me. Now here's the fatal problem. His nouveau bed partner is the former mistress of the senator from Oklahoma, who will also be here, but . . . with *his wife*, a shrew if you ever saw one. And, God help him, she would kill him if she ever found out about his double-dipping. Very hush hush was the Oklahoma senator's affair. Well, my dear, I simply can't handle all this intrigue. Catastrophe might break out over the Sole Veronique. So I told him, the congressman that is, that another prominent lady had been invited as his dinner partner and that my table was completely arranged." Dolly said this breathlessly without giving Millicent a chance to break in until now.

"Well, what can I do to relieve your

frightful predicament?" Millicent ventured with a hint of sarcasm.

"You can be the prominent woman occupying the seat that I don't want his whoring lady friend to sit in," declared Dolly, as if that was perfectly obvious.

"No thank you," said Millicent definitely. "I love your dinners, but I have no intention of being the congressman's dinner partner. Better you should end up in the gossip columns than me."

"Oh Mill, you must, or I'll be a liar."

"Dolly dear, you already are. Sorry, chum, but I refuse to get you out of this one, and anyway, I'd be a dreadful choice. I'd probably spill the beans to the senator's wife by accident. Besides, Jeff's out of town and I'm busy tonight." The last remark she regretted the moment the words were out of her mouth, and she wondered why she had even added it.

"Then who shall I get?"

"I don't know. You must have some bitchy friend who would enjoy the *intrigue,*" she said jokingly.

"Of course, you're right, I do. Cissy! She's a bitch. She'd love it. I'll have to swear her to secrecy, though. Mill, you're an angel for helping me out."

"Nothing to it. Always glad to help a friend," said Millicent, with a look on her face that she was glad Dolly couldn't see.

"Oh, you do sound better, my dear. We'll have to get together soon. Good things must be happening. You must have lots to tell me."

Millicent wondered if Dolly's remark was a forecast of the future.

Unlike the sameness of other days where undue time was lavished on routine tasks and evenings came without surprise or purpose, this day had been filled with a sense of excitement and anticipation. Millicent felt like a giddy schoolgirl preparing for an absurdly romantic date, the sensation of being in the prime of life yet also being newly vulnerable.

In the mirror of her mind she saw the person she wanted to see. Someone daring enough to love and allow herself to be loved with carefree abandon. Yet she reminded herself that she was only going out to dinner, nothing more.

Bathing was a glorious sensuous experience. She examined her body as she had rarely done before. She separated the foaming bubbles and stroked her still firm breasts with a wonderful feeling of confidence. Age was dismissed from her mind. With one long, slim leg uplifted coquettishly, she balanced herself on her elbows and threw back her head like a child hoping to catch the raindrops. She wiggled her torso, an act of capricious sexuality for someone who had never yielded to her reckless fantasies. This was the only time she owned.

Her underwear was chosen carefully. Silks and laces, relegated to the back of the drawer for lack of interest or special occasions, were taken out. When she held up the deliciously wearable ivory satin chemise she actually blushed, wondering why the flimsy lingerie looked more seductive to her now than when she had bought it. The gorgeously simple Geoffrey Beene olive-beige suit was selected for its elegant understatement. It was not that she was overly concerned with looking her best. She had to feel her best.

Mr. Julian worked her in between his society regulars. "Mrs. Hart, your hair is a bloody mess. You look as if you slept on the floor. No wonder you had to see me today. *Je ne sais pas* what to do! But let's have a go at it."

Millicent went about the day's activities, lighthearted and smugly happy, not wanting introspection and reflection to decrease her mood. She shopped for extravagant presents for the children. A handsome Ted Lapidus sport jacket for Johnny, an authentic Burberry trenchcoat for Cory. What to get Allyson? She found an antique music box that played a Bach minuet that Allyson herself used to play with great delight during her piano-lesson years.

For Jeffrey, she wavered. She didn't want the gift to be an overly magnanimous gesture on her part that would excuse his guilt, even if he had any, she thought. Yet, she could not leave him out. Not feeling quite so generous, she bought Jeff a tie. Impulsively, she bought Roger a tie too, just a small token of appreciation for taking her to dinner, she told herself. She saw the pale blue tie with the small red-and-white sailboat while shopping in Neiman-Marcus, and she couldn't resist buying it. However, after reconsidering what meaning he would place on it, she left the gift home with the other presents.

Arriving at the hospital early, Millicent wondered whether she should wait in the lobby until the official visiting-hour time or go up unobtrusively and take the chance of interrupting Allyson's dinner, which was a precarious situation at best. She decided to go up, anxious to give her the music box.

Miss Waverly was sitting at the nurses' station, engaged in conversation, and did not see Millicent get off the elevator. Millicent did not want to interrupt, so she headed down the hall. Loud voices were coming from the room and she approached cautiously, wondering who Allyson was talking to. It was a man's voice but not that of Roger Graham.

The door was slightly ajar. She peeked in.

With his back to the door, a heavyset bushy-haired man was sitting in a wheelchair laughing. Allyson, pale as porcelain and with only eighty-two pounds on limbs that looked at light as a lyric, was shouting, "You know what you are? You're full of shit!"

Millicent was taken aback, not by Allyson's profanity, which no longer shocked her, but by her rudeness to an obviously friendly patient who had stopped in for a visit.

Just as she was about to make a hasty retreat, the man zipped around as though he had sensed her presence. His burly frame looked incongruous in a wheelchair. His body was thickset, with strapping shoulders and muscled arms bulging under a plaid open-necked sport shirt and white lab coat. Powerful hands clutched the wheels of the chair. But his legs were obviously lifeless.

"We have company, kiddo, so you'd better get your act together," he said with a disarming smile that parted the curly dark beard that seemed to cover his broad face.

Allyson's eyes shot to the door. "That's not company. That's my mother." She looked at Millicent as if she were an intrusive stranger. "Why are you here so early? I didn't expect you until later."

Millicent was embarrassed and apologetic. "I'm sorry dear. It is early, isn't it? I didn't think you'd have a visitor now. I can come back later." She knew she had walked in on something private, but she didn't know how to exit gracefully.

The man in the wheelchair waved her in. "No, come in, Mrs. Hart. It's time we met. I'm just about through, anyway.

Your daughter is pretty sassy today. She's giving me a headache."

Allyson responded to him with a grim look. "You had a headache when you came in, so don't blame it on me, buster."

He held up his palms in front of his chest. "Excuse me! I stand corrected. So you gave me a bigger headache. Aren't you going to introduce me, or did your manners disappear with your weight?"

"I'll have to get a file box for your zingers," Allyson said with a derisive smirk. "This is my mother, Millicent Hart. Mother, this is Michael Lyons, *the* Dr. Lyons."

Millicent gasped audibly. After a few seconds of embarrassing silence she said, "How do you do, Dr. Lyons? I'm very pleased to meet you."

"You don't look pleased," responded Michael Lyons in his typical direct manner. "You look shocked."

Millicent sputtered. "Do I? I guess I am. I had no idea when I saw you from the door that you were a doctor. I thought you were a patient."

"The wheelchair does that. It's all I can do to keep the new nurses from propelling me to a room. Come on in. Sit down.

Relax. We're through for today. You're a good-looking woman, Mrs. Hart. Not at all like Allyson described you." He turned his head toward the bed. "Allyson, why did you tell me your mother was fat?"

"I didn't say she was fat," Allyson said defensively. "I said she had a full figure."

He turned back to Millicent and swept his right hand through the air. "Her perception is cockeyed, Mrs. Hart. Anybody seems fat compared to her. You have a lovely figure and you're very attractive and don't, for God's sake, go on a diet. You're OK in my book."

"Michael, she doesn't need your approval. So stop flattering her."

He gave her a sly look. "Jealous, kiddo?"

Allyson gave him an offended look. "Don't try to be cute. Really now!"

Millicent stood like a statue. She couldn't believe this dialogue.

Dr. Lyons was aware of her incredulity and tried to put her at ease. "Hey, Mrs. Hart. It's not always like this. We usually get into some heavy psychiatric stuff. We just like to kid around. Our insults are a cover-up. We really do respect each other . . . I think. Your daughter has a great sardonic wit, so I make her use it. Makes the juices flow. She really likes me, don't you, kiddo?"

"Stop calling me kiddo," Allyson yelled. "I told you that before. I think you do it just to annoy me."

"When you gain thirty pounds, then I'll stop, *kiddo*."

Millicent cleared her throat. "Well, I am very glad to finally meet you, Dr. Lyons. And I am pleased with Allyson's progress. Dr. Graham has given you most of the credit for it."

"Thanks, I'll take it," said Michael Lyons, unabashedly. "But there's lots more work to be done, lots." He turned to Allyson. "Right, kiddo?"

"Right," answered Allyson in a deep voice that mocked his tone. She was holding back a smile.

Chapter 15

Dinner was a repeat of the night before in that it was French and a gastronomical delight, only far more extravagant. Roger Graham, without any pretense, had selected Jean-Pierre's to impress Millicent, and he told her so over an ethereal scallop mousse and a superb veal with morels in cream sauce accompanied by an expensive bottle of Château Calon Segur, 1961. He had heard that Washington's fashionable inner circle dined there as much for the warm attention owner Jean-Michel lavished on his guests as for its outstanding food and quiet ambience. He wanted the evening to be perfect, and it was.

Millicent was floating on a cloud, not caring whether anyone saw them together. She felt wantonly reckless as she looked around the dining room for a familiar face, as though daring anyone to question her presence with this man who was not her husband. She had actually planned to introduce Roger as her daughter's doctor if the chance meeting of a friend called for an introduction. But now, she even felt slightly disappointed at not recognizing any of the diners. The thought did not escape her that this carelessly free feeling was totally out of character for the discreet woman she believed herself to be.

Over coffee and dessert, Millicent finally brought up the subject of Dr. Michael Lyons. "Roger, why didn't you tell me about Dr. Lyons? At least, I would have been prepared. It must have been quite obvious to him that his appearance shocked me. I looked like a gaping child staring at a cripple. It was so embarrassing. I can't believe that you or Allyson, or even Miss Waverly, never thought to mention it."

"Millicent, it just never came up. Honestly, when I'm dealing with Mike, I don't think about it. I used to, when he first came to the hospital, but I don't anymore."

"What's wrong with him, Roger? Why

is he in a wheelchair?" she asked with concern.

"He's a paraplegic," Roger said solemnly.

"Was he in an accident?"

"Uh huh. Motorcycle accident when he was in college, before medical school. It takes some kind of courage to go through medical school sitting down. He told me he had a rough time getting in because they didn't believe he could make it. God knows, it's hard enough getting through medical school when you've got two good legs." Roger paused, thinking about what an accomplishment that was. "He's very unusual."

"That's an understatement," responded Millicent with a sense of admiration. "I've never met a doctor like him before. He gives the impression of someone who's perpetually embattled."

Roger nodded. "Perhaps this galvanizes him to do his best work. No, I've never met anyone like him before, either. But then I've never met a doctor who's a paraplegic. Millicent, I'm sorry you were embarrassed but trust me, Michael Lyons won't lose any sleep over it. He's used to people staring at him or mistaking him for a patient. By the way, I spoke to him this morning, and he feels pretty confident about Allyson. She may be able to go home next week. Believe it or not, they have very good rapport."

Millicent placed her hands on the table and smiled at him. "I know. I can tell. Under the superficial backbiting there's a lot of understanding and respect. It finally came through to me tonight. Maybe it's the handicap, something they have in common. Whatever it is, I'm grateful to him and . . . to you, too, Roger. In over six years, I've never really felt this way . . . that she would truly get well. Before, even though I had hope, deep down inside I knew I was kidding myself. That it was just another lull before a bigger storm. And it always was. I was constantly waiting for the next episode. The scenario was always the same. Except, each time it got worse, until now." Millicent cast her eyes down. "And if she had died this time, I think I would have died, too."

Roger reached across the table for her hand. "Millicent, she's not going to die, and don't think about it anymore. Allyson is far from well, but she will be, in time. Maybe not the same as before, probably different, and maybe even with some residual physical effects. And, of course, personality changes. But she's going to make it."

Later, they were sitting next to each other in the garden room adjacent to the terrace, warmly sheltered from the raw November weather. Moonlight spilled in from the bank of glass doors. Roger thought how the turmoil of life can quickly be forgotten amid such subdued elegance.

When he walked in he looked around thinking that if you could build and design yourself into happiness, this must be the way.

After dinner Millicent suggested they go back to the house, knowing that Regina and Homer were off for the night and not expecting Jeff to call. Even though she had never done anything like this before, she sensed that she would feel more secure on her own ground. A disquieting thought crept into her mind: *Would I have even brought Roger here if father and mother were not out in Florida?* She got rid of it immediately.

Roger was thoroughly unprepared for the grandeur of Millicent's house. They sat facing the lush winter garden, holding hands and drinking brandy. For Millicent, it was such a different feeling from last night, when she had felt awkward and guilty just being alone with Roger. As though all her inhibitions had been temporarily put aside, she savored these moments of tender and tantalizing intimacy, forgetting their mutual promises about this being a professional engagement.

The silence was broken. She had to ask: "Roger, when is Janet coming back?"

"Day after tomorrow." He waited, and she answered the question he could not bear to ask.

"So is Jeff. There was a message. He's in New York."

Roger straightened up and looked at Millicent seriously before asking, "Is your husband in New York on business?"

Millicent's mood changed. A troubled expression came into her eyes. "Not exactly." She paused and rubbed her hands together. "He went there on that pretext but . . . he's with someone else. I'm very sure of it."

Roger hesitated before asking the next logical question, "Am I here only because of that, because you want to get back at him for hurting you?''

There was another long silence. When Millicent spoke, her voice wavered. "I honestly don't know. My marriage hasn't been ideal for a long time. Lately, we've grown even more apart. Maybe it's the strain of Allyson's illness." Then she added quickly, "That may only be an easy excuse for our deeper problems. Whatever — I've been unhappy . . . lonely . . . for a long while. And finding out that Jeff's up there with another woman was a terrible blow. So I can't truthfully tell you that what I'm feeling right now isn't the result of the hurt. But I do know that this evening was glorious. In fact, the whole day was wonderful just thinking about being with you." She stopped. Her expression was sad. "I just don't know, Roger."

He moved closer and took her chin in his hand, making her eyes meet his. He smoothed her hair and kissed her gently on the cheek. With a burst of emotion, Millicent embraced him and they held each other for a long time.

"Millicent darling," he finally said. "Right now, nothing matters except what we both feel at this moment. It's as if all my life I've been looking for you. As time goes by, I hope you'll want me, for whatever reason, as much as I want you."

When he said that, she smiled, remembering a love scene from a movie that was as romantic to her now as it was in her youth. She stood up and arched her body, put her brandy on the table and said, "You sound like Humphrey Bogart in *Casablanca*." Then pensively, as though struck by a remarkably innovative thought, "I think I want you now. Shall we go upstairs?"

Roger got up, still holding his brandy glass, extended his arm in a grand gesture as though he were making a toast and in a very poor imitation of Bogart said, "Here's looking at you, kid." He put the glass down and placed his hands on the back of her shoulders, steering her through the door. "Lead the way, I'm right behind you."

In her own house, but not in her own bed, Millicent let Roger make love to her. She responded to his overwhelming desire as though she had been hypnotized. From that moment, they were like two astonished people, unable to believe their own senses, spellbound and lost in wonder. They fell easily into a passionate, intense lovemaking, as though each knew every pleasured sensation of the other's body from many acts of love. This was made all the more extraordinary by the fact that they were both relatively untouched people. Millicent had only known one man, and Roger had been with one woman for twelve years. He was a sensitive man, not an expert, not obsessive, but he showed a loving concern for gratifying her sensuousness that made her believe she deserved happiness. She felt a youthful passion when his body was on hers, pressing against her breasts and thighs, as though she was actually experiencing the fantasies she'd had as a young girl. It was so peaceful to feel free, uninhibited, that she clung to him long after the fervor of their lovemaking had ceased. He held her with gentle caring, sensing her need to prolong the enchantment.

After Roger left, when she was lying in her own bed, Millicent thought about the evening as though it had taken place in some distant time, unconnected to the life she now knew. The unexpected splendor of it had made her euphoric. For the very first time she thought of herself as a beautiful, desirable woman far removed from the roles of daughter, wife, and mother. She felt as if she had no past. It seemed like a dream, vivid but unreal. She knew it had happened, but she could hardly believe it had happened to her. Another person she did not know had taken over and become Millicent Hart. Afraid she would lose the dream, she didn't want sleep to come.

But sleep did come, until eight the next morning when the phone rang. Alarmed, she was almost afraid to pick it up. Who could be calling so early? she wondered. The hospital? Jeff? Joan again?

With trepidation she picked it up and heard an exuberant "Hello."

"Who is this?" Millicent asked anxiously.

"Who is this! I'm the gentleman who occupied your guest room last night. Remember?"

"Roger? Why are you calling so early? What's the matter?"

"I'm in love," he said matter-of-factly.

"Oh, Roger, stop that. Where are you?"

"At my office. But I can't see one patient until I know I have something to look forward to tonight. Say you'll see me this evening." He hesitated, but only momentarily. "This may be our last free night for . . ."

"Roger, I couldn't possibly do that." Her voice grew very serious as she thought about last night. "In fact, I can't ever see you again."

"Why not?"

"Because I've committed adultery."

"You have?" he said with surprise.

"Of course I have. And so have you."

"It didn't seem like that last night."

"Roger, don't you realize that what is thought of as ecstasy and passion when it's romantically dark becomes adultery in the light of day?"

"Are you embarrassed, Millicent?"

There was a long silence. Finally, she said, "I'm mortified. Aren't you?"

"No. The mortification hasn't sunk in. Why are you so mortified?" he asked, suppressing a chuckle.

"Because I'm fifty years old."

"Well, I'm forty-two," he said, as though indicating that the eight years

305

should not make such a difference in how they regarded sex.

"Roger, fifty-year-old women don't commit adultery for the first time."

"Who does then?"

"Young women, thirty, thirty-five at the most."

"You're just a late bloomer."

"Oh, Roger, be serious. It's so, so improper, inappropriate. I feel like . . . like Grandma Moses trying out for the Dallas Cheerleaders."

"I would never have thought of it that way."

"Roger, what are we going to do?"

"Meet again tonight."

"Are you out of your mind?"

"No. Since, as you say, we're already adulterers, we might as well make the most of it. Say you'll see me tonight, or I won't be able to make anyone well all day."

"I can't do that."

"Then you'll have a lot of sick people on your pretty conscience."

"Roger, why can't you realize the seriousness of what we've done?"

"My darling, you enjoy your guilt. Let me enjoy my soaring masculine ego. It still feels good."

"You're impossible! But very lovable. I'll see you at the hospital, I guess. But how can I face Allyson?"

"Don't wear your scarlet 'A' and she'll never know."

"I never realized you had such a sense of humor, Dr. Graham," she said with faint disapproval. "Seriously, Roger, what *are* we going to do?"

He paused, and his voice took on an earnest tone. "I don't know, Millicent, except that I can't give you up when I've just found you."

"But I can't go on seeing you like this when Jeff returns."

"Even after knowing that he was in New York with another woman?"

"Yes, even after knowing. How can I reproach him now, after last night?"

"And I can't hurt Janet. She doesn't deserve to be hurt. It looks like we've both come up against our own limitations." His voice became comforting. "But let's not think about it now, sweetheart. We'll find a way."

There was a moment of silence as Millicent sighed. She sounded uncertain. "I wonder . . . but no matter."

Chapter 16

As the weeks went by, Millicent settled into a new routine, much of which involved Allyson.

Allyson was home and looking better each day with the weight she was gaining and the soft brown hair that was finally beginning to look as if it belonged on her head. She was seeing Dr. Lyons four times a week and Dr. Graham once a week. She was demanding of Millicent's time and attention, questioning her whereabouts but, at the same time, openly resentful of her own dependency and Millicent's solicitousness. She talked about going back to college, getting a job, moving out of the house. But she knew it was just talk, because she still carried around burdens beyond herself, becoming frustrated at the lack of solutions. But Allyson had changed. No longer was she numbing her sensitivity to emotional realities with dulling sedatives like "I wish," "I hope," "Maybe," "If only." She was being forced to wrestle with her confused feelings. Dr. Lyons did not allow her to remain "stuck." Gradually, she was acquiring the "courage and determination" to take charge of her life. In analysis, she was beginning to understand hard truths about her impaired ability to function in an adult world. She was also beginning a valiant and disquieting quest for identity. She had to make peace with being adopted.

Millicent found she was not disappointed that the strong romantic love she had felt for Jeffrey disappeared. It had been replaced by a nonemotional conjugal state, the warmth of a long-standing relationship. And it was not just because Roger had come into her life. For many years, she had been holding on to the sentimental notion that a wife takes her strength from her husband. Now she realized that she had gradually been making her way through the bonds of dependency, struggling to exist on her own. Her whole being had been defined in relation to other people. She was tired of being protective of their lives and defensive of hers. Meeting Roger Graham only made her see how much she wanted the freedom to follow her own heart.

No more did she feel hurt and resentful by Jeff's obsessive devotion to work and his fling with Cynthia Ross. Her emotions were bound to another person who gave her brief moments of ecstatic fulfillment. The moments she and Roger spent together were brief indeed. An afternoon ride in the country. Measured glances during office visits with Allyson. A quick lunch at an out-of-the-way restaurant. A stolen hour in his office. No more was she consumed with the guilt of their relationship. While she was still struggling with her feelings, she too was learning to make peace.

Roger began to take Thursday afternoons off. Those hours became their only regular time together and they treated it with a sense of urgency, as though they had to make up for all the other hours of separation. When they were with each other they tried not to think of the future, committed as they were to the present. But it was the past they talked about the most.

Roger told her about growing up in Newton, a suburb of Boston, as the adored and only child of a doctor father and a mother who was an elementary-school principal. His was an ideal childhood, filled with love and respect, without great pressure. But everything about his life spelled achievement, from the day he was born until his graduation from Harvard Medical School twenty-seven years to the day after his father had graduated.

One cold, gray Thursday afternoon in the middle of December, they sat in Roger's empty office eating sandwiches from the carry-out in the medical building. Somehow the day reminded Roger of the times when, as a young boy, he and his father would just sit and talk. After the patients had left, he would go downstairs to his father's office on the ground floor of their big frame house, and they would talk about his father's early boyhood in Scotland and about what Roger wanted to be when he grew up.

"You know, Millicent, I can't figure out why I never had the desire to have children. Mine was such a perfect childhood, you'd think I'd want to pass it on to

311

another generation. Maybe it was too good to be duplicated. Until recently, I never thought much about children. Now I think about it a lot." His voice trailed off as he looked at her with uncertainty.

"Funny," said Millicent. "That's the one thing I wanted more than anything else — children. You see, my childhood was not all that perfect. So perhaps I was looking for a way to change the past instead of holding on to it." Her voice grew quiet. "But I never succeeded."

"You were a pretty unhappy kid, weren't you?" His question came out like a statement.

"I wasn't completely aware of how unhappy I was until I grew up. My father told me I was rich and privileged. And he also told me how to feel. It was as if I was observing life instead of being a part of it. There was pleasure all around me, so I was told, but I didn't seem to have the ability to experience it. So I pushed away the pangs of loneliness and insecurity with fantasies because I felt guilty about not feeling the way I was supposed to feel." Millicent stared at a framed medical diploma on the wall. "You became a doctor. I became a dreamer."

Millicent also talked with Dr. Bromley every week. "Am I wrong to continue seeing Roger . . . Dr. Graham?" Millicent asked with a puzzled expression.

"Do you mean are you evil or immoral for having an affair?" suggested Dr. Bromley.

Millicent put her head down and sucked in her breath. "Yes, I suppose that's what I really mean."

"You're only wrong, Millicent, if you're hurting yourself or someone who is an innocent bystander."

"Like his wife?" Millicent said timidly.

"Do you have a responsibility to his wife?"

"Not really. I've never met her." She paused and thought for a moment. "Yet in a way I do, because I'm taking something away from her."

"No, I don't think you are," said Dr. Bromley in an assuring tone. "Whatever was lost between them was apparently gone before you met Roger. And you haven't taken him away, not yet. If that comes to pass, then you do have a problem and that's when you have to examine your feelings about your responsibility to another person. But what about your husband? What's your relationship with him now?"

"Oddly enough, it's very peaceful." Millicent then seemed to flounder for an explanation. "It's hard to describe, but it's as though the fight has gone out of our marriage. We're not exactly close — I guess you might say we're living separate lives in a way — and yet the strain is gone. Jeff is working very hard. He's away a lot, but when we're together it's as if . . ." she groped for the words, ". . . as if we're trying to be kind to each other."

Dr. Bromley was very direct. "Do you feel you are deceiving him?" she asked.

The psychiatrist's words made Millicent flinch. "At first, I did. But then, as his relationship with Cynthia Ross persisted — and I think it's still going on — I felt less guilty, because I had been deceived."

"That could be your real problem. A marriage that persists with revenge can, in itself, become immoral. But I don't get the feeling that your relationship with Roger Graham is completely based on that."

"No, it really isn't. Not at all." Millicent said this quickly and without reservation. "Oh, at first I wanted to get even with Jeff, and that may even have led me to consider seeing Roger. In my mind I rationalized that Jeff had driven me to it. I was terribly hurt, but that passed. Now it's much more than that."

"Is it love?" Dr. Bromley asked more bluntly. "Do you love Roger Graham?"

Millicent let out her breath slowly, hugging her arms to her chest. "I don't know," she said. "Sometimes I feel it's all a dream, and sometimes it feels very real. But when I'm with him, I'm able to shut out the world." Her voice became hesitant, as though she were reluctant to confess her thoughts. "I know I love feeling . . . well . . . young again, sought after. I was never really pursued before . . . not like this. I guess I just love feeling as though I have a self, a unique self. It gives me a sense of power." Then she looked at Dr. Bromley with a timid expression. "Am I acting like a silly old woman?"

The psychiatrist responded, "No, my dear, more like a middle-aged woman trying to become autonomous. But don't deceive yourself into thinking that a lifetime of bondage can be released by emotional union with another person. The change has to come from you and you alone. And don't confuse dreams with reality, or your struggle to find yourself will end in another kind of dependency — on illusions."

Chapter 17

On December 15, Millicent realized that neither Cory nor Johnny had told her when to expect them home for the Christmas holidays. It was Jeff who called this to her attention on one of the rare evenings he was home early.

They were in the library having drinks before dinner. The vague sense of emptiness and desolation generated when they were together was not present tonight. A roaring fire blazed in the hearth as the dusky tones of a winter's night enveloped the room. It was a time of tranquility, and Jeffrey Hart seemed unusually content.

He had just returned from a business trip to London and Zurich. The John J. Bolt enterprises had become international under his leadership. He was flying all over the world to oversee their corporate holdings and making more frequent trips to New York to take care of other "business." Millicent had stopped questioning his absences from home. She accepted their marital status — cordial and attentive but detached — because she wasn't sure now that she wanted it any other way. Their relationship had become reconciled to a mutual rearrangement of priorities. Not that they had discussed it and decided that this was the way they were going to live. Quite the contrary, they clung to superficial conversation to prevent the slightest confrontation. Over the past few months, it had just evolved into this kind of marriage.

But tonight Jeff was in a mellow mood, as though he was calling a truce to the distance between them. He looked relaxed, with a martini in his hand and spread out on the sofa with his feet propped up, gazing into the fire.

"Mill, when are the kids coming home? I want to plan my schedule so I'll be here during Christmas. I have to go back to Switzerland, but I'd like to spend part of the holidays here when everyone's home."

Millicent scratched her head as though she were puzzled. "I don't really know. I spoke to Cory last week and Johnny about ten days ago, and they were both so busy preparing for exams that they never told me, and I forgot to ask. I'll call tonight or tomorrow and find out for sure. Oh, Jeff, I am looking forward to everyone being here this Christmas now that Allyson's home."

"Me too," said Jeff with a look of nostalgia. "Last Christmas was pretty awful with Allyson so sick. Gosh, Millicent, I can't tell you how good it feels to see her starting to look human again. Do you know what she did tonight?" His voice started to break a little. "When I came home, she ran down the stairs and gave me a hug and a kiss. She hasn't done that for a long time." He took a swallow of his drink and stared into the fire. "You've been through hell, haven't you?"

Millicent closed her eyes to hold back the tears. "I guess I have, but it's been nothing compared with the hell Allyson's been through." Her voice trembled. "Jeff, help see her through this."

Without looking at her, he said, "Don't worry, hon, I will. It may not seem like it, but I haven't forgotten her."

Tonight was one of those nights when

Millicent considered the marriage arrangement with doubt. Unwelcome questions invaded her thoughts: *When did we stop being close? When did we start feeling betrayed? When did our marriage start hurting?*

She had not seen Roger in almost a week, and her sublimated anxieties came to the surface when Roger wasn't around to offer the kind of support she needed. *Am I ever going to get my life together?* she asked herself. The struggle of conscience was not completely resolved. Without his gentle touch, she was brought back to reality.

The next morning she called the college, knowing Johnny would be in class, but anxious to leave a message. The dorm clerk answered and told her that John Hart had moved out two months ago, where he did not know. The unexpected news was staggering. How could she not know? But then it came to her that she had always left Johnny's messages with his roommate, and Johnny had returned the calls. She had not reached him directly in the past months. Where could he be living, and why hadn't he told them? More to the point, why did he lie? Filled with the inquietude of maternal apprehension, she called Jeff at the office, hoping he would allay her fears. He was out, so she called Cory at Smith.

"Cory, have you heard from Johnny? Have you seen him recently?"

"No, mother, not for a while. In fact, I spent a weekend in Boston a few weeks ago but never saw him. I saw his roommate, Justin, and he acted kind of funny when I asked him where Johnny was. He didn't want to say. Why? Haven't you heard from him?"

"Yes, I've heard from him, not often, but he does return my calls eventually. But now the dorm clerk says he doesn't live there anymore and I'm worried to death. He did call last week but he never said a word about having moved. Where could he be living?"

"Probably with a cute little preppy."

"I don't think so. He would have told me."

"Oh, come on now!" said Cory with astonishment in her voice. "Of course he wouldn't. And it's pretty obvious that he didn't if he hasn't been in the dorm for a couple of months."

"Well, where could he be? And who should I call?"

"Forget it, mom. You'll hear from him when he runs out of bucks. Leave him alone to run his own life."

"Corinne, can't you understand that I'm not just trying to pry. I'm really worried. This is not like Johnny."

"Sure, mother, sure, I understand. Say, did I ever thank you for the smashing raincoat? Love it, really. Hey, do you know what? Nana and granddad sent me three crates of oranges from Florida. Tons and tons of them. They must think vitamin C is a new kind of contraceptive. Isn't that wild?"

"Oh Cory, really! By the way, when are you coming in? I don't want you to leave at the last minute and get caught in the Christmas rush."

"Can't say exactly. I've got a pile of work to finish. Probably a few days before Christmas. Just don't worry. And don't expect me until I arrive. I may drive down."

"Cory . . . be careful. Drive carefully, please."

Just as Millicent was about to call the

dean she heard Homer opening the door and exclaiming, "Master Johnny! Welcome home. Merry Christmas. We weren't expecting you. Here, let me take your bags."

The coincidence left Millicent dumbfounded.

She rushed from the library with a surge of relief, grabbed her son in her arms and started to cry.

"Hey, mom! What's with you? I haven't been to war. Are you really that glad to see me or has someone died?"

"Oh, Johnny," she said, wiping away the tears. "Where have you been?"

"Where have I been?" he repeated with bewilderment. "At school, of course."

"But I just called your dormitory and they said you don't live there. So that's why I'm asking. Where have you been living?"

"I just spoke to you last week," he said, ignoring the questions. "Look, I'm beat. Can't we talk later?"

Millicent stood back and looked at him with a curious expression. "Johnny, what's going on? And why did you come home early in the middle of exams? Is something wrong?"

"No, mother. Why do you always suspect the worst?" he said by way of chastising her and offsetting his defensive position. "I just got through early. I have some papers to do and I can do them here. Look, nothing's wrong. Can we please talk later? I want to go to my room and get out of these grubby clothes. I'm really tired. I've been driving all night. Say, where's Allyson? Is she home? How's she doing? I'm anxious to see her." With that he bolted up the stairs.

Millicent was not at all relieved. Once his safety had been assured, other fears engulfed her. His evasiveness only added to her original apprehension.

Allyson's room was in a corner of the second floor overlooking the garden level, giving it a feeling of being far from the center of the house, and this detachment was enhanced by a balcony of its own, reached through a French window. She liked the privacy. She was sitting on the bed, leaning against the floral tufted headboard and listening to a Mozart concerto. She took pride in her skeletonlike appearance. At least she was in control of one area of her life.

She stayed in her room most of the time, because she was tired of people asking her how she felt. It had been the number-one question since she came home, and it was asked so frequently that it had lost any meaning. Allyson felt it was not prompted by genuine concern but by habit. She had the distinct impression that everybody was "sick" of her "sickness," so she had made a conscious decision to stay out of the way and reverse the order of attention that had been directed to her. Anyway, she didn't really believe she was sick, not in the true sense. On the contrary, she felt she was doing something positive about her life. But even Dr. Lyons couldn't get her to say exactly what this was.

She heard footsteps, then a knock on the door, and Johnny came barging in.

"Allyson, wow! You've got hair! It looks great."

"Johnny, where did you come from? How come you're home? Mother never said you were coming."

"She didn't know. I just blew in. How goes it? You look good, you really do. A hundred percent better. How do you feel?"

"I'm OK, Johnny," she said, trying to

put some conviction in her voice. "How about you? Are you OK?" she asked cautiously.

He squinted his eyes and rubbed his forehead. "I don't know, Al. I sure as hell don't know."

"Feel like telling me about it?"

He blew out his breath. "I don't feel like telling anybody about it, including myself. I wish it would just go away. Look, I'm going to jump in the shower and then change my clothes. Maybe by then I'll get my head together. I'll be back after a while."

Afterward she sat on the bed and wondered what Johnny had to tell. It seemed to Allyson that this room was always the place where he told her his "secrets" when they were kids. Johnny would come in when she was doing her homework, and with the saddest face, he'd say he had a secret to tell her. Then, almost immediately, he would change his mind and say he had better not talk about it and begin walking out of the room. Allyson would put down her books and coax him to spill it out. The ritual took about four persuasive pleadings before he would tell her. The secrets usually had to do with his fears: A friend ignored him for another friend; a little girl told him that his ears were too big; he came in last in the race; his father scolded him; his grandfather wasn't satisfied with his report card; he was afraid to go to sleep because he had nightmares about amazon monsters.

Allyson, who was only three years older than he, would assume a maternal role and comfort him by making up stories about all the horrible things that would befall the people who had mistreated him. Johnny would feel appeased. Unfortunately, the stories didn't prevent his nightmares.

Allyson realized that they had lost contact with each other when she was fifteen and had started mistrusting everyone.

He returned to her room clean but with the same look of dejection on his boyish face. He sat next to her on the bed, staring through the window. She knew the feeling — the need to talk without direct eye contact with the listener. Again she had to persuade him to open up.

"Johnny, something's really bothering you. Tell me what's wrong. Honestly, it can't be all that bad." In a spurt of energy and compassion Allyson said, "Tell you what, I'll make up a great story about whoever is bugging you. Just like old times, huh?"

He tried to smile, but the expression faded. "I don't want to bother you, Al. Don't think I don't know what you've been through. It's just that I didn't know how to reach you. For the life of me, I could never understand what was going on in your head that would affect your body so much. I wanted you to know that I cared, but I guess it was just easier to run away. I'm sorry, Allyson. I should have given you more support."

"Look, Johnny, don't you start feeling guilty, too. I don't want anyone else to wallow in self-reproach. I've got enough of that to deal with already. And I'm finally coming around to realizing that whatever has to be done, I've got to do it myself. With help, of course. But now it's up to me. So I don't want to talk about me. I do that practically every day with the doctor. Let's get to you. What happened? What are you running away from?"

He let out a sigh so heavy that it shook the bed. "My wife."

Allyson jumped. "Your wife! You're not married!"

"Yes, I am," he said sadly.

"Jesus Christ Almighty! You're married! When?"

"A few months ago."

"And no one knows?" her tone was incredulous.

"Just a few people in Boston. I never intended to keep it a secret, honestly. I was going to tell mother and dad, all of you, but somehow I couldn't."

"And the worse it got, the harder it was for you to admit it?" Allyson asked rhetorically.

"For sure. How'd you know?"

"Well, it's obvious that you didn't run away from the girl of your dreams. How bad is it and who is she? You'd better fill me in. Johnny, was she pregnant? Is that why you married her? Is she in your class?"

"Allyson, she doesn't have any class. Jesus! That's a rotten thing to say, isn't it? No, she wasn't pregnant. She wasn't anything. She was just there. Always there. And I must have been out of my fucking mind!'' he said as he pounded his fist into the palm of his other hand.

Allyson was disturbed by his outburst. Johnny was not one to show strong emotion readily. "Why did you marry her?" she asked.

It was almost a plaintive cry. "Because I thought I was in love with her, and because she wanted me to marry her, so much! She said she needed me. I guess I needed her more." His hands were circling the air in agitation. "Allyson, she did crazy things to me. Flattering me and building me up like I was some Greek god. She was the first girl . . . woman who ever acted like I was something special." He looked as if he was pleading for her to understand. "How can I begin to explain to you how she made me feel? Like . . . like . . ."

Allyson finished his thought: "Like a real man?"

His hands dropped. "Yeah. Like I was the most important man in the world. Does that shock you?"

"No, Johnny, but it shocks me that you felt you had to marry her. Why?"

"Because I had this terrible need to

belong to someone and so did Sandy. And she's had such a rough life, it just wouldn't have been fair to live with her . . . and take from her . . . and give nothing in return. She said she needed some dignity." Johnny fell silent, then suddenly added as an afterthought, as if it explained everything, "She's a waitress."

"What's that got to do with anything?" asked Allyson.

"I mean she's not a student. She's an older waitress."

"How old?"

"Twenty-seven."

"Is she pretty?"

"I thought she was a knockout."

"But you don't think so anymore?"

"Al, I don't know what I think anymore except that I made a terrible mistake. Two weeks after we got married, everything changed. Before, she was so easy and full of fun. Now she's on top of me all the time, pulling pieces from me. She won't let me alone. She doesn't give me room to breathe. It's as if she's holding on to me for dear life, as though if she lets me out of her sight, I'm going to abandon her." He dropped his head forlornly. "And I guess I have. But, Al, I couldn't study or sleep or anything. She's so damned possessive and jealous." He paused and breathed hard. "I feel as if I'm suffocating."

Puzzled, Allyson said, "Johnny, I don't understand. You must have thought she was great before you married her."

"I did, Al, I did. Believe me I did. I really thought this was what I wanted out of life."

"It sounds like you didn't do much thinking, Johnny. You just did a lot of feeling. What are you going to do?"

"I don't know. I don't even know why I came home. That's not going to solve anything. But I had to get away from Sandy and the kids to try to think this thing through."

Allyson was incredulous. "Kids! What kids?"

"Her kids. She's got a boy and a girl. They're real nice kids. She was married before."

"Jesus Johnny. You'd better tell mother and dad."

"I know, but what can I tell them? Especially dad. That I've shattered my life at twenty? Look what I've done to Sandy. I've messed up her life, too."

"Don't be so dramatic," commanded Allyson. "You haven't shattered your life. I know. I'm an authority on that. When you shatter your life, the pieces can't be put back. Yours can. As for Sandy . . . well, I don't know. Don't worry, Johnny, we'll think of something."

As they sat in the library, Millicent had a haunting illusion of déjà vu. All the characters except the main one were the same. This time, the protagonist was Johnny instead of Cory.

It was the worst kind of luck, she thought, that her parents had walked in, practically right off the plane from Florida to spend Christmas with them, while Johnny was breaking the news about his marriage.

They were all in a state of disbelief, and John J. Bolt was furious. "Where do you come off pulling a crazy stunt like that? The whole world's changed. Young people don't get married anymore. They all live together like animals in a pack. But not you! Oh no, not you! You have to be different. Different and stupid. The big noble, honorable schoolboy has to be different! Only this time, my boy, you screwed up. You screwed up good! My God, boy, where's your sense?'' His suntanned face turned as red as the blazer he wore, and he headed for the bar.

"Your grandfather's right, Johnny. It makes no sense. You don't know a thing about her background. Why, she's not even a college girl,'' said Constance, as she delicately wiped her brow.

"She's not even nothing!'' shouted Jeffrey, who was pacing back and forth. "No . . . no, I take that back. She's something all right. She's a cheap little gold digger who saw dollar signs written all over your big, panting body.''

Johnny sat there in somber reflection. No one could possibly understand the alienation he felt toward those who were closest to him. He had been the quiet son, the one who took orders without resistance, who never gave them any grief. Now they were all worlds apart from him. What could they know about the misery he was going through?

But Millicent knew. Her face was taut and strained as she looked at her son. Her clenched knuckles turned white as she smoldered at the double standard they all presented. Why didn't Cory marry the boy who got her disgracefully pregnant? That's what they all asked. But now it was quite the opposite. Why couldn't Johnny just live with this girl? No boy in his right mind has to get married.

She longed to reach out to him, to gently put her arms around him and soothe him as she had done when he was a little boy. But how could she comfort this distraught young man who blamed himself for denying reality?

Suddenly she heard Jeff's voice echoing all the thoughts she was thinking: "You had everything to make you happy, but you couldn't allow it. You inherited all the good things of the earth and then waited for someone to take them away from you. Mainly, your youth and your freedom. Why, Johnny? Why?"

Johnny looked up at Jeffrey and started to speak but couldn't. He realized that he wanted his father to be aware of his discontent if only to blemish the charmed life of this charming man he wanted so desperately to emulate but believed he never could. *How can I ever compete with him, live up to his expectations?* Johnny asked himself. *My God, the man's too good to be true. At fifty-one he looks more like my brother than my father. How did he acquire all that confidence? And look at grandfather. How did he become so successful and vital and so sure of himself? Why didn't it rub off on me?*

Johnny heard John J. Bolt's expansive voice come out of the air: "You are the possessor of a proud and unique heritage, just like your father says, Johnny-boy, and you want to turn your back on it. Yes, sir! It's pure and simple. You are not duty-bound!"

It did not stop. The exasperated look on Jeffrey's face told Johnny what was coming. The words got angrier as Jeff lashed out at him for being headstrong and impulsive and inconsiderate of the family name. Johnny could have handled that because he felt he deserved it. But no, it was Jeff's smoothness and rationality as he lectured his son on using better judgment and less emotionality in dealing with people. And all those subtle remarks suggesting that he didn't deserve the advantages he was getting, considering his lack of interest in one day taking over the family business.

That's when Johnny's rage exploded: "Will both of you please cut that condescending crap! I'm sick and tired of being treated like a fourteen-year-old moron!"

John J. Bolt looked at him with piercing eyes. "Then act like an adult, a Harvard man, and a responsible member of this family!"

Johnny pounded his fist in the arm of the chair. "And, of course, a responsible member of this family only associates with the right people," said Johnny with bitter sarcasm. "No way does the social register allow us to marry a waitress instead of a debutante. My God, the bloodline would be corrupted forever. But if by chance one of 'us' right people does stray from the fold, then 'pater' and 'grandpater' just start twisting the screws on 'little sonny boy' until he knuckles under and comes begging for forgiveness for getting out of line. Where do you come off being so high and mighty?"

"Now you just hold off a minute and stop shooting your foul-mouthed accusations where they don't belong." Jeffrey was angry, but calmly so. "Your blame is as inappropriate as your disrespect. I don't believe you married this girl out of any great love. Very probably, you married her in a rash moment. Your marriage, like

337

most impulsive actions, was likely done out of defiance. To what, God only knows. And if you will remember, *my son,* only an hour ago you were the one who said you were pretty damn miserable to be saddled with a wife at twenty years of age. And if you will also try to remember, it was you who said this very night, to me and your mother, what a terrible mistake you had made getting involved with someone you had nothing in common with, except if I may add, sex. You're the one who feels trapped by all this responsibility. So don't play the suffering victim routine with me. I think you would be only too glad for us to relieve you of your mistake.''

Johnny cupped his face in his hands to hide the tears that were brimming at the corners of his eyes. "You really know how to rub it in, don't you?''

"No, that's not my intention," said Jeff with calm and assurance. "I do not want to rub it in. I want to discuss it and come up with a solution. You got into this mess by being a self-indulgent jerk. But to get out of it, you need some clear thinking. And the time has come for all of us to discuss the matter and decide what to do.''

"Damn it!" Johnny shouted as he lifted his head. "Why do you always want to discuss everything to death?"

John J. Bolt interrupted before Jeff could respond. "Damn it to you, boy! Because that's the logical and businesslike way to get yourself out when you're between a rock and a hard place. And if you're ever going to take your rightful place in Bolt Construction, then you'd better damned well learn how to discuss."

Millicent could no longer restrain herself. She went to Johnny and bowed at his knees and put her arms around him.

It was decided that Johnny should get a divorce. John J. Bolt would send his lawyers to Boston to take care of the necessary legalities. Johnny would move back to the dormitory. And if Sandy contested and claimed desertion, a proper settlement would be made.

"I don't think the little lady will object too strenuously when she's confronted by our imposing team, especially when she sees the checkbook in hand. It shall be done with dispatch and decorum. Now that that's settled, let's get into the Christmas spirit and have a drink and consider the matter closed." John J. Bolt had spoken.

Jeff agreed, and Constance was relieved.

"My heavens, Millicent, you do look pale. You should have joined us in Palm Beach. It's been a remarkably good social season. Did you ever meet my dearest friend, the countess? Fascinating woman. We entertained for her, and if I do say so myself, *your mother* hasn't lost her touch. It was an outstanding party. Everyone said so. Wasn't it, John?"

"Yes, Constance, outstanding. Quite outstanding."

Johnny looked at his mother with an expression of defeat. He excused himself and went upstairs. Millicent started after him and then reconsidered. She sensed his need to be alone.

John J. and Jeffrey quickly became involved in shop talk, and Jeff animatedly filled his father-in-law in on all their current business dealings in spite of the fact that they had talked every day long distance.

Millicent pretended interest in her mother's ceaseless derisive chatter about the nouveau riche social celebrities of Palm Beach and their impressively decorated condominiums. But the voice inside her head was violently protesting: *If you don't leave, I'm going to scream.*

Johnny lay sprawled on his bed, face down, feeling alone and isolated. His whole body was seized with a terrible shake. He felt like a yo-yo becoming unglued. His father's words still stung. But now they made him feel more confused than angry. *There is too much sense in what Jeff said. I've always made a big thing about not caring what happens to the business. Oh sure, willing to live off it, but not caring. Dad's right about that. If I don't care, then I have no right to take from it. Am I willing to turn my back on tradition? Do I want to walk away from the business, from everything it represents, and not be a part of it? Am I that weak, that incapable, that I can't at least carry on what's taken two generations to build up?*

And did I marry Sandy out of rebellion against an image that I couldn't live up to? Was I acting like a sex-starved adolescent who wanted to believe that I was as good as she said I was? Am I breaking the ties with the family and isolating myself just so I don't have to deal with my own faults? Am I really playing the "poor little rich boy" so I won't have to face up to reality and . . . compete?

That was a rotten thing to do, marrying Sandy, he admitted to himself. *Rotten for her and her children. Honorable schoolboy, huh? I cheated her and I lied to myself. But most of all, I took away her dignity. Is there some kind of meaning to all this irony?*

Allyson came into the room slowly. Her large brown eyes were sad and sunken behind the jutting bones. She sat next to him and patted his back until the trembling motions subsided.

Without looking up, in a fluttery, distorted voice, he asked, "Did you hear?"

"I heard," she answered with a sigh. "But you never told them about the kids."

Johnny rolled over on his back and stared at the shadows on the ceiling. "I know. I felt like I was in enemy territory. I would have if nana and grandfather hadn't come in. I just couldn't get it out. That would have made me look like more of a jerk, I guess."

"Do you think she'll give you a divorce,

Johnny?"

"Why not? What good am I to her now? After hurting her like this, why would she want to stay married to me? I deserted her, just like her other husband did."

Chapter 18

Somehow Johnny's distress abated. Being home granted him a respite he had never found there before. And being out of Sandy's possessive sight gave him a false sense of freedom, as though she and her children had blown away. He was almost convinced that he could return to Cambridge and pick up life as it was before he had met her. He now knew that whatever fears had pushed him to her would be welcomed back if only she would release him from his commitment.

He and Allyson resumed their closeness. She let him ventilate his feelings in much the same way Dr. Lyons had been doing with her. They talked of the naked truth of their emotions, those that had been locked up in their hearts and souls for as long as they could remember. And

Allyson let out her anger and resentment for being adopted — for having been "given up" — and her sadness for never having known the mother who gave birth to her. On long walks in the crisp air, through Rock Creek Park and the deserted gardens of Dumbarton Oaks, Johnny told her of his fears and insecurities about having to "assume the throne" as he called it, and not being able to live up to what he presumed was expected of him.

"Allyson, that whole empire may come tumbling down if I take over. I just don't have the 'balls' dad and grandfather have. Can you understand that? I'm just not made from the same stuff they are. They're hard as steel, inside and out. I'm nothing compared to them, nothing."

"How do you know that? You don't, Johnny. And if it's not for you, the business that is, then what makes you think you have to take over? If you don't want it, walk away. Do what you want. Become what you want. You haven't made any contracts with your life. Just because it's *there* doesn't mean you have to take it. Let it end with dad."

He looked more confused than ever. "I can't."

"Why not?" pressed Allyson.

"Because I want it." He added ironically, "I really want one day to be president of Bolt Construction Company, and . . . I want to carry on for dad."

"Then what's stopping you?"

He reluctantly admitted: "I'm . . . I'm scared."

"Johnny, I'm scared too," confessed Allyson. "I've come to believe that everybody is scared of something. We all think we live alone in fear, but the truth of the matter is that our fears are the same as everyone else's. Only the circumstances are different. Don't you see, I'm afraid of what I have to become, too. But, Johnny, believe me, you can overcome your fears if only you'll face up to what you expect of yourself and not what everyone else expects of you."

"But all that power . . . it scares me, because there's so much power. I don't know if I can handle it." He stopped talking and they walked a while in silence. Then, "You know, I think that's why I married Sandy. I was running away from my own fears and trying to put an end to what was expected of me. In a way, I guess I was saying, 'Look, everybody, I don't have what it takes to be what *you* want me to be or even to be what *I* want to be. So this is it. Don't expect any more. Give up on me.' " He was silent again, and they continued to walk.

Then Allyson spoke to him directly, as though she were commanding him to understand. "Johnny, you have to face up to Sandy. You can't just discard her like *they* want you to. It's not fair. You've got to explain to her why you can't stay married."

He shook his head back and forth as if acknowledging the enormous difficulty of that burden. He sounded breathless when he responded. "I know that now. I dread it, but I know what I have to do. I'm going right back after Christmas and try to make her see how wrong the whole thing was."

Chapter 19

Millicent had not slumped into morose musings at the prospect of extricating her son from his brief but disastrous marriage. She would let her father's lawyers handle the divorce because she was too depleted, mentally and physically, to cope with this situation that Johnny had brought to them.

Most regrettably, she recognized her inability to deal with the situation fairly — emotionally detached and with the same compassion for the girl he had married as for Johnny. Her son's happiness was at stake and it was too much to commiserate with a woman she didn't even know. Like a balloon ready to burst, her own life had expanded with other people's needs. She felt she had reached her limit.

In thinking about herself and her son, she remembered a line of Emerson's she had read in college. Its truth struck her with a force that she never saw as a young girl: "One thing only has been lent / To youth and age in common — discontent. . . ."

She wondered how one survived the illusions of youth and the disenchantments of middle age. She now knew that you survive because you have no choice. You just move on.

Cory came home the day before Christmas, and the house was again filled with people and noise. For once, Cory's helter-skelter life of boyfriends and causes became a grateful distraction. A large tree was delivered and set up in the hall, to be trimmed in the traditional manner on Christmas eve. Even Allyson left the solitude of her room and joined in the preparations for Christmas.

On Christmas day, the Harts and John and Constance Bolt were assembled for dinner in the grand Regency dining room to carry out the ritual of family solidarity that was still a meaningful part of their lives.

Regina had cooked a wonderful meal of traditional favorites. There was a golden-brown turkey with stuffing and cranberry sauce. A large glazed ham decorated with pineapples was in the center of the table, surrounded by candied sweet potatoes and mushrooms. There were salads and relishes and hot buttered rolls. A silver platter held stuffed acorn squash, a vibrant green and orange display. There were fruits and nuts and a glorious hot apple pie and a rich pumpkin pie covered with whipped cream. Homer served it with all the polish and dignity befitting the occasion. Lending sparkling accents were Baccarat goblets, antique candlesticks, Tiffany flatware and Wedgewood china that had been hidden behind glass for much too long, thought Millicent.

All of this helped to achieve the perfect look, a harmonious setting. The house looked happy. It looked festive and perfect and, to an unsuspecting visitor, it told that happy people lived here.

What makes certain rooms memorable? Millicent wondered as she looked with warmth at her family gathered around the large oak dining table. *Isn't it, above all, a sense of the people who inhabit them and who have made them uniquely their own?* Collections of memories formed an important part of her life. Eating together made up their happiest times until Allyson got sick. The gracious formality of this room, full of personal things, its old Waterford chandelier dominating the high ceiling, had about it an unmistakable air of contentment and well-being. It was easy for Millicent to believe that life in this house went on much the same as it always had.

Millicent's house had a holiday spirit, and she was determined that nothing should spoil this rare evening, not the intrusive feelings she had for Roger, not the reflections she cast upon Jeffrey, not even Cory's contentious enthusiasm about marching to Congress tomorrow to protest the nuclear arms race.

Allyson had joined them reluctantly, but once she was at the table, she seemed glad to be there. She sat quietly and ate sparingly, but enough to give the impression that she was not reverting to fasting. Johnny had lost some of his agitation now that he had come to terms with his future and had, without too much persuasion, accepted the family's intervention in bailing him out of his marriage to Sandy.

Jeffrey sat at the head of the table but shared the patriarchal role with his father-in-law, who sat at the opposite end where Millicent usually sat when John J. Bolt was not present.

Cory had marched in a pro-abortion rally only days ago and was still primed for another protest march. During dessert, she explained why her feminist group had to escalate their campaign against the anti-abortionists.

"Don't you see, they want to nationalize a woman's womb! Those antiquated, religious, moralistic nuts are hell-bent on putting this country back a hundred years by trying *again* to outlaw abortion, either by amending the Constitution or by enacting federal legislation." Her face was fiery with excitement. "Do you all realize that at least one million women a year will be forced to have illegal abortions if these sanctimonious 'right-to-lifers' get their way?"

"And no doubt, young lady, you will continue to contribute to those figures," said John J. Bolt with stinging acrimony, as he shoved another piece of pie into his mouth.

But Cory was not to be dissuaded by personal digs. Nuclear war, she announced, was even a graver concern than abortion rights. The fate of the world was her cause, she told them, and "her" supporters were mushrooming in numbers like the deadly clouds they were determined to prevent. They were united in forestalling a nuclear holocaust. Her vehement arguments were countered by John Bolt and Jeffrey as being stupidly emotional and overly simplistic.

"I wish you kids would stop protesting and start thinking," said Jeff, who was now stirred up. "You're all pathetically short on suggestions as to how to contain Soviet aggression. My God, don't you realize that the Russians are threatening our very survival! They've got enough bombs to blow us into oblivion. What else can we do but build up our own defenses so they'll think twice about starting a nuclear war?"

"We can march for survival until the anti-nuclear movement becomes a real force," said Cory with pride.

John J. Bolt shook his fork at her and smugly reminded Cory that she was unpatriotic. "I think it's damn presumptious for you college kids, who never lifted a finger for flag or country, to tell the president of these United States what to do to protect our great nation."

Cory responded loudly, "Nuclear arms control is too important to be left to politicians."

Her grandfather gave her a disparaging look and grunted.

Millicent begged them to calm down. A heated argument was just beginning, with Cory and Johnny advocating an end to the nuclear arms race and Jeff and John Bolt defending nuclear armament, when the doorbell rang. It was somewhat jarring coming in the midst of the tempestuous discussion, and they all looked at one another with expectation. Even Regina, who was in the kitchen but listening with great interest to every word being spoken at the dinner table, jumped when she heard the chimes.

Homer went to the door and they all fell silent as they listened for recognizable voices. They heard mutterings of a brief conversation and anxiously waited for Homer to return.

He came back and seemed embarrassed as he walked quickly to Jeffrey's place. "Mr. Hart, uh . . . there's a lady out there. She says she wants to see Mister Johnny. She says her name is . . . that her name is Mrs. Hart and . . . she has two little children with her."

They all looked at one another in stunned amazement, but Johnny smacked the palms of his hands to each side of his head and let out an uncontrollable gasp. "Jesus Christ, it's *her*. She's here!"

Jeff turned to Johnny and asserted with an unsympathetic, ironic smile, "I take it this *Mrs. Hart* is your wife." Then he turned to Homer. "Did you say there were children with her?"

"Yes sir, two children, a boy and a girl."

The silence was dramatic as they turned to Johnny for an explanation. All except Allyson, who looked down at her plate while sharing her brother's suffering.

"I'll take care of this," announced Jeff as he started up from his chair.

"No," said Millicent as she got up. "You stay here. All of you. I'll see what she wants."

"Millicent, let me handle this," said Jeff, trying to control his voice.

"No, Jeff, not this time. I can handle it. Stay here. Please stay here," she insisted.

At once John J. Bolt was on his feet. He threw his napkin on the table. "Now just wait a minute! I'll take care of this matter! The very audacity of that woman coming here, and on Christmas day! Millicent, you sit down!"

Millicent gulped as she felt her heart rise and fall. "No, father! *I* will be the one to see her. *You* sit down!" she demanded.

John J. Bolt's eyes bulged in disbelief, as did all the other eyes that followed her out of the dining room and into the reception hall until she was out of their sight.

Sandy stood transfixed on the marble floor of the entrance hall. Darlene and Stanley, dressed in travel-weary Sunday church clothes, were at her side, wide-eyed and dazzled by the Christmas tree despite the long, tiresome train ride from Boston.

Before approaching them, a fleeting thought of amazement raced through Millicent's mind: *This woman, these children, can't possibly be connected to Johnny. There must be some mistake.*

But she moved toward them and cordially extended her hand. "I'm Millicent Hart, John's mother. You must be Sandy."

"I *am* and I'm Johnny's *wife*. And that's Darlene and this here's Stanley and we've come to see *my husband.*"

Millicent struggled slowly with her words. "Johnny's here but . . . but I think it best that we talk first, Sandy. I'm rather surprised you're here. We all are. And I . . . I had no idea you had children."

"It appears you got no idea of a lot of things, Mrs. Hart. And that's exactly why I've come, to straighten things out and take Johnny back home. He shouldn't have left like he did. I'm his wife and he shouldn't have walked out on me and the kids."

"Johnny's not going back, Sandy." Millicent clenched her hands weakly. "He'll return to college but not to . . . to wherever you've been living. I don't mean to be so blunt, but he's left for good. The marriage was a . . . a very bad mistake. Surely you must know that."

Sandy glared at her and hunched her shoulders higher. "I don't know nothin' of the kind. His place is with me and the children, especially on Christmas. And he shouldn't be running home to you like some little boy. We haven't been livin' in sin like a lot of college people do these days. We got married for keeps, and he's got to come back and do right by us. You got no business to interfere in our happiness. Johnny belongs to us."

If Sandy had intended to hurt Millicent with her last remark, she succeeded. Millicent's tone became tight and resentful. "I'm afraid he doesn't feel that way. He believes he made a serious mistake. He's very young, you know."

"Well, he didn't think so at the time. And he was old enough to know what he was doing then, so he didn't grow no younger. You go tell him that me and the kids are waiting and we want to see him, now."

Millicent managed to recover her decorum. "Please, Sandy, let's talk first. Then you can see him. Have your children had dinner?"

Before Sandy could answer, both children quickly said, "No."

"Would it be all right with you," Millicent asked kindly, "if the children went in and had dinner while we went into the library and talked?"

Stanley and Darlene looked up at Sandy beseechingly until she finally said, "Well,

I guess so. They are pretty tired and hungry."

"Fine," said Millicent. "I'll take the children to my housekeeper and she'll be only too happy to take care of them while we talk."

Millicent led Darlene and Stanley to the kitchen and placed them in Regina's capable hands. She deliberately avoided the dining room, as much for the children's sake as for Johnny's.

Stiffly, Sandy sat in a straight-back chair in the library, facing Millicent but not looking directly at her. The cold, hard-pinched expression on her face concealed the nervous flutterings pricking her chest. Now that she was exposed to the awesome grandeur of Johnny's background, she was not as ready for a fight as she had been on the train. Knowing about it and actually seeing it were quite different. The carefully rehearsed offensive attack that she had prepared in Boston and that had escalated to outright anger during the train ride, had dissipated. She felt threatened by the elegant setting and by Millicent's status.

They sat silent. Sandy was thinking her own thoughts, while Millicent was searching for the right words that would avoid an emotionally charged situation between herself and this stranger who was her daughter-in-law.

Millicent searched the younger woman's face, trying to find a way to reach out to her. But she began badly.

"Sandy, why did you marry Johnny?" she asked.

The question seemed to startle Sandy, and she faced Millicent with piercing belligerence.

"Just what's that supposed to mean?"

Even before Sandy answered, Millicent knew it would evoke a hostile reaction, and when it did, she tried to soften the question with an explanation.

"Johnny is young, very young, only twenty and not exactly mature . . . at least, I would think, not by your standards. You're older, you were married, and now I find out you have children. Why would you want him as your husband?"

The explanation came out worse than the question and Sandy snapped back, "Ain't you really saying, Mrs. Hart, why would he want me as *his wife?*"

Millicent tried to avoid the confrontation that was about to erupt. "What I mean, my dear, is that Johnny is too young, too unsophisticated to offer you the kind of stability, the kind of home you need for . . . well . . . any sort of family life. I'm sure your children are your first consideration."

Sandy began nervously twisting the small diamond engagement ring Johnny had given her at the height of his enchantment. She looked unsteady and slightly confused. "What do you know about what I need or what my children need? Right now we need Johnny because we're his responsibility. He said that before we got married and I sure intend to hold him to that."

"But, Sandy, don't your children have a father? They're his responsibility, not Johnny's."

Sandy was furious. "Of course my children got a father, and we were legally married."

"Then why isn't he helping to care for them?"

Sandy bristled. "I don't think that's any of your business."

Millicent bit her lip and was contrite when she answered. "No, you're perfectly right. That isn't any of my business, and

I'm sorry for saying it. But, Sandy, all I am trying to point out is that I don't think it's fair for you to hold Johnny responsible for the well-being of your family. He's only a boy himself, and he apparently rushed into this marriage without much thought. He's still in college and not at all capable of taking on the kind of responsibility you obviously expect of him."

There was unconcealed rage in Sandy's response. "Is that so? Your little boy's not *capable*, huh? Really? Well, your son's mighty capable in bed, and he sure is capable with those fancy words when he's telling me how much he loves me and how I make him feel happier than anybody ever made him feel in his whole, entire life. And he's real capable when it comes to taking what he wants, which was pretty often before we got married. I guess something awful big must of been missing in his life that you all weren't *capable* of giving him or else he wouldn't have jumped so fast right into my arms. And you better believe that's exactly what he did. Oh, he's *capable*, all right, in taking just as much as I had to give. So I'm inclined to think that he does owe us something and that he is responsible for us." There was a long pause. "And what's more, I explained all that to those big-shot lawyers his grandfather sent up yesterday."

Millicent was uncomprehending. "Are you saying that you won't give him a divorce and that you want him back knowing full well that he doesn't want to come back and that the marriage would be a disaster under these circumstances? Sandy, you can't stop him from leaving you or getting a divorce."

"I can stop him from getting off so easy, that's what I can do. I can make it tough, real tough."

Millicent suddenly understood. "What do you want?"

"I want more than what those lawyers wanted to give me. They thought they were dealing with some dumb country girl who didn't know the time of day. Well, lady, that just ain't the situation. When you claw your way up from a hellhole, you learn a thing or two. I learned early, there's no free lunch for me, and there's not going to be for your Johnny. I paid for everything in my life. You betcha I paid. I got nothin' for nothin'. And why people like you always expect to get a free ride beats me. Your kind sure does think you're *entitled.*"

Millicent was lost for words. Her shame at the truth of what this woman was saying forced her silence.

Sandy continued to vent her pent-up rage against society directly at Millicent: "I'm a waitress, Mrs. Hart. I've been one for years. Do you know who's the worst tippers? Rich people. That's right, the richer they are, the more service they think they're entitled to. Only they don't expect to pay for it. They got some crazy notion that people like serving them for nothin'. Like they're entitled to be treated special. Some poor student comes in and gets a lousy beer and gives me a bigger tip than your society boys who drink scotch all night. And you want to hear something funny? Rich people expect me to feel flattered when they order me around. And it never occurs to them that maybe I expect something, too. Like respect."

Millicent folded her hands in front of her chest defensively.

"Sandy, we're not like that and my son isn't, either. You're very upset, and understandably so, but I can't believe that Johnny did this deliberately to hurt you.

He's just young and impulsive and obviously wasn't considering the seriousness of marriage. He wasn't ready to make a lasting commitment." She knew it sounded weak and defensive and the knowledge depressed her, because it was close to the truth.

Sandy leaned forward in her chair and smiled knowingly. "Well, I was," she said indignantly. "When we stood before that justice of the peace, your Johnny did just that, committed himself. And nobody twisted his arm. This was no game we was playing with each other. I expected it to be for keeps. Can I tell you something, Mrs. Hart? I'm tired. I'm real tired of men not carrying out their commitments. You see, I'm getting to where I believe that I'm entitled, too."

Millicent was stunned by Sandy's tirade of cynicism. She felt a surge of pity and a sense of shame at what this woman must have suffered in her young life. After a few moments of silence, each avoiding the other's eyes, Millicent got up, went to her desk, slowly opened the top drawer, and took out a very large, flat checkbook. She opened it, took the pen from the holder, and then turned toward Sandy, who was watching her intently.

"How much do you want?" she asked almost apologetically.

The lawyers had offered her $5,000. Sandy had carefully figured that she would ask for $20,000 and settle for $10,000 after they bargained with her. But when Millicent asked so casually, Sandy blurted out, "Twenty-five thousand."

Millicent never flinched. She wrote a check for $25,000 and held it out for Sandy, who was so completely taken by surprise that Millicent had to put it in her hands.

Sandy took the windfall with reluctance. All the fight had gone out of her. Heavy despair had set in, and she looked up at Millicent with her lips parted, wanting to explain, even wanting to lower the amount. Pain and guilt were written all over her face. She held the check in her hand and then extended it to Millicent as if she was meekly offering to return it.

Millicent waved it away.

Worldlessly, Sandy got up and started for the door. Her shoulders drooped and her gait was slow and unsteady.

Millicent asked, "Would you like to see Johnny now? I'll send him in."

With her back to Millicent, Sandy answered and she sounded dismally defeated. "No, ma'am, I don't think so. We probably wouldn't have much to say to each other. I'll just collect the children and be on my way."

"Sandy, I'm sorry. I'm so very sorry."

On the day after Christmas, Millicent and Johnny were the only ones at home. Jeffrey was at the office, preparing to leave for Switzerland. Cory had joined her college friends at Lafayette Park, across from the White House, in a demonstration to protest the nuclear arms race. Allyson was engaged in a psychiatric session with Dr. Michael Lyons. Homecomings, for any family members, were always difficult for her. Homer and Regina had left for their Christmas vacation. And John and Constance Bolt, much to Millicent's relief, were on a plane for Florida to resume their winter sojourn in Palm Beach.

After spending a sleepless night, with Sandy weighing heavily on her mind, Millicent became increasingly disturbed about her son's irresponsible and capricious marriage and separation. She wished that Johnny could understand what he had done was far more serious than merely making a bad choice.

Millicent did not tell Jeff and Johnny that she had given Sandy the money. She thought about this as she sat in the garden room, warmed by the mid-morning sun that was bright and crystal on this clear winter day. The money she gave to Sandy was from her private funds, inherited money, generally disbursed to various charities. Never before had she thought about having to account for it. Now she felt a tinge of dishonesty in not fully disclosing the outcome of Sandy's visit. Telling them about Sandy's real purpose in coming, she rationalized, could destroy her son's last shred of self-respect. Her father would have become enraged and insisted on legal intimidations more suitable to a business failure than to a human misfortune. Jeff would call it extortion and think her a fool for playing into Sandy's greedy hands. That she could take. What she could not bear was to see the added humiliation Johnny would suffer in his father's eyes when Jeff said the inevitable, "I told you so." Jeffrey Hart had become one of those confident people who believe that, no matter what happens, he always knew it would.

How could she explain to them her own inscrutable conviction that this angry young woman who had come for payment deserved compensation. Injustice had been done, Millicent decided, and damages must be paid.

What disturbed her sense of propriety this morning was that she was assuming her son's responsibility, prolonging his immaturity, giving in to pure maternal emotion. She vowed this would be the last time she would protect him from the consequences of his mistakes. But even as she made this pledge, she faltered in her conviction. So strong were her protective feelings for her children that she doubted her own courage to stand by with any sense of detachment as they suffered the penalty of their blunders.

Torn between anger and frustration, she decided to tell Johnny. Millicent found him in the kitchen eating a bowl of cereal and looking very glum. She sat down beside him.

"John, I want to talk to you," she said very seriously.

"I thought you would," he responded as he listlessly continued to eat. "In fact,

I expected it last night."

"No, last night was not the time for it. I wanted to speak to you alone. And furthermore, I had some thinking to do."

Millicent started slowly. "Your marriage to Sandy was more than a mistake, more than just using poor judgment. It would have been a shabby thing to do to any woman . . . walking out without giving the marriage any kind of chance just because in a few months it became intolerable for you . . . but . . ."

"But, mother," he interrupted, "if I had stayed a year, it wouldn't have made any difference. I knew, almost immediately, that it could never work, and I've never been more sure of anything in my life."

"Wait," Millicent said crossly as she held up her hand. "Hear me out. That's not the point. The point is, it would have been a terrible thing to do to any girl, but to do this to someone like Sandy, who apparently already suffered a bad marriage and a very rough life and who has in all probability been the sole support of those two children, well that was shameful. . . . I'd go so far as to say rather contemptible."

Johnny looked at his mother in shock.

Never had she accused him of anything like this before. He hadn't expected sympathy. But he didn't expect an abusive bawling out, either. His jaw tightened and he stared into space.

Millicent continued: "You don't prove your manhood on someone who has been kicked around by too many men already. Women like Sandy become very vulnerable to even a kind word, or, *even* a commitment they know deep down inside is . . . a lie."

Johnny's fingers clenched into fists, and he shook them in front of him as he tried to defend himself. "Don't say that! I wasn't lying. At the time, I honestly thought I was in love with her."

Millicent then shook her finger at him. "No, that's not good enough! What you didn't think about was your future and just as important . . . her future. You were simply determined to satisfy your fragile ego. But what about her fragile ego? John, you weren't just involved with a woman. You were involved with a very unhappy and bitter woman, and you were involved with a family. But the saddest thing is that you took unfair advantage of someone who trusted you."

Johnny looked at her with a puzzled smirk, as if Millicent didn't know what she was talking about. "How can you say that? Sandy's no innocent babe in the woods. She's been around, plenty."

"You don't understand, Johnny. She trusted you to raise her standard of life. She was looking to you to give her respect. You must have promised her that in some way."

"That's her sin, not mine," he said smugly.

"Your sin," said Millicent emphatically, "was in dazzling her with the expectation of respectability. That's what she trusted you to do. You don't smash a person's expectations and then expect them to agreeably return to life as before."

Johnny lowered his head in remorse. Then he held up his palms as though admitting failure. "OK, OK, everything you say is true. I was wrong for what I did and how I tried to get out of it. But my God, mom! What *was* I supposed to do? You can't know how miserable it was. She wouldn't let me live! She was so damn possessive."

With her eyes flashing, Millicent stared at him. "I don't know what you were supposed to do! That's something you should have figured out yourself. All I'm trying to impress on you is that marriage is serious business and divorce is an adult failure. It's not for children."

Johnny cupped his mouth with his hand and sucked in his breath. He turned away in depressing silence.

"Johnny, I've said my piece. I'm not going to belabor the point. But I do feel compelled to tell you that when Sandy left here yesterday, I gave her some money. I wasn't going to say anything to you, but that would have been wrong."

Furious, he jumped up and knocked his fist on the table. "For Christ's sake! Why did you do that? You had no right to."

Millicent was surprisingly calm. "I felt I did. It was only fair."

He asked anxiously, "How much did you give her?"

She hesitated. "Twenty-five thousand dollars."

"Holy cow!"

Johnny sat down, dazed, slumping into the kitchen chair. He ran his fingers through his hair again and again.

Neither of them spoke for a miserably long time. Millicent remained silent, leaving him to struggle with his conscience, and she with hers.

Finally he said, "Mom, I'll pay you back."

"No," Millicent protested. "That's not necessary and that's not my reason for telling you. I did it because *I* wanted to and because *I* felt it had to be done. It was my decision."

He shook his head as if to insist. "No, somehow I'll pay you back. It's my responsibility and I owe you. I didn't ask for advice in getting married. I didn't even discuss it with you, so I have no right to let you bail me out completely." Tears came to his eyes. "Mom, it's about time I started paying back. Maybe dad's right. I've been living on the edge of this family for too long."

Millicent reached for his hand. "If I've been too hard on you, I'm sorry. But it had to be said. I can't keep so much inside of me anymore. I forgive you. Now you forgive yourself. Remember that you're very young."

He sounded weary. "I don't think I'll ever be young again."

Chapter 20

It was twelve noon on Thursday, the fifth of January. Exhausted, Millicent sought the tranquillity of her sitting room, a sheltered place to withdraw from the frenetic pace of the morning's activities.

Cory and Johnny had left for the return trip to their respective schools, but not without Cory involving the entire household in frantic last-minute packing and delays, and searching for misplaced articles that assumed unusual importance only because they were lost. Cory personified chaotic disorder. She always seemed to go back to college with more luggage than she brought.

And Johnny left with a crown of gloom and a resurgence of his anxieties. Sandy's surprise appearance crushed his wishful fantasy that she would vanish from his life and cease to be. Now he could not altogether withdraw behind his defenses. He was still legally married to a woman for whom he had no feeling other than shame.

The thought that he had once felt love and passion for her made him cringe. The divorce was still ahead, and until that unpleasant business was over, she would be a constant reminder of his immaturity and rebelliousness. He longed for the freedom of the past, which he could not believe was in actuality only a matter of months ago. After learning of the payoff to his estranged wife, he was pitched into further self-condemnation. Johnny was tougher on himself than he was on Sandy for her greed. The price of freedom from this marriage was guilt and recrimination. He knew he would have to find a new beginning, and a way to restore his mother's trust in him.

At two o'clock that day, Millicent planned to see Roger for the first time in weeks. During the holidays, their Thursdays had been spent apart. Millicent was busy with the family, and Roger had gone to Bermuda alone.

Elated at the prospect of seeing him,

she lost her weariness. Their alliance had become an escape, and it satisfied a craving for excitement. A warmth of feeling for Roger came over her as she dressed. She took the mink coat that she seldom wore out of the closet. She would wear it today, she decided, to suggest that she cared.

Allyson came through the sitting room carrying a book. She frowned at the sight of Millicent dressing. "Are you going out?" she asked with annoyance.

"Only for a few hours. I'll be back for dinner, and since no one is home tonight, how about the two of us having dinner out?"

"I don't think so. I'm not hungry today," she said, as though not eating was something unusual for her.

Millicent didn't coax. "All right, then. We'll fix something here. There are plenty of leftovers."

Allyson appeared surprised that Millicent did not try to persuade her. So she reconsidered. "Well, I'll see later. Perhaps by then I will be in a mood to go out," she said. Then, as an afterthought, "By the way, when's dad coming back from Switzerland?"

"In about a week. He has to go to

London, too."

"I don't suppose you know that he invited me to go with him," Allyson said with a tone of smug triumph.

"No, I didn't," replied Millicent, suspecting that Allyson was trying to make some kind of statement.

"Well, he did. But I'm not up to it yet. Anyway, I wouldn't want to leave you alone."

Millicent arched her eyebrows and smiled as Allyson walked to the door.

"I'll be expecting you back by five," Allyson called as she left the room.

Millicent sighed and wondered what that was all about. Under her breath she said, "I think I have a new caretaker."

The George Washington Parkway on the Virginia side is a heavily wooded area that overlooks the Potomac River. It is a breathtakingly beautiful drive, especially in the spring. Now the trees were barren, affording a spectacular view of the river and the houses and boat docks that lined the Washington side.

Roger and Millicent drove along nonchalantly, then parked in a scenic overlook with the spires of Georgetown

University and the Potomac Palisades in sight. The weather was only moderately cold for January, but the popular parking area was empty of sightseers.

After stopping, they exchanged cursory and disinterested questions about their respective holidays. And then came a moment of absolute quiet, as if the realization of being together, alone, had just set in. Spontaneously, they flew into each other's arms and embraced awkwardly because the bucket seats made it almost impossible to get close enough with any comfort.

They burst out laughing, feeling more at ease now.

''Cars are not made for loving anymore,'' said Roger, with a boyish grin.

"Oh," said Millicent acting surprised. "Is that what you did on dates? I think we used to refer to it as 'petting.' Although I'm sorry to say, that wasn't my life-style."

"It wasn't exactly mine either," Roger said as he took her hand in his and kissed it. "I told you, I was once terribly shy with girls." He looked at her longingly. "I have an urgent need to make up for lost time."

Millicent became quietly pensive while

his words sifted down through the labyrinth of years. "Can we, Roger?" she asked.

He looked puzzled. "Can we what?"

"Make up for lost time. Is that what we're trying to do?"

He seemed to understand what she meant, yet he didn't answer. He bent over and kissed her cheek and then nuzzled his face in her neck. He sat up and said, "I'm just grateful for what we have." Then he asked, "Did you miss me?"

"Very much."

"Do you love me?" he asked.

"I love being with you."

"Is that the same?" he wanted to know.

Millicent felt strange. Mixed emotions were being pulled from her. Then she smiled at him and squeezed his hand. "I dream about you. Is that romantic enough?"

Her words lifted him. "For now, that's enough. Later . . . who knows?" His hand went under her coat and his fingers brushed against her breast. "Millicent, I adore you."

Her body was throbbing. Her senses were aroused. With difficulty, she managed control and straightened her position. She also changed the subject. "Tell me about Bermuda. What did you do there?"

"Think about you, sweetheart."

She gave him a slightly exasperated look. "Other than that?"

"Oh, I sailed and went diving. It was very nice . . . great, in fact," he admitted. "Come with me sometime, Millicent. Will you?"

Her eyes were dreamy. She lifted her hand to her chin. "Maybe someday." The reverie was suddenly broken by an oppressively gray cloud that swept the sky. "But right now I'm cold, and I have to get back."

Disappointed, he asked. "You mean . . . this is it for the day?"

"Afraid so. Allyson is expecting me for dinner."

Roger became sadly distant. Millicent wanted to soften the letdown. She suddenly remembered that Allyson had reluctantly agreed to go to a concert on Friday night with her old music teacher, a woman who had been very kind to her during her illness.

"But I'm free tomorrow night," she said. Then she asked sheepishly, "Are you?"

"I could be," he answered with pleasure.

A dozen long-stemmed red roses were delivered the next morning. When Allyson saw them she admired their beauty and told Millicent how wonderfully thoughtful her father was to have arranged to have them sent while he was in Europe. She also told her she was lucky to have a husband like Jeff.

Millicent neither confirmed nor denied Allyson's assumption. And she didn't show her the card: "Can we do some 'petting' tonight?"

Chapter 21

February weather in Washington is unpredictable and inconsistent. A week of snow and bitter cold can be followed by a hiatus of premature springtime.

It was early afternoon on Tuesday. The day was unseasonably warm and bright, and the air was crystal clear, as though spring had joyously jumped out and announced the closing of winter.

Millicent took advantage of the day to enjoy the garden. She slumped lethargically on the terrace lounge, wanting no alternatives other than peace and privacy.

The past two months had been made up of alternating layers of happiness and despair. Allyson was improving, but Johnny had become more withdrawn. Communication with him had become difficult. Roger was committed to loving her ardently, and she found this both irresistibly pleasing and yet strangely disturbing. Jeff seemed committed to nothing more than maintaining the status quo, as if a wrong move could topple his solid structure. And Millicent found she was still committed to everybody and everything, though with a certain distance.

Millicent tried not to think about that as she sat facing the afternoon sun. But her thoughts slipped in and out, denying her the peace she craved. Dreamily, she lost the heavy thud in her heart, turning common unhappiness into diverting fantasies. In her mind, Roger was pictured standing at the far corner of the garden as though his body had floated through the brick ivy-trellised wall. He started to come toward her, and she sat up with a start. The surprise caught her voice and she could barely get it out.

"Roger, where did you come from? What are you doing here?"

"The gate was open. I drove by, somehow knowing you'd be here. I had to see you, Millicent. I couldn't wait until Thursday. I brought you a rose."

"Roger, you shouldn't be here."

"I couldn't stay away, darling. You

haven't called."

"I know, but Jeff's been home and there's been a lot of company. He's had clients here. It's hectic. Roger, please go. I don't want anyone to find you here."

"You're ashamed of me, aren't you, Millicent?"

"Ashamed! That's ridiculous. Why would I be ashamed?"

"I'm not good enough for you, is that it? I can never give you anything compared to all this." His arms swept the air.

"Roger, what are you talking about? Why would I want you to give me anything?"

"You don't even want my love, do you? You think we have nothing in common."

"Roger, please go. You're just confusing me. I don't even know what to say."

"I'm not going until you promise me one thing."

"And just what may that be, Dr. Graham?" asked Jeff, who was standing beside them, having appeared without as much as a footstep of warning.

Roger faced Jeff proudly. "That she promises, Mr. Hart, that she won't let her absence from me break our intimacy."

"It's broken, gone," responded Jeff as

he protectively placed his hand on Millicent's shoulder.

"Not so fast," shot back Roger. "I've come for what I'm entitled to."

"You're not entitled to anything, doctor, is he Millicent?"

Millicent was stunned into silence as she looked from Jeff to Roger. So Jeff went on, "Tell him, dear, tell him that my claim is greater than his. He can't have anything from you. We have to keep it in the family, right?"

"Wrong, Mr. Hart. She can't have her love back. It belongs to me now."

"I think you'd better leave, Dr. Graham," said Jeffrey, with controlled anger. "It's almost time for dinner."

"I hope you understand, Mr. Hart, that I am a desperate man."

"And I hope you understand, doctor, that it's time to eat. You do eat, don't you?" asked Jeff with smug condescension.

This outraged Roger. He looked first to Millicent, then back to Jeff with fiery eyes. He took a gleaming silver scalpel from his breast pocket and lunged the steel blade into Jeffrey's chest without a second's hesitation.

Jeff let out a gasp and between rasping breaths uttered, "I knew it would come to this," as if it were a whispered curse. As the blood trickled from Jeff's body onto Millicent's blouse, he fell across her lap.

Roger watched Millicent's face as it became a horrified contortion. "I shouldn't have taken his life," said Roger, contrite and self-accusing. "My darling Millicent, will you forgive me? I only meant to make him disappear. That was clumsy of me, I will admit. I should have aimed lower." With delicate gentleness, Roger placed the rose on Jeffrey's body.

An agonizing scream finally emerged from Millicent's constricted throat.

"Mother, mother!" Allyson had to shout to make herself heard over Millicent's screams. "What's wrong? Why are you yelling?"

Millicent's cries suddenly stopped, but fear made her voice shrill. "Where are they? Is he dead?" She asked breathlessly. "Why would he kill him?"

"Mother," said Allyson in a reassuring tone, "you must have fallen asleep and had a bad dream. You're OK. Nobody got killed. And no one else is here."

"Are you sure?" asked Millicent miserably as she wiped the imaginary stains from her blouse without looking down. "Are you sure?" she asked again.

"Yes, I'm sure," said Allyson, as she sat down beside her. "I was coming into the house when I heard you screaming. I couldn't imagine what had happened. You were just dreaming. I guess it was a nightmare. What was it about? You looked really scared. Do you want me to get you something? Regina and Homer went out. Do you want something to drink or a pill or something?"

Millicent did not answer. She fought back the tears as she tried to erase the image from her mind. They sat in silence while Allyson held her hand. Allyson realized she could not reach her in this mood. All the same, she finally said, "I'm good at interpreting dreams. Tell me yours. I'll help you figure out what's bothering you."

Millicent sat upright. She shook her head slowly. Her voice was quiet. "No, it's probably nothing. I can't even remember much of it now," she said, lying. *Was it possible that this horrifying dream was a scenario with any real meaning?* It was wild and illogical in retrospect, but the potency of feeling persisted.

Allyson watched her face. She wondered what, exactly, had precipitated that violent cry that still made her mother look frightened.

Millicent looked at Allyson's face, too. The dream momentarily faded from her mind. Allyson was only beginning to resemble the pretty girl she once was. She was still unusually thin, but the hollow look of gaunt despair was gone and there was flesh covering the fragile bones. Her hair was short, coming back gradually, but it looked natural and there was color in her face. Not the rosy-cheeked look of youth. But not the no-color look that fades into a hospital bed.

"Do you want to go in? It's getting chilly again. Or if you like, I'll sit with you," murmured Allyson.

"I'd like that very much," said Millicent as she squeezed Allyson's hand. "I'm very tired, and I don't know why." Millicent's mind was beginning to function again. She realized that her daughter was well enough to give her strength.

In a matter of days, it turned bitter cold

again. But it was warm in Dr. Bromley's office, so warm that Millicent was perspiring. The thought ran through her head that older people must turn up the thermostat a notch every time they have another birthday. *When I am old and cold, will I still have a lover to keep me warm?*

In spite of herself she smiled, and Dr. Bromley asked her what was so funny.

"Nothing really," Millicent said, embarrassed by her thoughts.

"Does that mean you're in a good mood?" asked the psychiatrist, aware that it was a leading question.

Millicent sighed and sat back in the chair. She folded her arms and then unfolded them, then she shifted uneasily. "I'm in a dreamy mood . . ." She caught herself. "I mean I'm in a confused mood."

Dr. Bromley looked at her in silence for a moment. Then she said, "Tell me about your confusing dream."

Millicent was taken aback. "How did you know?"

"Easy," laughed the psychiatrist. "I'm used to listening to slips of the tongue. No, I'm not a mind reader, my dear. I only deal in clues." Dr. Bromley asked gently, "Can you tell me about it?"

Millicent described the dream and the intensity of feelings that persisted and continued to disturb her. It was still so vivid, unlike other dreams that slip away at the moment of awakening. When she finished, she asked with serious curiosity, "What do you make of it?"

"And what *do you* make of it?" countered Dr. Bromley.

Millicent rubbed her hands over her mouth and said, "I'm obviously mixed up about my feelings. I guess you could say I have a classic case of ambivalence. I continue the affair with Roger and I continue my marriage to Jeff." She paused and then tightened up with agitation. "I feel like I'm on a seesaw, right in the middle where I can't get off. I imagine that's why Roger appeared so angry in the dream . . . because I can't make up my mind."

Dr. Bromley sat back and hesitated a moment before saying, "Perhaps *you* are the one who is really angry. You know the old expression: 'I was so mad I could have murdered him.' "

Millicent said, "Why am I the angry one? In reality, I'm wronging both of them

. . . Roger and Jeff."

"Maybe you're still angry at your husband for rejecting you, for not being there for you, for withdrawing into other satisfactions. For disillusioning you. Could that be why you had Roger kill him for you?"

Millicent answered, sounding uneasy. "Why would I want Roger to . . . to do that?"

"It could be that you're mad at both of them. Jeff for turning you over to Roger. Roger for causing your conflicts and guilty feelings." Dr. Bromley leaned forward. Her look was intense. "But why aren't you angry at your father?"

Millicent grimaced. A shiver went through her body. Her voice wavered. "Because . . . we're two of a kind. I've become a mirror of my father."

"No, you haven't!" Dr. Bromley was emphatic. "You're fusing together all the dominant men in your life. You feel betrayed. You've lost your trust in them. They all cause you so much heartache, don't they?"

Millicent nodded but looked perplexed. "It's all so cloudy. I think my mind plays tricks on me because . . ." There was a look of instant insight on her face. "Because I feel it's wrong to be angry at the people I love."

"Oh yes," Dr. Bromley agreed. "And, subconsciously, if you could get rid of them, you might not feel so angry with yourself." The doctor pointed to her own chest. "That's where the rage is, my dear, deep down inside. And that's real ambivalence."

Millicent dropped her head in her hands. For minutes she did not move.

She heard Dr. Bromley's voice: "My dear, you are changing, and it's not easy."

When Millicent looked up, she saw that Dr. Bromley was eagerly waiting for her to respond. "All of a sudden," she said plaintively, "I feel as if my private world is turned upside down. Nothing is the way it was." She paused. "Who *can* you love?"

"Ah, that's a question!" said Dr. Bromley.

Chapter 22

Disgruntled, Allyson stepped off the scale, waiting for Dr. Graham's short weekly lecture. She pulled the sheet closely around her slight frame.

"Well, you're almost up to stylishly thin, Allyson. Ninety-two pounds." He said this as he made notes on her chart. "You're getting there, but not fast enough. Can I treat you to a Hershey bar to speed up your progress?" He opened his desk drawer and took out the candy from his stash of sweets, reserved for extra busy days of missing lunches.

Allyson took it reluctantly. "Why does everyone still try to feed me?"

"Because you don't eat," he said matter-of-factly.

"That's not fair," she said with annoyance. "I am eating now. I never miss a meal."

Roger Graham leaned against the wall and put his hands in the pockets of his white lab coat. "But you're not eating enough. I'm impatient with how slowly you're gaining." He tried to offset her irritation with light humor. "You see, young lady, if you get fat, then you'll make me look good."

Allyson narrowed her eyes. "I don't want to get fat!"

"I know. I'm only joking, Allyson. But you still don't see yourself as terribly thin, very much underweight, do you?"

"No. I don't see myself as skinny, like the rest of you do. I feel like you are all telling me lies, childish lies that you don't even take the trouble to make convincing." She paused, as if she was about to make a confession. "But I also know that it must be true, that I'm thin . . . emaciated, or why would I end up in the hospital, dying of starvation?" She stopped for a second, and her voice took on a more positive tone. "But I'm getting better. So stop bugging me, Dr. Graham. You'll see. I'll turn out to be one of your most successful cases, and then you can write me up in the medical journal. How about this for a title: 'Sixty-Pound Weakling Becomes Star as Fat Lady in the Circus'?"

"Don't get cute with me or I'll report you to Dr. Lyons." She flushed and began putting on her clothes, hoping the doctor would leave the examining room.

But he didn't, and he became very serious. "Allyson, have you gotten your period yet?"

"No. Does that mean that I'm pregnant?" she answered, trying to make his serious question sound flippant.

"It means I want to do some more tests on you to find out why you haven't started menstruating again."

"Maybe you should do some tests on my mother, too. She doesn't look so good."

Without thinking, Roger raised his voice and asked anxiously, "Why, what's wrong with Millicent? Is she sick? Tell me what's wrong."

For a moment she didn't respond. The interest aroused by her mentioning this fact made her wonder why he looked disturbed. "I'm not sure anything is wrong. I don't mean she's sick exactly. She just seems so tired and kind of worried. And I think she has very bad dreams."

"Come on, Allyson," Roger said with relief but also with the kind of exasperation an adult reserves for a naïve child. "You've got to admit that the past few years haven't exactly been a bed of roses for her. And I'm not just talking about your illness. With all that she's been through with your brother and sister and the rest of the family, is it any wonder she's worn out? She's probably just plain exhausted. Perhaps I should call her and urge her to come in for a checkup. What exactly has been bothering her? Tell me about it."

A shadow crossed Allyson's face, and her eyes widened. She wanted to ask, *Why do you care? And what do you know about Johnny and Cory?* What bothered her was that his tone had changed from that of the impersonal but concerned doctor asking about a patient's welfare to what was more like a very close friend anxious to know about details. But she had not formed the conclusion that there was a relationship between him and her mother.

"Hi, kiddo, take your usual seat and start talking. I've just got to put these files away or I'll catch hell from that bitchy secretary." Dr. Lyons said this as he opened the file drawer with one hand and stuffed half a baloney sandwich into his mouth with the other.

Allyson stood there watching Michael Lyons and then announced with irritation, "I can't talk while you're messing around with those file drawers."

"Don't worry, you have my undivided attention. I can do ten things at one time and still catch every word you say. Hey, do you want a sandwich? I have an extra one."

"No, I don't want a sandwich and I don't want a candy bar!" snapped Allyson.

"I don't have any candy bars. It's baloney or nothing." Dr. Lyons stopped what he was doing and spun his wheelchair in a semicircle. "Say, what's eating you today? You look mad as hell." A sudden glow crossed his face. "That's a good pun, isn't it? . . . 'What's eating you?' . . . Sort of like a Freudian slip. I get such a bang when I say things like that accidentally. It makes me feel like I'm one of my own patients."

He paused, waiting for a laugh or a smile, but he got no response except a sullen look as Allyson slipped into the cushy leather chair facing him and folded her arms across her chest, as though she were making a statement of defiance.

He leaned back and firmly gripped the handles of his chair. "OK, I repeat, seriously, 'What's eating you?' And this time I want an answer."

Allyson looked as if she was ready to explode. "I'm sick and tired of people offering me food!"

"You mean to tell me that you're really this ticked off because I wanted to give you a baloney sandwich?" His face had a bemused expression.

"Oh, I don't know," answered Allyson, her anger somewhat diffused. "It's just that Dr. Graham insisted I take a candy bar and then you wanted to give me a sandwich. . . . Oh, I don't know, it made me feel like . . ."

"Like we were conning you," he finished the thought for her. "Like we were treating you like a baby, trying to stuff the pablum into your mouth while diverting your attention?"

"Something like that," she said, without looking at him.

She stared out the window, and he let

her remain silent. Eventually she looked at him and exclaimed, "I'm tired of being different. Why did God make me different? I want to be like everyone else!"

With a sympathetically ironic smile, he said, "I'm tired of being different, too. But 'them's the breaks,' kiddo."

She winced with shame. "Oh, Michael. I'm sorry. Look who I'm complaining to about being different. You must think I'm awful."

"Yeah, sometimes I do," he said with a wry smile on his face. "But most of the time I don't. Remember one thing, Allyson, I'm a physical cripple because of my own stupidity. Nobody made me ride a motorcycle at ninety miles an hour on a rainy night. And nobody made you stop eating. We weren't born that way. We had the power to stop ourselves. Maybe not the will, but we had the power. So I doubt if God will accept the blame for us. He's already got his hands full with guilt about the millions of poor souls who never had a chance from day one."

"Well, I never had a chance," Allyson insisted. "Who asked me if I wanted to be adopted? Who asked me if I was willing to swap families?"

"Nobody," he replied sternly. "But I'll bet you a hundred to one that you got the better deal by that very fact."

She reacted by shaking her head swiftly, decisively. "No, that's not true. You're like all the rest. You think I should be grateful. That just because I'm in a family with a lot of money, I'm better off than I would have been with my *real* mother and father."

"What I'm saying," retorted Dr. Lyons amiably, "is that when a mother feels forced — for whatever reasons or circumstances — to give up a child she has given birth to, that child is probably, very probably, better off with a family who needs and wants her and loves her than she would be by remaining with a mother who, obviously, is not capable of taking care of her. And I'm not just talking about money. But listen to me, kiddo, don't knock the money. Because if you're going to be sick, it's a lot more comfortable lying in a nice private hospital room with private nurses and caring doctors who charge a bundle to bring you back from the dead than it is lying in a ward with nurses who are too busy to give you a bed pan on time or sit and spoon-feed soup down your throat.

And believe me, waiting your turn in a clinic isn't a fun way to spend the day. So all I'm saying is that if you had to be adopted, you're damned lucky the money came with it."

"You *don't understand*," protested Allyson. "The money doesn't make up for what I am."

"Maybe I don't understand," agreed Michael Lyons. "What are you?"

Allysons's eyes were now fixed on him. "I'm adopted. I'm different. I'm an unknown quantity. I don't belong! I don't look like them. I don't think like them. I don't act like them. I'm not one of them! They come from money, from position, from background. I come from nowhere! Whatever they are, they're whole. But me . . . half of me is missing."

"And how does that make you feel, Allyson?"

"Like a charity case! Like a hungry, lost child picked up off the streets and fattened up out of pity."

Michael put his thick hands behind his bushy head and stared at her. "So you decided to reject their 'charity' and their 'pity' by refusing their worldly goods, especially their food? Which, by the way, you literally threw up in their faces."

"No, no, I didn't consciously reject anything," she objected passionately. "I wanted to be just like them. I wanted to be one of them more than anything else in the world. I knew I couldn't pick up and go back where I came from. There was nothing to go back to." She paused, now suddenly wistful. "I wanted so much to be included. I just wanted to be magically transformed into their bloodline, their heritage. I wanted to be worthwhile, to be real."

He watched her small face, full of fear as the inner truth rose to the surface. And he sensed the unforgivable differentness she felt within her, differentness that had set her apart from the family that loved her. Sympathetically and softly, with none of the brashness he customarily used as the prodding psychiatrist, he asked, "When did you first start feeling . . . 'unreal'? Tell me when you started feeling this way."

"I don't know," she answered in a voice of puzzlement and pain. "Maybe when I was ten or twelve. I don't exactly know. Perhaps it was when the girls at school asked me questions. Somehow, they all knew I was adopted. I don't even remember if I told them or they just knew. But I sensed that they felt I was different, not like one of them."

"Allyson, after a while that's also how one can come to see oneself and . . ."

"And," she quickly said, "it is the beginning of craziness."

Dr. Lyons continued throwing out provocative suggestions. "Is that when the 'good little girl,' the 'smart little girl' became more comfortable with failure?"

Allyson shifted in her chair. Her fragile, bony shoulders dropped and her hands fell limply in her lap.

He waited. She shook her head.

"No, that came later," she said quietly. "The feelings were there, but the craziness came later."

"Do you mean, Allyson, that you felt you would be more appealing to your family in a state of deterioration?"

She seemed amazed by the odd question. "Oh God, I don't know. I get so mixed up with how I feel. One minute I want them to love and accept me and the next minute I want them to push me away because I'm so weird. I want to dye my hair blond and look like Cory. I want my father's nose. I want Johnny's eyes. And then I want none of them, nothing from them."

Michael Lyons grasped the wheels of his chair and moved closer to her. "And what did you want from your mother, Allyson?" She became very quiet, and he broke the silence by asking again, "Allyson, what did you want from your mother?"

The expression on her face was one of outrage. "I wanted her to stop killing me with kindness!"

"Why, Allyson?" he urged.

There was a haunted quality to her response. "Because that made me feel different. It proved I was different."

"Didn't that just prove her love for you?"

Her hands were clenched tightly. "Not to me it didn't! I didn't want to be treated better than the others." Then she said wistfully, "She never even punished me."

"So you had to punish yourself, and them too?" Michael asked, knowing he would not get an answer.

"I didn't want to be loved more than the others, as if she had to convince me that I belonged. It made me feel special, not special good, but like an outsider. Like a guest in the house who's excused for everything. You know, the guest breaks your best piece of china and you tell them to forget it, it's nothing, just to make them feel good, to wipe away the embarrassment. Well, you don't do that with children, your *own* children. It became so . . . so unnatural."

"Allyson, you're thinking about all this in retrospect. Your memories have become a process of selection to justify the trauma of your actions, of your feelings. It's a way of getting an awful lot of mileage out of what you consider your personal misery. Hasn't it become somewhat of an exaggeration?"

"Of course it's an exaggeration," she said. "Feelings always are."

"You're so right," he agreed. "And speaking of exaggeration, go open the door of the coat closet."

Allyson looked at him suspiciously. "Why?"

"Don't ask why," he said impatiently. "Just do it."

She knew he had an ulterior motive. Michael Lyons never did anything without a purpose. But his look was insistent, and he was gesturing with his hands for her to do it. So she uncurled her legs and got up and walked to the closet, opening the door cautiously, as if she expected a snake to jump out. Attached to the inside of the door was a full-length mirror.

Michael said, "I just put up the mirror especially for you. Look at yourself."

A terrible fear gripped her and she spun around and yelled, "You stinking son of a bitch! What's this all about?"

"It's about exaggerations," he said, without reacting to her anger. "What do you see?"

She was furious. "None of your goddamned business!" She stood in front of the mirror, defiant and rigid, waiting for him to come back at her with his anger.

To her surprise, he gave her a sympathetically ironic smile and said calmly, "Allyson, it is my business. And it's time for you to start dealing with reality, no matter how painful it is. What do you see in that mirror?"

She stared at her image, and her body grew limp. She felt as if she would dissolve in a puddle of water, like a piece of ice. The reflection of a very narrow figure was unmistakable, despite the baggy slacks and bulky knit sweater. Her head still appeared too large for its body, but her skin had a clear, translucent smoothness and she was almost pretty again.

When she finally spoke, her voice was thin and weak. "You want me to say that I see a skeleton, an ugly bag of bones. But I don't. I see a body that I like a lot better than the one that belonged to the chubby little girl who always felt apart from everyone." She turned around and faced him. "And that's the truth."

Michael Lyons propelled himself across the room and positioned his chair in front of the glass next to her.

Looking at her reflection, he said, "Nothing happens magically, Allyson. Just being aware of the problem is the beginning of solving it. One day you'll look in that mirror and see the person you really are and you're going to like her. Trust me, kiddo, you're going to be swell." All the while, he wanted to tell her that she was pretty, especially when she was angry.

Chapter 23

The dreaminess descended on him soon after Allyson left the office. Daydreaming was a state Roger Graham suppressed by keeping very busy with office patients and hospital visits and medical journals. This regulated way of life staved off his imagination, and loneliness. But the general stream of men and women who filed through his office with their physical ailments in tow was not working for him today.

With his thoughts elsewhere, he listened politely as patients elaborated on their aches and pains. His naturally compassionate manner became one of disinterest. His distraction increased, and he rushed an old patient with arthritis out the door before the gentleman half finished with his list of complaints.

He dialed Millicent's number, praying out loud for her to be home. The relief came as Homer called her to the phone and when he heard her voice, he began to feel elated. "Millicent, I'm in the middle of office hours and I've only got a minute, but I had to talk to you."

"Roger, is anything wrong?"

The questions came in a rush of anxiety. "Millicent, are you all right? Allyson said you weren't well. I'm worried about you. Will you see me this evening? Can you get out?"

"I'm fine, Roger. I don't know what made Allyson tell you I wasn't well." She said this knowing Allyson must have mentioned something about the dream.

His tone lightened. "I guess I overreacted to something she said. No matter. Glad you're OK." He tried to sound casual. "Is there any chance you could see me tonight? I could give you a checkup just to be sure you're all right."

She laughed. "I'd like to, but I can't. Jeff is bringing people for dinner tonight. Business associates. I have to be here. But maybe . . ." She stopped, not knowing what to suggest.

"Then tomorrow. I'll cancel my afternoon appointments. How about it?"

She hesitated. "It's tempting, Roger, but . . . but maybe we should wait till Thursday. It's only two days away."

He caught the ambivalence in her voice. "You're right," he said. "It's too late to call people. It's just that I . . . I miss you."

"I miss you too, Roger." Her tone was unemotional.

"Do you?" he asked. Then, "You don't sound convincing."

She tried harder. "No, I really do. I'm just very anxious about this dinner tonight. I don't know the people. And it's rather important . . . for Jeff."

There was a moment's pause. "Darling, I love you," he said.

She wanted to say, "I love you too," but the words would not come out, and yet she could hear them in her mind.

"I'd better get back to my patients." His voice sounded professional. "The waiting room is probably piled up. I'll see you Thursday, then?"

"Yes, Thursday," she responded. Then, as an afterthought, "Roger, I'll bring lunch. Something special."

Millicent put down the phone, aware

that there was a tremor in her hand. She wondered why she felt so nervous about Roger's call. She did not delude herself that their relationship was causing her only moral qualms. The risk she was taking was real, and suddenly it terrified her.

Jeffrey was having an affair with Cynthia Ross. She knew this almost with certainty. Several weeks ago, on an impulse, she'd called the St. Regis when Jeff was supposed to be in New York. He wasn't there. A company executive was using the suite and he told her that Jeff had left for Washington that morning. But Jeff didn't return until the next day, and his explanation was vague. It had devastated her self-esteem all over again. But this knowledge still did not resolve her own conscience, nor her fright. The double standard of infidelity was a permanent fixture in her psyche. It had nothing to do with intellectual reasoning. Emotional habits hold fast, and women of her generation were conditioned by the men of their generation to believe that a philandering husband's best possession is a sympathetic wife. Not that she had accepted Jeff's infatuations in the past as a matter of course. Yet she never really confronted them. In the early years of her marriage, she merely put up with them and hoped that he would change. Which he did, to some extent. But the hurt was there, seldom surfacing, mostly bottled up, waiting for the next chance episode of infidelity to break the calm. Meanwhile, the marriage had assumed a stability. Immobility had locked her in, and that's the way it would have continued but for Roger Graham. Roger's amorous attentions filled a void in her life. And she couldn't deny how the sex made her feel. Each encounter was an ecstasy of life, a mystic trance that made troubles disappear.

So what was the risk? She went over the possibilities again and again. *If Jeff found out, he might divorce her. A woman of her age had to be married or widowed. Again the double standard that was no longer considered a reasonable, rational alternative in this day and age. Just a traditional hang-up. But of course, he would never divorce her. He was as married to the Bolt Corporation as he was to her, and that relationship was forever. Worse yet, he might magnanimously forgive her and feel free to pursue Cynthia and other women.*

Her father would find out and pile scorn and shame upon her. Never mind that his life was anything but virtuous. The children would not side with her, even though their lives were conventionally unconventional. That's not for mothers. Mothers are not supposed to throw caution to the wind. Mothers are a custom, not an aberration.

And what about Roger? He's the sweetest, kindest man I have ever known. What other person has ever shared his dreams with me? He needs me and I need him. Isn't that what life's all about?

I am not a risk taker, Millicent explained to herself as though there were two beings within her, one reacting and the other analyzing the inner conflict. *What risk?* she asked again. *The risk of upsetting a marriage. Good or bad, it's still a marriage, and it does have a certain form and substance that give me reassurance. It's a safe place to be. And I have fears. Maybe I fear nothing more than a change of circumstances. Or independence. Perhaps I'm afraid of the exposure to family and friends who become hostile when you act out your special hopes and dreams. I don't want to be surrounded by that small world of people who become your critics and judges and make you feel strangely solitary in their presence.*

The inner dialogue went on until Millicent felt paralyzed by the excessive self-doubt.

That evening the Harts entertained the British Weckworth brothers, Billy and Olin, and their wives, Cicely and Peggy, with the studied elegance Millicent disliked but gave in to when Jeff insisted on impressing impressive clients. The Weckworths were British contractors who owned a multinational corporation and were seeking international financing. John Bolt and Jeffrey were very interested in a loan syndication for an industrial complex on the outskirts of London that would expand their foreign-based subsidiaries. The Weckworths had the technical know-how but needed an infusion of American capital. They came to the States for meetings with Jeff and John Bolt and with another giant corporate power in New York.

So John and Constance were at the dinner as was the bachelor Sheldon Carpenter, their boring but brilliant tax lawyer. Against Jeff's better judgment, Millicent had invited Dolly Henderson as Sheldon's dinner partner. Jeff thought that Dolly's overwhelming personality was too much for the staid Britishers and for Sheldon, who lacked the barest social graces and could rarely hold a conversation that did not include taxation. But Millicent convinced him that Dolly was the perfect foil for Sheldon, since she could be trusted to talk to a deaf mute without stopping. Also, she could be counted on to add some zest to the otherwise dull evening of business talk that Millicent feared this one might very well be. Dolly's incongruity of ideas never seemed to put off strangers because she said them so fast and so convincingly. And since the Weckworth wives, Cicely and Peggy, were along for pleasure rather than business, they might enjoy someone as exuberant as Dolly.

Regina, with the help of her cousin Hilda, a gifted cook, had prepared a superb dinner worthy of royalty. It started with perfectly executed medallions of lobster with mussels aubergine, which the distinguished English guests consumed with dignified gusto. There was a delectable filet of beef rare with mushrooms and golden roast potatoes, crusty outside, tender and moist within. The crowning touch was Hilda's English trifle, made with raspberries and frothy mounds of whipped cream. It all added up to food with a very splendid taste, enhanced by the very fine Burgundies selected from Jeffrey's wine cellar.

Table talk was light and confined to exchanging pleasantries on the relative merits of England and the United States. Jeff had to admit that having Dolly at the table, with her inexhaustible verbosity, did liven up the languid group. Sheldon Carpenter said nothing, but he ate with a vengeance, as though this was his first decent meal in weeks.

It was 1:15 A.M. Millicent sat on the edge of the bed in her nightgown, gazing into space and holding a bottle of cleansing cream in her hand. She was deciding whether she had the energy to go through with her nightly ritual or she should just let her face go quickly to bed. The evening had been successful but exhausting.

Jeffrey came out of the bathroom rubbing his neck with a towel. He looked tired too, but happy. He sat down beside Millicent and ran his fingers over her shoulders. "Thanks for the great dinner, hon. It went perfect. I think it was just what Billy and Olin needed to come over to our side." He smiled. "They're impressed by family solidarity."

Millicent returned a weary smile. "Well, I'm glad it's over. I hope the wives enjoyed it, too. If you think Dolly's a talker, you should listen to Cicely and Peggy for two hours."

As they got into bed they both heaved sighs of pleasure. Millicent lay on her back and Jeff on his side, facing away from her. In a sleepy voice he said, "You always come through for me, Mill."

She turned toward him, close to his back, and put her right arm around his chest. She felt the muscles tighten in his thigh as her leg pressed against his. He grasped her hand, and they fell asleep that way.

Chapter 24

It was a perfect afternoon in April, with a brilliant blue sky and bright sunshine bouncing off the rolling hills of the Virginia hunting country, where time has virtually stood still for two centuries. Although the nation's capital is less than an hour's drive away, the bustle of Washington is forgotten as the rustic but imposing estates come into view.

Roger and Millicent had driven down to Middleburg, the quiet hamlet in the grassy Virginia countryside where enormous wealth is hidden behind neatly fenced horse farms and stately homes. Crisp white fences frame endless acres of magnificently manicured paddocks.

Leisurely, they strolled down the main street of Middleburg, stopping in the shops that cater to the understated horsey set like the Mellons and the Bruces and the Whitneys, Virginia's gracious, slightly stiff upper crust.

Roger and Millicent could easily have been taken for one of the typical middle-aged "FFVs" — First Family Virginians — the entitled aristocracy, except for their clothes, which lacked the "seedy touch" common to those who lived in the faded plantation houses of their forebears. Middleburg inhabitants admire shabby grandeur both in houses and people.

If they appeared as a married couple, happy in the physical pleasure of just being close, it was because that was the fantasy both were engaged in as they walked hand in hand on the old cobblestones.

Everyone has a special moment in time that belongs only to him. For Roger, this was the moment when fantasies of peace and bliss drifted around in his mind. He looked up and the sleek blue sky seemed motionless, smooth and lustrous, as if it had been polished in the heavens. In the distance, he saw the faint outline of the Blue Ridge Mountains. He knew he would always remember this interlude with the same emotional intensity he now felt.

In fact, the pleasure made Millicent feel

so euphoric that she deliberately dismissed all conflicts from her mind, relishing the great tenderness she felt for Roger. The idea of a Prince Charming carrying her away seemed more than imaginary. It could happen, she thought.

They had an early dinner at the Red Fox Tavern, the traditional gathering spot for area horsemen. The handsome stone inn, with its exposed beams and massive hand-hewn posts, had provided food and shelter to travelers since 1726. A plaque in the dining hall proclaimed that George Washington had stopped here for refreshments when he was only sixteen.

After finishing the regional favorites — crab cakes and peanut soup and pecan pie — they lingered over coffee, and Millicent almost forgot the uncertainties she'd had before coming. When the check came, the realization that she must talk to Roger about their relationship returned. The truth was that she had serious doubts about whether they belonged together. Still, they were getting deeper and deeper into a situation that seemed insoluble.

"Roger, I have something to tell you. I've been putting it off all day."

Somehow he knew what she was trying

to say. "Millicent, don't shut me out of your life."

She looked at him pleadingly. "Roger, please understand. I don't want to. These months with you have been wonderful. Even this afternoon. But that's because I haven't allowed myself to think beyond that. Now I must. I have commitments and so do you. I don't know if I can complicate my life with this kind of relationship anymore. But there's something that's bothering me even more. Roger dear, this isn't fair to you. I let you drift in and out of my life at my convenience. You answer my needs but I don't think I have . . . well, anything permanent to offer you."

Millicent waited. Roger took a deep breath and was about to say something when the waiter returned with his change. Silently, he got up and she followed. He went to the desk and asked the clerk if he had an available room. Millicent moved back instinctively, demurely, as though she was waiting for the clerk to demand to see their wedding license before responding. But the young man never looked at her and replied pleasantly, "You're in luck, sir. We had a cancellation today, and we seldom do with only six guest rooms." The clerk handed Roger the key, and he gripped Millicent's hand firmly, holding it as if they had been together all their lives, and led her up the oak stairs.

The room had an eighteenth-century atmosphere, with its canopied four-poster bed, braided rug, antique writing desk and working fireplace. There was no television in sight to interrupt the colonial tranquility.

Millicent sat down on the quilt-covered bed and with a sense of embarrassment asked, "What am I doing here?"

Roger looked at her lovingly. "You're giving me something permanent. At least, that's how it feels now. If it turns out to be nothing more than a memory, it will still have been a permanent part of my life. This is *my* need."

Millicent sighed, closed her eyes and lay back on the bed. She let the tension in her muscles loosen. Nothing was clear. The moments were getting hazier. Reality was fading. The inner qualms were slipping away.

Despite her conscience, she denied him nothing. Their love-making was strong and passionate, as though this one encounter was their last and had to serve for a lifetime of memories. His fiery body was all over her, but with a powerful grace. She felt a primitive excitement with every sensuous gesture. She was transported through space and time until she was a young virgin being seduced, feeling shame because she wanted more.

The pleasure continued as they lay quietly in each other's arms, not talking, barely moving, content to be close. After a long while, he whispered softly, as his fingers moved gently over her body, "You know I'm yours. I'm as committed to you as if I had never been married to anyone else. I love you, Millicent, more than I've ever dreamed I could love another person, and I can't give you up. So please, don't give me up. I need you. I want to believe that we need each other. I wish . . . I wish, it could even be more than this."

Millicent sat up and gathered the sheet around her breasts. She became uncomfortably aware of the surroundings. Roger's declaration had broken the spell. The fleeting thought crossed her mind that she had never been here with Jeffrey and the image of his face was there. Suddenly the future was spread out before her.

"Roger darling, have you any idea how confused I am? In my mind, if not my heart, I had resolved what was the right thing to do. I came here with all the determination I could gather. I was going to tell you that I can't complicate my life with this kind of relationship anymore. I don't know how to live two separate lives. But look what I've done. I've let you make love to me with a kind of intimacy that I didn't know could exist between two people. What I've done doesn't make any sense. Now I'm so full of doubt that I don't know which way to turn. I really have lost my head completely."

"I hope it's over me," he said with a broad smile.

"Be serious, Roger," she pleaded. "Don't make it more difficult for me than it already is."

His tone became earnest. "I am serious, Millicent. I want nothing more than for you to be hopelessly and madly in love with me."

Millicent felt nervous. She gathered the sheet more closely around her. "I don't even know how to respond to that. How would you feel . . ." She took in her breath. ". . . if I told you that all I want, Roger, is to be loved?"

"Isn't it the same thing, Millicent?"

"I don't think so. And that's why this isn't fair to you."

"Millicent darling, let me be the judge of that. For now, just let me love you."

At the very moment that Millicent was lying in Roger's arms, her sister Joan was calling from Italy. Homer told her that Millicent was not at home, but Joan sounded so excited that he called Allyson to the phone.

"Aunt Joan, this is Allyson. Mother's not here. She'll be back later. How are you?"

"Hello, darling. I'm fine, marvelous, never felt better in my life. And I look like a million dollars. Everyone says so. I've lost *beaucoup* weight. This spa is the absolutely perfect place to diet without feeling deprived. *Quel magnifique,* Corinne."

Idiot, Allyson thought.

"This is Allyson, Aunt Joan, not Corinne."

"Of course, you're all beautiful. Darling, I must speak to your mother. I'm getting married, and I want my *only* sister at the wedding. I couldn't bear to get married without family around. You come too and bring your little boyfriend, but don't tell your grandfather. He would just spoil everything."

"Aunt Joan, I thought you were already married."

"My dear, I've been 'already married' loads of times. But this one is for keeps. He's a perfect dream. He's a doctor at the spa. Well, he's not exactly a doctor, more like a Hindu therapist, but he's cured me of everything. He's simply marvelous."

"Aunt Joan, I don't think you should get married before discussing it with mother. You'd better hold off and think about it carefully before doing anything. It's a serious step."

"How right you are, dear. It's terribly serious. But I can't wait. I'm madly in love, and Indians are impatient. They're not at all contemplative like you hear. Anyway, he's an absolute charmer. Sanjay knows positively everything about the body, and he's been marvelous for me. I drink *nothing* but alkaline-sulphate spring water. It tastes like bitter saltwater, but oh my God, the therapeutic effect! Sanjay insists on a quart a day. I feel so . . . well, so cleansed. Oh, I must tell you about the underwater massages that relieve the tension points in my head and the phytocosmetica, a kind of acupuncture without needles and the . . ."

Allyson cut in. "Aunt Joan, just listen. I'll have mother call you tonight or tomorrow. Just don't do anything until she gets in touch with you. Give me your number in France and she'll call."

"Oh, I'm not in France. I moved on. I'm at Montecatini."

"Where is that?"

"In Italy, of course, in the splendid hills of Tuscany, where the thermal waters cure even infertility. Now take down the number of this glorious spa, because it's listed nowhere, and tell your mother to call her little sister straightaway . . . Ciao."

Allyson stayed by the phone long after their voices had faded away. She thought, *She's like a constant irritation. But so sad.* Feeling a terrible emptiness, Allyson spoke aloud the wrenching words that came immediately to mind: "Just like me."

Just before ten, Millicent slipped quietly

into the large stone house on Belmont Road. Like a guilty child who had defied her curfew, she ascended the stairs soundlessly, having first removed her shoes. No more than three or four steps had been taken when she saw Allyson, in her pajamas, at the top of the staircase. Allyson, thin and gaunt, was standing defiantly, arms folded, head tilted and staring down at her with close interest.

"Where have you been?" Allyson called loudly.

Millicent smiled nervously and wondered if somehow Allyson knew exactly where she had been.

Allyson knew nothing more than that Millicent was sneaking into the house, an act as unlikely as anything Allyson could think of in connection with her mother, who led a blameless life.

Millicent continued up the stairs without answering.

Allyson smiled to show that she suspected something not quite right and waited for an explanation. When none was given, she followed Millicent into her bedroom.

Furious at her mother's silence, she asked abrasively. "Well?"

"Well what?" Millicent responded with defense, but equally caustic.

"I think you owe me an explanation," Allyson said indignantly.

Millicent looked at her daughter and shook her head. "No, that's where you are wrong. I don't owe *you* any explanation. I'm the *mother* here, and I'm much too old to give excuses or explanations."

Allyson, shocked by this anger, changed her tone to one of concern. "Well, I was worried."

"Why? Didn't Homer tell you I called and said I'd be late?"

Millicent heard the whine in Allyson's voice and the guilt returned to her penitent mind. "I didn't intend to worry you. The time just got away from me." Determined not to explain, she did so anyway and felt even more guilty making up excuses. "The time just got away from me. I was at Dolly's and there were old friends I hadn't seen in ages. And . . . well . . . we got to talking and I was enjoying all the news . . . and the time slipped by."

"And, of course, you knew daddy was out of town."

Millicent winced but ignored the implication. "Anyway, I'm here now and fine.

So you can go to bed. I'm sorry I worried you, dear."

The explanation did not satisfy Allyson, but she let it drop.

"Don't you want to hear the news?"

Millicent frowned. "What news? Is something wrong with Cory or Johnny? Did they call?"

"No, but Aunt Joan did," said Allyson, with an affected smile.

"Joan called? From where? Has anything happened to her?"

"She called from Italy." Allyson paused so as to draw out the news. "No, nothing's happened to her except that . . . she's 'madly in love' and she's getting married."

The news took Millicent's breath away, just as Allyson had imagined it would. "Married! Again?" she exclaimed.

"Yes, again. To an Indian faith healer who's cured her, of what I'm not sure, with bitter saltwater, and she wants you to come to the wedding. She invited me, too."

"Oh my God!" said Millicent. "That girl must be out of her mind."

"She sounded very excited and said not to tell grandfather."

Millicent arched an eyebrow. "I just bet she did. Did you say she called from Italy? I thought she was in France."

"She was. She changes locations as fast as husbands," said Allyson, enjoying her role as harbinger of this intriguing information. "She's in a place called Monte . . . here, I wrote it down, Montecatini. She's taking the *cure* there and staying at the Grand Hotel, where she drinks all that saltwater with her guru. And she said she looks 'marvelous." She left the number. She said she wants 'family' around when she gets married. Mother, are you going?"

Milicent could not conceal her contempt. "If I go, it will be to see that there *isn't* any wedding." She paced around the room nervously. There was exasperation in her voice. "Good grief, what is the matter with her? Flitting around Europe, picking up husbands as if they were souvenirs to be bought and discarded! Why is she always so anxious to get married?"

Allyson's voice became serious. "Maybe because she's so lonely."

Millicent looked at her daughter with surprise. "She doesn't have to be. She could come home."

"Perhaps she can't come home because that's where her real loneliness is, mother. She might be chasing a dream."

Millicent looked troubled and realized what Allyson was really saying. She didn't want to accept this theory about her sister, but she could not dismiss it. She had just never thought about it that way. Ironically, Allyson had hit on the truth. Although everyone always said Joan should come home, no one really wanted her to. It was easier on all of them to have her stay away. Having her out of sight, traipsing about Europe with boyfriends and husbands and being pampered in luxurious spas, allowed the family to forget her complexes and her embarrassing behavior. *Oh sure, I worry about Joan and feel guilty about her*, thought Millicent, *but only when she calls it to my attention. Most of the time, I feel a sense of relief knowing she's too far away for me to be involved. Certainly father couldn't take seeing the woman she's become. When she visits, he seems to be in constant pain. Denial is his way of dealing with Joan. He expects perfection from everyone, especially his family, and when they don't live up to his expectations, when they don't show his strength, he judges them harshly. But Joan was his darling. Now, the only emotion he appears to have whenever her name is mentioned is . . . is pain.*

But what about me? I haven't been too sympathetic to Joan, either. Who am I to have such a low level of tolerance for weakness? Unconsciously, I've been self-righteous about my sister, never trying to figure out the real reasons for her self-destructive side. Maybe I couldn't face it, either. I did resent her, more than I knew. She was so beautiful, but so selfish and irresponsible, and unaware of my feelings. She was my enemy and I didn't know why.
Millicent wanted to weep.

Allyson's gentle touch on her mother's arm brought her back to reality. She covered the hand with her own and sighed regretfully.

"Perhaps you're right, Allyson. She may be very lonely. I don't want her to suffer loneliness. But I wish I understood her."

She kissed Allyson lightly on the forehead. "I'll call her in the morning and then decide what to do. Go back to bed, dear."

Millicent slept soundly, as though to block out the guilt she felt toward herself and the guilt she felt for her sister. Staying with Roger, succumbing to temptation against all her better judgment, then hearing about Joan's impulsive marriage plans with a feeling of contempt rather than compassion, had revealed her own hidden weakness with startling clarity.

Everyone wants to be loved, she thought, *and getting a little love never satisfies the craving. It does just the opposite. It becomes an addiction. Doesn't Jeff want this from me, too?*

The next morning she called Joan at the Grand Hotel in Montecatini but was told by a very solicitous Italian attendant, who reverted to perfect English as soon as he realized he was talking to an American, that "the signora was taking the marvelous water of Tettuchio" at its impressive source nearby. Relieved by the postponement, Millicent proceeded to fortify herself with morning exercises, a hot bath, and a pot of strong coffee. Then she waited for the call, unsure of how to dissuade her sister from this new matrimonial venture.

Hours later Joan telephoned, exhilarated from the therapeutic regimen of bitter saltwater and underwater massages. She gave a breathless account of the bubbling hot springs, and Millicent found it difficult to divert her enthusiasm to the purpose of the transatlantic call. After repeated requests to Joan to hold off on this ill-conceived marriage, Millicent resorted to shouting orders, over and over, for Joan to do nothing until she could get over there. This, Joan finally promised to do.

Millicent hung up the phone with the stunning realization that at the start of the call she had never intended to go to Italy. Certainly not now of all times, but she was fully committed.

As though Joan's call had set off a chain reaction of uneasiness, Millicent felt compelled to call Johnny and Cory and her parents in Florida, just to make contact with her family. She couldn't even repress the impulse to call Jeff in New York, knowing that she would not reach him. But she left a message, and that made her feel better.

Meanwhile, in Massachusetts, John Bolt Hart was overcome with exhaustion. His entire body ached, as though it had been struggling with an illness. He wanted nothing more than not to move off his bed for at least an hour. When he was called to the phone, he moaned and shuffled off slowly, because his back felt as if it would break in two.

Millicent was on the phone, surprised and happy to find him in. She kept asking him why he sounded so tired, and he just said he was working hard this semester. No mention was made of Sandy, and she suspected that he was more depressed than tired.

But Johnny was not depressed. For the first time in months, he had become accustomed to living without self-reproach. Since returning to Cambridge, he had been working on a construction job in nearby Waltham. He went to classes in the morning and worked on rebuilding a church in the afternoons.

When he returned to school in January, Johnny had been sure of only one thing: He had to pay back the money his mother had given to Sandy. Getting a job wasn't easy, he found out, and making a substantial dent in the $25,000 was next to impossible. But he was determined to make a start. He had no special skills, and unemployment was high in Massachusetts. But he saw an ad for part-time work at a construction site. The low hourly wage didn't attract too many people, and he was hired after he convinced the foreman that he knew something about the construction business. Since the work was mainly renovation and since his particular job was carrying building materials and helping the more experienced brick layers, he managed to stay on the job.

Although each day he was more weary than the day before, he found he enjoyed physical labor. Not being a natural athlete, he had almost convinced himself that he was incapable of using his body in this way. He had the satisfaction of looking in the mirror and seeing muscles develop like small ripples all over his sun-baked arms and chest.

He lay in his bed wondering whether he had stumbled into a career or had chosen one.

Chapter 25

Millicent sat with her father and mother in their living room overlooking the murky waters of the Potomac. They had returned from Florida that very morning looking suntanned and vigorous. But now they appeared somber.

John J. Bolt remained unusually quiet as she told them about Joan. She went through the formalities of seeking parental advice, although she already knew what had to be done. Her father indeed looked pained, as though a thorn that could not be removed was pricking the one sensitive part of his hard exterior. Her mother fluttered about, wiping nonexistent dust from two Regency tables. She would have preferred not to have been a part of this conversation. She spoke of Joan as though her younger daughter was still a schoolgirl, having never embarked on a life of drink and escape, and collecting husbands. Constance's allusions to other times and other places were inappropriate, echoing the glamour and security of years gone by, as if the upcoming event were a debutante ball, not a fifth marriage.

Only when there was a long silence did John Bolt finally speak, tentatively, as if he was unsure of himself. "Millicent, you'll just have to go to Italy and put a stop to this nonsense once and for all. If I were ten years younger, I would go myself. But I'm afraid age is catching up with me. I admit it. That girl is beyond me. She messes up her life as fast as we can untangle her from the last scrape. I didn't tell you about the nasty business in Cannes. She was passing bad checks. She overdrew her account, then went on a wild spending spree with some Parisian gigolo. I don't have to tell you what an awful mess *that* was. The French authorities were not very sympathetic, even when we covered her debts."

"Well, perhaps her allowance isn't adequate, John. *You know* how high prices are in Europe," interposed Constance, by way of steering her husband's critical appraisal to a more reasonable explanation.

John J. Bolt looked at his wife with undisguised annoyance. "My good woman, her allowance is *more* than adequate, adequate enough for an entire family to live on unstintingly. I might add, lavishly. So don't lecture me on inflation," he told her.

Constance suffered his displeasure. "I only meant that Joan is not used to budgeting. She . . . she isn't good with financial matters and . . . and she probably didn't realize how much costs have gone up and . . ."

"Constance! Drop it! This is all beside the point. The issue here is whether Millicent should go to Italy and stop these impulsive escapades once and for all. Frankly, the thought of subsidizing one more foreigner makes my blood boil. When will it ever be *enough* with that girl?"

"If I do talk her out of marrying this man, father, should I bring her home?" asked Millicent with hesitation.

John J. Bolt slumped in his chair, his large frame losing the look of power. Quite suddenly he appeared older than usual, and vulnerable to age. In later life, he was not able to spare himself unhappiness by refusing to feel guilty as was his habit for most of his seventy-five years. This was a question he did not want to be asked. His quiet indecision puzzled Millicent. This was not like him.

"Father, should I try to convince Joan to come back for good? She's been away so long. I'm not sure where her home should be and whether I have any right to tell her where or how to live. She's not a child, and I have the feeling that we're acting as if she were."

"Believe me, Millicent, she is," said John Bolt as he looked away with forlorn weariness. Then, evading her questions, he said with resignation, "Do what you think best. Just go . . . and do what you think best."

Millicent went to Italy and Allyson went with her. Their plans coincided with Jeffrey's business trip to London for further negotiations with the Weckworth brothers.

Jeff persuaded Millicent to fly over with him on the Concorde before going to Italy. It seemed to mean a lot to him for them to travel together and she wondered why, because they had been living in a state of civilized estrangement. Jeff was individually absorbed but acted as though they lived in mutual harmony. She had gone along with this pretense, thinking her affair with Roger was coming to an end. But her most recent infidelity convinced her that she could not end their relationship. Neither could her marriage continue in this farcical way. The deceit and guilt were turning her inward, making her a victim of her own hate. No longer could she remain at the mercy of her social environment. It was a burden she could not carry anymore.

The thought of dissolving her marriage was almost unbearable. And yet she found that she was not strong enough to give up Roger. She thought about what would happen if she did leave Jeff. She would have to accept the devastating consequences. Her father's wrath, her husband's scorn, her children's disappointment in her. Another wife's hurt. How could she prepare herself for all that? It was too much to sort out, and she put this dilemma aside. For now, she had to attend to one last piece of family business.

But how could she stop Joan from this foolish act when she could not stop herself?

Unexpectedly, Allyson asked to go with her. Allyson had gone nowhere, except to the offices of Dr. Lyons and Dr. Graham, for so long now; she almost refused to socialize. Millicent was pleasantly surprised by her request. In fact she was delighted, not only because it was the first sign that Allyson was returning to some sort of normal existence, but because she selfishly wanted her along as a buffer between herself and Joan.

Allyson rather casually mentioned that Dr. Lyons was going to a medical meeting in Canada, and since her appointments with him would be cancelled, it would be a good time to go. Millicent sensed that Allyson was afraid of being alone with herself, without the support of her psychiatrist or her mother. Her appearance had improved to the point that people had stopped staring with horror. Her body was still narrow and scanty, but she had lost her emaciated look. And life and warmth had come back to her eyes. Jeff agreed that the trip would be good for her, although he had misgivings about subjecting Allyson to the absurdities of his sister-in-law. Allyson had no such qualms. She was anxious to see her capricious aunt. In a peculiar way, she identified with her and was more than curious about what made Joan tick. Although she hadn't seen her in years, she found herself silently defending Joan whenever anyone in the family alluded to her bizarre behavior. She thought of her as a wayward child and wanted her to come home.

The Harts arrived at Heathrow Airport and said their good-byes quickly as a limousine was waiting for Jeff. From London, Millicent and Allyson flew to Rome and then to Florence, the cultural haven not far from the magnificent spa at Montecatini.

Allyson was in awe of Italy. Where in the world but there can you find both cobbled roads where Roman chariots clattered and super highways with cosmopolitan contessas driving sports cars?

Millicent and Allyson agreed with Joan on one thing. The place was extraordinary. The Grand Hotel provided surroundings that would make the most overindulgent alcoholic or glutton swear off debauchery just for the special pleasure of their suggested ten-day cure. The marble halls were filled with movie stars, royalty, and the ordinary international super rich, all of whom sincerely believed that they needed a respite from the strains of their luxurious lives. The natural beauty of the region, with its blue Tuscan sky and the hills beyond, made physical fitness seem like a joy instead of a chore. And the curative powers of the waters of Montecatini have had considerable help from the elaborate amenities afforded the fortunate patrons. Every morning a basket of fresh-cut flowers is delivered to each guest. Exotic fruit drinks are served all day beneath the splendor of frescoed ceilings and rare marbles, along with divine potato chips you have to taste to believe, made daily by their own chefs. If the rooms at the Grand Hotel seem fit for a king . . . one may indeed have preceded the present guest. Caviar is the afternoon snack, as is smoked salmon flown in from Scotland. If anyone should suffer from boredom there is tennis on the grounds, swimming in the garden pool, or harness racing at the Montecatini track. If that isn't enough, there is excellent shopping at luxury boutiques in Montecatini or in Pisa or Florence. Even the exercise leotards, all bearing designer labels, are provided by the spa, and all exercises and treatments are watched over by a trained therapist or nurse. A hotel is a place to stay, but the Grand Hotel is a place to remember. It would be difficult not to luxuriate in this pampered existence where the languid days slip by as effortlessly as sunbeams.

Millicent was jarred by the incongruity of a health resort being this opulent. Not Allyson. She found it amusing that people who spent their lives in pursuit of relaxation and escape should be in need of more structured relaxing treatments. She compared it with the stark hospital room where she too had found escape.

Joan was not there when they arrived. She was at the hot springs, taking one of the four Montecatini alkaline-sulphate waters, which Millicent and Allyson found, all neatly bottled and labeled, in their lavishly appointed suite.

Joan returned, exhilarated and over-joyed that they had actually come. She swept into the room and greeted them with enthusiasm. She hugged and kissed them on each cheek and then circled the room, pointing out each exquisite decoration as though she had personally provided guest quarters for them in her own house.

Allyson had been nervous about her appearance, wondering what Joan would say to her. Would she remember the chubby, pretty little girl she once was and make some overly sympathetic remark about her looks? Worse yet, would she ask about the embarrassing details of the illness that had wasted away her body? But Joan hardly noticed at first and when she did, she mentioned it in a nonchalant way.

When she finally sat down, she looked at Allyson as though it suddenly dawned on her that the young girl had been sick. Her only comment was to the effect that Allyson was lucky not to have a weight problem and that if you had to get sick, wasn't anorexia the perfect illness.

Millicent wondered whether Joan was simply incapable of focusing on anyone else's problems or was being deliberately casual in an effort to be kind. She had to admit that Joan looked better than she had in years. *But that could be,* she said to herself, *due more to the fact that liquor was not allowed at the spa than to anything else. Whatever it was, the beauty that once was Joan, was again apparent.* But her sister's excessive enthusiasm was frightening. She had witnessed Joan's artificial euphoria too many times in the past. Her "perfect solutions" would suddenly drop with a thud. The cyclic mood could swing back to dissipation and depression. The feeling of well-being would be replaced by confusion. Joan's highs and lows came and went like the weather, expected but unpredictable.

Joan leaned forward and clasped her hands together like an eager child. "Millicent, before you do another thing you must meet Sanjay. You'll adore him as I do. We'll have cocktails together before dinner. Cocktails? Fancy fruit drinks in champagne glasses. Allyson child, you'll love him, too. He's so lean. He'll charm the pants off you, but don't be fooled by that. *Tout au contraire.* Underneath, he is deep, very deep."

"I'm sure he is, Joan," said Millicent. "I'm very anxious to meet him. But I think Allyson should rest first. She hasn't been too well."

Joan appeared delighted. "Then you've

brought her to the right place. She'll be cured in no time. I'll have Sanjay prescribe something for her. Millicent, you simply would not believe what that wonderful man knows about the human body. Allyson can rest while we plan my wedding."

"Joan." There was a long pause as Millicent awkwardly searched for the right words. "That's really why I'm here. I don't think there should be any wedding plans until we've had a chance to talk about . . . about why you're so anxious to get married again. Why, you hardly know this man."

"My dear sister, I am getting married because I'm crazy in love. What's there to talk about? I know everything about Sanjay that's important. He's very healthy." She looked at Millicent now with a look that blended confusion and hostility. "In other words, you didn't come just to attend my wedding. Millicent, did daddy tell you to stop me from marrying Sanjay? I just bet he gave you strict instructions to whisk me away. Did he?"

Millicent was quick to defend her father. "Father is only thinking about your welfare, Joan. He just doesn't want you to make another mistake by rushing into one more unhappy marriage."

Joan had acquired an indeterminable accent during her years of living abroad. She spoke English with a British sound, but not pure British. The accent was more of a blend of affectations, with French and Italian influences that were almost natural after such long usage. But it was definitely an upper-crust European voice. From it, a stranger would be hard put to determine Joan's origins, seldom guessing that she had been born and raised in the United States.

But now when she spoke, all affectations disappeared. It was pure American. "My welfare! What bull! Who are you trying to kid? *He's* worried about my welfare? Crap! John J. Bolt doesn't give a damn about other people's welfare. He's just worried about his pocketbook. No, I take that back. He's worried about losing his power over me. He can't stand not being in control."

"Joan, what are you saying? You're not making sense. Of course, he's worried about your welfare and your happiness. He always has been. And as for the money, you're completely wrong. He could have cut that off a long time ago if he wanted to control you. The money has never stopped coming, has it? And when he dies the rest of it will come to you, no matter what. Why are you so hard on him? Why are you so suspicious of his motives?"

Joan placed one hand on her hip and glared at Millicent. "Why have I lived in Europe all these years?"

"Why?" Millicent repeated. "I don't know why. I guess because you chose to. And don't forget that it was his money that allowed you to live the way you wanted to. Joan, you sound as if you've stayed away because of father. Don't use him as your excuse. You know perfectly well that he loves his family more than anything else in the world." She paused a moment, and the image of Martha Carrington came into her mind. "Sure, I know his faults. He's powerful and controlling, and of course, righteously moralistic about other people's behavior. But he does love us and wants the best for us and for mother. He always has. And Joan, you *were* his favorite child. You've got to admit that."

Joan heaved a deep sigh. "Yes, I was

his favorite child, but you are his favorite daughter."

Millicent looked at her sister intently, not understanding what she meant.

Both Millicent and Joan seemed to have forgotten that Allyson was in the room, quietly watching them with a subtle sense of pleasure.

"Listen to me, Joan," Millicent said almost pleadingly. "Father and mother are just . . . well, just naturally concerned about you, as I am."

Joan's voice quickly reverted to a casual cosmopolitan manner. "My dear sister, what in the world is there to be concerned about?" She said this as though she had lived the most normal of lives.

"You don't exactly call marrying five times a normal way of life. We have a great deal of concern."

Joan haughtily corrected her. "I have been married *only* four times. The fifth is the one you're trying to prevent. Or is it daddy? You never answered my question. Did daddy send you to stop me?"

Millicent hesitated. "He wanted me to come. But I wanted to be here, too. Because I don't want you to rush into something rash again that will . . ."

"That will mess up my life? Oh Millicent, Millicent, come now. We're not children with the rest of our lives ahead of us anymore. We're middle-aged women, much as I do everything in my power to deny it. Most of our lives are behind us. My mess is done. All I want is a few more years of love and fun. And not being alone. I can't live without a man. You have one. Why don't you think I should, too?"

If only Joan knew what was going on in her mind. Yes, she had a man, but not the one Joan thought she had. *Here I am preaching to my sister about not ruining her life and I am seriously considering messing up mine. And my husband's and my children's, not to mention the anguish I'll cause my parents. I've got plenty of principles and common sense for other people. Why am I so generous in giving away what I need most myself?*

It was the realization of Allyson's presence that broke up the conversation. "Dear child," said Joan, typically in character again. "You look positively exhausted. Without a moment's delay, I want you to drink a full glass of *tamerici* and have a proper rest before dinner." Quite adroitly and with a flourish, she opened a bottle that stood on the gilt-edged coffee table and poured a glass of the bitter stuff into a crystal glass. "Drink it down, love," Joan ordered as she handed Allyson the glass.

Allyson made a funny face and was about to protest. But Joan was adamant.

"Drink! This one is especially superb for brittle bones. Drink, and in one glorious gulp!"

Allyson took one long gulp and said, "My God, this stuff is putrid!"

Joan looked in the direction of the water that was trickling down Allyson's chin onto the oriental carpet. "The taste is unimportant for now. You'll grow to savor it. Finish it all. It is precious!"

Allyson screwed up her face and drank. She finished the water and clutched her throat, then she made a gulping sound of total misery. "Aunt Joan, if I die from poisoning, you realize this is going to be on your conscience."

"My conscience is not only clear, dear girl, it is nourished because I have the complete satisfaction of knowing that you are being purified. Poison! *Tout au contraire*. This shall wash the poison from your body that has been corrupted by God knows what! Now go lie down and take the bottle to bed with you. Finish it and prepare for the revelation of your young life."

Then Joan turned to Millicent. "Cocktails at seven and dinner at eight. Sanjay will receive you then, after his evening meditation."

Allyson stretched out on the bed and finished the bottle of bitter saltwater to please Joan and for curiosity as to its effects. Then she slept for an hour. When she awoke she felt completely rested and somewhat euphoric, as though she had indeed been given a magic potion.

Folding doors in her room opened to a balcony and a tranquil Italian vista of a brick courtyard with a bright mosaic of plants in terra-cotta pots and a medley of spring flowers. A small decorative fountain in the center spashed mellifluous sounds. Allyson sat on the balcony in the late afternoon sun, while Millicent slept in the other bedroom. With analytical reasoning that had become finely honed through her many psychiatric sessions with Michael Lyons, she dismissed the idea of miracle saltwaters and attributed the unusual effect to the power of suggestion. Not haveing met Sanjay, she wondered if that was his power, too — the ability to manipulate vulnerable people like Joan with hypnotic suggestions. Already she did not trust him. No matter. It was all an engaging interlude in her young life, one that had been dull and depressing with so much introspection. Allyson liked the diversion.

But the self-contemplation continued. Her thoughts turned to Michael Lyons, because she missed the brash but caring doctor who was making her see that pain is no excuse for withdrawing from life. He certainly had not.

In their last session before she left for Italy, Michael had talked about himself, which was unusual. He rarely mentioned his background to Allyson. When she would ask subtle questions and try to pry information from him out of curiosity, he would dismiss her inquiries with, "I'm the psychiatrist and you're the patient, so don't try to exert your control by getting me to identify with you."

But in this last session, he did reveal something of his history. Allyson was experiencing acute separation anxiety in that last meeting, and she was frightened of leaving and losing her psychiatrist's constant support. She doubted whether she would be able to cope in a strange environment with unfamiliar people. Out of anxiety and fear, she began to cry. Dr. Lyons was sympathetic. For the first time, he told her of his own fears and somehow pieces of his life unfolded.

He told her that he was the only child of German parents who had survived the horrors of a concentration camp. Michael Lyons was loved and indulged by these two overprotective people who felt guilty about just being alive when their entire families had perished. They spoiled him way beyond their means and he grew up in a suburb of Chicago as an undisciplined teenager and a bright but indifferent college student. The motorcycle accident that left him a paraplegic was the culmination of a succession of wild and willful acts that had always made him the center of attention.

Just as the accident changed his physical life forever, the year he spent in the hospital also changed his goals. Eventually, he gained a purpose. And it was his meek, usually spiritless father who gave him the will not only to live but to make a fulfilling life for himself. Every day his modest, long-suffering father would come to the hospital after closing up his dry-cleaning store and tell Michael, who wanted to die, of the atrocities he had endured in the concentration camp at Auschwitz. Haunting and horrible memories that had never been talked about before, merely alluded to. Only then did Michael learn of the actual terrors of his parents' lives in Europe that had been buried in their souls. And only later could he understand what allowed his father to reveal that which he had deliberately kept hidden from his son. It was as if his father was telling him: "If I could survive, then you can, too."

Once when Michael screamed out in anger at his own condition and wished himself dead, his father stood over him and said, "I shall not let you die. Whatever strength I have left is yours. Whatever hope I have, take from me. You must live, otherwise there is no purpose in my having lived."

And at that moment of reflection, Allyson realized that she had been getting her strength and hope from

Michael Lyons.

The Persian-carpeted lounge was filled with perfectly dressed people, all suntanned and glowing, confident that they were buying more good years of health and youth.

Joan, looking elegant in flowing blue chiffon, was sitting on a red satin settee and drinking *tettuccio* water. She waved them toward her with a dramatic gesture, her hand with the glass sweeping the air. Not a drop spilled. "Millicent, Allyson dear, come join me," she called out. "I've ordered marvelous fruit juices for you. Sanjay will be here shortly."

They sat down and gazed around at the opulent setting and the magnificent-looking people who were milling about.

"Did you rest well?" asked Joan. "Oh dear child, you do look so much better. I for one think you should stop dieting. But you know what the late Mrs. Paley used to say. 'No one can ever be too rich or too thin.' Well, that's exactly how she died, poor thing — too rich and too thin. Millicent, you must shape up. Women who have been married to the same man all their lives tend to let themselves go.

Darling, with a gorgeous husband like yours, you must learn to keep fit. Mother certainly knew that. Oh, but you were never like mother, were you, dear? So I've made arrangements for you to start the cure tomorrow, *coûte que coûte.* I shall foot the bill. You have appointments for the sauna and Scotch showers and stretching on the Swedish bars, and an herbal oil massage, and of course, you'll go to the *tettuccio* pavilion for the waters and . . ."

Millicent held up her hands. "Joan, please, hold it. Don't make any plans for me. I didn't come here to restore my health. I came just to be with you. And all that activity sounds exhausting."

"Well, I wouldn't mind taking 'the cure' as long as I'm here," said Allyson. "It might be fun."

Millicent looked at Allyson with surprise. She never thought her daughter would be willing to expose her body to strangers.

"Good girl," said Joan, turning her attention to Allyson. "I'll sign you up for everything, cost what it may, including Tai Ch'i. But, of course, only after Sanjay analyzes your body and determines your reserves. Then he'll map out a complete regimen. Oh, my God. You'll be divinely healthy!" Joan said enthusiastically.

But Allyson suddenly lost some of her enthusiasm for the cure. "Does he have to examine me?"

"Only the mind, dear, only your mind. Sanjay has the uncanny power of sensing one's physical needs immediately. His sensitivity is extraordinary. Believe me, he will be *in touch* with your entire being the moment he meets you."

"Joan, Allyson hasn't been well," said Millicent, as though it was necessary to remind her sister. "I really don't think your friend, uh, Sanjay, is acquainted enough with Allyson's health problems to prescribe for her. Without realizing it, of course, he could do her more harm than good."

"Nonsense! Sanjay wil infuse her very marrow with unbelievable feelings of well-being. I can't begin to tell you about all the magical qualities Sanjay possesses. His perception is unfailing. You'll see. And there he is! Oh, Millicent, isn't he glorious?"

Sanjay walked toward them with a slow, stately stride. Although of medium height, he gave the impression of being tall. Like a fine-spun dancer, his body was slender but not sparse. He wore an immaculate white tunic with pearl buttons and straight silk trousers without a crease or a wrinkle. On his head was a white turban in the style of an Indian rajah. It was a handsome face, bronzed as that of his countrymen, but his features were those of an English aristocrat. The white of his outfit made his dark skin glisten. The dazzling sight was not lost on Millicent or Allyson. Nor on the other people in the room. Despite the fascinating congregation of famous people at the Grand Hotel, heads turned when Sanjay entered.

When Sanjay joined them, he made a slight bow, extending his hands, one to Millicent and one to Allyson, at the same time. They both concentrated on the spiritualistic glow in his penetrating gray eyes. Joan watched with rapt interest, because she knew that Millicent was sensing the strange kind of dignity that surrounded Sanjay.

Happiness, for many, is getting approval. For Joan, it had always been that way. Now it was public admiration that she needed. Sanjay provided it by openly showing that he was attached to her. She basked in the envy of the other women at the spa.

He introduced himself, conscious of the effect he was producing. "I am Sanjay. I have looked forward to this moment of meeting. Mrs. Hart, pay attention to your dreams. And, Allyson Hart, remember that you must have the pull of discontent to become something. Have you enjoyed your beverages?"

He moved toward Joan and kissed her hand, while his eyes made contact with hers. "Shall we go in for dinner, my dearest?"

As he thought proper, Sanjay offered Millicent his arm, and they walked into the dining room together, Allyson and Joan following close behind.

The dining room looked as if it belonged in a palace. Even the scale of the room was palatial. The grandeur seemed to come from another century. The profusion of gold and silver and crystal sent off sparkling facets in all directions. Strains of lilting music drifted from a platform that was almost hidden by tall palms. Enough waiters were at attention to see to every guest individually. Flame red roses stood with limpid beauty in Waterford vases in the center of each dining table next to crystal decanters of the famous waters. Porthault linen covered the tables. This splendid room and its very fine accompaniments provided a backdrop for the most opulent of life-styles. The food was not only absolutely superb but beautifully served and presented as well.

Millicent had been totally unprepared for her reaction to Sanjay. Listening to him during dinner, she thought: *How objective he is, how extremely sensible. His ideas are like shooting stars, bright and illuminating.*

Allyson was equally charmed, more like entranced, by this young, cultured Indian who seemed to possess the wisdom of the ages and the calm of a man who is completely at peace with himself. He talked of many subjects with ease and familiarity. But Allyson spoke, too. For his noble face always reflected appreciation of anything she added to the conversation. During dinner, she acted as though her mistrust of him had disappeared.

The dinner turned into almost a mystical event, and Allyson and Millicent talked about the experience long into the night. They admitted to each other that they had been spellbound by Sanjay and were more than curious about his background.

Oddly enough, the next few days were exactly as Joan had planned. With Sanjay's constant guidance, Millicent and Allyson engaged in the traditional spa activities. Although exhausted at the end of each day, they felt healthy and invigorated. And the bitter therapeutic waters became almost palatable.

They looked forward to their evenings with Joan and Sanjay; she, animated and vivacious; he, serene and philosophical, and noncommittal about his past. Polite questions about India or his background received vague answers. Somehow this only added to the mystery of his charm at first. But Allyson was not completely captivated by Sanjay. She remained suspicious of his motives and kept reminding Millicent of their purpose in coming to Italy. She urged her to talk to Joan alone, to persuade her to put off the marriage until she knew more about Sanjay.

But Millicent was seldom alone with

Joan. And when she was, and would try to initiate serious talk about the forthcoming marriage, Sanjay would unexpectedly appear and offer advice on their health with praise for their progress. She could not bring herself to seriously disturb the unaccustomed and pervasive feelings of well-being she felt coming from Joan. So after a few days, she said nothing more about postponing the marriage.

In the midst of the whirlwind of activity at Montecatini, Millicent found she missed Roger very much, especially when she lay in her bed at night, alone with her thoughts. *Absence does make the heart grow even fonder,* she mused. So many of the agonizing doubts and reservations about their relationship were forgotten as she realized that it was possible for her to love this man very deeply if only she had the courage to live life purposefully.

The "ten-day cure" at the Grand Hotel went by like a delightful holiday. The purpose of the trip to Montecatini was quite lost, consigned to oblivion. Millicent found herself caught up in Joan's enthusiasm, and behaving like a loving parent, she could not bear to spoil her sister's newfound happiness. She was also reluctant to break the feeling of closeness that had developed between them. She told herself that Joan adored Sanjay and he was apparently good for her. Wasn't Joan healthier and more content than she had been for years? She had stopped drinking. And Sanjay seemed truly concerned about her. Millicent wanted to believe that this marriage would work out.

On an afternoon at the end of their stay, Millicent and Allyson sat on the balcony watching the blazing sun set brilliantly over the hills of Tuscany. It had been an exciting day after a wonderful excursion to Florence, the treasure chest of Italian art. Millicent had shown Allyson Michelangelo's celebrated statue of David at the Accademia and the other Renaissance masterpieces throughout Florence. They sat in awe-inspiring silence, thinking of the beauty of the past and the peace it brought to them at this moment. But Allyson broke the reverential spell they were absorbed in by voicing reservations about why Sanjay would be anxious to marry Joan.

"After all, mother, he's got to be around twenty years younger than she is. And he's so handsome and brilliant, why he could have any woman he wanted. Do you think it's because he knows she's going to come into a bundle?"

"Oh, I don't think so, Allyson. From what he's told us, it sounds as if he comes from a very prominent family in India, and wealthy too."

"Mother, he's told us nothing. You're only assuming that because of the way he acts, because of the aura he's created about himself."

Millicent did not want to agree with Allyson's doubts. "But he's highly educated and extremely knowledgeable about everything."

"That doeesn't mean anything. Poor people are smart, too. And charming and clever and cunning," she added cynically. "I just can't believe that somebody like Sanjay could be that crazy about Aunt Joan."

Guiltily, Millicent immediately thought Allyson was referring to the difference in their ages. "Why darling, lots of younger men fall in love with older women. It's become perfectly acceptable. And you must admit that Joan is still very attractive, and when she's feeling good, like now, she's extremely charming herself.

Middle-aged people can still be very desirable. And as I said, it's not uncommon for a young man to fall in love with an older woman." Millicent said this with conviction, as though she were pleading a cause of her generation.

Allyson was still very skeptical. "But this is no ordinary middle-aged woman marrying a younger man because she's so damned flattered that he's attracted to her. Or that he's marrying her because, well, maybe because he's looking for a mother figure. Aunt Joan's looking for a fantasy life with a gorgeous swami who will take complete charge of her life, and most likely her bank account. Sanjay is not your run-of-the-mill young lover. He's almost a mythical figure, like a character in a romantic novel."

Millicent was not surprised by Allyson's skepticism, but she still said, "I thought you liked Sanjay. You certainly acted like you did."

"It's not that I don't like him," said Allyson. "He's so full of charm, how could you help but be attracted to him? But I still have this awful feeling that we've been taken in by . . . I don't exactly know what."

She then became vehement. "Nobody really knows anything about Sanjay except that he has some rare fascination that's unbelievably powerful. To me, that's frightening. It's like he's cast a spell on all of us. Really! And I don't mind admitting that at first he had me mesmerized. But I sure wouldn't want to marry him or let anyone I love marry him. I think the whole thing is very scary."

"Allyson, I do have my own reservations about Sanjay, but I think you're exaggerating the mystery of him. Just because we don't know about his background doesn't mean he's immoral or unethical or after Joan for some fiendish reason. He's just very different. He's from another culture that we are totally unfamiliar with."

Allyson seemed perturbed. "So what you're saying is that you think it's OK for them to get married now? You sure have changed your mind since we've been here."

Millicent sighed. Her voice sounded doubtful. "Yes, I guess I have changed my mind somewhat. But it's more than that. I just don't think I have the right to tell Joan how to live her life. If it's another mistake, well then, we'll just have to deal with it. But I hope with all my heart that it isn't. It's just that she's so happy and content, and if I try to break up this marriage that she seems to want so much, what do I have to offer her in its place? What do I tell her to do? Go roam around Europe and find more young men to keep her from being lonely? She would very likely start drinking again and be worse off then before. And she would probably go ahead and marry him anyway, even if I did everything possible to discourage her, and then where would our relationship be? She'd be angry at me for interfering in what she truly believes will finally be the right marriage for her. How can I deny her this happiness, even if it may not last?" Millicent paused and put her hand under her chin in contemplation. "Allyson, what would you do if you were in my place?"

Allyson did not hesitate. "I would take her home, back to the States. I would get her away from here as fast as possible. The whole place is unreal, and so is that smooth Indian. Good God, mother! When she wakes up from this dream world she's in, she's going to come face-to-face with a nightmare. This won't be just another rotten marriage. It could be her final disaster. Aunt Joan's too gullible, too trusting. That man is not good for her. There's something awfully sinister about him. Don't you see it? How can you let her destroy herself?"

"How can I stop her?" Millicent's heart ached as she looked at her daughter. "Allyson dear, you know better than anyone that, for whatever reasons, some people are self-destructive and it takes a miracle to save them."

Nevertheless, Millicent did attempt to persuade Joan to give the marriage more thought and return to Washington. She knew it was a futile gesture, trying to convince Joan to wait, because she knew exactly what was in Joan's mind before she expressed it.

"Give it more thought? Ridiculous! I don't want to lose Sanjay. He's the best thing that's happened to me in a long, long time," Joan told her. "I want to be eternally under his care."

Millicent tried to be convincing. "If he really loves you, Joan, he'll wait. A few weeks, a month, can't make that much difference."

Joan looked at her sister with astonishment. "Can't it! Just time enought for one of those love-starved socialites to get their hands on him. Who do you think comes to this spa! Oh no, as soon as Sanjay makes the arrangements, we *shall* be married. The sooner the better."

"Then when will it be?" Millicent asked with resignation.

"Soon. I was hoping we could be married this week, before you leave. Oh, I do want you to be at my wedding, Millicent. You haven't been at many of my weddings, have you? Sanjay has to return to India, only for a few days, to take care of some kind of business and to, well . . . to clear the marriage with his family. Indian tradition and all that, you know, getting the family's permission. Just a formality. Then we'll get married next week in Florence at the most exquisite little church that's centuries old. Millicent, say you approve, give me your blessing."

"Does it really matter to you?" Millicent asked plaintively.

"Of course it does," said Joan. "You are my very closest family. Except daddy."

"Then come home with me and discuss it with mother and father," said Millicent, almost pleading. "Why, you can even bring Sanjay. Let them meet him first. There's always time to get married."

Joan became sullen and determined. "No," she said. "There is no time. And daddy would never approve of Sanjay. They are much too much alike. Really! They are. You wouldn't think so, but they are very similar in some rather peculiar way. Millicent, that's an awfully bad idea. Daddy must not meet Sanjay. Not now. Perhaps later, when we have a child."

Millicent looked at her sister with shock and clasped her hand to her chest. "Joan, what are you saying? A child? You're almost fifty years old."

Joan gave a bitter laugh. "Well, it's not completely impossible. It does happen, especially when one is in good health. And I am *not* fifty and won't be for *years*." she said caustically. Her mood changed suddenly, and her eyes grew strangely bright. "Millicent, you do want me to be happy, don't you?"

"Of course I do, Joan. That's all I want for you. You know that."

"Then give me your blessing," Joan

entreated.

"Do you want me to stay for the wedding?" Millicent asked, thinking that might be what Joan really wanted.

"No, that's not necessary. It's just as well that you don't. Too much fuss and bother. It will be more intimate without family. Just Sanjay and I."

Millicent was confused. She did not understand. For some reason or other, Joan had completely changed her mind. But now, what seemed more important than Joan's future with this unusual man was her present state of well-being.

"Then I do give you my blessing," said Millicent. "I can only hope that you will both be very happy, and blessed."

Joan passed her hand over her forehead and smiled. She thought for a moment. Then she said, "Isn't Sanjay absolutely divine?"

Millicent heaved a deep sigh. What was the use of saying anything except exactly what Joan wanted to hear. "Yes," she answered slowly. "Sanjay is divine."

Chapter 26

Going home was filled with a familiar wave of apprehension. Speculating about her future, Millicent wondered about Roger's place in her life, and she knew that the time would soon come to make a decision.

Also, there was a sense of failure. Little was accomplished in Italy as far as straightening out Joan's life went. Millicent would have to tell her father he was about to acquire another son-in-law, one more foreign than he had ever imagined. She felt she had done nothing more than sanction another irrational phase of human folly, which had become the pattern of Joan's existence. And she worried about Allyson's reaction.

Allyson still believed that they were leaving Joan in the hands of not only a persuasive charmer but an unpredictable menacing force. During the flight back to the States, they talked about Millicent's predicament. Although her own battle with irrationality and confusion was still painfully close, Allyson realized that relatives are often in the least favorable position to save members of their family. Joan did not seek advice, nor did she want it. She wanted approval, and that's what she got. Benefiting from advice requires more insight and understanding than giving it. Allyson recalled her conversation with Dr. Lyons. So many times he had repeated the old maxim. "One of the most important signs of maturity is the realization and acceptance of the fact that no one will ever fully understand." She did not understand Joan. She was not sure she understood her mother's actions lately. And she was certain that no one understood her own mental alienation. For sure, no one would understand her feelings toward Michael Lyons, least of all him.

Roger called as soon as Millicent returned. "I can't begin to tell you how much I missed you," he said. "I felt as if we were the ones who should have been in Italy together."

"I missed you too . . . very much," Millicent admitted, now in a reflective mood. "And I had the same fantasy. The two of us in some gloriously romantic place like Italy. Oh, Roger, it's beautiful there and meant for people who . . . who mean something special to each other. The two of us . . . it would have been nice," she said dreamily.

"Millicent, if not Italy, would you consider a weekend in Bermuda?" he asked anxiously, as though plans had been whirling around in his mind for weeks.

She considered the idea only for a moment. "Roger, how is that possible? How could I get away for a whole weekend?"

"I don't know," he said, then added, "By extending it into weeks or even more and perhaps . . . making it into a honeymoon. Then it could be Italy or any other place in the world." Roger was finding it difficult to hide his feelings.

There was an embarrassed pause. *Am I ready for that?* she wondered aloud, knowing the answer could only come from her own heart.

Spring is a short season in Washington. Already the sticky, humid summer air was moving in. Millicent arrived at Dr. Bromley's Georgetown office feeling uncomfortably warm and nervous. Dr. Frances Bromley seemed unaffected by the weather. The moods of her patients affected her more than the changing seasons did. She sensed a change in Millicent since she had seen her before her trip to Italy. She was not familiar with this new attitude of responsibility for Joan.

"Why do you feel responsible for your sister's mixed-up life?" the analyst asked.

A shadow crossed Millicent's face when she answered. "Because someone has to feel responsible."

"Let that someone be your mother or your father or her former husbands or even Joan herself. Already, it seems to me, you have taken on more than your share of people to be responsible for. Now you want to accept full responsibility for your sister's eccentric behavior. Why?"

Millicent wanted to explain, but she didn't know if she could adequately interpret the change in her feelings about Joan. "It's as if my father, who has always been like the Rock of Gibraltar and the most powerful force in our lives, is relinquishing his position."

"And you feel you have to assume his role?" Dr. Bromley asked, not fully understanding Millicent's reasoning.

Millicent looked perplexed herself. "No, it's not quite that *I have to*. It's as if the control *is* in my hands. I don't think I'm putting it in the right words. But it is a different feeling, one that I've never had before, and it's more than a sense of guilt about my sister." She paused, looked around, and then went on. "It's as if she needs taking care of, and I never fully realized how desperate her need is. It's also as if I'm ready for it, though I still don't really understand her."

"Are you saying, Millicent, that you are experiencing a change in yourself rather than a change in your family, your sister?" Dr. Bromley prodded.

Millicent hesitated before answering. "All I know is that the relationship between Joan and me has changed and it feels . . . it feels right. What will come of it, I can't say, because I certainly did not accomplish my purpose in going to Italy. But the rift between us, I hope, is over. Though I don't understand her misery, I sense it. For the first time, I can feel for her."

Millicent became strangely silent. Then the old feeling of guilt that she wore like a crown of sorrow seemed to return as she said, "I just wish I knew why Joan is so intent on living a life of constant contradictions. She went to the spa to restore herself, then she falls in love with a man who I don't think is any more ready than her other husbands to offer her a commitment. And I couldn't persuade her to even postpone the marriage. She lives such a disordered life." Then she sat quietly, thinking of her own situation with Roger.

Dr. Bromley looked at her carefully. "Millicent, my dear. There is sweet and sour and good and evil. But life, I'm sorry to say, is not that clear-cut. It is a jumble of disorder, of disharmony. And you are trying to make order out of confusion by holding yourself accountable for everyone's scattered parts. It won't work."

Dr. Bromley waited for a response, and when none came she sat back and changed her tone abruptly. "Do you love Roger?"

Millicent was startled by the question, which seemed to have no relevance to what they were discussing. She moved uneasily in her chair. Her answer was strange: "I think so. I loved him in Italy."

"Then you do not love your husband?" asked Dr. Bromley sharply, as though she wanted that fact well established.

Millicent looked confused, then disturbed, by the direct question. "It's not that I don't love him . . . it's . . ." She paused and took a deep breath. "I did love Jeffrey. I truly did. What I feel for Roger is . . . not the same. Loving a man at this time of life is . . . is so very different."

Dr. Bromley continued to question her. "Can you accept the consequences of leaving your husband? Can you put up with the anger and guilt you'll be subjected to?"

Her face flushed. "How can I know that now?" she responded, as though the ambivalence were pulling her apart.

"Do you feel that the rest of your time here on earth is sacred?"

Millicent was again bewildered. Then she said, "Yes, I believe that."

"Then don't turn away from it. Stop thinking and start feeling. Face life honestly and accept the risk. My dear Millicent, there is no safe place to hide, not even behind guilt and responsibility. Make a choice and try to live with it. Lower your expectations. There are no certified guarantees in life. Not yours, not mine. There are only choices. But whatever choice you do make, be sure it's a real one. A fantasy in Italy or Bermuda or even in a garden cannot sustain you for life. Sooner or later, all dreams fade away."

Allyson was in Dr. Lyon's office, feeling very awkward. This was her first visit in three weeks. Nothing seemed to be forthcoming. The continuity from daily contact had been broken. Dr. Lyons attributed it to that fact.

"It's like starting over," he explained. "You have to get warmed up and begin again. A unique relationship develops between a psychiatrist and a patient, especially when they are in touch on almost a daily basis. An interruption of even a few weeks decelerates the momentum. The patient puts on the mental brakes. You've had time to mull over all the private things that have been said here and wonder if too much has been revealed. You have second thoughts about what's been going on in this room, don't you, Allyson?"

Allyson bit her lower lip and then spoke slowly. "That may be your psychological assessment, but it's not mine."

"Then let's hear yours, professor," he said with a bite, as he wheeled his chair closer to hers.

She said nothing, and he waited as was his custom. Michael Lyons stared at her face, which was turned to the window. He knew she would speak eventually.

"It's not the same anymore," she said, without looking around.

"No, it isn't. I just told you that. You've closed your mind to me. You're afraid. But it will open again. Now the rhythm is irregular. It will take time and practice to get it going again. We'll work on it. Meanwhile, tell me about Italy and that snazzy place you went to while I was working my butt off. What did you do there? What's your mother's sister like? Tell me about the 'beautiful people,' and then we'll go from the ridiculous to the sublime."

Allyson told him. Fragments, anecdotes, descriptions of Montecatini and Joan and Sanjay. All about the frivolity and fantasy that the place represented to fulfill a psychological need.

"Sounds like a fool's paradise," said Michael Lyons with a big smile.

"It is," said Allyson. "But the man my

aunt is marrying, or has already married, is no fool."

"No, probably not. The Indian man sounds like a pretty smart cookie. But that's a problem you can do very little about. Let's get back to you."

Dr. Lyons went on to ask her about her thoughts when she was away. "What did you think about while you were hobnobbing with the idle rich in their garden of Eden?" he said with light sarcasm.

She sat silently and considered the question. Then she said, in a voice that was barely audible, "You."

"Me?"

"Yes, you," she repeated, somewhat embarrassed.

"Well, at least you acted foolish in the right place," said Michael Lyons, trying to turn her response into a joke. Now he was feeling awkward.

"Seriously, Allyson," he went on, "what went through your mind while all this business with your aunt and her boyfriend was going on?"

"You," she said again, more in control.

This time, the psychiatrist turned away. For a minute he lost his composure and flushed, realizing where all this was leading.

It was Allyson who finally broke the silence. "Michael, you might as well know what I know. I am . . ." she lowered her head slightly and coughed. "I'm in love with you." She paused and looked up. "But please . . . please don't give me a psychiatric explanation of why I am or tell me that it's natural for a patient to fall in love with her psychiatrist or that it's some form of transference that always happens in analysis. I really am in love with you. Not as a patient but as a woman. And don't tell me that we'll work it through and that I'll get over it. That's not the way it is."

Allyson waited for him to make some flip remark, as he usually did whenever she got this intense about something he disagreed with. He would throw in a joke with a little well-placed sarcasm and get her back on track to the feelings she should be talking about. She waited for him to take her from the ridiculous to the sublime.

When he said nothing, she interpreted his silence as embarrassment. Allyson sat uncomfortably for a few minutes, rubbing her hands in her lap. Then she came straight to the point. "Michael, I didn't know it for certain until I was away from you. I didn't just miss you," she paused, "I longed for you. I did a hundred other things, but you never left my mind." She stopped and sighed several times. "I guess this places you in a pretty difficult position. I'm sorry. Sort of puts an end to our professional relationship, doesn't it? I don't think I should come back anymore."

She looked at him with her large, sad eyes and then uncurled her legs from under her body. She started to get up and leave.

Dr. Michael Lyon's pulse was beating double time. Without turning, he spoke to her in a voice that was wavering: "If you don't come back, I'll . . . I'll come and get you . . . because I can't think of my life without you."

Allyson stopped and reacted with surprise.

He turned around and faced her. Tears were falling onto his beard. "I love you too, kiddo, and that's no psychiatric crap. So I guess you're right, we'd better end the professional relationship." There was a poignant quality to his plea. "But how about starting a more personal one?"

Michael opened his burly arms and Allyson, wide-eyed and elated, rushed into them.

Chapter 27

Remembering the words of Dr. Bromley, Millicent felt troubled. It had been easy to love Roger in Italy and tell herself that she wanted to spend the rest of her life with him. But now she had doubts as to how to put the whole thing in motion. She started to laugh. All of a sudden it seemed funny to be worrying about how to leave your husband and go off with another man.

What if she actually did get a divorce? What do you do? she asked herself. *What do other people do?* she wondered. *Do you write a note? Do you set the scene with soft lights and candles, like a proposal of marriage, only in reverse? If it actually came to a separation, how would she break the news to Jeff? Is there a special etiquette or proper words that simplify the whole ugly business? When would she tell her father, the children? How would they react? No one would understand. Perhaps she should talk to someone who's been through this. No, this is ridiculous,* she told herself. *Dr. Bromley's right. You don't make a choice between fantasy and reality. But what,* she said aloud, *is the* real *part of my life?*

Even Roger did not fully understand her misgivings. For him, this was no fantasy. "Millicent darling, we've talked about your qualms, all your doubts and mine, too. I know we can live with them, but not without each other. I've made a soul-searching decision, and it's not impulsive. I've given it a lot of thought. I want you to seriously consider marrying me. If not now, then later. I can wait. What I can't do is go on this way not knowing whether we have a future together. I've got to have some hope."

Millicent felt truly scared, as though she were being backed into a corner. And yet she knew Roger was not doing that intentionally. He was a dear and patient man who only wanted to hold on to the happiness he had found.

"Roger, why do you want me when I'm

not sure what I really want?"

"How can I answer that, Millicent? All I can say is that I feel . . . deep down inside . . . you want me as much as I want you."

They were sitting in the park across from Roger's office. People were milling all about on this warm sunny day. But Millicent was totally unaware of her surroundings. Her entire being was involved in searching for the truth.

"Roger, if I were to . . ." she could hardly say the words, "one day, marry you, think how many lives would be turned upside down. You have a wife, and I don't for a minute underestimate how hard it will be on her, but I have a whole family to consider, besides a husband. So many dependent people. And they're all going to be very angry and terribly hurt by this decision. But most of all, they'll be shocked."

Roger sat on the bench with his hands clenched between his outstretched legs. "I know that, Millicent, but the task doesn't become easier if it's done with reluctance. We're in it together, for the rest of our lives, and we'll just have to accept their hurt and anger and criticism and whatever else they throw at us. Sure it's a terrible risk. Don't think I don't know that. I knew it the minute I fell in love with you. But isn't a lifetime of love worth the risk?"

The "risk" that Dr. Bromley presented and Roger affirmed was now upon her. No more contemplation and "what ifs." No more giving in to pangs of conscience while she wallowed in indecision. She made up her mind to talk to Jeff that night.

Their marriage had to be reevaluated. Either she would have a different kind of marriage with the same man or newfound fulfillment. *I'm not asking for total devotion,* she told herself, *but I can't go on with a loveless marriage. And I can't go on being unfaithful to Jeff, and to myself. As for Roger, it's not fair to hold him with vague promises any longer.* She would have it out with Jeff, calmly and maturely, and they would come to an understanding.

It was a perfect evening for telling your husband to either love you or leave you, she thought with irony, as she waited in the library for Jeff to come home. Allyson was out, where she did not know, but she wasn't worried. Allyson seemed positively radiant and would only say that she had "plans" and would tell her about them later. Homer and Regina were off for the evening. Both Cory and Johnny had called to say they would finish classes next week and would then decide on their summer plans.

She waited in the library, nervously going over and over in her mind what she would say. She was well rehearsed. All kinds of imaginary reactions had been anticipated, and she was prepared. She was prepared for anger or indifference. She was prepared to reveal her affair with Roger and for Jeff to confirm his with Cynthia Ross, and she even anticipated the excuses and accusations that might come out of the confessions. She was also prepared to rush into Jeffrey's arms and vow to restore their shaky marriage.

Jeff walked in the door and slammed it hard, making known his state of agitation. "Mill, I'm home," he called out. "God, but I'm bushed. I feel like I'm going to explode. Fix me a scotch while I change, and make it a big one. This has been some kind of day!"

I certainly picked the right time for a calm discussion, Millicent thought with irony, somewhat amused at herself. *This will really* finish *his day. My timing is off as usual. But there will never be a good time for something like this.* So she fixed him a double scotch and then decided on one for herself, as fortification.

Jeff came into the library in casual clothes, gave her a quick kiss on the cheek and grabbed the drink. He took a long swallow before plopping down on the leather couch. The pressure of a miserable day was written all over his face.

"It started off rotten, and it ended rotten," he said, as though he had been cursed.

"Listen to this," he went on. "That whole English deal is about to go up in smoke. The Weckworth brothers have been wheeling and dealing behind our backs with a syndicate in New York, and I have to go back to London tomorrow and try to straighten it out. We've already invested a fortune in speculation. On top of that, we were hit with a lawsuit because of that building that collapsed in Leesburg last year. The one where the construction workers were hurt. We already established that the subcontractor was at fault. But now the subcontractor filed a third-party complaint against us, claiming that we were at least contributorily negligent and demanding contributions if the verdict should go against them on the principal complaint. As if that wasn't enough, your 'good old buddy' Martha Carrington spoke to reporters, against my specific instructions not to, about the case and intimated that the subcontractor, the cement company, is a wholly owned subsidiary of Bolt Constructon, which makes us liable. That woman is Attila the Hun! She doesn't know what the hell she's talking about. And now we've been put in the compromising position of having to deny it. I swear, I think she's getting senile. When I told J. J., he nearly hit the roof. You know how he is about bad publicity. Well, I guess that's one where only the lawyers are going to come out winners. We'll probably have to settle big to keep it from dragging on."

Millicent listened impassively, without interrupting.

Jeffrey yawned and then sighed. "Hon, make me another drink, will you, just a light one. Then we'll have dinner. I need a little more time to unwind. And tell

Homer to pack me a bag for tomorrow. Just enough for a day or two in London. It's going to be a quick trip this time. Either a yes or no from those two horse traders. And when my secretary calls, tell her to have the car here at seven-thirty and have all the papers ready. We'll stop by the office on the way to Dulles and pick them up. How was your day, Mill? Not like mine I bet. Gee, it's good to have you back. You never told me what happened in Italy. Did you disengage your sister?"

Millicent went to bar. As she was fixing Jeff another drink, she said to herself: *Now. Just let it out before he starts in again. No more distractions. This is it.*

She stood there with her hand on the glass, concentrating on the row of liquor bottles. "Jeff, there's something I have to talk to you about. I'm sorry it comes at a time when you're having so many problems at the office and just before leaving for London. I didn't think you would have to go back so soon. But we have to talk . . . about our marriage . . . because I simply cannot go on this way any longer. We've been living like perfect strangers and at the same time acting as though nothing is wrong when everything is wrong." Suddenly her voice became shrill. "Yes, whether you admit it or not, our marriage is a shambles!" She caught herself and her voice became calmer. "I know about Cynthia Ross, and before you deny it or offer excuses, I have something to tell you. I've been seeing someone myself, a man I think I could be . . . happy with. A man who says he loves me very much and Jeff . . . I need that love. I needed it from you, but if you can't give it to me then . . . then, God, I can't believe I'm saying all this." Millicent paused a second and gulped. "Jeff, isn't there some way we can talk about what we both want out of life and come to an understanding? I guess what I'm trying to get you to say is . . . is that you still love me and don't want me to leave."

She waited for Jeff's reaction. A shout, a gasp, a plea, even a nasty scene with uncontrolled fury, anything, before she had the courage to turn around and face either his wrath or his affirmation of love. She wondered if Jeff could tell how hard her heart was beating. Why did this dignified silence seem to last forever? She turned around. "Jeff, you know it hasn't been good between us for a long time. Let's talk about it, something we should have done years ago. Jeff, say something. Why . . ."

Millicent stared in disbelief. Jeff was stretched prone on the couch, sound asleep. The almost empty glass lay on the carpet, below his outstretched hand. Slowly, drops of scotch trickled out. His mouth was partly opened as he drifted down the tides of sleep. He started to snore, very loud and very strident.

Millicent walked over and stared down at him. "You never heard a word I said. You don't even know that I'm thinking of leaving you." She picked up the glass, more from habit than from concern about the carpet.

Upstairs, she packed his suitcase and put in on the hall bench, where Homer always placed his luggage.

The phone rang and it was Miss French, the secretary, awaiting instructions. Millicent gave her the message as though it was the only important thing on her mind.

Then she took a blanket from the linen closet and went downstairs. Jeff was deep in sleep. She removed his shoes and placed his dangling right arm across his chest. As she covered him with the blanket, he let out a loud snore and it startled her. For a moment there was a strange smile on her lips. Somehow, she thought bitterly, he always gets his way.

With a weary sigh, she walked out of the library and went upstairs to bed.

Chapter 28

The day was just about to begin. Sitting in her dressing room, Millicent heard the crunch of gravel on the driveway. She looked out the window and saw the company limousine pull up. Moments later she heard muted voices and watched Jeff enter the car as the chauffeur and Homer exchanged instructions. It was exactly seven-thirty by the small Louis XV cartel clock on the dressing-room table. She had no memory of hearing Jeff come upstairs during the night. In an unusual act of resignation, she had taken a sleeping pill, surrendering to the futility of trying to do things decently and in order.

At eight o'clock the phone rang. It was John J. Bolt and she was surprised by his early call, suspecting something was wrong but too emotionally discouraged after last night to show genuine concern. "Millicent, I want you to meet me for lunch today," he said immediately.

"Oh, father, I'm not up to it. Can we make it another day?"

"No," he said rather abruptly. "I haven't had a chance to hear in detail about . . . about Joan, and I would appreciate a report about your trip to Italy."

The thought struck her that he was speaking to her as if she were an employee, asking, but really demanding, an up-date on a business transaction.

When she didn't respond right away, he said, "There are some financial arrangements I plan to make and before I do, I must talk to you. I would like everything to be in order."

Reluctantly, she agreed to meet him at his office at noon.

The time dragged as Millicent worked at her desk. Bills and papers were piled in a thick stack. She would keep her mind on trivia until eleven-thirty. Then she would go downtown and meet her father at his office. Aware of an uneasy feeling coming over her, as though she had a premonition that told her to be on guard,

Millicent found it difficult to concentrate on her financial matters. Whether it was the unfinished business with Jeffrey or the anticipation of seeing her father and telling him about Joan, she didn't know. It was a very strange feeling, as if she were at odds with her destiny and that fate was dragging her down an unwilling path.

She heard Allyson's voice call out and silently she said, *What now?* She was in no mood for her daughter's problems this morning. Allyson was standing in the doorway of the sitting room.

"I have to talk to you!" she said, sounding very excited.

"Allyson, can we talk later? I want to finish these bills before noon. I have to meet grandfather for lunch."

"No, I have to talk to you now or I'll simply burst."

Millicent looked at her in surprise. It was rare for Allyson to be so animated and demanding.

"Well, don't burst on me, not today, heaven forbid. What's on your mind that can't possibly wait?"

"Mother, put down that pen and look at me. I want your full attention."

Millicent looked up. "All right, you

have it. What's the matter?"

"Nothing's the matter," Allyson said with an amused smile. "That's just it. I mean everything is great, absolutely wonderful. I'm going to get married."

Millicent sat absolutely stunned as she looked into her daughter's starry eyes.

"Good lord!" she exclaimed. "You too!"

"Oh not now, not for a while yet," Allyson assured her. "But certainly sometime in the not-too-distant future, we plan to be married."

Millicent was visibly upset, unsure about what was going on. "Allyson, are you out of your mind? You haven't seen a boy in years. Why are you saying this?"

"Because it's true." Allyson smiled and clasped her hands together. "And I have too been seeing someone, on a very regular basis, and we're crazy in love."

Without thinking, Millicent blurted, "Crazy is right! Who is he?"

"Michael Lyons," said Allyson, beaming.

Millicent looked at her suspiciously. "Dr. Lyons? Dr. Lyons your psychiatrist?"

"Yes, Dr. Michael Lyons," Allyson repeated emphatically as she raised her eyebrows. "But he's not my psychiatrist anymore. He's my fiancé."

Millicent caught her breath. "Oh, Allyson, you really are serious, aren't you? I don't know what to say. This is all so sudden, and I hardly know the man. Isn't this unethical or something . . ." Millicent sputtered, as the realization began to sink in.

Allyson bent down and gave her a tight hug. "Mother, be happy for me. He's the most wonderful man in the world and he loves me. He really loves me!"

Millicent knew she should be ecstatic, especially since only a few months ago Allyson had all but given up on living. But all she could feel was unbelievable shock. It was the last thing in the world she had expected to hear. There were a hundred questions going through her mind about this turn of events, but she was too numb to focus on the right ones. What came out was sheer nonsense, and she knew it the minute it was said.

"Since Dr. Lyons . . . Michael . . . is in a wheelchair, where will you be married?"

"Oh, mother!" Then Allyson laughed. "For heaven's sake, we'll be married in the same place where everyone else gets married. Here or in church or wherever they allow people who can't walk," she said with amused sarcasm.

Millicent started laughing too, then she began to cry. She hugged Allyson tenderly and patted her on the back.

"Oh, honey, it's all too much to take in. Give me time to get used to it. Yes, I'm happy, very happy. It's wonderful, really wonderful! You are well, my darling." Suddenly she stopped and gained her composure.

"Allyson, we must have Michael over for dinner next week when everyone is here. No one in the family knows him. Where are his parents? I must get in touch with his parents. It's only proper. Oh dear, there's so much to do and think about."

It occurred to Millicent almost immediately that by next week the Hart family might not be intact. What kind of a dinner party do you give to announce an engagement and a separation?

As Millicent drove to the Bolt Building, her head was spinning like a whirlpool. She felt disconnected. There was no awareness of where she was or what she was doing. The driving was mechanical.

How could I be so astonishingly ignorant of what was going on right under my nose? she asked herself. The fact that she had been so involved with Roger did not, in her eyes, excuse the lack of sensibility to the turn of events that were shaping Allyson's life. With the astonishment came a sense of fear. A shiver raced through her body. She had another premonition that she would remember this day for the rest of her life. And not only because Allyson had told her that she was going to marry Michael Lyons. The foreboding was casting its shadow. It was frighteningly close.

Meanwhile, John J. Bolt was in his marvelously spacious office having an extremely unpleasant argument with his secretary emeritus. Martha Carrington was on her way to lunch when he called her in to reprimand her for shooting her mouth off to the reporters. He was sick and tired of what he perceived as the exaggerated importance she gave herself. He intended to tell her, once and for all, that she was not the spokesman for the company. He would also remind her that Bolt Construction had a perfectly fine public-relations department that handled all publicity and this was no longer her domain and hadn't been in years. He was aware that Martha acted as though the company was still a small business, but these were not "the good old days" that she always referred to, and he would remind her of that, too. Then, as an afterthought, he decided that this was as good a time as any to take Jeff's advice: retire Martha.

Martha was splendidly turned out. She wore a black linen suit and carried a Gucci handbag that cost more than most secretaries' weekly salaries. She dressed for the office as other people dress for tea at the White House. She was not beautiful, but her elegant, flattering clothes were a distraction from her imperfections.

Martha Carrington was seething. Her vehemence was directed at the white-haired man who sat impatiently behind his desk, waiting to get the matter over with. "I implied nothing, John. I merely gave the papers information that is already on public record. Had I been secretive, they would have been doubly suspicious. And I resent Jeffrey's insinuation that I am disloyal! Who the hell does that young upstart think he is telling me what to do or what not to do when it comes to the company?"

John J. Bolt sat in his massive executive chair watching Martha pace back and forth like a caged animal. Her anger was unmitigated. But in his usual deliberate manner, he came to the point harshly. "Martha, no one questions your loyalty, only your judgment. At our age, it sometimes gets a bit fuzzy. But that's over and done with. The factor here is that Jeff *is* running the company, and doing a damned fine job, I might add. I am the boss and always will be, but . . ."

"Then why don't you act like the boss?" she interrupted, "and get your son-in-law off my back? I am finding it increasingly difficult to get along with that man. And I will not abide his disrespect any longer. Honestly, John, his arrogance is too much. He comes in here as an office boy and acts as if he created Bolt Construction."

"Martha, that was almost thirty years ago," he said impatiently. "Jeffrey Hart is president of this company, and as such he has the power of all decisions. I think it's time you understood that. You are living in the past, and the past is *over*."

Martha smiled reproachfully, "You've made that perfectly clear, John! Oh, how you've made that clear. Well, *you* may have forgotten what we did together to build this business, but not *me*." Suddenly her anger subsided, and a look of nostalgia crossed her face. "John, do you remember how we worked to build up the company? The times we stayed in the old office all night, figuring up costs and production and getting our bids down? Those were such great times. We had special hopes that no one else could share. *We* created this empire, John. You and me. We had a dream, and *we* fulfilled it. And we had something beautiful between us, something that no two people ever had. There was such a closeness. I remember every moment we spent together."

John J. Bolt spread out his hands on the desk, and his eyes bored into her as if his heart had been chilled by indifference. "You remember too much, Martha! Now let's get down to business. Constance and I will be leaving for the Vineyard in a few weeks, and I want this matter settled before I go. Martha, it's time you retired. It's as simple as that. You have been an honored employee of Bolt Construction for over forty years and you deserve a rest. You've earned it. No one expects anymore than what you have already given. Without a doubt, we owe you a great deal for your faithful service, and you shall be handsomely rewarded. Your pension will commence as of the first of June, together with a *very* sizable monthly stipend. We take care of our own, you can be sure of that. There will be a dinner in your honor with an appropriate testimonial. I think Miss Thornton can arrange that reasonably well. Now that that's settled, I think you can start clearing up loose ends and turning over your files to Thornton and Buckley."

Martha stood motionless. The color was gone from her face. Her blazing eyes were wide and full of hatred. Suddenly a vitally important part of her existence was being threatened and she had to fight back. "You can't be serious!" she yelled. "You can't discard me like an old servant. You are not my master! And I *am not* just an employee. I *am* your partner. Do you hear? I am your partner and I will not be treated otherwise, by you or Jeffrey Hart. I worked beside you! I suffered beside you. We lay together and shared each other's dreams and passions. I will not relinquish my position!"

Martha's voice was getting louder and more hysterical. "Oh no, this can never do! Never! Pay attention, John Bolt. You threw me out of your bed and out of your heart but you cannot, *cannot,* do you understand, throw me out of your company with a pension and a dinner and expect me to go on living. This *is* my life! This is *my* dream, too."

"Martha, control yourself," demanded John J. Bolt. "This unseemly behavior does not become you. It is undignified, to say the least."

"You bastard!" she shouted. "You throw me out like garbage and then expect me to slink away with dignity. Dignity! You just took it all away, John Bolt."

He watched the flushed, angered elderly woman across the room. He found it hard to believe that he had once been madly in love with her. "You are making this increasingly difficult for me," he said with an attempt at self-control. "And the presumption that you have an equal voice in the policies of this company is unwarranted and ridiculous, if you will forgive me for saying so."

"I forgive you nothing!" The veins stood out in her temples. "For years, I created a totally forgiving world in which any slight effort you made, any crumb of affection you gave, was all that was demanded. Well, the time has come for the high and mighty to pay his dues."

Her unbridled anger soon turned into wild irrationality. "You are not going to get off scot-free and be allowed to forget your 'faithful employee' after a chicken dinner and a silver plaque. You can be sure of that!"

John J. Bolt slammed his fist down on the desk as he rose from his chair. The emotional escalation openly disgusted him, but he kept his voice under control. "Martha, this ugly display of emotion does you a disservice and tries my patience. I will hear *no more!*"

"Oh, but you *will* hear more, *John J. Bolt*," she said, with an air of smug condescension, "because I am not *finished*. Not *finished* at all. I have a great deal more to . . ."

"You're crazy, Martha!" he roared as his temper got the better of him. "Stark, raving mad, and I think it's time to put an end to this distasteful conversation."

He sat back down at his desk and busied himself with shuffling papers as he waited for her to go. When she did not, he looked up and tried to dismiss her from the room by saying, "I have work to do."

Defiantly, she walked close to the desk. He felt her presence, and the fury in him turned his face to scarlet. He looked up, ready to order her out of his office in no uncertain terms. What he saw made his eyes bulge in horror.

Martha was standing on the other side of the desk pointing a small pearl-handled revolver at his chest. Her handbag lay open in front of her. It was the very same gun that he had given her twenty-eight years ago after her apartment had been burglarized.

John J. Bolt gripped the arms of the chair in which he sat. His heart beat painfully. He felt quite sick. He knew he had only seconds to talk her out of this life-threatening situation. And he talked.

"You're right, Martha. Perfectly right. I do owe you a debt of gratitude for all your years of devotion. The company owes you. I don't know what got into me. I've been harsh and thoughtless, but it's only because I'm tired. You know the pressure

I've been under for the past few weeks. You'll stay with the company as long as you want to. Of course you'll stay. We need you. We couldn't possibly manage without you. And I'll talk to Jeff as soon as he returns from England. I had no idea he was harassing you. That's unforgivable. I'll certainly have a word with him. You're absolutely right, this will never do. *I* am in charge, and I shall correct the situation immediately. Say you'll stay, Martha, and give me the gun."

Martha continued to stare as he talked, her gray eyes shadowed. The gun was steady in her hand.

Taking advantage of her momentarily stunned condition, he went on. Gone was his haughty superiority. "Martha darling, try to remember how much we loved each other. The nights we spent in each other's arms were glorious. You think I've forgotten? Never! I can still feel your body close to mine. There was no one quite like you. The passion I had for you has never left me. I still have it. Believe me, we can be together again like young lovers. It's not too late. Sex can still be sweet, can't it, Martha?"

She searched his eyes for several

moments. It was as if she wanted to carefully think about his words. When she spoke, there was a terrible irony in her voice. "No, John."

"Why?" he pleaded.

"Let's just say that at my age, vengeance is as sweet as sex," she said triumphantly.

"Don't do this, Martha," he whispered, barely able to speak.

"I must, John," she said with a cool calm. "But oh my beloved, it is still quite an effort not to think of you with affection."

She fired the gun, and a scream pierced the room. A blind red rage flashed in her brain and sent a signal through the nerves to her fingers. A second and third shot followed, even though his body was already twisted back against the swivel chair with blood flowing from his neck and chest. Even though John J. Bolt's eyes were already wide open with death.

Moments of silence, a cry of agony, and then a fourth shot was fired.

It began to rain, just a light drizzle, but dark clouds appeared and quite suddenly shut out the sunlight. Millicent pulled up in front of the huge Bolt Building, which took up almost an entire city block on K

Street. She had no recollection of driving there, but her dreamy mood was shattered instantly.

The parking attendant was not in front but in a matter of seconds a line of police cars with flashing lights and two ambulances, sirens blasting, circled the entrance. Millicent's pulse quickened. The cops yelled at her to move her car, but she ignored them and ran into the building with a sense of urgency that she knew was warranted.

Throngs of curious people were already gathering in the lobby, hoping to see what was exciting enough to bring out the police force so early in the day.

She pushed her way to the elevator but was held back by a police officer. The frantic building guard recognized her, and she was quickly whisked into the elevator by the policeman. She rode to the tenth floor with a feeling of overwhelming fright and sorrow, waiting for the inevitable.

The elevator door opened to a scene of eerie chaos. A few secretaries were crying hysterically. Some people seemed suspended in motion at their desks. She saw blurred figures in open spaces. One man was slumped over the Xerox machine, sobbing quietly. Sheldon Carpenter, the nontalking tax lawyer, was moaning and wailing as though he had been torn apart. All this was above the noise and confusion that was coming from John J. Bolt's office.

Millicent made her way there clutching her throat, trying to stifle the cries that were starting in her chest. There were at least a dozen people in the room, and they all seemed to be shouting the same instruction: "Don't touch anything!"

Millicent was stopped at the open door by a uniformed officer, but she saw Martha's body immediately. She lay sprawled in front of the desk face downward, her right hand clutching the gun. Blood was still oozing through her gray hair. When Millicent looked up and saw the freakish contortion of her father with his head snapped back against the chair and his glazed eyes fixed on the ceiling, she cried out and slumped to the floor.

The image of that room would remain with her forever.

Chapter 29

The night was agony. Everyone gathered in a state of shock in the large stone house on Belmont Road. Still numb and emotionally paralyzed, Millicent sat on the living-room sofa clutching Allyson's hand and thinking that this was a scene that must be existing in her imagination. Friends and relatives, people from the office, even political figures, came and went. But none of it seemed real.

Constance, heavily sedated, lay in the upstairs guest room with a nurse to watch over her.

Detectives had been to the house earlier to verify facts and relationships, asking personal questions about John J. Bolt and Martha Carrington.

A flood of queries from the business community was being handled by the public-relations department of Bolt Construction.

Reporters surrounded the house, stopping anyone they could for a few more grisly details to add to the sordid murder-suicide exposé that would appear in tomorrow's *Washington Post*. In a city accustomed to electrifying news, this was still considered first-rate front page scandal.

Dolly Henderson seemed to be enjoying the excitement of the tragedy, though she expressed shock and sympathy to everyone who entered the house. She acted as if she were in charge, screening those people she considered worthy of approaching Millicent with a few words of comfort and praise for her departed father.

Homer and Regina were in and out of the kitchen making endless pots of coffee and enough food to nourish the horror-stricken assemblage.

Corinne and Johnny arrived near midnight.

The office staff were trying to reach Jeff, who had barely arrived in London.

Joan had to be notified. Allyson called the spa at Montecatini to find out whether they knew where she was and was surprised to learn that she was still there. She told Joan the devastating news, expecting a hysterical reaction or some far-out spiritual reponse, but astonishingly enough, Joan remained composed and lucid. She would take the next plane out of Italy and be in Washington tomorrow, she said. She even showed genuine concern for Millicent and Constance and in a rather strange way told Allyson to tell Millicent not to be too sad.

Everyone else reacted with stunned horror. They were completely dumbfounded. The events of the day were shockingly unbelievable. What kind of insanity could have driven Martha Carrington to commit such an evil act of violence? John J. Bolt was a great man and would be long remembered. It was all a nightmare too terrible to comprehend.

The morning brought a measure of reality. There were funeral arrangements to be made for John J. Bolt. And something had to be done with Martha Carrington's body.

On this day, which was Tuesday, Dr. Michael Lyons came into the Hart house for the first time and took over. Allyson had called him immediately. He arrived in the morning in his wheelchair, introduced himself with simple candor, and gave the Harts the support and direction they so desperately needed. By the end of the day he was an acknowledged member of the family.

Michael called Martha's sister in Ohio and then made arrangements for her body to be sent there for private burial in the family plot. He went with Johnny and a company executive to the funeral parlor. Funeral and burial arrangements, scheduled for Thursday, were made for John J. Bolt. Michael picked out the casket and selected flowers and hymns for the service. He even decided on the attire in which the man would be buried.

Initially it was decided that a small, rather private funeral was called for. Under the circumstances, more than that did not seem appropriate. This was not an ordinary death, however. John J. Bolt had been an important man, an empire builder, with an extensive and impressive list of connections all over the country. His friends and associates would never consider letting him go to his grave without fanfare. Hundreds of people would find it unthinkable not to publicly lament his passing at the great Washington Cathedral. The family gave in to outside pressure. John J. Bolt would have a proper funeral like any other Washington dignitary.

Throughout the day, Michael Lyons acted as psychiatrist and family adviser, giving strength and advice and comfort, especially to Constance, whose grief knew no bounds. The death of her husband, upon whom she was totally dependent, would have been awful enough had he died of natural causes. But for John J. Bolt, her acknowledged tower of strength, to die violently at the hands of his trusted employee and have the sordid murder splashed in headlines was absolutely unbearable. The innuendos in the paper did not escape her, despite her wretched state.

"Lies, lies, all of it lies!" Constance said to Michael as she sat in bed crying pitifully and holding the newspaper that she had demanded to see. She felt violated and vowed never to be seen in public again after the funeral.

Roger Graham came to the house. His presence was not thought unusual. It was the decent thing to do, for a physician to visit the bereaved family. He spoke with Allyson and was reassured that she had not regressed physically. He looked in on Constance, who could never get enough sympathy. He was not surprised to see Dr. Lyons. He had suspected that Allyson was falling in love with the young psychiatrist.

Then he sat by Millicent and talked to her quietly as he held her hand in the most professional way. All agreed that Millicent needed the calm attention of a doctor to get her through the heartache of the next few days. She looked plagued by emotional emptiness.

Dolly told Cory that Dr. Graham would not let Millicent yield to despair. "Isn't it dear of Dr. Graham to stop in and comfort your mother, Cory? Millicent is the foundation of this family, like a towering oak, and she must not give in to the wretched gossip that's spreading all over town about your grandfather, God rest his soul, and that astonishingly mad, mad woman."

"Dolly, do you believe there really was something between grandfather and his secretary?" asked Cory, seeking an expert opinion.

"Heavens no! Newspapers dream up anything they want just to sell a story.

They simply imply and the readers infer the worst. Idle gossip, child. That old woman obviously just went berserk and, unfortunately, had a gun handy. It's not uncommon, you know, with crime being what it is. I wouldn't be without one myself. Gracious, who would ever want to kill your grandfather? He was so handsome and rich. Everyone worshiped him." Dolly seemed terribly moved and dabbed at the tears in her eyes.

Cory look unconvinced.

Roger wanted to speak more than words of consolation to Millicent. He did not intend to let her private agonies tip the balance away from their plans for the future. "Darling, this whole business is so horrible for you. I wish there was something I could do to wipe out what you've been through."

"Roger, I've never seen a dead person before. The sight of my father in that grotesque position will haunt me as long as I live. And Martha, poor Martha . . . on the floor, with blood all over." Millicent cupped her face in her hands and shook from the vivid memory of that image.

"Millicent, you won't forget it, but you

will learn to accept it, because there's nothing anyone can do. It certainly makes clear how precious life is and how it can be taken away from you in a flash. Doesn't this make you see how we have to live life to the fullest? Together, we have so much to live for. And this is one tragedy that you can't take the blame for. It had nothing to do with you."

She sat and thought. "I'm not so sure of that. Somebody should have protected Martha from the misery of old age."

Dolly came over with hot tea. She loved taking care of Millicent. "Mill dear, listen to the good doctor. He knows what he's talking about. We must all bear up at a time like this. Your father would have wanted us to be strong. He was such a tower of strength himself. Dr. Graham, did you know John Bolt? He was an uncompromising man. He lived fearlessly, and he died fearlessly. Like a soldier in battle. Would you like some tea, doctor? And we have the most divine cookies. Ridgewell's sent them in."

Jeffrey Hart arrived home on Wednesday. Millicent was appalled by his appearance. He was pale and hollow-eyed because of sleeplessness and the worst kind of anguish. In London, he had cried privately, but now he sobbed openly in Millicent's arms.

He had loved John J. Bolt more than anyone else in the world. Jeffrey Hart had taken him on as a father, never having loved or respected his own father, who was a lifelong failure in Jeff's eyes. He had patterned his life after this giant of industry who had given him the opportunity to be successful beyond his wildest dreams. But now his mentor who had carefully shown him the way was dead, and Jeff felt responsible.

"If I hadn't pushed him to get rid of Martha, he'd be alive today. This just didn't happen, Millicent. I brought it about."

"Jeff, that's not true," said Millicent, trying desperately to relieve his guilt. "You know as well as I do that father was not someone who could be persuaded to do anything he didn't want to do. This was his decision, not yours. It had to come sooner or later. He had taken a back seat in the company, and he felt that Martha should do the same. The secretaries heard them arguing about that. And I know he wanted Martha to retire. He told mother that before you ever mentioned it. Jeff, you can't assume any responsibility for his death. Martha assumed it all by taking her own life. We must leave it at that."

She held him, cradling him in her arms until his sobs subsided and his rigid body went limp.

"Millicent . . . I loved him."

"I know, Jeff. I think you loved him more than we did. You understood him as we never did. We were terrified of him. Jeff, I want you to know that so much happened before you ever came into his life, things that went on between Martha and father that somehow led to this. That's why you must not blame yourself. Jeff, your remorse is unfounded. It was only between them."

Of all things, nothing is so strange as regret, she thought, *because sins or misdeeds when done are done without mercy, in the name of principle. But principles lose their substance when they foster human sorrow. But then it's too late. Everything has changed.*

Joan arrived exasperated and weary. Everyone waited for her to break down as soon as the realization of her father's death hit her, but she acted as though she had returned for a visit rather than a funeral. Her only reference to a death in the family had to do with what she would wear to the funeral service.

"Lord, you all look dreadful. Millicent, must I wear a black dress tomorrow? I hope not. You know I simply fade away in black."

Chapter 30

By all standards, it was an impressive funeral.

Three structures dominate the Washington, D.C. skyline. The United States Capitol, the Washington Monument, and the Gloria in Excelsis Tower of the National Cathedral, which soars over 300 feet in the air.

Hundreds assembled in the Bethlehem Chapel of the great Gothic church to pay their last respects to John J. Bolt. This lovely chapel, designed to tell the story of the nativity of Christ, is so resplendent in architecture that the people gathered there this day looked more like sightseers than mourners as they gazed around, taking in the extraordinary splendor. Everywhere there is beauty and history. Carved figures of King David with his harp and of John the Baptist are just a few of the heroic figures immortalized in the niches of the granite walls. Four massive columns surround the ornate altar, with its stone carvings of the four evangelists: St. Matthew, St. Mark, St. Luke, and ironically, St. John.

It is a glorious setting in which to extol the goodness of a great man. The bishop did that splendidly. His sermon gave John J. Bolt virtues in death that the man never possessed in life. He spoke of his kindness and sensitivity, his humility and morality. No mention was made of the way he died except to say that it was premature.

The service was marked by a magnificently lavish ceremony and display. It evoked a strong emotional response from everyone except Joan, who carefully peeled off her nail polish during the sermon.

Back at Millicent's house, a small reception was held, and the family heard more words of praise for the father and husband they had just buried.

It was Jeff who suggested that they seriously consider giving a large sum of money to an area university to build a business school in the name of John J. Bolt.

It was Cory who thought that the money

should go for a rape crisis center. Allyson said the money should be donated to a hospital. Constance liked the idea of giving a million dollars to the Kennedy Center for the Performing Arts, with the stipulation that a large bust of her late husband be placed next to that of the fallen president John F. Kennedy. Dolly felt that a statue of the man on horseback would be appropriate for the lobby of the Bolt Building.

It was Joan who told them that no matter what they did to commemorate the memory of her father, she hoped that none of the money would come out of her inheritance.

During a quiet moment after dinner, when the rest of the family had retreated to other rooms to seek seclusion from the enormously pressure-filled day, Allyson and Michael found themselves alone at the dinner table with Joan, who wanted anything but solitude. She was nervous and talkative and when she offhandedly mentioned Sanjay, Allyson pounced on the chance to ask about his whereabouts.

"Aunt Joan, why didn't Sanjay come to grandfather's funeral with you?"

"Because his concern is with life, not

death," she said falteringly, "although he does, of course, strongly believe in the hereafter, a belief I cannot share because I couldn't bear to think of daddy watching over us, wherever he may possibly be."

"Does that bother you?" asked Michael cautiously, trying not to sound too analytical, "to think that your father still has a presence?"

"Indeed it does," said Joan without hesitation. "At least when he was alive I knew where he was and I could absent myself."

"You mean it makes you uncomfortable to think that he may yet be involved with your life?" asked Michael in a rhetorical tone.

"Of course, doctor. A disapproving spirit is far worse than a critical mortal, because one cannot run away from a ghost. It's like . . . well, if you'll pardon the comparison, like never being allowed to go to the bathroom with any degree of privacy. One could become positively obsessed with flushing the toilet before leaving the seat."

Michael blinked, not exactly following Joan's analogy. Allyson felt it was the right time to ask more about Sanjay.

"Aunt Joan, you haven't told us. Are you married?"

She didn't reply. There was an uncomfortable silence in the large dining room. Joan self-consciously played with a coffee spoon on the table. Michael started to change the subject, and Allyson regretted asking. But finally Joan did answer.

"No dear. I did not get married. Sanjay went off to India to tend to business affairs and to consult his family, so I thought, and that's the last I've seen of him. We've spoken, but his mood has changed. It would appear . . . that there exists . . . a rather delicate problem." She paused with some embarrassment. "You see . . . it would seem . . . that he is already married, always was, to someone in India. And, even in his rather peculiar culture, they do regard another marriage without divorce as . . . bigamy."

"So," she continued in a more light-hearted vein, "I may just have to search the monasteries of Italy for a husband. I do believe that the monks are the only eligible men left in Europe."

With hardly a pause, Joan turned to Michael. "Doctor, how is it that you've managed to stay unmarried? Is it because you're an invalid? I would think that your handicap would be more in the nature of an asset. Women absolutely adore taking care of helpless men."

Michael was momentarily startled by Joan's bluntness.

Allyson was angry and defensive. "Michael is *not* handicapped!"

"Of course he is, darling," insisted Joan. "But aren't we all, in some form or another?" She looked from Allyson to Michael.

He ran his fingers through his hair and laughed as though he found her frankness amusing. "I'm appropriately shocked by your honesty," he said, "but I think you're confusing 'handicapped' with being weak and vulnerable. Psychiatrists' offices are a lot more filled with people whose minds are fragile than with those whose limbs are not working right. And I might add, so are expensive *spas*."

Joan lowered her eyes demurely and appeared properly chastened. Then she looked up and smiled. "Touché, doctor, touché."

"To answer your question," Michael went on, "I didn't get married because I was waiting for someone like Allyson to come along."

"Oh really," said Joan with a bemused smile and a touch of irony in her voice. "And what does this dear girl have to offer you that no other lovely young lady had?"

"A strong spine. A combination of fragility and strength that I find very attractive in a woman," said Michael, glancing at Allyson adoringly. "She was very easy to fall in love with." Then he leaned back in his wheelchair and with a sardonic grin added, "And, of course, she had money. That's very attractive in a woman, too, as I'm sure you know, Joanie."

"My dear young man," said Joan with a good-natured smile, "shall we call a truce? I think I've met my match."

Then Joan turned to Allyson, who all the while was watching them with skeptical silence. "Oh, if your doctor were older, I would bloody well give you a run for your money." Joan meant this as a compliment.

Meanwhile, Millicent came upon Jeff in the upstairs sitting room. He was sitting alone in the dark. All his thoughts were bent on the loss of John J. Bolt. No one dreamed what went on in Jeffrey Hart. He felt afraid and powerless, as though his courage and strength had vanished with the remains of the man he mourned. The gnawing grief within him had visibly altered his appearance. His face looked older and his body smaller.

Millicent turned on the lamp. He did not look up. He sat motionless, consumed with self-torment. Once more she saw his anguished face. It was ash pale.

"Martha killed him, not you," she said simply. "Blaming yourself won't bring him back or get rid of your undeserved guilt. Of all the things that have gone wrong in our lives and of which we could claim responsibility, this is not one of them. Jeff, please don't eat yourself up with remorse. You have other things to think about. The whole company now depends on you. You must not feel this way. You've got to carry on."

Jeff was not to be parted from his guilt. "I don't need you to tell me how to feel, or to absolve my conscience. And I don't have to be reminded of my responsibility to the company. Who do you think has been running things for God knows how long?"

Millicent was instantly apologetic. "I'm sorry, Jeff. All I meant was that self-accusation serves no end. Don't make yourself a victim, too." There was an edge of desperation in her speech. "I've been through this myself with Allyson and that's *not* what helped her get well. . . . I know I'm saying this badly . . . but what I'm trying to tell you is that you are *needed*, needed more than ever, now that father is gone. And whatever you think you might have done to cause what happened, forgive yourself."

Jeff looked at her, then sighed quietly. "Can *you* forgive me, Millicent? Do you still need me?"

She could not answer. She gazed at him sympathetically.

"We both need time, Jeff, time to get through this terrible ordeal."

The words came slowly. "I'm talking about our marriage, Millicent."

She looked at him with a touch of bitterness. "Why now, Jeff, when you should . . . when we should have been talking about . . . about our relationship a long time ago?"

He took a deep breath. "Because I finally realized it's time to restore what we had." He paused and looked away. "I thought about that at the funeral." Without explaining what he suspected she already knew, he repeated himself directly. "I guess I'm asking for forgiveness."

Millicent felt a lump in her throat. At this moment she could not bring herself to tell him about Roger because she was swamped with uncertainties. She only alluded to what was in her mind. "I suspect we've both committed a painful breach of marital trust. I should be asking for forgiveness, too."

Chapter 31

Days passed. People still came to pay homage to John J. Bolt. Letters, donations, and tributes continued to pour in. But getting on with living was what mattered to most people.

For strangers, even for friends, the tragedy of death is indifference once the immediate shock is gone. A death in the family lingers only for the family that is left — a mother or a child or a wife or a sister, those whose lives will forever be diminished by the loss.

Had John J. Bolt died a natural death, there might have been a different reaction by his family. There would have been sadness for the loss of the patriarch, but pleasant memories mixed with a sense of order would have established a family bond, like the old guard passing and the new guard carrying on. There would have been a framework to enable them to deal with their deep and painful emotions.

But murder in a family is a different story. The taint touches everyone like a mark of disgrace and builds up walls of emotions that cannot be shared. Theirs became a house of strangers, each concerned with his or her own individual means of survival.

Jeffrey went back to work like a man who volunteers to go to prison on the grounds of moral responsibility. Bolt Construction would never again be the same without his revered leader. The fire of his ambition was flickering.

Cory returned to Smith to take her final exams and to plan for the rape crisis center that would be her senior project. She and her classmates were establishing the center in a small town in Massachusetts.

Johnny did not go back to Harvard. He had already decided to drop out after his second year and work full time. The death of his grandfather provided the impetus to join Bolt Construction. He told his father he wanted to come into the business and learn it from the bottom up. At first, Jeffrey tried to persuade him to finish college, but when he realized that Johnny had made up his mind about working, he readily accepted him. He saw his son not as a reflection of himself but as a replacement of John J. Bolt, and it was a comfort to have Johnny's support.

Allyson found herself in charge of the house and caretaker to her grandmother. Constance, incurably inured to luxury and dependency, yet not without a sense of pride, discharged the nurse-companion hired to console her, saying she needed no one to lean upon in time of crisis. Instead, she transferred her demands to Allyson.

Millicent suffered from a paralysis of the spirit that sapped her energy and rendered her incapable of presiding over a busy household. She became too exhausted to think, despite her lack of activity. Most of the decisions she deferred to Allyson. Her weakened state and heartbreak came not only from the death of her father, who had so profoundly influenced her life, but from the loss of her beloved friend Martha, whose life remained a tragedy to the very end. The realization that she would never again see Martha, never have the opportunity to resolve their estrangement, was devastating in its finality. Unresolved alienation between the living and the dead is never buried with the corpse. It remains to haunt the living. Millicent harbored no bitterness toward Martha, only a deep pity.

Joan was bored. A house in mourning is austere and lonely once the company leaves. Meals offer the only diversion. Constance would have liked Joan at her side, administering to her grief. Millicent wanted her sister to grieve openly and share the past with her in order to keep alive the memory of their father.

Joan would have none of that. She was anxious to leave and get back to Italy or France, where her past was more recent. The only reason she remained after the funeral was to learn the contents of the will, which was in the hands of the lawyers, and to sign some necessary papers. She made no pretenses for staying, and this callous attitude finally got the best of Millicent in an unprecedented fit of anger.

With the morning came rain and mist, the kind of oppressive Washington weather that ushers in the summer. Millicent and Joan sat in the sun-room and drank coffee. Constance was asleep, and

Allyson was marketing with Regina.

"Millicent," said Joan with an air of impatience, "could you possibly get that lawyer, Mr. Watson, to hurry along with the will? He insists I stay and sign some documents. It could go on for days, weeks even, at the rate he's going. I called him this morning, and he gave me absolutely no clue as to when they'd be ready."

Millicent looked at her coldly. "I'm sure he's working as quickly as possible. There's a great deal to do in probating a will."

"Well, I know *that!*" she said indignantly. "But the only thing I have to do is sign some papers. I don't expect him to hand over the money today. He can send it to me later. I intend to stay in touch, for heaven's sake."

"Is that all you're thinking about at a time like this, the money?" Millicent asked, deliberately angry.

Joan seemed unmoved. "What else is there?"

"What else is there!" Millicent repeated with outrage. "Your father is dead, murdered! Your mother is devastated and cries all day. Jeff is consumed with grief and heartache and has to continue running a business that is, if you've forgotten, supporting *you*. Our whole family is torn apart. Oh, my God! I don't believe this. And all you care about is how much money is coming to you. Joan, you haven't shown one drop of compassion since you walked into this house. What in God's name do you have in place of a heart?"

Despite the tirade, Joan remained unaffected. "Would it make you feel better if I ranted and raved and pulled out my hair?" she asked sarcastically.

"By God, yes!" screamed Millicent. "At least then I'd know that you're not made of stone."

Joan continued to drink her coffee, unshaken by this last remark. The moment of tension passed.

"Joan, I honestly cannot for the life of me understand what's going on inside of you. I want to understand but . . . I just don't. Father gave you *everything*, including his love. Can't you even grieve for him, just a little?"

"I can, but I won't," said Joan calmly, but with defiance.

Millicent looked at her sister in amazement. "You act as though you're relieved. Yes, you seem relieved that he's dead."

Joan looked Millicent squarely in the eyes. "I am," she retorted, "and that's something you will never understand, sister dear. So no more lectures about my 'heart of stone.' I've booked an afternoon flight to Rome. Tell dear Mr. Watson that I shall provide him with my address and he can send the papers to me. I'll tell mother that I'm leaving and spend a few hours with her before I go. Would you be good enough to have Homer drive me to the airport at two? I'll go up and pack now."

Millicent tried to suppress her anger and failed. When Joan started to get up from the table, Millicent took hold of her arm and pushed her down. The coffee spilled over Joan's robe.

"Now look what you've done!" said Joan with exasperation, as she grabbed a napkin to sop up the liquid running down her lap "Coffee is the devil to get out of silk! I'm sure it's ruined for good. And I adore this robe. Sanjay sent it from India."

"Damn the robe!" Millicent shouted. "Once and for all, tell me what the hell is the matter with you. How dare you say that you're relieved that father is dead! He deserved better from you, even in death!"

546

Joan looked at Millicent with cold, icy eyes. "Drop it, Millicent. Enough! This conversation ended a few minutes ago. And I choose to forget what has been said. I am going upstairs."

Millicent looked at Joan imploringly. "Don't go this way," she said softly. "I couldn't bear it. We've lost so much already. Let's not lose each other." A flash of remembrance came into her mind, and she became excited as she related it to Joan. "Joan, do you remember the time father bought you the pony? Mother didn't want you to have it because she was afraid you'd get hurt. You were so little then. And you cried for days. And father was so upset that he left the office and came home and took you to the stables, where the pony was waiting for you. He caught the devil from mother, one of the few times she really got mad at him, but he said it was worth it just to see you happy again." Millicent became almost sad and hesitated before saying, "And I was jealous of you because I never felt he loved me in the same way that he loved you."

Joan gazed at Millicent with haunting eyes. "You had nothing to be jealous about, Millicent. He knew you were strong."

Millicent reached over and gently took her hand. Her voice was filled with nostalgia. "Joan, can you really forget what you once felt for father? That's all I'm asking. That you try to remember the feelings of love you had for him."

As if Millicent suddenly struck a raw nerve, Joan's body grew rigid and her eyes opened wide as she stared at the raindrops splashing against the window. A faraway look crossed her face.

" 'There are some feelings time cannot benumb,' " she recited in a monotone.

Millicent was puzzled. She suddenly sat up. "What did you say?"

Just as suddenly Joan returned to reality. "Oh nothing, nothing at all."

"No, it *was* something," Millicent insisted. "That's a line from a poem I learned in school. I remember because I taught it to you. It's by Byron, isn't it?"

Joan appeared foggy. "Yes, I guess so."

"Joan, whatever father did to hurt you, whatever it was that still bothers you, forgive him. You were always 'daddy's little girl.' Remember? I know he was overbearing and sometimes harsh and controlling, but he meant well. It was only in your best interest."

Joan looked at her with fury in her eyes. "My best interest! Are *you* crazy?"

Joan began to laugh hysterically. " 'Daddy's girl! Daddy's girl! Daddy's girl! Daddy's girl!' " She chanted it over and over as her voice got shriller and more mocking.

Millicent didn't know what to say or do. She put both hands on Joan's arm, attempting to calm her.

Joan pushed Millicent's hands away with force and turned to her with a glazed expression. Then she said, "Oh, I was 'daddy's girl' all right! For years, I was 'daddy's girl.' Every time he crawled into bed beside me, he would say that."

Millicent sat frozen in horror as Joan's voice grew babyish, doll-like, as she recalled a voice out of her past: "You're daddy's pretty little girl and you want to make daddy happy, don't you? Then we won't say anything to mommy or sister. This will be our little secret. Whatever we do will just be between daddy and Joanie. You'll never tell anybody, will you, baby? No, of course not. Because you're daddy's girl and you love him, and he loves you very much. And daddy will buy you something very special tomorrow because you make him so happy. Now take off your nightie like a good little girl and I'll . . ."

Millicent clasped her hands over her ears trying to block out the agony of that terrible little voice. The shock on her face was complete.

"No, no, no, stop!" shrieked Millicent. "Oh my God, Joan, please stop!" She was sobbing uncontrollably.

Then the cries began to come from Joan, wretched cries from the depths of her soul, as she relived her suffering.

"I was so rotten, Millicent, so filthy rotten!" Joan put both her hands over her face in anguish.

Millicent took her sister in her arms, and the wall of misunderstanding between them fell away. Choked with pity, half crying the words, she said in sober sadness "No, no, you weren't, *he* was. Oh, the hell you must have gone through! Joan dearest, you *don't* have to forgive him, ever."

As Millicent held her sobbing sister and felt the sounds of pain coming from Joan's body, she was aware that a monstrous image of her father was shaping itself in her mind.

A rage came over Millicent as she put Joan to bed. She wanted to scream, to curse her father, and shout to the world what a pathetic man he was. She was appalled by this impulse and quickly suppressed it, teling herself that he deserved her pity, not her scorn. It would have been wrong to hate her father now that he was dead.

Joan looked like a broken woman who had quite suddenly disintegrated once the silence of her secret guilt came to an end. She lay in bed whimpering like a hurt animal, and Millicent became apprehensive about her physical and mental well-being.

Allyson arrived home and found Millicent hovering over Joan, trying to ease the agitation that wracked her sister's body.

Allyson looked amazingly mature and frighteningly serious. "What's wrong with Aunt Joan? She looks awful. And what is she mumbling about?"

"Quiet, dear," Millicent whispered. "She's . . . just not well. It's all been too much for her."

As if their minds flowed together, Allyson said, "I guess a lifetime of running has finally ended. Poor Joan, she had to take the leap to reality too fast."

Millicent looked concerned. A wave of panic came over her. "I really don't know what to do."

"Call a doctor immediately," said Allyson emphatically.

Ordinarily, Millicent would not have to be told what to do in any given situation. She had been one of those people who always took action, no matter what doubts came into play, never believing that a problem would resolve itself. But her natural instincts had been consumed first by sorrow, then by unrestrained anger.

"Yes, you're right. She needs a doctor," Millicent said, her bewilderment over.

"I'll call Dr. Graham," said Allyson.

"No, don't do that!"

"Why not?"

"It's not a good idea. Call Dr. Sarbanes. He knows the family."

"Mother, Dr. Sarbanes must be a hundred years old," said Allyson, exaggerating to make her point. "He certainly looks it. He could barely make it to grandfather's funeral. And he's most certainly *not* psychiatrically oriented. I'm calling Dr. Graham. He'll know what to do."

After Roger examined Joan, he joined

Millicent and Allyson in the library. "Your sister's sleeping quietly now. I gave her a mild sedative, and I'm going to leave a prescription. Nothing too strong. It will just have a tranquilizing effect, to calm her down. I think she'll be all right. She just seems to be extremely upset and disoriented. I rather imagine your father's death suddenly hit her with full force, or is there something else, *Mrs. Hart?*"

Allyson watched as their eyes met in recognition. The gleam was unmistakable.

Millicent turned away from him and tried to assemble her thoughts. "Joan's always been a very nervous person. But I've never seen her like this. Yes, it's probably a delayed reaction to the tension."

"Was she very close to your father?" he asked.

She looked at him suspiciously. "Very close."

On occasions, and this was one of them, Allyson had sensed that Dr. Graham and Millicent had private things to say to each other. But unlike the other times, this did not concern her own state of health. And unlike the other times, she was not curious about what they discussed, although she was very interested in Joan's welfare. But she didn't want to know about any more complications. Life was much too involved already, and she recognized that feelings were getting too deep. She had learned from Michael how to protect herself.

"I'll just go upstairs and check on Aunt Joan," said Allyson, and she was gone.

Now Millicent was unprotected, and Roger was very aware of this. "Millicent, Joan will be fine, really. The shock will pass."

"Will it?" Millicent asked with a trace of cynicism.

"It will unless there's more wrong with her than your father's death," said Roger suspiciously.

"There's so much more wrong than I ever imagined, Roger . . ." She stopped abruptly, afraid she would reveal what was still so astonishingly horrifying.

He looked at her knowingly. He started to say something, then thought better of it.

"Roger, how are you?" Millicent asked with concern. "I've been so involved with my own problems . . . in fact, you've been so involved with all our problems, that I'm afraid I haven't been thinking of how you must feel."

He cleared his throat. It was obviously an effort for him to say what was on his mind. "Millicent, I know this is neither the time nor the place to discuss our future. But I have the sinking feeling that there may never be any. Troubles usually don't stop with a single event, as I've found out. One bad situation generates another, and before you know it, you stop looking for happiness and think it's enough just to survive. I don't want it to be that way with us." The last statement was almost in the form of a question.

"Roger, what can I tell you?" she said helplessly. "As for our future, well, you're expecting me to think logically when my world, at this moment, is completely illogical. My life is so turned around that I'm positively reeling. It's like being in a revolving door that doesn't stop spinning. I'm thoroughly confused because so much has happened in such a short space of time." She paused and reflected. "As for us, I don't think I'm capable of thinking clearly."

"Millicent, I'm not presenting an ultimatum," he said apologetically. "It's nothing like that. It's just that at times I

get so damned frustrated. I want . . ."
He started to say more but pulled back.
"Please forget it. It seems as if I'm always
putting a choice before you, and the
choices are never that simple." His face
suddenly brightened. "Don't worry,
Millicent, we'll work things out." He took
her hand and squeezed it between his. "I
have to go." He leaned over and whispered, "I love you a lot."

Millicent gazed at Roger, and for a
moment she felt complete happiness
knowing that someone wanted and needed
her, just for love. After Roger left, she
took a few minutes to sit alone and think.
Why did she feel such conflict? What was
the matter with her? Why couldn't she
just tell him that she loved him? That
when she lay in bed at night, she would
pray for the soul of her poor father and
for the deliverance of her tortured
husband, but that her body would still
become hot and explosive and full of
sexual hunger that she could not control,
despite the somber prayers that were in
her troubled mind.

Why didn't she let him know that when
this ugly business had faded into a bad
memory she would come to him? Why

didn't she ask Roger to wait for her? That's really all he wanted to hear.

Why did Jeff ask her to forgive him? That only confused her all the more.

Chapter 32

Time passed without anyone noticing it. Hours became days and then it was a full week since John J. Bolt had been shot to death.

Constance and Joan were still with Millicent in the house on Belmont Road, and although their separate sorrows did not lessen, they began to take control of their emotions.

Constance talked about returning to her apartment at the Watergate but when Millicent agreed with her, she began to cry and presented all the reasons why she could not go back. "How can I return there without John? I think I would simply die myself, walking in there all alone and knowing that he's never coming back. Never to hear his sweet, gentle voice again. As long as I don't go there, I feel he's going to return."

"Father's not coming back and you must face that fact, mother. And the sooner you go home and pick up your life, the better it will be for you."

"Pick up my life!" Constance said, sounding injured. "What life do I have left? A poor widow on her own at the mercy of all those vicious gossips who will never allow me to forget that my husband died at the hands of a deranged *employee* whom he never should have hired in the first place. Millicent, if I do go back to that empty place, I shall lock the door and never step foot outside, except perhaps on the terrace. My life is over, don't you see that?"

"No, mother, I don't. You've had a terrible time. It's been horrid, but you must go on living, because that's what life is all about." She forced herself to say, "Father would have wanted you to go on without him. He cared very much about his family. And he loved you very much."

Constance's face brightened. "Yes, he did, didn't he? Well, perhaps I shall go on now that I have a great purpose."

"I don't understand," Millicent said.

Constance's eyebrows went up. "My

purpose, our pupose, must be to preserve your father's memory."

"How can we do that?"

"By getting started on his memorial. The name of John J. Bolt must *never* be desecrated again," Constance said with bitter emphasis.

It was the long talks with Michael that helped Joan with her terrible, aching sadness. Allyson persuaded Joan to go down to the garden each day and sit with him during the dusky hours of twilight and just talk. Nothing of seeming substance was discussed, not the specifics of her forbidding past, only generalized lamentations that often brought forth the agony of reluctant tears. With all his warm understanding and gentle professional guidance, Joan gradually unburdened herself of some of the misery and self-doubts that churned beneath the surface of her frivolous exterior. That, and the sweet spring evenings, started the healing process.

At first, Joan held back by announcing to Michael that it was no use talking to him or to anyone else for that matter, because no one could understand how she felt about the sequence of events that had brought her to her present state. Although she was careful not to reveal her secret humiliation, she told him that there was a futility in trying to translate her feelings into words.

"How can I explain to you how I feel when you've never felt this way?" Joan challenged him.

"My experience is not the same as yours," Michael said, "and my background is as different from yours as day from night, Joanie. But I do have one thing that you can relate to. I've got the most terrific imagination. Believe me. It's the truth. I can put myself into the shoes of anyone I talk to, and that's why I'm such a good psychiatrist. I don't always have 'heart', and sometimes I'm short on patience, but I've got the best damn imagination in the whole world."

Joan gave Michael a wilting look. "And you no doubt possess the most colossal male ego, despite your obvious *handicap*," she retorted with sarcasm, "a handicap that would ordinarily deflate any normal, self-respecting European male from London to the Riviera. But, alas, American men are not normal. They don't know who their ancestors are, so they have nothing to live up to. I am a miserable human being, doctor. So leave me be!"

Michael shrugged his shoulders. "I will if you want me to, but you're a talkative woman, Joanie. And there's no one else around to talk to. So take me, *handicapped* as I am, or leave me, unless you'd rather converse with your mother."

"Heaven forbid!" said Joan in a voice meant to be deliberately disapproving. "She's the last person in the world I want to pour out my heart to. Constance Bolt is perfectly marvelous for advice on fashions and entertaining. Unfortunately, or perhaps fortunately, she's not a deep thinker and never gives much thought to the origins of depression. To put it kindly, I would not consider mother a vastly complex creature." Joan paused for effect. "Yes, Michael, you've uncovered my pervasive weakness. I am a compulsive talker who desperately needs an admiring and attentive listener, even when I am quite aware that the other person probably doesn't understand a word I'm saying." She smiled, as though she were laughing at herself. "Like the Polish woman on the plane who was subjected to my French and Italian for hours on end even though the languages were incomprehensible to her. That she was a captive audience did not daunt me in the least. See how I'm running on despite my melancholy. So fire away, Dr. Lyons, and test your *brilliant* psychiatric theories on me, at least those you haven't thrust upon dear, unsuspecting Allyson. I'll very probably end up telling you just about everything that I've endeavored to keep hidden for a lifetime. Would you like to know about the Indian who jilted me for his wife?"

But Michael did not ask many questions. He and Joan would spend an hour or two with each other before dinner in the quiet of the garden. He let her ventilate her feelings. And somehow, without disturbing her privacy, he got across to her that instead of experiencing and confronting her angry feelings consciously, she turned them inward, into weapons of her own destruction. And even now, the release of anger was taking its form as rage against herself. She had lived a life of simmering fury, he told her, and she had chosen, subconsciously, to live with a problem she could not solve rather than look for a solution she could understand.

Intuitively, he understood her feelings without probing into the reasons.

"Joanie, you've been moving around in an extended euphoria, giving the impression that you're as high as the proverbial kite, while all the while, you've been denying any realistic problems. One big, massive denial of what's really an underlying depressive state. Do you follow me, Joanie?"

"I follow you, doctor. And stop calling me Joanie. My third-grade teacher called me that, and I spit at her."

"You see," he went on, "it's been one great, grandiose scheme of avoiding those ambivalent love-hate feelings that we all have toward our parents. That is, until the bubble burst and your defenses went with it. Now you feel weak and scared and full of lots of unresolved guilt about being a vulnerable woman. Maybe you can finally stop trying to 'kill the pain,' Joanie. Don't struggle so much. 'Go with it!' "

Joan grew very fond of Michael Lyons, and one day she would tell him that he was the most "unhandicapped" person she had ever met.

Millicent sat in Mr. Watson's office

listening to the lawyer explain the terms of John J. Bolt's will.

"Mrs. Hart, you are a very wealthy woman. Your father left one third of his personal estate to your mother and two thirds to you and your sister. Your children, of course, have been amply provided for by the trust funds John Bolt set up years back. However, Bolt Construction Company is not part of your inheritance. I assume you know that it is a closely held corporation whereby the shares were held by only two people, and there were no outside investors. Your father owned seventy-five percent of the stock and your husband twenty-five percent. It was more like an incorporated partnership. And your father left all his corporate holdings to your husband, Jeffrey Hart. I must say, I as rather dismayed by your husband's reaction to this well-deserved windfall. He accepted with good grace, of course, but he appeared less than pleased by John Bolt's, shall we say, vote of confidence in his ability to carry on Bolt enterprises. Quite naturally, no one takes pleasure in profiting from the death of another. So his reaction may be attributed to the unfortunate chain of circumstances. However, as your father often said, Jeffrey Hart would unquestionably have been his successor under any circumstances."

As Mr. Watson continued to explain the remaining bequests and the intricacies of settling such a large estate, Millicent's predominant feeling was one of relief.

At least father made it easier for me to consider dissolving my marriage. If I do go through with it, my conscience may be the hardest thing to deal with. It should make the burden of guilt a little more bearable. This is as good a trade-off as I could possibly hope for. Jeff may lose me, but he gains an empire. If there is a void, it will be filled with the one thing Jeff wanted more than anything else. Bolt Construction Company. God, how can I think this way? Even in my head, it sounds so calculating.

Millicent was forced to look at aspects of herself she had never considered before. All those years of being a dutiful daughter, a devoted wife, an indulgent and compliant mother, a decision maker, might be coming to an end. She was possibly on her way to a second chance at the future. Marriage to Roger could be the start of a new existence because, regardless of her age, she would be a bride. The other life would be over. Priorities would change. As for her children, they would remain a very important part of her life, but no more would they be her entire life. She gave serious thought to what her life would be like if she married Roger. It would be an adventure, and her identity would change. She strongly suspected that it was already changing.

Life is not constant, she thought, as she recognized her human yearning to alter her destiny. A sense of romantic excitement came over her when she realized that she did not have to be locked into the same relationships. She was ready, so ready, to give up the central theme around which her entire life seemed to revolve — nurturing her family. Underneath the powerful force to take care of others was a need for someone to take care of her. Independence, she realized, is also not constant. She had discovered a contradictory and crucial truth about herself, one she had no desire to suppress. She wanted to be femininely dependent, like a delicate woman of another century. The fantasy of a strong knight in shining armor spiriting her away was the most pleasing thought she could possibly imagine. This made her wonder whether she had fallen in love with an illusion, an imaginary person whom she had invented to fulfill her own wishes and desires.

Chapter 33

Millicent left Mr. Watson's office and hurried to the French restaurant across the street from George Washington Hospital and around the corner from Roger's office. La Gaulois is the perfect place to meet for lunch when you don't want to be noticed. Not that it's quiet and out of the way like a secret rendezvous. Quite the opposite. Noise and crowds and bustling commotion give the little bistro an undeniable French charm. But one leaves never remembering the anonymous faces that fill the restaurant.

From his place on the other side of the table, Roger Graham looked at Millicent, and she looked back. In that brief moment, there was an unmistakable loving communication.

"You look happy, Millicent."

"In a way I am, and I guess I have father to thank. He did me a great favor by leaving the company to Jeff. He was always father's heir apparent, but now it's definite and that makes it easier for . . ." She hesitated and then changed her thought. "Anyway, I won't have to be involved with the business. Jeff owns it all now. He'll have what he wants and . . ."

"And I'll have you, I hope," Roger interjected. "Millicent, does this mean that you've made a decision about us?"

She shifted uneasily in her chair. "Roger, I've given it a great deal of thought, and I'm not sure . . ." She stopped abruptly and looked into Roger's face. Suddenly she realized she could no longer refuse to make a commitment. "I think I have," she said. As the idea took hold, she became more enthusiastic, elated. "Yes, I think we could be very happy together." She smiled at him and reached for his hand.

Looking at her as if in a dream, he said at last, "Then how would you like to spend your honeymoon on a boat, sailing into the sunset, just the two of us?"

Her fantasy stirred, Millicent leaned back and closed her eyes in a dreamy way.

"Roger dear, right now I would gladly spend a lifetime on a boat, on a mountaintop, in a cabin in the woods . . . any place where we could be alone and put this whole miserable year behind us."

"Great!" he said, as the realization of what he heard sank in. "Then we'll start making plans right away. You see, I've been looking at boats, and I have my eye on this . . ."

"Not so fast," she interrupted, lifting her hand from his grasp. "You seem to have forgotten that Jeff doesn't know about us yet. Not that I don't think he suspects. He would have to be stupid not to know something is going on. And he's far from stupid."

"Well, when are you going to tell him?"

"Very soon, this weekend for sure."

"And then?" he asked, hesitatingly.

"And then I'll go to my lawyer and find out what I have to do to start divorce proceedings. I'm sure it will mean a separation for a certain period of time before the divorce becomes final."

They sat for a few moments in silence until Millicent said very seriously, "Roger, there are so many things to work out, and I must ask you to let me do whatever I have to in order that this whole unpleasant business runs smoothly and with as little bad feeling as possible under the circumstances. No matter what I've been saying, I really don't want to run away. I want to leave with a certain amount of dignity and peace of mind."

Roger looked at her adoringly. "Whatever you say, sweetheart. But let me help, in any way I can."

"After I tell Jeff, I think it would be best to leave the house for a while. I've decided to open father's place at Martha's Vineyard and take mother and Joan there for the summer."

Roger's face fell at the thought of Millicent leaving for three months.

"Roger darling," she said, trying to reassure him, "it's better this way. Jeff will have a chance to get used to the idea. And at a time like this, I certainly can't ask him to move out. And I need . . . I need a little time myself. Furthermore, I simply have to get mother and Joan into some sort of reasonable state before sending them out on their own. Johnny will be working, and Corinne can come up to the Vineyard if she wants to, but then again, she probably has summer plans already. As for Allyson, she can stay with Jeff and Johnny, as I seriously doubt that she would want to come with us and leave Michael. Oddly enough, she's the one I'm most worried about telling. I would never forgive myself if this sets her back and brings on the anorexic condition again."

"I don't think you have to worry about Allyson," said Roger in a professional tone. "She's grown with responsibility. And she's got Michael, and he's the best thing that ever happened to her."

"He's the best thing that happened to all of us," said Millicent. "He's been an absolute angel to mother and Joan. I don't know how we could have gotten through this week without him. He's a remarkable young man, and I thank God every day, and you, Roger, for sending him to Allyson. I honestly don't think I could even think of leaving if she didn't have Michael."

Roger asked hesitantly, "Will Jeff have someone?"

Millicent was suddenly shaken. A vague image of Cynthia Ross appeared in her mind. "I'm not sure. And I won't ask, because I don't want to know the answer. My leaving Jeff has to be a decision based on my love for you and not on any feelings of retaliation."

"But would knowing that he does have someone make it easier for you?" he asked, his tone solicitous and gentle.

"All I know, Roger, is that I have finally made the commitment, and there's no turning back. Perhaps father's death did it, just as you said at the house. But what about Janet? When will you tell her?"

"I already have. Janet knows," said Roger with finality.

Millicent frowned and clutched her palms on the table, troubled by the thought that Roger's wife knew that she, Millicent, existed. That she was now "the other woman" breaking up a marriage.

"Oh, Roger," she said sadly and slowly, "*that*, I can't bear. She must hate me."

Roger became very serious. "No, she doesn't hate you, and she doesn't hate me. She didn't even ask who you were. Millicent, what I'm about to say is not by way of lightening your guilt or justifying our actions. Janet seemed almost relieved. Naturally surprised, but very relieved, as if she were finally free to do what she's been doing all along, but without any encumbrances. Look, her world is made up of science and research. There isn't room in it for anything else, not even a husband who she sees a few times a week. Do you kown what she said when I told her? She said that she hoped *I* would find happiness, because it had always bothered her that she had found *hers* long ago and she knew I was still searching. It was almost as if she was trying to tell me that our marriage, any marriage for her, had been a mistake, because her career is the only thing she really loves."

"I'd still like to meet her someday and tell her I'm sorry," said Millicent.

Roger looked almost amused. "Knowing Janet, she wouldn't remember what there was to be sorry about."

Still repenting and still reproaching, Millicent asked, "Are we doing the right thing? Tell me we are, because I desperately need reassurance."

Roger took her hand again and looked into her eyes and reassured her. "I can only hope we are. And if we live long enough and love each other enough, then we'll know it was right. It's as simple as that."

"Roger, suddenly it all seems too simple."

Millicent looked away and allowed her mind to drift into the future.

Roger looked at her carefully, as though he couldn't believe these happy moments would last. He smiled at her and asked, "What are you thinking about?"

Millicent returned his smile. "Oh, I wasn't really thinking. I was dreaming. Dreams are dancing around in my head."

She paused as if to consider her own words. Then her eyes brightened as a long forgotten image came into her mind. She started talking like an eager storyteller who doesn't want to forget the memory again. "When I was a child, eight or nine at the most, mother and father took Joan and me to Palm Beach for the Christmas holidays. We stayed at the old Breakers Hotel, a magnificent baronial place then in the heyday of its popularity. There was a huge fountain in the main garden, one of those elaborate spouting fountains all in white stone with carved cherubs dangling on the sides. After dark they turned on colored lights, and the waters became illuminated with every color of the rainbow. To me it was sheer magic, and I became fascinated as the sprays changed from one glorious shade to another.

"One night, when mother and father were in the ballroom for a big party and I was supposed to be asleep, an irresistible longing to see the fountain took possession of me. I slipped into mother's room and gathered up her bright silk scarves and wrapped them around my body until I looked like a flowing mummy. I stole quietly down to the garden to watch the colored waters and before I knew it, I was dancing around that fantastic fountain like the water nymph Arethusa in Greek mythology. I felt beautiful and gloriously free with the scarves blowing in the wind. Then someone in the hotel spotted me and informed my father that his 'demented' child was running around the lawn like a naked elf, and I was quickly whisked to my room by my embarrassed parents, who scolded me within an inch of my life for making them the laughing stock of that fancy hotel.

"When my father asked me why I would do such a crazy thing, I told him that I had had a wonderful dream that I could change into a spring of water and become part of that beautiful fountain, and that I was just trying to make the dream come true.

"Father became very serious and told me that dreams are not the stuff of 'people like us,' dreams are for 'fools and failures.' Those were his words. He said that I must stop dreaming and start achieving." A slight smirk crossed his face. "And of course, Roger, I always obeyed him."

She lowered her head, and a look of embarrassment came over her for having told him the story.

"When did you start dreaming again, Millicent?" Before she could answer, he impulsively said, "When you met me?"

She was silent for a moment. Tears filled the corners of her eyes and she sounded wistful when she answered, "When I met you, the dreams would come but I would push them away. But when father died, I somehow felt that I was free to dream again." She paused and, as if scolding herself, said, "That sounds rather ridiculous, doesn't it, as though his death released me."

Chapter 34

At the very moment that Millicent and Roger were finishing lunch, Jeffrey Hart was sitting in his office dictating a letter to his secretary. It had been a relatively quiet but productive morning, and Jeff felt in somewhat better spirits now that he was again immersed in work.

In midsentence, he stopped talking as though preoccupied and thinking ahead. Claudia French sat upright in her chair, pencil poised, waiting for him to continue. A strange look came over Jeffrey's face, as though he were in pain, and he squirmed in his chair. Quickly, Claudia cast her eyes down to the stenographic pad in her lap, always exact in what not to notice. She was well aware of Jeff's depression since old Mr. Bolt had died, and she attributed the look of distress to thoughts about his father-in-law. When she heard deep sighs, she feared he was about to say something emotional, and she sat up straighter, attempting to control her uneasiness.

She brought her eyes up when Jeff said, "God, it feels like an elephant is standing on my chest."

She immediately became concerned when Jeff suddenly moved around in his chair, becoming anxious and restless. He was breathing heavily and clutching his chest. Not knowing what to say, she stood up and reached for the carafe of water on the desk. But Jeff's breathing got deeper, and he became mildly delirious. Within a second, he swung around and toppled to the floor, still holding his hand against his chest.

Claudia screamed, and people from the outer office rushed in, the horrible memory of John Bolt's death still fresh in their minds.

Somone yelled, "Call a doctor." Others said, "Get the rescue squad." And while the pandemonium ensued and people rushed to the phones, a young office boy pushed his way through and knelt beside the gasping man, who was now making rattling sounds. Jeff's face was deathlike, and his eyes had a ground-glass appearance, without luster.

The young man put his face next to Jeff's, as if he were listening for breath sounds, then he felt the carotid pulse in the neck. With immediate precision, he started cardiopulmonary resuscitation, blowing quick breaths into Jeff's mouth and then compressing on his chest and alternating between frequent ventilations in the mouth and more poundings on the sternum.

Everyone stood around in stunned awe as Willie Knight worked feverishly over a man he hardly knew. In five minutes paramedics arrived and continued the cardiac compressions as the young man, dripping with perspiration, moved out of the way.

The medics put an oxygen mask over Jeffrey's face and lifted him on a board before putting him on the stretcher, all the while compressing his chest and trying desperately to keep life in him. Within minutes he was in the ambulance, receiving pure oxygen and being rushed to George Washington University Hospital, a few blocks from the Bolt

Building on K Street.

By one of those odd coincidences of timing that people later speak about as fate, Millicent was walking across Pennsylvania Avenue from the restaurant just as the ambulance circled the driveway of the emergency room of the hospital. She was returning to her car on Twenty-third Street, barely having bid Roger a lingering good-bye. She felt unusually contented, almost euphoric, because she was now clear as to where her life was headed.

When she saw the ambulance, she paid no more attention to it than any other mildly curious person passing on the street. But when she saw a long, black limousine pull up behind the flashing van, and there was no mistaking who the car belonged to, she stood paralyzed with terror. The personalized license plates on the front of the limousine said BOLT.

The company chauffeur jumped out of the car, followed by Johnny, Sheldon Carpenter, and Miss French, the secretary. Johnny ran ahead, but the others moved cautiously behind the stretcher through the electric doors, and Millicent knew for certain, without trying to see, that Jeff was on that stretcher.

Millicent rushed in and grabbed Miss French's arm, "What happened?" she asked breathlessly.

Miss French was startled by Millicent's sudden appearance. "Oh, Mrs. Hart, thank heaven they found you. I can't believe this is happening. It's like doom took over the company."

"What *did* happen?" pressed Millicent urgently.

"Mr. Hart had a heart attack, right in his office, right in the middle of dictating a letter." The distraught Miss French broke down and cried on Millicent's shoulder.

Jeff was rushed into the back area of the emergency room as Millicent stood helplessly at the front. She heard someone call out "acute myocardial infarction" and watched what looked like organized frenzy with Johnny standing solemnly in the background.

Doctors and nurses, in greens and whites, hovered around her husband, each performing designated functions like a crack drill team. She saw them cut away Jeff's clothes with the rip of a surgical scissors. Nurses slapped electrocardiogram discs all over his body to monitor the heart rate. An anesthetist passed a tube down his mouth into the trachea, still keeping the oxygen going. A resident started the I.V. to get his blood pressure up. Arterial blood gases were drawn. All the while, the emergency room chief was running the show, dictating orders to the other doctors and nurses. What seemed like mass confusion turned into precise action to keep Jeffrey Hart alive.

Suddenly the EKG monitor showed a flat line indicating cardiac standstill. The patient was quickly given epinephrine and calcium. His heart then went into an arrhythmia, and the chief doctor called for the shock paddles and told everyone to stand clear.

The paddles were placed on Jeff's chest, a button was pushed, and electricity flowed through his almost lifeless body. For an instant, the body jerked and convulsed on the table. No change was registered on the scope. The electrical procedure was repeated, and the normally tense room became a mountain of tension.

The resident, whose hand had been palpating the femoral artery at the top of Jeff's leg, said that he could feel a pulse, though it was still very weak. All eyes looked to the gas bag attached to the ventilation unit as it began to inflate and deflate, showing that Jeffrey was beginning to breathe on his own once again. With nervous caution, the chief doctor said the patient was stabilized but still in very critical condition. Without a minute's delay, he was rushed to the coronary-care unit, where the fight to save Jeffrey Hart's life would go on.

Millicent was still standing in the front of the emergency room, next to Miss French and Sheldon Carpenter. She was shaken out of her hypnotic state by a terrible, wretching sound. She turned her head and saw Sheldon Carpenter vomiting all over the emergency-room floor.

For a week, Jeffrey stayed in the coronary-care unit, hovering between life and death. The family vigil at George Washington Hospital temporarily blotted out the events of John Bolt's death. Every hour, one member of the family was cautiously allowed in, for a few strained moments, to view the sleeping patient, who remained unaware of their presence.

With the miracles of nature and medical science, Jeffrey Hart stayed alive and slowly responded. He was transferred to a private room, and the long recovery of his abused heart began.

Millicent's days were consumed with little else apart from waiting. It all seemed like an ironic repeat of her vigil with Allyson.

When Jeff realized where he was and what had happened, he slumped into deep depression. So she remained near by, encouraging him back to life as she had done with Allyson.

Meanwhile, the others found their proper places. With reluctance, Cory took Joan to Martha's Vineyard for the summer. Joan needed a quiet place to restore her fragile mind, away from her mother, whom she secretly blamed for her tarnished youth. She was convinced that Constance had known everything and chose to look the other way. Cory volunteered for the custodial job, despite the fact that she was anxious to start the rape crisis center. Without realizing the implication, Corinne Bolt Hart was as duty-bound as all the others.

Constance was no tower of strength. In fact, she resented the family's proccupation with Jeff, which drew their sympathies away from her and from the preservation of John J. Bolt's memory. Alllyson cared for Constance and continued to be in charge of the house. Allyson and Michael's love grew stronger each day, but marriage was out of the question until some form of stability returned to all their lives. Allyson was too busy managing the shattered Hart family to start another one. She and Michael agreed to wait until next spring to get married.

As for Johnny, the decision he had made to come into the company just before Jeff's heart attack seemed preordained and convinced him of his destiny. He knew that he would one day step into the shoes of his father and grandfather and carry on the family business. Meanwhile, he would work long and hard and learn, while the executives of Bolt Construction took over. And so the company went on. Not as before without the sure and brilliant business minds of John J. Bolt and Jeffrey Hart. But, nevertheless, with Johnny there, a continuity prevailed, and business went on as usual.

Dolly Henderson became Millicent's frequent companion at the hospital, bringing a ray of lighthearted giddiness to an otherwise somber scene. Millicent welcomed the departure from her own introspection. She had intended to spend the summer separating herself from Jeff and preparing for another stage in her life. Instead, she spent the summer at her husband's side, nurturing him back to health and forgetting that she had her own life to live.

Chapter 35

Almost as easily as it had begun, the Washington summer faded to autumn.

It was in Millicent's garden, in October, just as the leaves began to fall, that she and Roger Graham talked about their future, a future in which they would not be together.

Jeffrey had finally come home from the hospital for another long period of convalescence. Coronary artery bypass surgery had been performed after it was determined that the vessels that supplied his heart with blood were blocked. One day he might lead a relatively normal life. But for now, each day was lived with caution and care.

Millicent and Roger sat in the garden while upstairs Jeffrey lay under the watchful eye of the nurse who had been with him since the day he returned home, after spending more than four months in the hospital. It was a strained encounter for both of them, and Millicent would forever remember this day with a sense of loss greater than any she had ever known.

They had seen each other infrequently during the summer. Roger would look for Millicent in the halls of the hospital or drop by Jeffrey's room on the pretense of inquiring about his condition, asking the right medical questions that any interested doctor would ask about a friend. But his purpose, of course, was to see Millicent, to keep the sparks of their love from diminishing.

Roger harbored secret thoughts that Jeff would die and then Millicent would come to him, naturally and without guilt. But Roger felt his own guilt. As a doctor, such an idea was completely unethical. As a righteous man, such an idea was morally wrong. Still, the notion continued to run through his mind as he longed for this woman who loved him but sat by her husband's side, month afer month, until the summer turned into fall.

"I'm glad Jeff's better," said Roger

sincerely but feebly.

Millicent heaved a deep sigh. "He's got a long way to go, but his doctors feel that he's going to make it. Oh, he'll have to completely change his way of living and give up this obsession with work. But now that Johnny's learning the business, perhaps he'll realize that the company is more permanent than he is. It won't be easy for a man like Jeff to relinquish the least bit of power and responsibility, even to his own son."

"When do they think he can go back to work?" asked Roger.

"In a few months, if all goes well."

"And until then, Millicent?"

"I'll stay with him, and then take him away for a rest, someplace warm and quiet."

"So where does that leave us?" Roger asked, with a touch of sarcasm.

Millicent didn't reply.

Roger found himself saying, "We were lovers once. Remember? We made promises to each other."

Millicent sat with her hands folded and gazed straight ahead with a worried frown, but otherwise she maintained the same stoic poise she displayed at the hospital throughout the summer.

Without looking at him she said, "Don't speak about those times, Roger, they're over."

"Why?" he entreated. "I waited this long. I can wait again, if only you'll tell me to wait. If only you'll give me some sign that you still love me."

Millicent turned toward him and took his hands in hers, as he had once done when she, too, was feeling the utter futility of her own life.

"Roger, I can't ask you to wait because I don't know what will be. Perhaps later, much later . . . no, that's not exactly true. I'm kidding myself. I do know. Right now, Jeffrey needs me. As for later, I think he will need me more than ever." She said this without her usual modesty but with a sense of resignation.

Roger was not comprehending. "Once he's back on his feet, things will be different. Millicent, he'll have his work, and life will go on pretty much as before."

"No, Roger. It won't be as before. That I know. It will never be the same for him. Jeff is a dynamic man, just like my father was. Second best will never be good enough. His vitality and strength are gone, and with it his youth, which he held on to with a passion. He's going to have to face being a middle-aged man with a serious heart condition and lead a different kind of life in order to stay alive. He's always going to be frightened of another heart attack. He will never feel young again, and for Jeffrey, it was important to be able to do ten times what any other man half his age could do." Millicent paused, and the look on her face begged for understanding. "Roger, Jeff needs me to grow old with him. Can you grasp what I'm saying?"

"No, I'm afraid I can't. Are you telling me that you're going to stay with him out of pity?"

She shook her head. "No, Roger, I could not do that. Jeff would never accept pity from anyone, least of all from me. I'm staying because I have no choice," said Millicent with sorrow in her eyes.

Roger slumped wearily in the wicker chair and passed his fingers through his hair. "That's nonsense and you know it," he insisted. "You do have a choice. Maybe not now, but certainly in a few months. Don't you think I know how sick he was? But the probability is that he can live a normal life if he takes care of himself."

"I'm not talking about his physical condition."

"Then what the hell are you talking about?" shouted Roger with frustration.

Millicent wasn't put off by his anger. "This is hard to put into words because it's something I feel more than I know. I'm talking about the threat to his independence, his aggressiveness, his ability to compete . . . in every way. He can't win anymore, and he can't continue to achieve. He's got to give up the expectations he has for himself. He's also got to let go of his power, and for Jeff, that means growing old. He's going to suffer a great loss."

Roger looked at her uncertainly. "Are you saying that if you leave him, he won't make it?"

Millicent was silent for a moment as she tried to put her thoughts in order. "I know Jeff because I knew my father. You see, Roger, I married a man strangely like my father, a man who would desperately deny any dependency needs. They never admit human weakness. The difference is, I'm not like my mother."

Roger looked at her with confusion.

"What are you trying to explain?"

"I'm trying to say that my marriage is *not* over. There's still unfinished business. And as long as there is, you and I could never have a meaningful life together."

"I still don't get it," Roger said with utter despair.

"I'm not sure I do, either. I just know that there is a bond between Jeff and me, a commitment if you will, that still exists, and I can't break it. The realization of it all came out of this crisis. And if I left him now, I would suffer as much of a sense of loss as Jeff would."

Roger looked at her intently. "I think you're trying to tell me, in a very peculiar way, that you don't love me."

Millicent closed her eyes tightly and swallowed the small sobs in her throat. She waited for what seemed like an eternity and then said to him, "If I told you that, it would only be a lie, perhaps a kind lie, but nevertheless a false way to make you want to forget me." Millicent's eyes glistened with tears, and after a while she said, "Love? How do you explain love? I'm not sure I know what it is, but I don't think it's the only emotion that arouses our passion. I am passionately committed to my husband. Not to the man he was, but to the man he will be. Roger, if things had been different, I would have gone off with you to the ends of the earth."

Roger got up and stood with his hands in his pockets, looking down at the grass. He kept his head bowed as he said bitterly, "Then there's nothing more to say, is there? You've made your decision."

"I know this sounds implausible to you," she said, "but the decision was made for me. I had no control over it."

He looked up and with a deep note of pathos said, "I wish I could stop loving you, Millicent."

"Roger, you will, one day you will," she said through her tears. She paused slightly, her gaze never leaving his face. "You are the dearest man. You meant so much to me."

Chapter 36

When she lived in the big colonial house in the elite enclave of Spring Valley, the garden was Millicent's childhood haven of peace and privacy. Again, her garden was her gauge. It was something of a time warp, like being in a nineteenth century country retreat, far removed from the most urbanized society of Washington. There, among the vibrant swaths of azaleas and purple wisteria vines, she could withdraw from the demands and competition of the family within the house. She remembered feeling like a part of an Impressionist painting.

Summers at the shingled cottage on Martha's Vineyard offered different memories. A wonderful natural garden of daisies and cornflowers overlooking the sea made her feel free and adventurous, like one of the first settlers of the island. At dusk, when sailboats came home to anchor, she would stand in the garden and look out at the long stretches of sand and water and imagine herself the child of an old whaling captain of another century. Far beyond the blue horizon, she saw voyages and she dreamed of stepping back in time.

The garden at Palm Beach, where winter holidays were often spent, was formal and beautifully manicured, and hedged in by tall boxwoods. The feeling was lonely and cloistered. Its only saving grace was a small old-fashioned secret garden at the side of the pink palacelike house that had marvelous tropical citrus trees. There, Millicent could shut out the sheer perfection that symbolized this incredible Florida resort. Unlike her father and mother and Joan, she never felt she belonged to this corridor of time.

Now she was in her own rambling and informal garden that was crammed with a profusion of roses. White and pink dogwoods made it look like a perfect spring garden, although there had never been a plan to it. The design just had that quality of looking inevitable.

Her garden was a place filled with a great many reminders of her life in years past, and it had a way of giving her all sorts of new ideas about what she hoped to do in the future. This is where she would disappear to read undisturbed or to think.

The garden was where she had said good-bye to Roger last fall. Since then, it was where she sat with Jeff on so many days and nursed him back to health. Today it was the focus of human activity. Allyson and Michael were getting married. It was a glorious spring day for a wedding.

She sat quietly among the guests, the melting violin strains of *Liebestod* playing in the background, waiting for the wedding procession to begin.

For the first time since that afternoon in October when she had last seen Roger, almost seven months ago, Millicent did not push away the images and emotions that she had struggled to forget. She thought about her father, Martha and Roger Graham. And how different her life was now that they were gone from it.

The touch of Jeffrey's hand on hers brought Millicent out of her private thoughts. Turning, she saw tears brimming in his eyes. She leaned over and kissed him lightly on the cheek as she gently wiped the corners of his eyes with her lace handkerchief. The loving gesture was not lost on the family seated around them.

Cory looked beautiful, and for this occasion she had discarded the elegant rummage-sale look that was her image. Her blond hair was piled on top of her head with sprigs of spring flowers. Not generally one for ordinary sentimentality, Cory squeezed Joan's hand. In turn, Joan put her arm around Constance, who was weeping quietly beside her. This was the first time Joan had made any physical contact with her mother since John J. Bolt's death.

Sitting in back of Jeff, Johnny patted his father on the back affectionately. At the touch of his hand, an odd communication seemed to pass between father and son.

Dolly, in flowing flowered chiffon and a fabulous straw hat that obscured everyone's view, cried openly but elegantly. "My cup runneth over. I shall simply die from happiness," she said to anyone who was listening. Dolly never did understand the charm of understatment.

Millicent clutched Jeff's hand. It was warm with perspiration. He was not the same Jeffrey Hart of a year ago. And he never would be. That physically astonishing body had lost its aura of vitality and youthfulness. Though perfectly tanned, his face was clearly lined. He finally looked his age. By his own admission, he had become a man of contemplation rather than action.

The familiar sound of the Trumpet Voluntary Wedding March began. Instinctively, everyone turned to watch the bride and groom approach the altar, which was beautifully decorated with looped garlands of flowers. It was not the usual wedding procession. No attendants led the way.

Allyson, in white organdy, with a sparkle in her eyes and a lively glow in her cheeks, walked slowly beside Michael's wheelchair. She bore little resemblance to the anorexic young woman with the vacant expression whom Dr. Michael Lyons had first seen over a year ago.

Allyson and Michael might have appreciated the irony of the guests' emotional outpour had they not been so busily engaged in exchanging their usual barbs.

"I bet they all think that I'm marrying you for your money," whispered Michael, cocky and cynical.

"Well, are you?" asked Allyson, in hushed sarcasm.

"Yeah, I am," he answered with a wry smile.

"Good," confided Allyson in a whisper. "That makes us even. Because I'm marrying you for perpetual psychiatric care, and I like to pay my own way. You see, I'm liberated."

"You're crazy, kiddo," he said out of the corner of his mouth.

"So are you," said Allyson with flippancy. "Otherwise, why would you be wearing green argyle socks with a tuxedo? Honestly, Michael, you're going to have to start getting your act together."

Embarrassed, Michael glanced down at the footrest of his wheelchair in disbelief. Totally in character, he indeed had on bright green and yellow argyle socks, highly visible in a wheelchair.

Chapter 37

She stood in the rain, trembling, looking up at the old Georgetown brownstone. The desire to come had faded away when she saw the house.

She felt at odds with herself. *Why am I here? What can Dr. Bromley tell me that I haven't told myself? Emotionally, I'm all right. A year ago I made peace with myself, and I'm not sorry. The sad moments of the past have been put away. Or have they?*

The autumn leaves were wet and slippery under her feet. She pulled the hood of her coat over her damp hair. She stood in the rain, her hands in her pockets, looking up at the door. It had been long over a year since she had come to this house seeking solace. Why was she back? Perhaps it was merely to be quite sure that she was now left in peace. Or was it a wish, a wistful yearning to return to certain moments of the past?

Actually, it was the picture postcard that had prompted Millicent to call Dr. Bromley for an appointment. The scene on the front of the card was foreign and indistinguishable, but the writing on the other side was plainly Roger's. No signature. Just two lines:

"I'm sailing to the 'ends of the earth.'

"I live for yesterday or tomorrow because there is no now."

That was all. But it was enough to make her long suppressed desires erupt with a fire that left her miserably weak.

"I don't need to go in and rehash memories that no longer belong in my life," she said, hardly realizing that she was speaking aloud.

Somehow she made herself go up the steps. As soon as she rang the doorbell, Millicent pictured the elderly psychiatrist standing at the top of the stairway.

She waited for the sound of the buzzer that would automatically unlock the front door. Instead, the door opened and an anonymous woman came out. Strangely beautiful in a theatrical way, but with a look of long suffering that belied her years, the woman was as surprised as Millicent when they faced each other. In spite of the awkward moment, the patient going out and the one coming in stood staring at each other, each wondering what dark mysteries of their lives had brought them to the psychiatrist's office.

The other woman suddenly turned away and hurried down the stone steps into the rain. As she reached the bottom step, her right foot landed on some wet leaves and she lost her balance. Millicent gasped as she watched her fall. She called to the figure sprawled on the pavement. "Did you hurt yourself? Can I help you?"

Then she started down the steps herself with the idea of helping the unknown woman, who looked more startled than hurt. As she saw Millicent approach, the woman quickly jumped up from the side-walk as though to avoid the offer of help. Without looking back, she fairly dashed down the street, her soiled wet coat, half on and half off, flying behind her. In a minute, she was out of sight. Millicent stared even after she was gone, and she had a strange feeling that she was looking into the past, at herself. With a shrug, she turned and went back up through the open door.

Dr. Frances Bromley was waiting at the top of the inside stairs. She looked very much the same, and she held out her hand as though to welcome back an old friend.

"I'm glad you called. It's been a long time. I've wondered about you. Oh, that was so terrible about your father. What a tragic situation! I read about it in the papers."

Millicent shook her hand and greeted her warmly but said nothing in response. She did not want to think about her father. He was part of her very soul, but she didn't want him as part of her life. In her own mind, she had relegated him to heaven.

Dr. Bromley picked up on this immediately. As she led Millicent into her office she said, "We can't change the past, so let's hear about you, my dear." As they sat down, she said, "I hear that Roger Graham gave up his practice and left the country. Where does that leave you?"

Millicent folded her hands and said matter-of-factly, "With a sick husband."

"Then let's start with that. What happened that you should trade a sick daughter for a sick husband and give up a lover in the bargain?''

Millicent dropped her shoulders and glanced around the familiarly comfortable office as she groped for words. She didn't know where to begin, again.

After a long silence, Dr. Bromley asked: "How is Allyson? I take it she's well."

Millicent's face lit up. "She's more than well. She's married. To a fine young doctor, a psychiatrist too. Do you know him? Dr. Michael Lyons."

"I've heard of him. Everyone has. A psychiatrist in a wheelchair is unusual . . . even among the *unusual*." And she laughed out loud, as though poking fun at herself. "That's wonderful, truly wonderful about your daughter. I'm so happy for her, and for you. Children can bring us the greatest heartache ever, but also the greatest happiness. And your husband? Jeffrey? What's wrong?"

Millicent told her about Jeff. The aftermath of the shooting. The guilt and the estrangement. The heart attack. The long months in the hospital and his slow convalescence. And then she showed Dr. Bromley the postcard, already worn from being read so many times. And all the feelings about Roger poured out.

"It was never over," said Millicent sadly, "but it was resolved. And now I feel so . . . so left out." As if speaking to herself, she said, "I missed the chance to . . ." Her words trailed off and she stopped.

Quite surprisingly, Dr. Bromley did not respond to the poignant statement. Instead, she pulled herself up from the worn leather chair and walked to the other side of the room. She took a very ordinary picture off the wall. The scene was one of blue water and white foamy waves with a small sailboat against a heavenly sky in the background. She handed her the picture. Millicent looked bewildered but took it when she realized Dr. Bromley's insistence.

"Think of yourself in that boat, sailing alone with Roger, out in the middle of nowhere, with nothing to distract you but sky and water and the man you believe you love."

Millicent held the frame with both hands and stared at the picture intensely, allowing her mind and body to become part of an illusion. For minutes she was transfixed. Not until Dr. Bromley spoke did she look up.

"How does it feel to be out there?"

"Glorious!" answered Millicent, still immersed in her imagination.

"Then why didn't you leave Jeffrey and go off with Roger and feel 'glorious' for the rest of your life?"

Still holding the picture, Millicent said, "Because I couldn't *make* myself leave Jeff. He needed me. Not my money, not my father's business. Just *me*. And . . . and I rather imagine that because he needed me, I needed him."

"But now you doubt what you did. Is that it? That little postcard has stirred up all the emotions you had carefully submerged. And you're not only nostalgic for Roger but you're angry with yourself for being the person you *are*."

Millicent nodded in affirmation but said nothing as she looked at the picture again.

"Read the inscription at the bottom."

For a moment, Millicent didn't know what Dr. Bromley was referring to. She looked more closely and saw the small writing near the edge of the frame.

"Read it out loud," coaxed Dr. Bromley. "It's a translation from Latin by the Roman poet Horace."

Millicent squinted and read the ancient words: " 'They who cross the sea change their skies but not their natures.' "

Millicent looked up at Dr. Bromley until their eyes met, and a knowing look crossed her face, as if she suddenly understood what the psychiatrist was trying to get her to see for herself.

Dr. Bromley took the picture and put it back on its worn hook on the wall. She returned to her chair and confronted Millicent. "For you, my dear, it would not have been 'glorious.' Oh, maybe for a day or a week or even a month. But not forever. Your *nature* would not have allowed it. You did the right thing because you gave in to what was natural for you. Odd as it may seem, you followed your heart."

Millicent walked outside and stood leaning against the old Georgetown lamp post. The skies had cleared, and the late afternoon sun was making an effort to break through the clouds. Her hand was in her pocket, holding on to the postcard. She started to crush it but then loosened her grip. Roger could never be completely erased from her mind, but she was determined not to think of him now. She would put him back at sea, and one day, when it would not hurt so much, she would take out the postcard and allow herself to dream of another intimate moment.

For now, she would think ahead, of what this year or the next might bring.

Allyson and Michael adopted a baby boy. Allyson told Millicent that fate played a nice trick on her because it was only right that someone who knew what it felt like to be an adopted child should have one herself. "I don't want the experience to be wasted," she said to her mother. "I want it to mean something to someone else. I want to return some of the love that I got to another child. My very own."

Johnny continued to struggle with the empire that was thrust upon him before he was ready for it. One day he would be worthy of his position as head of Bolt Construction, and he would be mature enough to become a responsible husband.

Cory started not one but five rape crisis centers. Joan was her partner, providing much of her inheritance and all of her time to Cory's causes, whether they be rape, abortion, women's rights, or child abuse.

Joan's involvement was a result of the relationship she and Cory had established that summer at Martha's Vineyard. Cory's causes became Joan's causes because Joan was ready. Joan would never wear another designer gown or visit another European country or take another husband. Joan became as totally immersed as her young niece, and her grace, vitality, and fighting spirit were assets that ensured their success.

John J. Bolt would be long remembered. Constance would see to that. That his life had ended so violently did not detract from the worthwhile monuments that would be built in his memory. With the same zest and enthusiasm that she had given to her artistic philanthropies, such as the National Symphony and the Corcoran Art Gallery, Constance would immortalize the name of her husband. Two universities would receive a business school and a library in his honor. His likeness would be enshrined in marble in the lobby of the Bolt Building. Scholarships would be given. Donations would flood the various charities. A wing of Children's Hospital would be added as the Bolt Pavilion, and Constance would say to the large audience gathered at the dedication ceremonies: "This is a most fitting tribute to my husband, because in his lifetime, John J. Bolt's one true concern was for children. This is his legacy to the future. If he were here today, this building would make him prouder than any other building he had ever erected in our beautiful city."

As for Millicent and Jeffrey, they could finally live together in peace and harmony settling into a comfortable routine of pleasure and satisfaction. They became a family.

And one day, as Millicent and Jeffrey sat in the garden watching their grandson play on the grass, she suddenly realized that she was happy just being there. She felt strangely optimistic, as though the past was fading and the future was before her.

Jeff reached for her hand and said, "How would you like to go on a special sort of vacation I've been thinking about?"

"What did you have in mind?" she asked with interest.

"Sailing."

"Sailing," she repeated, taken aback with a painful twinge.

"Uh huh, sailing through the Greek Islands," he said. "Just you and me and a captain and a cook who can't speak English."

Millicent's heart began to beat rapidly as a wave of nostalgia swept over her, and she wondered whatever made him suggest that.

"What do you think?" asked Jeff eagerly.

For a moment she could not answer. Then, feeling acutely conscious of his need for her and thinking she had never seen him more content, she replied as though his idea was inspired: "I think that would be glorious!"

"Me too," he said, as he leaned over and kissed her on the cheek. "We'll do nothing but pay attention to each other and look at the scenery."

Then something caught her eye. Millicent looked straight ahead, and the expression on her face was one of complete surprise.

She started to laugh as she said to Jeff, "But for now, you'd better pay attention to your grandson. He's pulling up all the tulips."

Little Jeffrey Hart Lyons looked up with

a sheepish grin, as he methodically plucked the flowers Millicent had planted in the garden.

THORNDIKE PRESS HOPES you
have enjoyed this Large Print
book. All our Large Print titles
are designed for the easiest
reading, and all our books are
made to last. Other Thorndike
Press Large Print books are
available at your library,
through selected bookstores, or
directly from the publisher. For
more information about our
current and upcoming Large
Print titles, please send your
name and address to:

THORNDIKE PRESS
ONE MILE ROAD
P.O. Box 157
THORNDIKE, MAINE 04986

There is no obligation, of course.